EVERGREEN

Also by Marissa Doyle

Between Silk and Sand

The Leland Sisters series:
Bewitching Season
Betraying Season
Courtship and Curses
Charles Bewitched

EVERGREEN

MARISSA DOYLE

EVERGREEN
Copyright © 2019 by Marissa Doyle

All rights reserved. No part or the whole of this book may be reproduced, distributed, transmitted, or utilized (other than for reading by the intended reader) in any form without the prior written permission of the author, except in the case of brief quotations embodied in critical reviews and certain other non-commercial uses permitted by copyright law. The unauthorized reproduction of this copyrighted work is illegal, and punishable by law.

Published by Book View Café Publishing Cooperative
P.O. Box 1624
Cedar Crest, NM 87008-1624

ISBN: 978-1-61138-827-5

Cover design by Ravenborn
Interior design by Marissa Doyle

This is a work of fiction. Names, characters, places, and events are fictitious and/or are used fictitiously, and are solely the product of the author's imagination. Any similarity to real persons, living or dead, places, businesses, companies, institutions, events, or locales is completely coincidental.

www.bookviewcafe.com
www.marissadoyle.com

To Lily and Lou

ONE

Chestnut Hill, Massachusetts
July 1901

"Dorothy? Come help me, won't you?" Grace Boisvert beckoned to her younger sister from the bathroom doorway. She wore an old brown flannel wrapper, and her long, freshly washed hair dripped down her back. "And stop making all that noise or you'll wake Grand-mère."

"Nothing wakes Grand-mère when she's napping after lunch. Not even me." Dorothy paused in her headlong gallop down the upstairs hall, brown braids flying—she'd been re-reading *Black Beauty* for the seventeenth time—and looked bright-eyed at Grace. "What do you want help with? And why don't you want Grand-mère to know what you're doing?"

Why couldn't she have had a less perceptive little sister? Fortunately she'd learned from experience the best way to handle Dorothy: she put a finger over her pursed lips and raised an eyebrow.

It worked every time; Dorothy tiptoed to her. "What is it?" she whispered.

Grace closed the door behind them. "I need to do my hair."

Dorothy perched on the mahogany lid of the toilet. "So why are you doing it while Grand-mère's asleep?"

"Because I want to try something different." Grace paused, but it was too late to reconsider. All she could do was hope Dorothy would be interested enough that she wouldn't tattle. It would be a shame if she did, because this purchase had cost three weeks' pocket money. She pulled a small, paper-wrapped parcel from one of the deep pockets of her robe.

"Ooh, what is it?" Dorothy craned to see it.

"I got it in town at Jordan Marsh." Grace unwrapped the parcel to reveal a bottle with an elaborate gilded label.

"'Mademoiselle's Secret. For the hair. Used by Famous Parisian Beauties since 1854,'" Dorothy read aloud. "'The Most Natural Tints Beyond Those Provided by Mother Nature.'" She looked up at Grace. "Why wouldn't Grand-mère like it? It's French, isn't it?"

Grace set the bottle on the marble counter by the sink and picked up her brush. "Yes, but it's not how she does it. I'm tired of her black-walnut-hull-and-coffee-bean stuff. It smells funny and stains horribly if you get it on your skin. I want to try something modern."

"Eighteen fifty-four isn't exactly modern, you know." Dorothy hopped up, took the bottle, pried the stopper from it, and sniffed. "But it does smell better."

"*Anything* smells better." Grace leaned toward the mirror, peering at her hairline. An eighth of an inch of rich green showed there. She should have done her hair days ago, but guests at lunch three days running had meant disruption to Grand-mère's nap schedule. "All right," she said briskly. "Hand me that pail, won't you?"

Dorothy complied. "When do you think my hair will start to turn green?"

"When it's ready. Don't be in a hurry to grow up. It's a rotten chore, having to dye it all the time. Not to mention wearing corsets and putting up with visits from the red-haired lady every month." Grace set the pail under the hot water tap in the sink and turned it on, then consulted the bottle of Mademoiselle's Secret—in "honeyed chestnut," which she'd chosen in honor of the enormous chestnut tree outside her bedroom window that sang her to sleep every night. "It says one cup per gallon of water—goodness, that'll be most of the bottle!—and to soak the hair until the desired shade is obtained—"

"What are you supposed to do? Stand on your head in the bucket?" Dorothy collapsed on the floor, snorting giggles.

"Hush!" Grace prodded her with one slippered foot. "Now, let's see…if we put the pail on the toilet lid, I can sort of bend over it, and you can make sure all my hair is in it and pour the stuff over the back of my head so it gets down to the roots." Then, because Dorothy was starting to look mutinous, she added, "And I'll help you do the same when it's your turn."

"No you won't. By the time it's my turn, you'll probably be off getting married or something." Dorothy glowered up at her.

Grace stopped reading the label and looked down at her sister. "Yes, I will. Even if I'm married I'll come and help you. You know I always keep my promises. Now, let's see how this works."

Without another word, Dorothy watched while she mixed the dye and helped her get all her hair into the pail, then carefully poured the liquid over the back of her head where it wasn't fully immersed.

"What are you using to pour it?" The lapels of Grace's wrapper had flopped down over her chin and ears, making it difficult to both see and hear. At least if Dorothy got any dye on her brown robe, no one would notice.

"Your tooth glass," Dorothy said cheerfully. "I hope it won't stain it. If it does, you can bury it in the trash dump and tell Mum you broke it."

Grace closed her eyes. *You're the one who asked her to help, Miss Clever Boots.*

"At least you don't have to do what Grand-mère did and rub your forearms with lemons to bleach out the green hair there," Dorothy continued. "I asked her why she didn't shave 'em instead, but she said that wouldn't be ladylike. I don't see how rubbing 'em with a lemon is, though."

"Neither do I." Maybe she should be a blonde instead, and sit in the sun with lemon in her hair. But she'd always dyed her hair brown, and becoming blonde would be far too noticeable. "I wish I knew how long I need to stand like thi—"

"Did I hear the doorbell?" Dorothy paused in mid-pour.

"No, it's just the ringing in my ears," Grace muttered. Standing bent over the toilet with her hair in a bucket was starting to make her dizzy.

"I'll go check."

Grace heard the *clink!* of the glass being set on the marble counter and the creak the lower door hinge always made when opening. "Dorothy, get back here!" she called, loudly as she dared. "Rose will answer the door!"

But it was too late. Dorothy was down the hall, shrieking, "Who is it, Rose?" over the banister down to the front hall. So much for Grand-mère's nap...and her French dye. Grace gathered up her hair and tried to squeeze as much liquid as possible from it, then wiped her hands on her brown robe before the dye could stain them.

Dorothy came thundering back down the hall and flung the bathroom door wide open. "Grace! It's Alice!"

"Alice?" Grace found a towel and wrapped it around her head, flipping it back as she stood up. "You're telling tales again, aren't you? Just like you did that time when you said Dick Aspinwall was at the door asking to take me skating."

"I'm not!" Dorothy had the grace to look sheepish. "She's really here!"

"She wasn't supposed to get here till the day after tomorrow!"

"She said she wanted to surprise you. Come on! She's dying to see you!"

Grace looked hard at her sister. She *appeared* sincere… Well, the only way she'd find out was to at least peek over the banister. "Mrs. Lee isn't here too, is she?" She hastily tipped the pail of dye down the toilet. Dared she flush it? No; Alice—if she was actually here—would hear it and tease her.

"No, just Alice. Come on!" Dorothy was practically dancing a jig. "She don't care if you're wearing your old wrapper. She told me so."

"Never mind—I'm coming up," an amused voice called from the stairs. "Where are you?"

"In here!" Dorothy danced back out into the hall, gesticulating. Grace grabbed the bottle of hair dye and plunged it into her pocket. The last thing she needed was Alice demanding to know why she was dyeing her hair—as close as they were, there were some things that had to be kept secret—like the fact that Alice's best friend was a dryad.

"Grace Boisvert! You are still in your robe. Are you just getting up? It must have been quite a party last night. Wish I'd been there." Alice appeared, dressed for travel in a canvas coat and hat with veil, in the bathroom doorway.

"No parties, goose. I was, er, washing my hair. When did you get here? Why didn't you tell me you were coming today?" Grace stepped forward to give her a quick hug. "I'm so glad you're here!"

Alice Lee Roosevelt was her dearest friend. She and Grace had known each other since they were babies and had been inseparable during Alice's twice-yearly long visits to her maternal grandparents, Mr. and Mrs. Lee, who lived next door. They wrote each other copious letters when Alice was away, and always picked right up where they'd left off when she arrived at the Lees'.

"Must have slipped my mind," Alice said apologetically, but her eyes glinted with mischief. "I say, it's not as old and tatty as mine," she added, holding Grace at arm's length and scrutinizing her robe.

"I'll bet you've got one made out of ermine and velvet, now that your papa's the vice-president!" Dorothy said from behind them, sounding awestruck.

"We don't go in for ermine and velvet robes in America, though I must say I wouldn't mind it if we did." Alice sighed. "By George, it's good to be back, if only for a few minutes, anyway. Life has been a whirlwind—you've no idea!"

"Lucky dog. I wish mine were. Let's go to my room." Grace tucked her arm in Alice's and propelled her down the hall. Dorothy seemed ready to follow after them, but a high, imperious voice from the end of the hall called, "Doro*thée*!" She pouted, but didn't dare disobey. When Grand-mère called, you went.

Once in her room, Grace shut the door behind them. "Very well—what's been so whirlwind-ish?" she demanded. "Have you already been to Washington? Your last letter was from New York."

Alice threw herself onto Grace's four-poster bed, careless of her modish hat and duster coat and the ruffled dotted swiss counterpane. "No Washington yet—Mother doesn't want to bring the children there until the fall. I'll miss New York terribly—I had such fun there this winter with Aunt Bye!—but Washington will be fun too if I have any say in the matter." She threw her hand across her brow in mock distress. "I came here directly from the station—well, I stopped to kiss Grandmother first—but I've so much to tell you, I don't know where to start."

"Why don't you start with telling me why you're here two days early and what you meant by 'if only for a few minutes?'" Grace settled in the low slipper chair by the fireplace grate. This was how they always sat—Alice on her bed, she on the chair. "Aren't you staying for a regular visit this time?"

Alice rolled onto her side, reaching up with one hand to pull out her hatpin and remove her large hat, now rather crushed. "Almost. I've got plans, and you're going to be part of them."

"What kind of plans?" Grace knew better than to say an unreserved *yes* to any of Alice's plans. Some of her previous ones had earned them scoldings and being sent to bed without supper—not that she regretted any of them, except maybe for the time they'd hidden the chicken in Mrs. Lee's parlor organ. But Alice had never shirked her share of their punishments.

"Wait till you hear!" Alice sat up. "Grace, how old are we?"

"Seventeen, of course. What does that—"

"Yes, seventeen—and you've already graduated from high school. Which means we're old enough to—to *do* things!"

"Like what things?"

"Like—oh…" Alice pretended to examine her fingernails. "Like go to Newport this summer? I've been invited to spend a few weeks there by a friend of my aunt's and I said yes, so long as I could bring you with me."

"Newport!" Grace sat up straighter in her chair. Newport, Rhode Island, was the summer playground of people like the Astors and the Vanderbilts—the richest people in America. Not to mention the most fashionable ones. And she and Alice had been invited to go there— "Oh my goodness, when? I thought you'd be going to Oyster Bay?"

"Mother and the children are there—that doesn't mean I must be too. Believe me, Mother and Father don't miss me in the least." She grimaced; Grace knew that her relationship with her stepmother was not an easy one. "Sometimes I think they're glad when I come up here. Oh, Grace, we'll have such fun! Think of the parties...and the boys!"

Grace *had* been thinking of them, but she wasn't sure what to think. Once, boys had simply been playmates—annoying ones at times who taunted because they could run races and climb trees without being encumbered by skirts, but also nice ones who pulled sleds back up snowy hills and reached for apples on higher branches. But that had changed, especially since she'd finished school and started wearing her hair up. Some of them had begun calling her Miss Boisvert instead of Grace and looking at her in a way that made Grand-mère scowl. Would the Newport boys do that too?

"What about boys?" she asked. "Do you like them?"

"They're more interesting than girls, a lot of the time," Alice retorted, then grinned. "Present company excluded, of course. They're fascinating creatures. My cousin Helen and I made a study of them last winter. You can get them to do the most ridiculous things if you want, and they don't even realize they're being ridiculous. Haven't you tried that yet?"

Grace was saved from answering by a knock, followed by Mum poking her head around the door. "May I?" she asked. "When I heard who was here—"

Alice rose immediately and went to her. "It's lovely to see you, Mrs. Boisvert."

Mum came into the room and solemnly shook her out-stretched hand, then laughed and folded her into a hug. "Just because you're a young lady doesn't mean you're allowed to be formal with me, miss! You're looking very smart, unlike my daughter wearing the wrapper I thought she'd gotten rid of months ago. Your grandmother said you'd be here today."

"Why am I always the last to know anything?" Grace couldn't help muttering crossly. And anyway, Mum *knew* this was her favorite robe.

"You didn't ask," Alice said over her shoulder, then turned back to Mum, wearing her most winsome smile. "Mrs. Boisvert, the most exciting thing's happened! A dear friend of my aunt Corinne has invited Grace and me to visit her in Newport this summer. Do say you'll let Grace come with me!"

Mum raised an eyebrow the tiniest bit. "It was hospitable of her to include Grace, but if I haven't met her, I'm afraid—"

"Oh, but you have! It's Mrs. George Rennell, and she says you met two years ago at some luncheon or something. She's writing to you directly—you should get her letter any moment now." She turned her you-*know*-you-can't-say-no-to-me look on Mum again.

Mum's smile didn't waver, but Grace could feel her doubt. "Yes, I do remember her, of course, but I'm not sure that Grace is ready for Newport."

"Of course she's ready. I am," Alice said, with the air of having stated an incontrovertible truth.

Mum had the presence of mind not to laugh. "Perhaps, but I worry that she'd find it intimidating. We don't move in such exalted social circles."

"Neither do I," Alice promptly replied. "But your family and mine are far older and more distinguished than the Astors and the Vanderbilts, and they know it. Please, Mrs. Boisvert? Grace, don't you want to go?"

Grace just managed not to shout yes! at the top of her voice. "May I please go, Mum? I'm sure Mrs. Rennell will take good care of us." There was no way that she was going to miss *Newport*.

Mum looked at her doubtfully, but merely said, "Hmm. Well, I should like to discuss it with Grace's father before I say anything more…and I shall have to receive Mrs. Rennell's letter too."

Alice beamed. "Oh, thank you, Mrs. Boisvert! I know we'll have a lovely time! Won't we, Grace?"

Mum blinked. "I didn't say—"

"And then won't you let Grace come to the Adirondacks with

us? Mother is taking us rooms at the Tahawus Club in August before we go to Washington. It will be awfully wholesome, and you're definitely acquainted with Mother, aren't you?" She smiled sweetly.

Mum shook her head, but was smiling as she turned toward the door. "I'll leave you two to your plotting." She paused in the doorway and looked at Alice. "Your grandmother once said that you could sell boots to a python. I'm beginning to understand what she meant."

As the door clicked shut behind her, Alice began to mime a victory dance. Grace jumped up and clapped her hand over her mouth before she could start whooping. "She didn't exactly say yes, in case you didn't notice," she murmured.

Alice pushed her hand away. "Don't worry. We'll convince her." She hesitated. "You do want to go, don't you?"

"More than anything," Grace said fiercely.

After Alice left—she really *had* only paused to peck Mrs. Lee on the cheek before coming to Grace's, and had to go back to properly greet her grandparents—Grace returned to the bathroom to check her hair and think about Alice's invitation.

Mum's assumption that she "wasn't ready" to go to Newport with Alice nettled her. She was so ready she could *taste* it. She unwrapped the towel from around her head and peered at her hairline in the mirror. Ha. No more green. So much for Grand-mère's old-fashioned ways of—

"Your Alice is gone?"

Grace jumped and half turned, clutching the towel. "Grand-mère! I didn't hear you come in."

"Hmm. That is because I haven't yet." Grand-mère stepped across the threshold into the bathroom and took the towel from

Grace. "You did your hair, I see." She wore a high-necked black silk dress and a heavy gold chain looped at her waist to hold her watch. The chain was festooned with her collection of charms and fobs. Grace wished she knew how she could walk so silently with all those jangling bits of gold on her.

"Er…yes. I didn't want to disturb you, but it was past time to do it," she said.

Grand-mère took her chin between her forefinger and thumb and tilted her face left and right. "You must start doing your eyebrows as well. A few drops, diluted with water, can be brushed on when you dye your hair. Every other time will probably be sufficient."

"I will next time, Grand-mère."

She nodded, her green-brown hazel eyes still fixed on Grace's face. "You are growing up, granddaughter."

Grace had never been able to figure out how to respond to statements like that. Yes, she was growing up. But she had been for a while now, in case Grand-mère hadn't noticed. After all, her hair had been growing in green since she was fourteen.

But Grand-mère didn't seem to need an answer. "It will be time to send you to France soon, I am thinking."

"France?" Grace jerked her chin from Grand-mère's hand.

"But of course. It is what we have always planned. You shall go to a finishing school in Paris in the autumn to improve your French and give you a little polish, and then you will be introduced to the dryad families in society there."

Grace stared at her. "Mum hasn't said anything about this!"

"No?" Grand-mère frowned. "Hmm. Well, perhaps I should not say anything more."

Talking back to Grand-mère was never done. *Almost* never. "When was this decided? Why hasn't anyone mentioned it to me?"

Grand-mère's frown grew more pronounced. "*Chut!* You

should have known it would happen. Your dear mother is from one of the few pure-blooded families on this side of the ocean, and there are no male offspring in her family of your generation. If we are to find you a husband, it will have to be in France. In *Bretagne*, preferably, where you will be able to find a forest worthy of you."

It suddenly felt as if all the air had left the room. Grace was barely starting to think about boys as something other than playmates, and here was Grand-mère talking about sending her to Brittany to marry one come fall and to settle into her forest. She was so concerned with preserving their family's lineage—their *bloodline* as she called it, which made Grace think of prize cattle.

"Grand-mère, I don't… I'm only seventeen! Why must I be in such a hurry? I've been thinking about applying to Wellesley or Radcliffe for next spring, once I'm eighteen—not getting married! And anyway, there must be other dryad families here…and in Italy and Austria and England and Germany—"

"Do not speak to me of *Germany*." Grand-mère nearly spat the word, and Grace winced. She should have known better than to mention Germany, which had humiliated France thirty years before in the Franco-Prussian War during which Grand-père had been killed. "We do not know any German families…but what is this?" Before Grace could stop her, Grand-mère had reached deftly into the pocket of her robe and extracted the bottle of Mademoiselle's Secret. She held it up and read the label. "'The Most Natural Tints Beyond Those Provided by Mother Nature.' Hmm."

Oh, no. Could this go any more wrong? "I can explain—"

But Grand-mère was already unstoppering the bottle. She sniffed it suspiciously, then poured a drop onto her finger and touched it to her tongue. "Ah. Black walnut extract," she said with satisfaction. "How clever to put it in a bottle, but I am sure it was very expensive. You are better off using my dye." She handed the bottle back to Grace. "You should get dressed. I believe your mother is having Mrs. Heath over to tea." She kissed Grace, then sailed out of the bathroom.

Grace looked at the bottle in her hand, then set it down on the counter with perhaps a little more force than was necessary. But she didn't care if it broke. Black walnut extract…she should have known. There was no escaping what she was, was there? Not even the smallest attempt to be her own person—finding her own way to conceal her green hair—could succeed.

Thousands of years ago, being a dryad had meant something. They had cared for the forests and kept them safe from both men and the stranger, nonhuman things that roamed the world. And even now, being a dryad could still be fun. Grace liked being able to talk to trees, to feel their slow thoughts and listen to their long songs and heal their illnesses. She liked that she could make plants do what she told them—it had been so tempting to make Mum's roses grow in blue, which she thought would be much prettier than some insipid pale pink, but she certainly would have caught it from her parents and Grand-mère. She liked that she could influence the weather—it never rained when the Boisverts held a garden party—and that she never got lost because she always knew where the sun was.

But she wondered now, at the dawn of the twentieth century, if their dryad magic mattered anymore. Why bother maintaining Grand-mère's precious bloodlines and keeping themselves apart, in this age of telephones and automobiles? She *had* to escape Grand-mère and the box she was trying to put her into, had to convince Mum and Papa to let her go to Newport.

TWO

T rue to Alice's word, the letter from Mrs. Rennell arrived in the next afternoon's post. Grace took it from Rose, their parlor maid, and brought it to her mother, who was freshening the flower arrangements in the library.

"It's Mrs. Rennell's invitation, I expect. Do tell me about her, Mum." Grace hung over the back of her mother's chair as she sat down and pulled out a hairpin to slit open the envelope. "Have you met her?"

"Yes, of course I have…I think. Now if you'll let me actually *read* it…" Mum rustled the heavily scented paper a little crossly, then gave in and held it so that Grace could read it as well:

My dear Mrs. Boisvert,

Although I cannot hope that you remember the occasion with the same pleasure that I do, I trust you will recall that we were introduced at a luncheon given by my sister-in-law, Mrs. Herbert Townley, two years ago this last May on the opening of Lilac Week at the Botanical Gardens.

"Ah. Yes, now I remember her," Mum said, half to herself. "What was she like?"

"Very handsomely dressed. She fidgeted a lot, though. She reminded me of a Pekinese that my cousin once had."

"Oh." Grace got a mental vision of a small, nervous dog wearing a Worth gown and enormous hat. She continued reading:

Though our acquaintance is (regrettably!) but slight, I hope that you will permit me to presume on it to invite your charming daughter to visit me in Newport. Miss Roosevelt, who will be staying with me, especially asked if Miss Boisvert might share her visit. Dear Alice would be heartbroken if her friend could not accompany her, and I should be heartbroken if dear Alice were disappointed. I quite dote upon the poor child, having known her aunt for so many years, and have longed to bring her for a nice, quiet, restful visit—

Grace snorted. If Mrs. Rennell thought dear Alice intended to be quiet and restful in Newport, she'd better think again.

—at my cottage. There are such splendid facilities for young people of our class to enjoy themselves here—tennis at the Casino and swimming at the beach club, not to mention concerts and dances to which it will be my pleasure to chaperone them.

A thought struck Grace. "Does she have children?"

"Let me see…" Mum knit her brow. "Two, as I recall. She had them rather late, so they're still small. Younger than Dorothy by a fair amount."

"Then why is she asking Alice and me to visit her?"

"The fact that Alice's father is the vice-president of the United States might have something to do with it," Grace's father said, coming into the room with the newspaper. He had a tall, well-built figure; all dryads were attractive, though Papa didn't have to worry about dyeing his hair—only female dryads' hair grew in green as they approached maturity. Which Grace thought was *completely* unfair.

"Cynic," Mum said, smiling up at him.

He paused to kiss both of them before sitting down in the chair on the other side of the fireplace. "No, just being a realist."

"Do you really think so?" Grace straightened and looked at him.

He unfolded his paper and opened it with a shake, but glanced up at her. "I'm afraid I do. If you're going to go to Newport—"

"So I *am* going!" She grinned at him.

"Ahem." Mum coughed gently.

He sent her an apologetic look, then turned his attention back to Grace. "*If* you're going to Newport, you should understand how things are— Oh, good afternoon, *Maman*. Hullo, Sapling."

Grand-mère glided into the room, followed by a sulky-looking Dorothy. "I have asked for tea to be brought," she announced, sitting on the sofa and waving Dorothy to a small, hard chair by a window. "Though I am not sure that Dorothée should be permitted to have any, since she seems to prefer to take her tea in the stable with the horses."

"Have you been eating oats again?" Mum asked her sternly. Papa hastily raised his newspaper, but not before Grace caught a glimpse of his twitching lips.

"I like 'em." Dorothy lifted her chin. "If they're good for the horses, why aren't they good for me? I'd rather be a horse than a tree any day!"

Grand-mère looked horrified, but Mum laughed. "With a long face and prominent teeth and very large hindquarters? Is that what you'd really rather be? Now, stop giving your grandmother palpitations, and stop eating the horses' oats. I'll ask Mrs. Toole to make oatmeal for breakfast for you if you'd like, but I think you ought to beg Grand-mère's pardon for being rude."

Dorothy glowered and blew through her lips, sounding exactly like Daisy, her pony. Mum shook her head, and Grand-mère glowered back at her.

"Horses who are badly behaved tend to have riding crops applied to their backsides," Papa said, emerging from his newspaper. He'd managed to bring his expression under control.

"I'm sorry I was rude, Grand-mère," Dorothy mumbled, and turned ostentatiously in her chair to gaze out the window.

It was time to change the subject before matters escalated. "Papa, what were you going to say about Newport?" Grace slipped to the floor beside Mum's chair and sat hugging her knees. Grand-mère sent her a disapproving look.

"Yes, Newport." He sighed. "It was a prominent port in the seventeenth and eighteenth centuries, but now its chief trade is in leisure and pleasure. It's... I don't know. A fantasy land, where the rich summer in enormous Italian palazzi and châteaux that look like they were exported straight from the Loire valley. Those houses—they call them "cottages" without the least sense of irony—say it all, I think."

"What do you mean?"

"They're not real," Mum said.

Papa nodded. "Exactly. What is a French castle doing on a rocky New England island? Life in Newport is all surface. This Mrs. Rennell happens to have a connection to the daughter of the new vice-president, so she's trotting her out to show her friends."

A knock on the door made him pause, and Rose came in with the tea tray, followed by the kitchen maid with a platter of cakes and bread and butter. After they'd left, Grace turned back to her father.

"Isn't that true about fashionable society anywhere?" she asked. "And what about us? We aren't human, but we pretend to be. Aren't we all surface too?"

"We pretend because we must. There's a difference." He lifted his hands helplessly. "How can I make you understand? The world is not so either-or, or so black and white."

"I do not think it is necessary for Grace to go," Grand-mère said, pouring tea. "Dorothée, bring this cup to your mother."

Mum accepted it with a wink, which removed some of the scowl from Dorothy's brow. "No, perhaps not *necessary...*" she said slowly, after taking a sip.

Grace held her breath.

"...but perhaps advisable. It would be good practice for if Grace goes to France in the fall. After all, she's just left off being a schoolgirl. Society in Paris, even among our own people, will be more intimidating even than Newport. Don't you think so, dear?" she asked Papa.

Grand-mère didn't move, but the set of her shoulders radiated disagreement. "It is too dangerous."

Papa raised his eyebrows. "That's a little extreme, don't you think?"

"No. Grace is too young to go among the humans alone. Especially the frivolous ones of Newport. What if one wants to marry her?"

Mum shrugged. "If one does, we say no."

"But what if she wants to marry him, eh? No—it is best if she keeps away from human society until she is safely married. She is a lovely girl, of course, as I was"—she patted her hair smugly—"and the young men will take notice. What if it goes to her head? She is only seventeen and her judgment is not yet that of a grown dryad."

"How old were you when you started thinking about marrying, Grand-mère?" Dorothy asked.

Unexpectedly, Grand-mère flushed an angry red. "I do not see that it is relevant to this discussion. If you cannot hold your tongue—"

"Dorothy, didn't we promise Mrs. Toole that we'd make

gingerbread for dessert tonight?" Grace said, scrambling to her feet. "Please excuse us." She jerked her head toward the door.

Dorothy didn't need to be asked twice. "Whew! What'd I say?" she whispered when they were safely in the hall.

"I don't know." Grace tucked her shirtwaist more firmly into her waistband. Why weren't ladies' clothes more forgiving about sitting on the floor? "Something set Grand-mère off, though, didn't it?"

"She hates me," Dorothy said gloomily.

Grace put an arm around her shoulders and led her down the hall. "No. I think she just doesn't understand you—us. I'll bet things were awfully different when she was a girl—why, that was a couple of centuries ago."

"I suppose." Dorothy looked up at Grace. "So do you think they'll let you go to Newport with Alice?"

"I don't know. But I'm going to corner Mum later and try to get a definite answer out of her."

Cornering her mother turned out to be easier than she expected. As they finished their gingerbread with whipped cream at the end of dinner and Rose had begun to clear the table, Mum announced, to no one in particular, "It's such a lovely evening, I think I'll go out for a breath of air."

"The roses need deadheading," Grand-mère said. "I'll get my gardening gloves."

"I was rather in the mood for a game of chess, *Maman*." Papa looked at Grand-mère.

Her eyes gleamed, but she replied with careful carelessness, "As you wish."

Grace waited a few moments until Grand-mère had retired to the library to play chess with Papa—she was a cutthroat player and loved to win—then slipped out the scullery door to the garden to follow after Mum.

It *was* a lovely night. The sky was cloudless, and the setting sun had painted it a vibrant red toward the west, fading through pink and yellow and into colorlessness in the east. A soft, fitful wind rustled the leaves. No mosquitoes marred the peace; the trees kept them at bay.

Their house was set on several acres, with formal gardens to the front of the house; a faint hint of rose and lily drifted on the breeze from that direction. But beyond the back lawn, itself dotted with tall chestnuts, was what amounted to a miniature forest—her mother's forest, which she was married to even more deeply than to Papa. Grace found her mother seated on one of the benches scattered under the trees there, waiting patiently with hands folded on her lap.

"I expected you'd want to talk," she said as Grace approached.

Grace sat down next to her, arranging the folds of her blue silk dress around her feet. Ever since she'd turned seventeen in March, she'd had to dress for dinner every night with Mum and Papa and Grand-mère. Most of the time she liked it, though she occasionally missed eating in the nursery with Dorothy and Cushy—Mrs. Cushman, their old nurse.

"Grand-mère says I must go to France in the fall and get married," she said, all in a rush. She'd planned a calm, adult-sounding speech to begin this discussion and couldn't remember a word of it now that the time had come.

Mum sighed. "Yes. I'm rather annoyed with her for bringing it up without consulting Papa or me first."

"You don't want me to go, then?"

"I didn't say that."

"Then what? Do you have plans for me as well, like Grand-mère?" So much for keeping her voice low and even as she'd planned, but she couldn't help it. "It would be nice if someone would let me know about them too, since it happens to be *my* life we're talking about."

Mum didn't scold her for speaking crossly, but took her hand and gave it a squeeze. "We were going to. Grand-mère spoke prematurely because this Newport visit worries her. But there are other choices too. What do *you* want?"

Grace couldn't help feeling taken aback. All through dinner she'd rehearsed this conversation in her mind, planning on standing up for her right to have a say in her life…and here was Mum, calmly asking her what she wanted. The annoying thing was that she had no idea what to reply.

"Er…I don't know," she mumbled.

"Do you want to marry and settle down to your forest?"

"Well, yes, of course…but not yet. I'd thought about college next year, maybe. If Sandy can, why can't I?" Her older brother, Alexander, who was visiting friends in Canada that summer, had just finished his first year at Harvard.

"Would you like to travel, too? We could go to the Continent for a few months—have our own little grand tour. Or maybe—"

"I want to go to Newport with Alice," Grace interrupted. "Can't I do that first, before we decide on anything else?"

Mum leaned back against the oak tree they sat under, and Grace realized it was one of her especial pets. She ran her hand across its bark in greeting and felt its slow, sleepy—the sun had nearly set, after all—greeting in return.

"I'm not sure," Mum finally said. "All of the not-very-complimentary things your father said about Newport are true. On the other hand, I can see why you'd want to go. I would have too, at your age."

"So?" Grace asked, expectantly.

"So…" Mum sighed again. "I'm not your age anymore. I'm much older and much more experienced, and I'm your mother. And I want to protect you from being hurt if I possibly can."

"Why should going to Newport hurt me?"

She could feel Mum's eyes on her in the twilight. "I know what happens in places like Newport in the summer. What if what Grand-mère is so worried about comes to pass, and you fall in love with a human boy?"

"Oh, *really*, Mum!" Grace cringed. Why was everyone thinking she was about to fall in love with the first male creature to cross her path?

Under her hand, which still rested on the tree, she felt a slow ripple of amusement. *You are a young animal, and that is what young animals do in the warm of the year,* the oak said to her.

"Not *this* young animal, thank you," she said firmly. "And the way Grand-mère goes on about no drop of human blood ever coursing through the veins of a Boisvert—it's positively Gothic."

"You know we couldn't approve of your marrying a human, at least while you are young," Mum continued. "What you choose to do after that is up to you, though we would never recommend your doing so. We live so long—what would it be like to know that your husband will age and die long before you ever reach that stage of your life? What about revealing what you are? It would be unfair to wait until after you're married to tell him that you aren't human, and unsafe to tell him before. What of children? You know that most children of dryad-human marriages don't survive past their first weeks. We are too different to breed well together. And finding your forest—will a human understand your need for that too?"

"I'm not planning on marrying one—"

"I'm sure you aren't, but do you truly understand what it means? Could you watch five out of six of your babies die? Or watch your husband grow old and feeble while you are still in your prime—or grow feeble too early yourself if you do not find your grove to settle in? No, don't answer," she said as Grace opened her mouth. "You can't understand yet. But you need to keep it in mind as you go out into the world."

"I *will*." Honestly, did they all think she had pine needles for brains? "But I wish Grand-mère would remember that it's the twentieth century. Just because Grand-père died young—"

"I would ask you to remember that Grand-mère lost both her husband and her forest," Mum said, her voice stern. "She was lucky to get out of Alsace alive with your father. An experience like that leaves scars; she wants to protect you from being hurt as well. And if I'm going to be honest, I agree with her, at least partly. What's keeping me from agreeing wholeheartedly is that there are other kinds of hurt."

"Like what?"

"Like the hurt of wondering what you've missed. It can make for a bitter old age." Mum shook her head and looked down at her hands.

Grace sat up straighter. "Mum?" she asked tentatively.

"What? Oh." Mum gave a small chuckle. "No, not me. I'm very happy that I married your father and settled here. But I've seen others."

Grace's head had begun to ache. She twisted on the bench to rest the side of her head against the tree and felt it reach out to her to soothe away the pain. "Thank you," she murmured, then said more loudly, "Mum, I know what you're saying is important. But right now, I don't want to fall in love or get married or find my grove. I just want to go to Newport with Alice and have fun."

"I know, dear." Mum spoke hesitantly. "And I think I'm prepared to risk your getting hurt one way in order to prevent your getting hurt in the other."

Her headache vanished. "Then I can go?"

"So long as you promise us that you'll be careful—and not only about young men."

Grace was too happy to bother pointing out that she'd gone through years of school with humans and had never had a problem. "I will—oh, Mum, thanks! And can I go with Alice to the Adirondacks too? That will be, uh…*safer* than Newport, won't it?"

"I expect it will." Mum rose. "I should go and write Mrs. Rennell so we can catch the morning post. And we'll have a lot of work to do with your wardrobe. You'll need some more day dresses and suits and a couple of evening dresses, I expect, and some hats. We'll have to go into town first thing tomorrow—" She stopped, and looking down at Grace, held out her hands. "Oh, sweetheart, you *will* be careful, won't you? You're such a lovely girl, and humans tend to be strongly drawn to us—*very* strongly," she added. "I'm afraid some boy will fall at your feet and—"

Grace took her hands and squeezed them gently. "I *promise*," she said quickly, both to reassure her and stop her from saying more. It was… Well, what did one say to things like that?

Mum smiled and squeezed back, then turned to make her way through the deepening dusk to the house. A few late fireflies lit up in greeting as she passed.

Grace hugged herself. "I'm going!" she murmured.

Why do you wish to leave here? the tree behind her asked. *Is this not where your roots are sunk?* It sounded forlorn.

Grace leaned back against its trunk. Talking was always easier when she could touch the tree. "Yes, my roots are here, but…" She reached up and patted the place where one of the tree's limbs began to branch off from its trunk. "But I have to grow too, just like you grow. Only my growing means I have to move around first. One day I'll plant my roots somewhere, like Mum has. But not yet."

A feeling of doubt was plain under her hand. *I know it is the way of humans. But you are kin to us as well. What if you forget that out there?*

She stood up abruptly. Sweet Yggdrasil, was she going to be lectured by everyone today? "I'm getting chilly. Good night." She patted the tree again and walked back through the deepening dusk toward the lights of the house, then broke into a skip. She was going to Newport!

THREE

The next two weeks passed in a blur of shopping: trips to the dressmaker, more trips to the dressmaker, visits to the milliner and to the glove and stocking counters at Jordan Marsh. Mum had been determined that she have a wardrobe that would pass muster in Newport, much to Grand-mère's disapproval.

Not that any of it—not even the dark blue wool bathing dress or the modest evening party frocks (blue chiffon, a pink taffeta that looked like rose petals, and two in obligatory white, one lace, one shantung silk)—were at all risqué or extravagant. Nevertheless, Grand-mère's disapproval had been constant, right up to the moment Papa and Mum and Alice's grandparents established them in a first-class compartment on the train to Newport, then stood waving goodbye on the platform as the train slowly chugged out of Boston's elegant new South Station.

Alice was already rummaging through the picnic basket Mum had handed them as they boarded. "Oh, good. Fried chicken. And sandwiches and lemonade. And cake! I'd forgotten what good picnics your Mrs. Toole packed. I think there's enough here for a trip to Chicago, never mind two or three hours to Newport."

"They don't want us leaving the compartment to go to the refreshment car. I'm surprised my grandmother didn't demand we bring a chaperone." Grace studied her reflection in the plate glass of the window as they passed under the shadow of a warehouse. Her new hat was just the thing—a dark tan straw adorned with puffs of gathered ivory ribbon, not too large, and tipped down toward her forehead at precisely the right elegant angle. It complemented her tan poplin walking suit and ivory silk shirtwaist perfectly.

"Well, honestly, there's two of us. We can chaperone each other." Alice grinned around the drumstick she'd started munching. "Of course, I'm not sure I'd trust myself to chaperone anyone."

Grace laughed. "Do you trust me to chaperone you?"

"Not a bit. We're going to have fun, I tell you! There won't be anyone to tell us not to."

To be fair, no one had ever really told them they couldn't have fun, but… "What about Mrs. Rennell?"

Alice wrinkled her nose. "Well, she can tell us, but we don't have to listen."

Grace blinked. That didn't sound like the Alice she knew; the pair of them had been…"enterprising" was the word Papa used to describe some of their escapades, but never defiant. "What will your parents have to say about that?"

"Frankly, I don't care. We're practically grown-ups by now, aren't we? And anyway, I'm the cuckoo in their nest, so why should they care what I do? Sometimes I wonder why they didn't leave me with my aunt after they got married, but Mother decided she had to be the perfect stepmother and take me in. I'm always on the outside looking in. Well, I'm tired of that. From now on, I'm looking out instead. They'd better look out too. I'm ready to find my own way…which means having fun!" She took a large bite of chicken.

Grace knew all this already—how Alice's mother had died when she was born and Mr. Roosevelt had left her to his sister to bring up. But there was an edge of bitterness in Alice's voice that hadn't been there before. It wasn't the first time she'd notice it; it had appeared several times while they were getting ready to leave for Newport, and even Mum had commented that Alice seemed "off" somehow. It made her glad she was going to be with Alice for this adventure.

"So," she asked casually, "what kind of fun did you mean to have?"

"Oh, you know. What we used to do when we were kids—running around having larks. But we're not supposed to do that now that we're proper young ladies." Alice pretended to fan herself with her drumstick. "It's a frightful bore."

"I want to be somewhere I haven't before," Grace said. "There's not much I haven't done or seen already in Chestnut Hill. I want to see new places. New *people*." Mum didn't like to leave her trees for long, and Papa always did what Mum wanted.

"Poor thing." Alice patted her knee. "Chestnut Hill has always been like a safe little cave for me, but I can see that if you're in a cave *all* the time, it would get dull. We'll make up for that. We'll try everything we can."

"Yachting? I've never been on anything larger than a rowboat." There was a jaunty yachting costume with a bloused waist and sailor collar and simply *adorable* hat in one of her trunks that she couldn't wait to wear.

"I suppose." Alice managed to open the window a few inches and toss out the remains of her drumstick. "I was thinking of something even more exciting."

"Like what?"

Her eyes glinted. "We'll have to wait and see what presents itself, won't we? Here, would you like a sandwich? Mmm, egg salad." She waved it at Grace.

Grace took it. "When you say exciting, do you mean...boys?"

"Why, Grace! What an idea!" Alice pretended to look shocked. Then she laughed. "Well, of course. I told you I'd been making a study of them this year."

"What did you learn?" Thank heavens Grand-mère wasn't here or she'd have a fit to hear them talking about boys. Really, it wasn't like she was going to chase them or anything. She was merely *interested*.

"Ha! I wondered when you'd ask! For one thing, they're not very subtle. If they like you, you'll know it—they act like big, slobbery spaniels, looking at you with their hearts in their eyes and their tongues hanging out of their mouths."

"Ew." Grace wrinkled her nose. Spaniels... This was not what she'd expected.

"Well, maybe not exactly. But sort of. The thing is, it's ridiculously easy to get them into that state. Captivating them, we call it."

"How?"

"Oh, there's lots you can do," Alice said airily. "The most important bit to remember is that you want to keep them off-balance at all times so that they don't start taking you for granted. Keep 'em guessing."

"Guessing. Right." That didn't sound too hard.

"Now, first thing, you have to choose your mark—"

"Who's Mark?"

Alice sighed. "It's slang. *Mark* means your chosen victim."

"Oh. Right." Grace hesitated, then asked, "So...how do you choose one?"

To her surprise, Alice didn't laugh. "It depends. Sometimes you might be bored and want to pass time—you know, have some fun with whoever happens to be around. Or you might really like one. Or you might want to flirt with one to make another one jealous. There's a lot to consider."

Hmm. Flirting out of sheer boredom didn't sound appealing. "And then?"

"Then you choose your method of attack, depending on your mark and what you want to do with him. If you're just having fun, you can do whatever enters your head: be admiring, so he gets the idea you think he's the most wonderful thing ever. You can take care of that with mostly words, but you've got to play the part as well. Give him a look."

"Like this?" Grace tried to make herself look bright and interested.

Alice looked disgusted. "No, *not* like that. You look like a first grader waiting to hand teacher an apple. Think *captivating*." She let her eyelids droop slightly, glancing up through her eyelashes and pouting her lips.

Grace couldn't help giggling. "That's awful! You look as though you're about to throw up."

"I beg your pardon, but it works every time. You should also pretend that the things he likes are just as fascinating to you. Be admiring all over the place."

"What if his hobby is train robbery?"

"Well, *really*, Grace, I'm not even going to bother answering that. And it's not only hobbies. If he wants to see himself as a man of the world, tell him how sophisticated he is. Reflect how he wants to see himself."

Grace thought about that. It would probably be a highly effective tactic...if one could bring oneself to do it. "Anything else?"

"That's the basics. Now, if you get tired of him, put on the snow-maiden face." She looked down her nose and pursed her lips into a disapproving knot. "It helps if you can imply boredom as well. That's usually done with raising one eyebrow a little."

"I hope no one's ever caught you practicing in the mirror."

"My brother Ted did once, but he ended up practicing with

me. You think only girls can do this?"

"I thought you said all boys were spaniels?"

"Almost all. There's a few who aren't. Now, if you're trying to make one jealous, then you need to be sweet as pie to his rival. Really overdo the admiration and pretend you don't even see the other. It drives 'em nuts."

Grace hesitated, then asked, "What…what if you actually do like one?"

Alice shrugged. "I don't know. It hasn't happened yet. But I'm sure there'll be plenty of boys for us to practice on, in case we do like any. Newport is one big party, and we'll be in the thick of it."

"I suppose that will depend on whether Mrs. Rennell—"

"I *told* you, I don't think we'll have to worry about her. I'll have her eating out of my hand in no time. She won't have the least idea of what we get up to."

Grace took a bite of her sandwich. She and Alice had gotten into any manner of scrapes as girls (and even now, as young ladies), running around Chestnut Hill like a pair of wild things. *The Trouble Twins,* Alice's grandfather had christened them years ago. But this felt different, somehow. Any trouble they'd gotten into then had been the result of sheer high spirits; it was one thing to launch pranks and another to set out to intentionally deceive well-meaning people. Or to trifle with their affections.

But if she was right, then everyone did it. Did that mean dryads would as well, when—*if*—Grand-mère had her way and they all went to France in the autumn? However, Alice had failed to address one question: if everyone played such games, then how did you know when someone really did like you?

"Grace?"

"Hmm?" Grace looked up from her sandwich.

Alice handed her a bottle of lemonade. "I—I'm glad you're here. It'll be just like always, won't it? We may be seventeen and all, but—"

"But we're still the Trouble Twins." Grace grinned at her.

"'Both for one, and all for fun!'" Alice chanted, and clinked her lemonade bottle against Grace's.

The train inched to a stop in Newport two hours later. As they stood on the platform, Alice scanned the crowd. "Oh, there she is. Put on your best sweet-young-thing face and follow my lead. Oh, Mrs. Rennell!" she called, waving vigorously. "We're over here!"

A small, fair-haired woman, dressed in a smart gray walking suit trimmed with dark blue braid and a large hat, was hurrying toward them, trailed by a pair of sturdy young men and a couple of railway porters.

"My dear Miss Roosevelt! There you are!" she said. Grace remembered her mother's comment about Pekinese and tried not to smile; Mrs. Rennell indeed had the same nervous air, turned-up nose, and bright, darting eyes. She didn't quite yip, but her voice was high and quick. "Was your journey all right? I was so worried something might happen. And Miss Boisvert—I would have known you anywhere, you're so like your lovely mother. How is she? And your family, Miss Roosevelt—did you leave them all well?"

"They're fi—" Alice began, but Mrs. Rennell didn't seem to notice. "Now, I brought a couple of my servants who'll take care of your things, and I thought we could drive by the Casino and take a peek in—we could even have luncheon there if you'd like. Unless you feel the need to freshen up?" It was clear she hoped they didn't.

"Not at all," Alice said. "We'd love to see the Casino, wouldn't we, Grace?"

"Oh, yes—quite!" Grace agreed.

Mrs. Rennell kept up a stream of chatter all the way to her

carriage. "You know, of course, that it isn't a *gambling* casino," she said, raising her parasol once they were settled in it. "That's just its name. I think it means something in Italian. It's simply a lovely social club. There's tennis, of course, and croquet, and horse shows, and the Sunday evening concerts and Thursday evening dances, and cards, and billiards for the men, and lots more. Why, there's even a theater. Oh, dear, it isn't going to rain, is it?" Mrs. Rennell peered above Grace's head at the sky.

Grace looked up behind her at a bank of gathering clouds and frowned. It was hard influencing their movement so close to the ocean, but she was able to nudge them farther north, past the town. "I shouldn't think so," she said.

"I do hope you're right— Oh, here we are," Mrs. Rennell said brightly as the carriage stopped in front of a long, two-storied building with multiple gables. It looked like a row of shops— striped canvas awnings over windows filled with goods were all that Grace could see as she climbed down to the street—but Mrs. Rennell led them past these to a broad arch which led to a covered passage, like a tunnel through the building. A second later, they emerged in a different world.

A large oval courtyard of perfectly manicured lawn spread out like a green velvet carpet before them; at its center, a fountain splashed. A clock tower rose to their left, and on either side, wings enclosed the oval of grass. Opposite them stretched a covered, crescent-shaped arcade, and beyond the arcade Grace could see more manicured grass.

"There! What do you think of our little club?" Mrs. Rennell asked, shepherding them along a paved walk to steps leading up to the arcade. A breeze blew through the trellises that formed its walls, fluttering the ivy that grew up it. Large oval openings looked out across the lawns, which Grace could see were traversed by curving paths that passed tennis courts chalked into the grass.

Grace let Alice make the appropriate responses and gazed out across the space, where here and there young trees shaded the path. The sight of them scattered about, separate from each other, reminded her that she was alone here, far from anyone of her kind...but wasn't that why she was here? To see new places and meet people other than her family? She hadn't expected, though, that meeting new people would somehow make her feel more alone. The trees looked sad to her, as trees planted for landscaping purposes rather than growing naturally always did. Maybe they would talk to her if she spoke to them.

"It's, er, so lovely—can't we go for a little walk?" she asked, interrupting Alice. "We've been cooped up in the train so long, some fresh air would be nice."

Mrs. Rennell blinked. "Well...yes, certainly you may. I'll run inside and see if they can't give us a table for lunch in the cafe. Miss Roosevelt?" She took firm hold of Alice's arm. Alice rolled her eyes but let her lead her away.

Grace descended the stairs from the arcade. The sun was hot on her shoulders and she wished she'd brought a parasol; instead of making her tanned, too much sun made her dryad skin more greenish. Maybe she shouldn't have been so quick to shoo those clouds away. She paused, then started down the path unwinding like a ribbon across the grass. A group of white-flannel-clad men with tennis racquets on their shoulders stumped cheerfully down the path ahead of her on their way to a court, while others were making their way slowly back toward the Casino, laughing and obviously rehashing their game.

"Ahh!"

An agonized, high-pitched cry made Grace turn. A boy in a navy blue jersey and gray knickers sprawled in a heap at the bottom of the stairs she had just come down. Tennis balls scattered in every direction, and a wire bucket rolled crazily to a stop past him—a ball boy, evidently, who'd tripped down the stairs.

Grace started toward him—he looked to be no older than nine—but at that moment a tall young man, hatless and dressed in white flannels and a white knitted vest and shirt with the sleeves rolled up his tanned forearms, leapt gracefully down the stairs. He landed like a panther in the grass next to the boy.

"Here, Master Peewit," Grace heard him say, as he lifted the boy to his feet and held him by the shoulders to steady him. "You're not broken, are you?"

"N-no, sir," the child quavered, digging his knuckles into his eyes to try to stop his tears.

"Brave lad! But just because we call you after a bird doesn't mean you can fly down steps, you know." He softened his scold with a wink.

This elicited a faint smile. "You just did, sir."

"Ah, but I know how to fly, you see." The young man surveyed him. "You're looking a little worse for wear." He whisked an immaculate handkerchief from his pocket and gave the boy's face a quick scrub. "There. That will do until we can pick up all the balls. Then you can run back inside and have Mrs. Soares in the kitchen check those scraped knees—"

"But the gentlemen there'll be wantin' 'em, sir!" the boy protested, pointing at the foursome, now nearly out of sight on one of the meandering paths.

"I'll bring them to them. You go along to the kitchen. I'll bet there might be a sausage roll or two on hand. They're capital for staving off the lingering effects of falls, I hear." He gave the boy a flashing white smile, startling in his tanned face, that made Grace's heart begin to beat a little faster, then fetched the bucket and started to pick up balls.

A couple of them had rolled toward Grace. She tucked her purse under her arm, bent to scoop them up, and ventured back up the path. "I think these are yours," she said, a little shyly.

The young man with the beautiful grin glanced up. Some of

his slightly-too-long, sun-lightened hair flopped down over his forehead, and he brushed it back as he straightened. Their gazes met, and under his straight brows his blue eyes widened. He took a step toward her, and another.

"Thank you," he said, holding out his hands. His voice no longer held the cheerfully authoritative tone he'd used with the boy; it was quieter and almost uncertain.

Grace dropped the balls into his waiting hands. One of her gloved fingers brushed his, and she saw him swallow hard.

"I—I've not seen you here before," he said.

"We only just arrived," she replied. "Right off the Boston train, in fact." Yes, let them talk commonplaces; she was too busy wondering why she felt like she already knew him—that she'd always known him—though she was sure they'd never met. If they had, she would have remembered that smile.

"The Boston train," he repeated. His hair had fallen over his forehead again, and she felt an irrational desire to reach up and brush it back.

"Hallo! Here she is, Mrs. Rennell!"

Grace glanced up. Beyond the young man was Mrs. Rennell, in her large hat and veil, descending the stairs from the arcade. Alice was close behind her.

"Thank you, Alice dear," Mrs. Rennell said. "We've got a lovely table for lun— Oh, good afternoon, Kit. I see you've met one of my houseguests already."

The young man's—Kit's—face seemed to change subtly. It was like he'd donned a mask—one that possessed his features but nevertheless seemed to conceal him. "Hello, Mrs. Rennell. I didn't know your guests were arriving today." He looked at Grace, and again she felt that shiver run through her as his eyes—still as intense and uncertain as they had been a moment ago—looked at her from behind the smooth mask. "We hadn't quite gotten to introductions yet."

"Well, I shall take care of that. Girls, this is Kit Rookwood—Christopher, I suppose I ought to say, though no one calls him that—"

"Only my father, when I've disappointed him," he said, smiling. The quirk of mischief in his smile didn't quite reach the rest of his face, Grace noticed.

"I doubt that happens often," Mrs. Rennell said archly. "Kit is a popular young man around here. Kit, this is Miss Roosevelt, and this is her friend Miss Boisvert, from Boston."

Grace saw his eyes move from Alice to her, and back again. They had suddenly gone blank, as if the mask had shifted to cover them too.

"Miss Roosevelt, I'm a great admirer of your father's books." He stepped forward to shake Alice's hand, and suddenly, somehow, they were all walking back toward the arcade, Kit Rookwood with Alice and her with Mrs. Rennell.

"Oh, good," Mrs. Rennell murmured to her. "I was hoping Kit would take a liking to dear Alice. He's most charming. Excellent company for a young lady."

Grace knew—or thought she did. She'd liked how he'd come to the rescue of the lad who'd tripped down the stairs. It would have been easy to pretend not to have seen him and continue on his way, but he hadn't. Still, it seemed...well, *odd* that he'd more or less ignored her after Mrs. Rennell introduced them. After the look they'd shared... She hadn't imagined it, had she?

Ahead of them Alice broke into a hearty laugh as they climbed the stairs. What were they talking about?

"Just fancy! Mr. Rookwood here is a *Yale* man," Alice called as she and Mrs. Rennell joined them on the arcade. "Do you think we should we even be speaking to him, Grace? What would my father say? And your brother?"

Before Grace could reply, Kit dropped to one knee at Alice's feet. "Oh, say it isn't so!" he declaimed. "To be banished from your presence over such a little thing as that?"

Alice laughed again, but this time she sounded coy. "Having gone to Yale shows a distinct lack of discernment, Mr. Rookwood. Any Harvard man will tell you that."

He sighed. "Will there be no winning my way back into your good graces?"

Alice actually blushed. "Well…"

He scrambled to his feet. "I solemnly swear I'll spend the rest of your visit atoning for my family's short-sighted decision not to send me to Harvard, and prove that even a Yale man can be civilized company."

"Civilized company?" She wrinkled her nose, trying not to laugh. "How dull."

"Very well. I'll be uncivilized company if you prefer." His eyes laughed back at hers. "I'm good at that too."

Mrs. Rennell tittered. "Kit, you're such a rogue. Now really, we must go claim our table for lunch."

"Of course, ma'am." He looked again at Alice. "If you play tennis, Miss Roosevelt, I hope you'll give me the pleasure of a game or three soon." He nodded to them, flashed a last grin at Alice, and vanished down the stairs to the courts.

Mrs. Rennell barely waited until he was out of earshot. Taking Alice's arm, she said, "My word, Alice—you don't mind if I call you by your Christian name, do you, my dear?—but you do seem to have charmed Kit Rookwood."

"Oh, I don't know," Alice said demurely. "And he's only a Yale man, after all." She winked at Grace, who managed a smile in return.

Sitting down at the prominent table Mrs. Rennell had found for them in the restaurant and perusing the menu permitted Grace a few quiet minutes to try to put in order her confused thoughts. What had happened? She'd thought Kit Rookwood had seemed…well, it had been as if something had somehow fallen into place when their eyes had met over the scatter of tennis balls on the grass. Or had she imagined it? Considering how he had behaved toward Alice, she must have.

Or…her heart sank a little. *This* must be what flirtation was all about. Alice was right: she obviously had a lot to learn…but it was too bad. She'd liked Kit Rookwood's kindness to the ball boy. And she liked his golden good looks, like summer personified, and the way the corners of his mouth quirked just so—

"Girls, look," Mrs. Rennell said in a stage whisper, tilting her head toward the entrance, where two middle-aged women stood surveying the diners. "That's Mrs. Fish and Mrs. Oelrichs. They're—"

But whatever it was they were remained unsaid for the moment, for the pair had swept into the room and were headed directly for them. Mrs. Rennell looked both delighted and terrified as they drew up to their table like a pair of ocean liners coming in to dock. "Good afternoon, Mrs.…er, ladies," she said, and Grace realized she was unsure whom to give precedence by greeting first.

One of them, short and with a well-corseted-in figure, gave a malicious smile, recognizing her dilemma. The other, equally short but less plump, with heavy-lidded eyes and a humorous quirk to her mouth, didn't even seem to hear her. "Hallo, then," she said without preamble to Mrs. Rennell. "Are these your guests you've been making sure everyone in town knows about? Which of you is the vice-president's daughter?"

"I'm Miss Roosevelt, ma'am," Alice said, looking wide-eyed.

"And who's this?"

"My friend Miss Grace Boisvert, of Boston."

"Oh," said the first woman. "*Boston.*" She pronounced it with a slight sneer.

"Don't be a snob, Tessie," the second woman said. "I like Boston. At least, I think I do."

"Have you even been there?"

"Quite possibly," the second woman replied. "If I haven't, I should go, if all the girls there are as pretty as you, lamb," she said to Grace. "I like pretty people. They're much easier to bear than ugly ones… Oh, wait! Yes, I have been to Boston. I bought some of my best pieces there. Give me good American furniture any day. Too much frou-frou French stuff in this town."

The woman she'd called Tessie sniffed. "We don't all share your tastes, Mamie."

"Which is good, or I'd have to pay more for my American things. I don't have the cash you and Alva do. Here, why don't you give a lunch for these two sometime this week, and that way I can talk to 'em and find out if they're worth inviting to my house. Wednesday would be convenient."

Tessie sputtered. "You might have asked if I already had plans!"

"You're right, I might have." She squinted at Mrs. Rennell. "You'll have to come too, won't you? All right, luncheon at Rosecliff on Wednesday if you don't mind wet plaster—the house still isn't finished. I guess we'll have to invite Alva too. Or we could forget to, and make her mad." She laughed loudly, took Tessie's arm, and propelled her from the table. "That Roosevelt girl's all right, I suppose, but her friend's quite stunning, don't you think?" she said to her friend as they swept back out of the room, not troubling to lower her voice.

They all sat in silence for a moment, as did most of the other diners in the room. Grace wondered if they were all as shocked as she was at the behavior of the woman addressed as Mamie. She'd been astonishingly rude, yet there had been no malice in either her words or manner—she merely seemed to say and do whatever was on her mind. "May I ask—" she started to say.

Mrs. Rennell took a deep breath. "Tessie Oelrichs and Mamie Fish are two of the leaders of society here, now that Mrs. Astor has retired from entertaining. Mrs. Belmont—Mrs. Alva Vanderbilt Belmont—is the third. Mrs. Fish is somewhat—somewhat *unusual*."

"That's one way to describe her," Alice murmured.

Now that the air seemed to have cleared a little, Mrs. Rennell lost her dazed look and began to light up. "Lunch at Rosecliff, with Mrs. Fish and Mrs. Belmont! I couldn't have asked for a better—" she began, then composed herself. "It's a nice compliment to you, Alice, and will guarantee that you'll receive lots of invitations while you're here."

"It sounded more like a compliment to Grace," Alice said. Grace looked at her quickly. She hadn't been hurt by Mrs. Fish's remark, had she? How could she, after entrancing Kit Rookwood so thoroughly?

As if her thought had summoned him, Grace caught sight of Mr. Rookwood, leading the ball boy who had fallen on the stairs toward a swinging door that must lead to the kitchens. He paused at the door, spoke to someone within, then gave the boy a gentle push and turned. Again their eyes met, but this time Grace quickly looked down at the napkin in her lap.

Mrs. Rennell, however, had spotted him. "Back again, Kit?" she called.

He came to their table. "It's hard to keep away, ma'am. Did Mrs. Oelrichs and Mrs. Fish find you? They were looking for you, so I directed them here."

"Yes, they did, thank you." Mrs. Rennell looked smug. "By the way, Kit, where are your parents? I should love for them to meet Miss Roosevelt."

"Mother had a fancy to see the Pan-American Exposition, so they're off to Buffalo for a few days. I expect they'll be back sometime soon—"

"Oh, I was there!" Alice interrupted. "My father opened the Exposition for President McKinley, who couldn't go because his wife was ill. I had a splendid time on the midway with the French ambassador—we went riding on camels and saw someone dancing the hoochie-koochie, even. Didn't you want to go too?"

He shrugged, then grinned at her. "Life's much more interesting right here, I'm finding. Well, I'll leave you to your lunch, ladies." He sauntered from the room, paused in the doorway to glance back at Alice, one eyebrow raised, then disappeared.

FOUR

"I wonder what one wears to the Sunday night concerts at the Casino?" Alice asked absently as she looked through the dresses hanging in her wardrobe that Wednesday afternoon. "Evening dress seems a little out of place, but I'm not sure what else to wear."

"Ask Mrs. Rennell," Grace said from the window seat, where she gazed out at the garden. The only trees out there were short, ornamental cultivars—no sturdy oaks or graceful elms. Their absence was unsettling. It had been hard to fall asleep at night without her chestnut at the window, murmuring a lullaby.

"Oh, I will. Eventually." She paused. "This yellow muslin will make me look about twelve if I don't do something about it. And it looked so grown-up back at my grandmother's. What are you staring at out there?"

"Nothing. Just thinking." This was what she'd wanted, wasn't it? To live like a human, not a dryad. She sighed and squared her shoulders. Surely there would be compensations, eventually—

"That's a terrible habit, you know. Young men don't like girls who think."

"Pooh." Grace made a face at her. "What did you think about today?"

Alice shrugged and set the yellow muslin aside. "Not much. Why?"

Lunch today at Rosecliff had been…well, unexpected. In several ways. For one thing, there was the house itself. Mrs. Rennell had made sure they drove by the grander "cottages" yesterday during their afternoon carriage ride—enormous, heavy, imposing places. But Mrs. Oelrichs' Rosecliff was cut from a different cloth. Modeled after a French palace, it was gleaming white and columned like a Greek temple. Inside, the white marble entrance hall was dominated by a heart-shaped staircase. It was beautiful, and Grace could not help saying to Mrs. Oelrichs, who awaited them in the salon doorway, "This must be the most perfect house I've ever seen!"

Behind her, Mrs. Fish laughed. "*That's* the way to make up to Tessie, pet!"

Mrs. Fish took it upon herself to introduce them to all the other ladies…and to Grace's surprise, they were very kind. To her further surprise, she and Alice were showered with dozens of invitations for the next three weeks. Now, perched in the window seat, she frowned.

"Alice, all these invitations… Doesn't it bother you that we probably only got them because you're your father's daughter?"

"Not particularly." Alice held another dress against herself in the mirror and grimaced at her reflection "Did you think it was solely due to our charms?"

"N-no." It was lowering, really, but what did she expect? Papa had warned her, after all. "I don't think they particularly cared for Mrs. Rennell."

Alice tossed the gown on her bed. "I do wish I could have one in black. It would be so deliciously inappropriate… Of course they don't care for her. She's a climber. She desperately wants to be a bigger fish than she is, and I'm part of her campaign to get accepted in better circles. If I'm invited everywhere, she'll have to be too. The nice thing about that, though, is that you will as well."

"I suppose. But it seems so…"

"Calculating? So what? After all, it was because of you that I was accepted in Chestnut Hill. Even though I was half a Lee, it didn't mean people had to be more than polite to me for my grandmother's sake. Now I'm returning the favor. Except that you don't need to ride on my coattails since Mrs. Fish seems to like you." She laid down the dress she was inspecting and came to sit next to Grace. "I'm used to it. This is the way it's been since Father came back from Cuba. You should hear what my brother says about what it's like at school, with boys wanting to be his friend so that they might get invited to meet Father. It doesn't mean that we can't use it to enjoy ourselves, though." She punched Grace lightly in the arm and jumped up, heading back to her wardrobe. "Let's get my things done, and then we'll start planning your clothes," she said over her shoulder.

Grace sat for a moment longer, struck by a thought. Maybe that was why Kit Rookwood — whom she hadn't been able to stop thinking about, for some reason — had seemed so taken with Alice: because he, too, was only interested in meeting the vice-president's daughter. Why, he'd as much said he knew Mrs. Rennell was expecting guests — had he thought *she* was Alice when they first met? That had to be it…but she couldn't help feeling disappointed. That look they'd shared — it still sent shivers through her. And he'd seemed different from most young men — at least, different from some of her brother's arrogant college friends. But maybe she'd been wrong about that.

◆·✦·❖·✦·◆

Mrs. Rennell was delighted with the results of the luncheon at

Rosecliff. She sat at the breakfast table the next morning gloating over the stack of invitations that had arrived in the mail.

"Look! Dear Mrs. Van Alen has invited us to a luncheon…oh, what fun, girls—an archery competition at Mrs. Rogers'…and dinner at the Goelets' next Saturday…you shall certainly be here, my dear, won't you?"

This last remark was directed toward Mr. Rennell, whose physical presence was indicated by a pair of hands holding a newspaper; periodically one of them would grope for a coffee cup and vanish with it behind the paper. He'd arrived last night from New York, where he did "something very important at Mr. Morgan's bank," according to Mrs. Rennell.

"I wanna do archery!" demanded young Master Parker Rennell, who'd joined them for breakfast along with his younger sister, Sarah, and their governess.

"Yes, yes, my love. Miss Hamm will take you out later to play with your bow and arrows. Oh, Mrs. Belmont is having another motor-car race—"

"I definitely want to go to that!" Alice said. "Don't you, Grace?"

"I wanna motor-car!" Parker shrieked.

"Filthy things," Mr. Rennell growled from behind his paper.

"Oh, I don't know," Mrs. Rennell said meditatively. "Lots of people who matter have them now. Let's see…another musicale, at Mrs. Wilson's…oh, a polo match, that's always exciting…and…my heavens, a ball at Mrs. Vander—" Mrs. Rennell stopped mid-sentence. She looked uneasily at Alice, who was sitting up very straight indeed.

"Did you say a ball?" she asked eagerly.

Grace waited for Parker to want to go to a ball, but he was finding it more interesting to spoon jam into the pockets of his trousers while Miss Hamm tried to coax Sarah into finishing her milk.

"Er…yes, but…" Mrs. Rennell turned red. "I fear we shall have to send our regrets to Mrs. Vanderbilt." The words obviously cost her an effort to say.

"Why, ma'am?" Grace asked, as Alice looked too thunderstruck to reply. Mrs. Rennell refusing a ball at one of the most exclusive houses in Newport?

"I…er…made a solemn promise to both your mothers that we wouldn't… Well, that we would keep to quieter evening entertainments. After all, you aren't really out yet, are you, my dears?" She waved a finger at them in an attempt at playfulness. "But goodness, we certainly have enough other things to do, don't we? I declare, we shan't have a moment's rest the next few weeks!"

Alice was too well brought up to argue with Mrs. Rennell but was barely able to contain herself as they went back upstairs to change into crisp white shirtwaists and canvas shoes before going to the Casino to play tennis.

"Did you know that we weren't allowed to go to balls?" she demanded, following Grace into her room and leaning against the closed door.

"No." Grace kicked off her slippers and started to unbutton her dress. "But I'm not surprised. It took enough convincing just to let me *come* here, much less go to balls."

"It's so…humiliating!" Alice began to pace up and down the room. "It's like they think we're children or something."

"But we're not really adults. We're sort of in between childhood and adulthood," Grace said, pausing. "It's—it's like we're actors waiting to be called on stage."

"Well, actors get to rehearse. How are we supposed to learn to be adults if they don't let us practice doing adult things?" Alice stopped pacing. "I know. I'm going to make me some magics to make sure we get to at least one ball while we're here. I don't think Mother wants me to have any fun at all."

Last spring and summer, when there had been talk of her father accepting the vice-presidential nomination or some other national public office, Alice had told her that she was determined to do something about the situation. Being vice-president—so second-best!—wasn't good enough for her father. Being governor-general of the Philippines, though, would be much grander…so she'd commenced on a course of what she called "making magics" to help bring this about. She'd never showed any of her magics to Grace, which was just as well: Grace wasn't sure she could maintain a straight face if she had. What would Alice say if she knew that Grace and her family were capable of real magic?

"So playing tennis with me at the Casino isn't fun?" Grace pretended to pout.

"Oh, stop that. You know it is, even when you beat me all the time. But I want to go to a ball—or several balls—while we're here. Don't you?"

"Well, yes," Grace admitted. If she were to be honest, she *did* want to see what one was like. Not from the vantage point of peering down through the banisters, as she had as a child when Mum had held parties at home, but there in the thick of it. Alice was right about rehearsing for adulthood.

"There, I knew you would! Well, I'm going to make it happen. See if I don't!" She looked at Grace. "Aren't you ready *yet?* Mrs. Rennell said she'd be ready to leave in twenty minutes—"

She dodged, laughing, as Grace threw one of her canvas shoes at her, and ducked round the door.

⋯⊹⋅⊱⊰⋅⊹⋯

An hour later Grace had managed to put Alice's magics and most everything else out of her head on a beautifully groomed grass tennis court at the Casino. She and Alice were gently lobbing a ball back and forth over the net so that they could chat if they felt like it. Alice was still complaining about her stepmother's stricture against balls, so Grace let her blow off steam, responding suitably whenever it was required but not really paying much attention.

It felt good to move and stretch. Grace realized that, whenever Mrs. Rennell was around, she held herself stiffly, probably out of sympathy to their highly strung hostess. It was a beautiful morning—no need for her to alter the weather today. Out of sheer high spirits she returned Alice's patted ball with a hard drive to the far side of the court that she knew Alice would never be able to return.

She was right. "Very funny, you," Alice called. "Just for that, you can go find where it went. Anyway, let's stop for a moment. I need to retie my shoes."

"All right," Grace said amiably and started round the net to the lawn beyond while Alice headed for a bench next to their court, strategically set in the shade of a small maple tree.

She hadn't gotten past the back line when a tall, white-flannelled figure came strolling toward her, racquet on shoulder, tossing a ball casually in one hand. "Lose something?" Kit Rookwood called. His smile brushed past her and came to rest on Alice, who hastily finished tying her shoe and leapt up to join Grace.

"Mr. Rookwood!" she said. "Is that our ball? You angel!"

"Well, not really," he replied, his smile widening. "At least, angel's not the role I usually aspire to. Are you done playing, Miss Roosevelt?"

Alice seemed to melt under the force of that grin. "Not at all. I had to tie my shoe and sent Grace to fetch our ball since she hit it so abominably past me—"

"I did not!" Grace was stung into retorting. "You missed the return!"

"Well, anyway, we're here." She smiled at him, head tilted to one side. "Are you playing this morning?"

"I'd like to," he said meaningfully.

"In that case, won't you play with us? If you're not busy, of course."

"I was hoping you'd say that. After all, you promised me a game."

"Did I?" Alice pretended to look vague, not very successfully—she was *never* vague.

"Need I remind you exactly when you promised that, Miss Roosevelt?"

"I'll go and have a seat, shall I?" Grace said to no one in particular, but they didn't even notice. She almost stomped over to the tree-shaded bench—insofar as one *could* stomp while wearing tennis shoes—and slumped onto it, her good mood all but evaporated. Well, *really*. Alice was suddenly acting as though she weren't even there, and Kit Rookwood wasn't any better. She watched while Kit squinted up at the sun and gallantly offered to change sides with Alice so that the glare wouldn't be in her eyes, then sent a gentle forehand over the net.

"Think I'm a softie, do you?" Alice called, hitting it back to him.

"Wouldn't dream of it," he replied, returning an incrementally harder shot.

"He's going to let her win. I know it," Grace muttered. Was this really how flirting went? Imagine a boy at home *letting* her win at tennis! Whenever anyone beat her, he'd jolly well earned it. It was one thing to let Dorothy win now and then…that's what you did with a little sister. But to let a person of one's own age win, as one would a child…well, it didn't imply much respect for the other person, did it? She'd expected better of him…but between this and his obvious making up to the vice-president's daughter, maybe she'd been wrong—

I have watched here for many years, and still I do not

understand, said the tree behind her.

"Oh!" Grace started. "Forgive me, cousin. I should have spoken," she added more quietly. She'd been so occupied with watching Alice and Kit that she'd forgotten her manners. It was nice to talk to a tree for a change. They were calm and gentle and didn't dissemble. "Greetings to you; it is a pleasure to rest in your shadow. What don't you understand?"

The tree was silent for a moment. A few of its upper leaves fluttered, then were still. *This thing men do—the sending of an object back and forth between them.*

"Tennis, you mean," Grace murmured. "It's not the only thing they do. It's a game—a pastime. It's done for enjoyment."

A 'pastime'. Does not all time pass, no matter what one does?

"I suppose it does." Alice was laughing at something Kit had said, and she wasn't sure if she'd wished she heard it or not.

Yes. The tree fell silent. Grace watched the play and wished Alice would try harder, but she kept missing balls that she would never have missed playing with her. She wasn't trying to let *him* win, was she? How funny, the pair of them doing their best to let the other win. Except it wasn't funny. It was nauseating.

It is strange, this tennis, the tree said.

"You're telling me," Grace muttered.

I have seen men who profess the greatest amity toward each other do this tennising. Yet when they tennis, it is clear that their amity is all on the surface, and they are tennising as a way to best each other. Do men often do one thing and use it to mean another?

"Happens all the time." Like right now. She settled herself more comfortably in the tree's shade and resigned herself to watching. It would be interesting to see who won this battle of wills.

To her surprise, Kit Rookwood did—that is, he managed to lose to Alice. It must have taken some doing on his part, for it was clear he was a strong player.

"Well played, Miss Roosevelt," he said as they shook hands over the net.

"Piffle." She tapped him with her racquet as they strolled toward Grace. "You let me win, you bad creature. I shall get a swelled head and be insufferable, and you'll deserve it." She pulled out her handkerchief and fanned herself with it.

He was immediately all concern. "Is it too warm for you? May I bring you a cool drink? Or escort you back to the piazza?"

"No, I want to sit in the shade for a few minutes." Her eyes lit on Grace on the bench, and she smiled. "I say, why don't you play Grace while I take her shady-looking seat?"

Grace sat up. Play him, after that? "Alice, I don't really —"

"Oh, humor me. You'll have to do a proper job of beating Mr. Rookwood, since he was so *gallant* as to let me do it badly." She sent him a sly sideways look.

Kit barely even glanced at Grace. "Are you sure you wouldn't rather go back to the club?" he asked Alice again. "It's really gotten quite warm —"

"I'm sure." Alice prodded Grace with her racket. "Go on. It's your turn."

Grace tried not to scowl as she rose. It would look childish to continue to refuse…and anyway, why shouldn't she play him, even if he was so…so *pusillanimous* as to intentionally lose? "Mr. Rookwood?" She looked at him.

"I'm waiting," Alice called. "Entertain me."

Kit bowed. "At once, ma'am." He didn't meet Grace's eyes as he escorted her back to the court. "Do you have a preferred side?"

Grace smiled sweetly. "I'll take this one." She indicated the side he'd played on. It would mean playing with the sun in her eyes, but she would rather be boiled in oil than accept any advantage from him.

She watched while he crossed to the other side of the court, catching Alice's eye and smiling at her as he took position behind the service line. She flexed lightly up onto her toes, waiting.

"Cooler over there?" he called to Alice, and served.

Did he even notice she was here on the other side of the net? Grace narrowed her eyes and returned his serve hard, just beyond his reach if he wasn't paying attention enough to meet it.

Alice laughed as the ball flew past him. "Oh, I'm quite cool. I think you're the one who's in hot water now, Mr. Rookwood."

He stalked off to retrieve the ball without replying, but by the time he returned, his smile was back. "I wish you would call me Kit. Every time you say 'Mr. Rookwood' I keep expecting to see my father."

"Very well, *Kit*," Alice drawled. "And you may call me…Miss Roosevelt." She laughed at his expression. "Oh, don't be silly. Of course you may call me Alice."

"Your serve, Mr. Rookwood," Grace said. He hadn't asked *her* to call him Kit, after all.

He hesitated and, for the first time that day, actually looked at her. She returned his regard steadily so that for a moment they stared at each other just as they had earlier that week, and again Grace felt that pull between them like an elastic band trying to snap them together. *What are you doing?* she wanted to ask him. *Who are you, really?*

And then he served.

The play that followed was fast and intense. Grace understood as soon as the ball crossed the net that he had no intention of letting her win, as he had Alice. And she'd been right: he was a good player. He hit hard and straight and controlled. But she was good too.

She won the first furiously played game. Alice laughed and clapped. "There you go, Kit. Beaten by two girls in one day. What a comedown!"

"It's not over yet," Kit replied lightly. "Best of three?" he said to Grace. She noticed that he was back to not quite meeting her eyes.

"If you wish," she replied.

He won the next game, though not easily. Grace knew she was tiring but she guessed that he must be also; he no longer took time to smile at Alice but concentrated wholly on the ball. As they prepared to start their last game, she remembered what the maple tree had said and smiled. It had been right about men and tennis, hadn't it?

Her smile seemed to unnerve Kit. He'd been about to serve, but paused before swinging his racquet up and took a few seconds to resettle his feet. He was off-balance for the rest of the game, which Grace won easily.

"Hurrah!" Alice jumped up. "I knew you'd do it, Grace!"

"Glad one of us did," Grace muttered to herself. She was hot and sweaty and her hair under her white straw boater felt like it was in danger of tumbling over her shoulders, but she couldn't suppress the fierce surge of triumph that welled up in her as she walked to the net toward Kit. Beyond him, she saw the maple's branches waving back and forth, as if an extremely localized gale was blowing around it. The sight made her smile again as she reached across the net to shake Kit's hand. "Thank you. You play very well."

He didn't offer his hand; in fact, he walked right past her as if he hadn't seen her. Grace felt herself flush and followed after him, fuming.

"Do all the girls in Boston play like her?" he asked Alice loudly. "Must be all the centuries of Puritan virtue. Cold baths and plain oatmeal and scratchy woolen long underwear."

Grace nearly came to a halt from sheer surprise. Why was he behaving so strangely? Surely not because she had beaten him...or was it?

Alice giggled. "Grace doesn't wear scratchy woolen long

underwear. Her grandmother orders their underthings from France. Lyons silk and lace, you know."

"Alice!" Grace wished a crack would open in the beautifully manicured grass at her feet and swallow her up. Or maybe swallow Alice up. Why was she discussing Grace's *underwear*, of all things, with him?

For a fleeting second, an odd expression crossed his face. Then he laughed harshly. "Not such a Puritan maiden after all, then."

Grace followed the pair back to the clubhouse, still fuming and not sure which of them she was more cross with. A few moments later, though, she knew.

"Thank you for the game," Kit said to Alice as he prepared to leave them on the piazza steps. Alice had invited him to join them for iced tea, but he'd claimed a prior engagement. "I hope we can do it again soon."

"Next time I hope you won't feel you have to play the gentleman and let me win," she pretended to scold.

"Who, me? I'd never do such a thing." He turned the full force of his smile on her, and Grace could practically see her melt under it. Then he half turned toward her. "That is…most of the time I wouldn't."

Before Grace could even sputter, he'd turned and started back down the path, whistling.

FIVE

Grace was determined not to dwell on Kit Rookwood's appalling rudeness, though over the next days she couldn't help remembering flashes of that morning. What had she done to make him behave so unpleasantly toward her? No one had ever been intentionally rude to her before. Especially no one to whom she'd at first felt so drawn; if she remembered his rudeness, she also remembered the looks they'd exchanged, both when they first met and during the horrible tennis game. That made it hurt even more.

If only he weren't so attractive and hadn't let her see his kindness to the ball boy. Then she could have labeled him insufferable and forgotten about him. But she couldn't—most especially because he was always underfoot. Whenever they went to the Casino (which was every day), he was there, playing tennis or listening to music at one of the daily concerts or lounging on the piazza, waiting to flash that smile that seemed to turn Alice into a blithering idiot.

And dancing. Though she'd ruled out balls in deference to Mrs. Roosevelt's wishes, Mrs. Rennell hadn't had the heart to forbid their attending the Thursday night dances at the Casino theatre ballroom. "After all, they're not really *balls*," she said by way of explanation. "They're simply friendly get-togethers where there also happens to be music and dancing."

"I'm sure you're right, ma'am," Alice agreed. "But I'm still determined that we're going to get to at least one real ball," she added under her breath to Grace.

To Grace's dismay, Kit Rookwood was standing inside the entrance to the Casino theatre when they arrived for their first Thursday evening dance. He looked as good in evening dress as he did in tennis flannels.

"Goodness, somebody's prompt," Alice greeted him.

"All the better to get first crack at your dance card," he said, letting his gaze sweep appreciatively over the décolletage of the yellow muslin gown she'd spent all morning lowering.

She blushed and tapped him with her fan. "I haven't even gotten one yet, silly."

"Now you have." He snatched one from a hovering usher. "I am nothing if not efficient." He began writing in it with the tiny pencil attached by a fine white silk cord.

Alice snatched it from him. "You're also nonsensical." She folded it hastily into her purse, but not before Grace had caught a glimpse of it. She looked away, not sure whether to laugh or be sick. Oh, *really!*

Mrs. Rennell had seen it too. She giggled. "Now, Kit, be fair. Other young men must have their chance to dance with Alice too."

"I thought I *was* being fair," he protested. "I only took every other dance. That's quite generous."

Mrs. Rennell took two programs from the smiling usher and handed them to Grace and Alice. "No more than two, you young scamp," she said to Kit.

He sighed and shook his head, then took Alice's program and

signed his name twice. "I still think mine was better." He handed it back to her.

"And?" She glanced meaningfully from him to Grace.

No. The last thing Grace wanted was to dance with him. She nearly put the dance program behind her back.

"And?" Kit echoed. He barely glanced toward her. "I didn't think Puritan maidens were allowed to dance. Oh, there's Reggie Vanderbilt. You'll excuse me a moment, won't you? I've been needing to talk to him." He threaded his way back into the crowd.

"Well, that was odd." Alice frowned after him.

"I'm sure he'll be back to claim his dances, dear," Mrs. Rennell said soothingly. "Shall we find a nice place to sit? Not that I expect you'll be sitting much. You both look very handsome tonight." She gave her arch little smile.

Grace let her direct them toward the row of chairs lining the room. Why was Kit insisting on continuing the silly Puritan business about her — But no. She was not going to let him ruin her evening.

She'd barely had time to sit down and smooth the skirt of her white lace dress underlaid with blue satin and start to examine the theatre — all classical white with elegant plaster moldings picked out in gold — when a tall young man, looking even taller in his black evening clothes, appeared before her.

"Good evening, Mrs. Rennell," he said, but he was looking directly at Grace. "I wondered if I might be presented to your friends."

Mrs. Rennell was only too happy to oblige. Grace waited for the young man, whose name turned out to be Tom Livingston, to turn to Alice as soon as he found out which of them was Colonel Roosevelt's daughter, but his gaze never wavered from her.

"Would…would you care to take the next dance with me, Miss Boisvert?" he asked after they'd made a few minutes of polite conversation. His slightly prominent ears turned red.

Alice's eyebrows shot up but she didn't say anything. Grace glanced at Mrs. Rennell, suddenly unsure of herself. Of course, she'd been to a few dances at home, but those were all with boys she knew. Dancing with them had been like dancing with her brother, Sandy. Mrs. Rennell beamed and nodded at her.

"Yes, thank you," Grace said, because she couldn't think of any other possible response, and let him take her hand and lead her out into the center of the room. She'd been asked to dance before Alice! Now all she had to do was get through it without tripping over her feet. Or his, for that matter.

Mr. Livingston turned out to be an adept dancer, however, and after a moment she found that she could relax as he guided her across the floor.

"How do you like Newport, Miss Boisvert?" he asked after they'd found their rhythm.

"I like it immensely." Thank goodness for Grand-mère's drills in how to make polite conversation. "We went down to the harbor to see the Fête on Tuesday—"

His warm brown eyes crinkled in enthusiasm. "I was there too, on my father's boat. What did you think of it?"

Grace tried not to grimace. They'd brought little Parker and Sarah and Miss Hamm with them to view the parade of sailors from the warships and Naval College and Spanish-American war veterans marching down the flag-bedecked streets. Parker had yelled himself hoarse, little Sarah had cried incessantly, overwhelmed by the noise and the crowds, and Alice had disappeared, only to turn up much later with Kit Rookwood in tow, both of them looking distinctly grubby. He'd taken her to the waterfront to watch the rowing races, she'd explained. Mrs. Rennell had scolded poor Miss Hamm for losing sight of Alice, which Grace thought unfair. If anyone should have been scolded for losing Alice, it was *her*.

"The fireworks were spectacular, and everything looked so

festive. Really, everything I've done or seen in Newport has been lovely," she said. "Alice—er, Miss Roosevelt and I have greatly enjoyed playing tennis here at the Casino."

"That's…well, actually, I've seen you playing," he said as if making a confession. "You're very good."

Grace felt herself blush with pleasure. "Thank you."

"I'd be happy to let you beat me any day if you ever need an opponent. In fact, I'd enjoy it. Will you be here all summer? The national championship is in late August, and I'd love to escort you to a game."

"Thank you, Mr. Livingston. It sounds exciting. But we are only here for a month."

"Oh." He looked downcast for a moment but then brightened. "But you're here for the Cup trials." She must have looked puzzled because he explained, "The America's Cup trials. Sailboat racing. We're going out to watch next week on my father's steam-yacht—make a bit of a party of it. Won't you come with us?"

Grace remembered her adorable yachting costume that she'd been dying to wear. "I'd love to—that is, if I'm not already supposed to be somewhere else," she added conscientiously. "May I check with Mrs. Rennell before I accept?"

"You're not only the prettiest girl here, you've probably got the nicest manners as well." He was looking at her with a…a *melting* sort of expression that made her feel somewhere between alarmed and amused. Was this what Alice had meant when she talked about boys as big, slobbering spaniels? Mr. Livingston wasn't drooling, thank goodness, but it didn't look out of the question.

At the end of the dance he brought her back to Mrs. Rennell, wrote his name on her card for another dance, then stood talking until another young man appeared beside him, intent on dancing with her. This dance went almost identically to her first…as did the next dance with another young man, and the one after that.

Grace wasn't sure how she felt about it; it was fun to be able to dance every dance, but by the sixth or seventh she'd begun to lose track of her partners. Had it been Frank who'd chattered away to her at great length about his motor-car and how fast he'd made the trip from Stamford, or Bert? Or had it been Springfield and not Stamford?

Grace smiled and fanned herself and made the appropriate responses, but realized with a small shock that she was bored. The dancing had been pleasant—the band was a good one, and all of the boys who'd partnered her had been good to excellent dancers—but she was still bored. Possibly it was because she was a stranger here and didn't know people well enough…but she also couldn't help thinking that these young men were all rather dull, for all their enthusiasm over sailboats and motor cars. Or maybe it was because of—

Just then, Alice danced by with Kit Rookwood. She winked at Grace as she passed. Kit glanced back as well, and his expression darkened as he looked from Grace to the young man partnering her so that he almost glared. Then Alice said something and he returned his attention to her, his brow clearing as he did.

Grace frowned at his back as he danced away. What had *that* been about? Oh, let her guess—maybe Puritan maidens weren't supposed to dance with good-looking young men at Casino dances. Well, she was no Puritan maiden, and if she wanted to dance with *twenty* boys it wasn't any of Kit Rookwood's business.

A few moments later, the dance ended. The latest motor-car enthusiast gave her up reluctantly as Tom Livingston returned for his second dance. "Me again, Miss Boisvert," he said cheerfully.

Hmm. Maybe it was time to see if she could follow Alice's Captivation directions. She smiled at him but let her eyelids droop provocatively, trying for the sultry look Alice had demonstrated. "Why, it's an old friend!"

Her smile seemed to stun him for a second or two. Then he

shook his head as if to clear it and took her proffered hand. He spoke less during this dance but kept looking down at her with a befuddled expression on his face, as if he weren't quite sure of what he was doing. Alice had been right! It worked!

"You're awfully quiet," she said after a long lull in the conversation. "Am I boring you?" Keep them off-balance, Alice had said.

"No! I'm..." He gazed at her for so long that she began to worry they'd dance into a wall. "I...I can't stop looking at you. You're... I wish there weren't all these people here." He paused and swallowed hard. "You wouldn't care to step out for some fresh air, would you? They say the moon is up."

Even through her corset she could feel his hand, resting on her back while they danced, tighten as he spoke. For a minute she felt a quaver of doubt—what was she doing to this nice young man who reminded her of the boys she'd grown up with? But then the words *Puritan maiden* reminded her.

"I'd love to." She lifted her chin and smiled at him again.

He nodded, and she wondered if it was because he couldn't speak—his Adam's apple under the collar of his shirt seemed to have taken on a life of its own. He danced them close to the entrance, then led her out into the cool, damp night.

The moon was indeed up; it was peeking over the roof of the theatre, round and bright. Grace was relieved to see they weren't the only ones who'd slipped out to enjoy each other's company in cooler, quieter surroundings—at least a dozen other couples strolled on the grass or the covered piazza leading to the court tennis building or stood close together, gazing skyward. She thought she caught a hint of movement in the shadow of the theatre building as well but decided it was best not to look too closely at what might be happening there.

Mr. Livingston steered her down the piazza, which didn't offer as much of a view of the moon...but moon watching didn't seem to be what was on his mind.

"This summer's been dull as dirt, till now. If only you'd arrived sooner—but you're here now." He caught up her hands and pressed them gently.

Oh, dear. Did Captivation happen so quickly? "Yes, and it's such fun!" she said enthusiastically, as if she hadn't noticed him squeezing her hands. "I *am* looking forward to going boating. Thank you so much for inviting me—"

"If I had my way, I'd just bring you." His voice had grown husky. "We'd go all the way to Block Island, just the two of us…or Bermuda…"

She stole a glance at him to see if he'd reached spaniel stage yet, and saw that he was staring down at her with an intensity that made her quail. Goodness, all she'd done was *smile* at him—

And then she heard Mum's voice in her head. *"Humans do tend to be strongly drawn to us… I'm afraid some boy will fall at your feet…"* Oh dear, was that it? Had she put on the dryad charm a little too hard? She hadn't meant to do anything of the sort to the poor boy—

"I've never met anyone like you." He gripped her hands more tightly and pulled her toward him. He wasn't going to try to *kiss* her, was he?

"Oh, I'm nobody special," she gabbled, turning her face to one side as his loomed toward her. It wasn't that she didn't like him, but she certainly had no wish to kiss a young man she'd met for the first time this evening. What could she say to stop him without causing a fuss or hurting his feelings…because really, this had been her fault? Oh, Mum…if only she'd explained a bit more clearly what she'd meant by humans being "strongly drawn" to dryads—

"Miss Boisvert…" He raised first one of her hands to his lips, then the other. It was a deliciously romantic gesture but she could not let it continue, especially as he was tilting his head down now, his eyes fixed on her lips. This would be a good time for someone to break in on their tête-à-tête—

"I can't see the moon. Might we walk, please?" she asked brightly.

Tom hesitated…and behind her Grace heard a voice say lazily, but with an icy edge, "Oh, I see. The *moon*. Is that why you're out here?"

For a second, Grace gripped Tom's hands as hard as he'd gripped hers. Yes, she'd desperately longed for someone to interrupt them…but why had it had to be Kit Rookwood?

Then she got angry. What was he doing out here anyway? Wasn't he busy flirting with Alice? That was probably what he *had* been doing—until he surprised them.

Tom cleared his throat. "Um, hello, Miss Roosevelt… Rookwood…nice evening, isn't it?"

"Looking at the moon seems like a perfectly good reason to be out here to me," said Alice's voice, which sounded amused, unlike the barely concealed anger in Kit's voice.

Grace disentangled her hands from Tom's and turned. Alice's grin was clear even in the dimness, but Kit's face was expressionless.

"Yes, we're here for the moon," she said to him haughtily. "And some peace and quiet. We Puritan maidens aren't used to all this heat and noise."

"No?" Kit said softly. "Could have fooled me." There was an odd note in his voice that Grace couldn't decipher.

Alice snorted a giggle into one gloved hand. "Now, Kit, don't be mean to my best friend."

Tom cleared his throat again, more loudly this time, and, taking Grace's hand, tucked it into his arm. "I don't know what you're on about, Rookwood, but if there's anything you wanted to say to Miss Boisvert, you can say it to me instead," he said sternly.

"I don't know why he'd care to say anything at all to me," she snapped. "After all, I'm not the daughter of the vi—" She stopped and bit her tongue before the rest of what she'd been about to say could spill out.

There was a silence…and then the moon rose high enough to illuminate the scene. Alice looked troubled, and Kit looked like he'd been carved from marble, so cold was his face. Oh, bother him! Even if he had been truly smitten by Alice and not by who her father was, he should be able to mind his manners toward Alice's friend.

"I should like to go inside now," Grace said to Tom. He didn't say anything, but nodded and led her past Alice and Kit. On the way she touched Alice's arm and smiled. Alice smiled back, but there was still a troubled look in her eyes.

They went back into the warmth and light of the theatre, for which Grace was grateful. Both trees and dryads found the full moon's light disquieting, and it certainly hadn't helped just now.

Before he brought her back to her seat, Tom pulled Grace aside. "I—I'm sorry about that," he said, a little shamefacedly. "It was all I could do not to plant Rookwood one right on the nose."

"It's all right. He doesn't bother me a bit," she lied.

"It's only…" Poor Tom was turning red. "Well…I'd already invited him to watch the Cup qualifiers, and…and I don't want him being rude to you again."

"Make sure you invite Miss Roosevelt as well. She'll keep him occupied." She gave him a cheerful smile—not a Captivating one—but he still looked at her with that besotted look in his eyes.

"I'll do that." He sighed. "I wish we hadn't been interrupted like that."

"Mmm." Grace took refuge in an indecipherable monosyllable. It didn't seem necessary to explain that some *other* type of interruption would have been fine as far as she was concerned.

To Grace's relief, the rest of the evening was uneventful—except for one thing. She noticed that Alice danced at least four or five times with Kit, rather than Mrs. Rennell's stipulated twice…and slipped outside more than once, the last time coming in looking both disheveled and demure, which was worrying. Alice only looked demure when she'd been up to something she shouldn't have been.

As she'd expected, Alice came to her room after they got home so that they could discuss the evening. "Well!" She flopped onto Grace's bed. "You made a conquest! That Mr. Livingston looked like he'd been hit over the head with a rock."

Grace was still at her dressing table, unpinning her hair. "I didn't mean to," she confessed. "You didn't warn me that it was so easy."

"Oh, some boys are like that." Alice waved her hand. "They drop like a ripe pear right into your lap as soon as you look at them. So what do you think? Do you like him?"

"He's nice, but…"

"But nothing. He'll do quite well to keep you amused while we're here. Did he invite you anywhere?"

How did Alice know these things? "He invited me—well, us— to go watch the yacht races in a day or two if the weather is fine."

"Oh, excellent!" She sat up and looked closely at Grace. "Did he kiss you?"

"Of course not!"

"Huh. Did he try to?"

"Well…I think he wanted to, but I didn't let him. He kissed my hands, but I didn't want him to do even that!"

Alice crowed. "Ha! Then why did you go outside with him? What do you think people go outside for at dances? To canoodle, of course. You must have known that—you're not that much of a wet-behind-the-ears."

Grace couldn't help squirming a little as she picked up her brush. She *had* known that…and she wasn't proud of herself for having led poor Tom Livingston on, just to annoy Kit Rookwood.

"Is that why you went out too? To canoodle with Mr. Rook-wood?"

Instead of laughing and denying it, Alice fell back onto the bed. "Oh, Grace—isn't he something?" she said to the ceiling. "He's sooo good-looking…and I swear, I've never had as much fun as I did with him tonight."

Grace tried not to let that declaration hurt. "What did you do that was such fun? Looking at the moon? I saw you go out with him again."

Alice giggled. "Yes, looking at the moon! I complained that I couldn't see it well enough, so he" —she sat up again and grinned at Grace—"so he dared me to climb up onto the roof of the piazza, and I did."

"Alice! In an evening dress?" Grace laughed, but she couldn't help being a little shocked, too. If they were almost grown-ups, as Alice had said, shouldn't they…well…*behave* like grown-ups? Climbing on the piazza roof was not what adults would do.

"Well, I couldn't very well take it off, could I?" She laughed again. "He climbed up there first to give me a hand up, and we had a splendid view of the moon and the Casino grounds and all the other people who were out there to canoodle. I should have brought a notebook and pencil—we could have started a nice little blackmail scheme from up there. It felt a little rickety when we started dancing on it, though."

Grace stopped brushing her hair. "On the roof of the piazza? What if it had broken or you had fallen off it and smashed your head?"

"Oh, stuff. I didn't fall, did I? And anyway, Kit wouldn't have let me."

"Hmmph." What was he up to, letting her do scatterbrained things like that? Grace remembered Alice on the train, talking about her vow to live her own way and make her own fun…except that her idea of fun these days would give her parents a severe case of the vapors and quite possibly land her in trouble. Had Kit sensed her longing to rebel and decided it would be amusing to aid and abet it?

Alice interrupted her thoughts. "Look, I know you don't much care for him," she said. "He *has* been a bit beastly to you, though I don't know why—he only shrugged when I asked him this evening—"

"I fully intend to avoid him as much as possible in future," Grace said—a little stiffly, she suspected. "I wish he'd do the same with me."

"I'll try to keep you apart." Alice's face creased into what could only be described as a fatuous smile. It didn't suit her. "Grace, he's...well, he's nothing like the boys my cousin Helen and I experimented on last year. He's so...oh, I don't know. So assured, and so much more mature—"

"Because climbing on the roof of the piazza is such a mature thing to do," Grace murmured, then wished she hadn't as Alice looked annoyed.

"All right, maybe we shouldn't have," she agreed irritably. "All I'm saying is that he's not like any other boy I know—oh! I didn't tell you. My magics worked! I've figured out how we're going to get to at least one ball while we're here."

Grace was glad for the change of subject. "Really? How?"

"Simple. We're going to make Mrs. Rennell give one herself. After all, she can't very well lock us in our rooms to keep us from attending if she does give one. And we won't *really* be going to a ball if she does—we'll just happen to be here while one is taking place."

Grace snorted. "You're wasted in Newport. You should be pleading cases in court."

"I'm sure Mrs. Rennell will see the reasonableness of it if we present it our way." Alice grinned. "And besides, she won't be able to resist the idea of inviting all the Newport nabobs...and they'll come, too, because of us."

"Because of *you*, you mean," Grace said dryly as she went back to brushing her hair.

Alice didn't look one whit abashed. "Well, of course!"

* * *

Dear Grace.

See. I told you I'd write back to you if you wrote to me.

It's realy boring here without you. at least when I can't go do stuff with Mary and Eunice and Anne. Then its all right. When you said you were going on a yacht we borrowed the Sears' rowboat and took it on the pond. but I don't think it was much like a yacht. Didn't I spell yacht nicely? Mum told me how. Are you having a good time? You sound like you are in your letters. which makes Grand-mère frown the way she does when she's angry. She wants you to come home. I do too. but I guess I'm not mad about it the way she is. I think you better not write about any boys when you send me letters. because Grand-mère reads them even though their my own PRIVATE corispondince and that's what made her mad. But Papa says you'l do fine because you have a good head on your sholders. Guess what! Daisy and I won a race! We beat Harry Clarke and his—

"Love letter, my pet?"

Grace started and nearly dropped Dorothy's letter. Mrs. Fish stood grinning at her under the fall of leaves of the weeping beech tree in Mrs. Berwind's garden, where she'd taken refuge from the hubbub of a garden party.

She probably shouldn't have brought the letter with her, but the post had arrived as they were leaving and she'd tucked it in her purse without thinking. Reading it now was a bad idea; it had given her a full-blown attack of homesickness. The beech had done nothing to dispel her mood; it was very vain of its appearance and could only talk of itself. It had even tried to snatch her letter away from her, because it felt she was not paying it proper attention. She longed for the trees of home, who were comfortable old friends and possessed of much better manners.

"No, not a love letter at all, ma'am." She rose from the bench under the tree's cascading boughs. "It's from my little sister."

Mrs. Fish grunted as she sat down next to Grace, set her parasol on point between her knees, and leaned on its handle. "Sit down and talk to me. A letter from your little sister's nothing to be proud of. It should be from some young man desperately in love with you at your age. No, don't get all missish and modest. You have more sense than that, which is probably why you're hiding here and not cooing at the flower beds."

Grace smiled as she sat down. The conversation among the ladies attending the party *was* insipid. ("Those pink begonias are very pink. And the white ones are very white," she'd heard one lady announce with an air of great profundity. Her companion had agreed with equal gravity.) Then again, it was a ladies' party, so there was no Kit Rookwood making her life unpleasant, which was a relief.

"It's a little hard sometimes, not knowing everyone—" she began.

"Oh, we're like a coop full of hens, scratching for the same old worms and cackling about the same things day in, day out." Mrs. Fish waved one hand at the crowd of mostly white-clad women. "Look at 'em! They even look like a flock of hens wandering around, except they don't do any good by manuring the lawn while they're at it."

Grace couldn't help giggling. Mrs. Fish looked at her approvingly. "That's why I like you. You're not stupid. Everyone else here is stupid. Too bad Harry Lehr isn't here to stir things up, but he's on his honeymoon with that girl he married. Nice little thing, but too insipid. Not at all like your Roosevelt friend."

Grace caught her sideways glance and felt a pang of trepidation. "Er, no…you can't say Alice is insipid."

Mrs. Fish nodded. "She was seen up on the roof at the theatre the other night," she said abruptly. "She and young Kit Rookwood, which surprises me as he's never been like that before. But sometimes people can have funny effects on other people."

Grace hesitated, then said, "I told her it was too much, and that she couldn't do anything like that again."

"Good girl. But that's not all she's done."

"What?" Grace exclaimed, then felt herself flush. "I'm sorry, ma'am, but I didn't know. Would you tell me what else she's—what else there is?"

"The pair of 'em stole a boat at the Harbor Fête the other day and crashed the rowing races. He rowed and she sat in the stern, shouting and throwing peanuts at the other boats."

So *that* was why Alice had looked so disheveled when they'd finally found her that day. Grace wanted to laugh but managed to keep her mouth mostly prim. Mrs. Fish, however, grinned.

"Oh, you don't have to hide it. I'm sure it was as funny as anything," she said. "But the local boys and the sailors from the visiting warships didn't take kindly to it. They did return the boat to its owner, though."

"Thank heavens for small mercies." Grace swallowed. "Anything else?"

Mrs. Fish's eyes lost their amused twinkle. "At Carrie Wilson's musicale last night, someone saw her and Rookwood sneak out, then sneak back in about twenty minutes later. His hair was mussed and his tie crooked, and she was disarranged as well."

"Oh." Grace closed her eyes. That *wasn't* funny. She and Mrs. Rennell had somehow gotten separated from Alice when it had been time to take their seats for the vocal concert—Miss Nellie Melba was singing—and though she'd seen Alice on the other side of the salon at the start of the concert and at the end, she hadn't paid much attention to the in-between. But to have been seen under those circumstances... Well, it was easy to jump to conclusions—conclusions that might well be true. The last thing a girl wanted was a reputation for being fast. Not only was it vulgar but it could follow her around for life and have an effect on her marriage prospects. Few men were interested in marrying a girl whose virtue and morals were suspect, and those who didn't care weren't necessarily the kind of men one wanted to marry. And if her parents heard, they'd *kill* her—or worse, try to send her to a strict finishing school, which would send Alice truly into rebellion.

And she could completely see Alice falling into Kit's clutches—or his arms—like that. She'd once told Grace that she was lucky if she got a quick handshake from her parents before she left to visit her grandparents or aunt for weeks or months on end. How alluring Kit's caresses would be to a girl who was rarely hugged or petted by anyone.

What should—or *could*—she do? Being a dryad was no help—in fact, being a dryad hadn't been of any help with anything in Newport, and at times (like with Tom Livingston) it had been a downright nuisance. Well, she'd wanted to see what it was like to live more as a human. Or was it more a matter of living in the adult world, with adult problems? No matter what, she had to do *something*.

Mrs. Fish had remained quiet while she thought. When Grace finally met her eyes, she asked, in a remarkably gentle voice, "Not out yet, are you two?"

"Well, sort of, almost." After all, they wore their skirts to the floor and put their hair up, even if they hadn't been formally presented to society.

"That's even more reason your friend should behave herself. Especially considering she's the vice-president's daughter."

"Please, Mrs. Fish—you won't tell anyone else about any of this, will you? I don't think she did any of it to make a spectacle of herself—well, not much. She's got too much energy bottled up inside her and no way to expend it, and—" She drew a deep breath. "And I don't think her parents will understand at all."

Mrs. Fish sighed. "I'll do my best to make sure the stories don't get around, but you must try to keep her on a shorter leash."

"I'll try, ma'am. Though I doubt anyone will ever be able to put a leash on Alice." She bit her lip, thinking. "Perhaps…perhaps I should try to talk with him and make him see the damage he's doing." Though she'd much rather chop off his head and dump his body in the harbor than speak two words to him in private.

"You could try." Her heavy-lidded eyes held a sudden sparkle of amusement. "You know, the whole problem would go away if he could find someone new to occupy his interest. Some lovely, sensible girl who wouldn't make a fool of herself over him."

"Yes, it would, but who— Oh!" Grace nearly fell off the bench. Mrs. Fish couldn't mean—couldn't mean that *she* should—

"Oh, I expect you know who. Well, I think I shall go admire the flower beds." She rose and put up her parasol. "Think about what I said, lamb," she added and ambled back toward the house.

SIX

Grace thought about it all right. Her first thought (and her second and third) was *never in a million years*. Try to draw Kit's attention away from Alice and onto herself? For one thing, Alice would kill her, or at least never speak to her again. Well, maybe she would, eventually; but in the short term, it would put a serious strain on their friendship — and they would be spending the next several weeks together, here in Newport and then in the Adirondacks. Kit was giving Alice something she hungered for: his attention. It would be cruel to take that from her — but it would be irresponsible to let him entice her into more bad behavior.

Still…could she even bring herself to do it? It wasn't that Kit wasn't attractive — in fact, it had bothered her a great deal that she thought him so good-looking, because of the way he'd been behaving toward her. But could she try to…to Captivate him when he'd been so unpleasant? Would it even be possible?

Of course it would be possible. Remember what you did to Tom Livingston without even really trying?

All right, that was true. Maybe being a dryad would come in handy after all. Mum would have a fit if she knew, not to mention

Grand-mère — ! But they would never have to find out.

Dealing with Alice if she were to entice Kit away from her, though…that would be the problem. Maybe she would try talking to him first. And if that didn't work, then she'd be forced to launch plan B.

Her opportunity to corner Kit came a day later, at Tom Livingston's yachting party.

As Grace checked her white captain's hat, complete with gold braid, in the front hall's mirror while they waited for the carriage to be brought round, Mrs. Rennell came down the stairs.

"You look lovely, my dear! And Alice is always perfectly dressed." She came to stand next to Grace and scrutinized her own reflection. "I do hope this hat is quite right for a boating party. I've never been invited — er, that is, I've not yet been able to attend one. It's not that I don't *adore* my children, but being a mother *does* restrict one's social life, you know."

Mrs. Rennell remained all atwitter as they were driven down to the dock where the Livingstons' motor launch would ferry them out to their yacht. It was a lovely day; the sky was a light, cloudless blue, and the harbor sparkled in the sunshine. Bunting and flags from the Harbor Fête a few days before still lent a dash of color to the weathered gray fishing shacks on the waterfront.

Tom Livingston was waiting at the dock, nautically handsome in a blue blazer and white flannel trousers. He greeted them all enthusiastically, but his face lit up as he took Grace's hand. "You look a perfect mariner."

"Then I must be a better actress than I thought. I've never set foot on anything bigger than the rowboat on Hammond Pond at home." A gust of wind caught at her hat, and she reached up to make sure it was still secure. "Will it be rough today? I'd hate to disgrace myself at your party."

He took firm hold of her arm as he helped her onto the launch. "Nothing worse than a fine, brisk breeze. Don't worry, I won't let anything happen to you. I've got a few more guests to escort, and then I promise I'll be your devoted servant." He squeezed her arm tenderly, then stepped back and snapped her a smart salute before leaping back onto the dock.

"That wasn't quite my concern," she whispered to Alice after they'd settled on the green-cushioned bench that filled the back perimeter of the launch.

"What is? Getting seasick and whoopsing all over poor Tom? Don't worry, I'll bet you ten dollars he'd still adore you even if you did." Alice surveyed the dock eagerly. "Where *is* that dratted boy?"

That dratted boy could only be one person. "Mr. Rookwood is coming?"

"I don't know why you insist on calling him that. Didn't he ask us to call him Kit?" Alice craned her neck to see past the crewmen who were casting them off from the dock.

"He asked *you* to," Grace said a little more shortly than she'd intended, because Alice turned to look at her, a frown gathering between her brows.

"Now who's being unpleasant?" she demanded. "Really, I don't know what the problem is between you two, but it won't get better if you continue to bear a grudge against the poor thing."

"Poor thing?" Grace stared at her. "He's the one who started it with his stupid Puritan maiden nonsense."

"How can he resist when you never fail to rise to it? Really, Grace, you should try to look at it from his point of view."

Grace struggled to count to ten before replying. She made it to four. "So you think it's my fault he persecutes me?"

"Yes, I do. If you didn't react, he wouldn't do it. It's perfectly obvious."

"It isn't any such thing!"

Alice's manner changed abruptly. "You know what I think? I think you're jealous." She patted Grace's hand. "It's perfectly understandable, since we've always been so close. But you've got to accept it was bound to happen that a man might someday come between us. It doesn't mean I like you any less because of Kit. We'll always be friends—don't you know that? Even if Kit and I..." She trailed into silence, blushing.

Grace forgot her irritation for a moment. Good heavens, was Alice that far gone over him that she was thinking about "always"?

She was saved from having to reply by a small cough from Mrs. Rennell, sitting across from them. "Excuse me, girls, but do one of you have any smelling salts? I seem to have forgotten mine," she asked, brightly enough. But Grace saw that her usually delicate complexion was more pasty white than porcelain.

"No, ma'am," Alice said. "Aren't you well?" Her voice was sympathetic, but Grace caught the edge of glee in it.

"Oh, quite!" Mrs. Rennell tried to smile, but only half of her mouth cooperated.

"No, I don't have any," Alice declared. "I've got a cast iron stomach, Father says. I can handle the bounciest seas."

At the word *bounciest*, poor Mrs. Rennell grew even paler. "I'm sorry, ma'am," Grace said. "I'm sure the Livingstons will have something on their boat if anyone should feel unwell."

Mrs. Rennell looked a little relieved. "Thank you, dear." She sat back and folded her lips tightly together, as if further speech would be unwise.

By the time they'd drawn alongside the Livingstons' steam-yacht, which seemed enormously long and high, like a great white wall topped with masts and a slender smokestack and the name *Princess Eleanor* in gold and black letters, Grace wasn't so sure she wouldn't be needing smelling salts herself. As she climbed the gangplank up to the ship's deck, a wave of dizziness passed over her, then was gone. But she sensed that it might still be lurking nearby. Please, let her not whoops all over poor Tom's spotless blazer!

Her equilibrium was not helped by the sight of Kit Rookwood, as smartly dressed (and, to her disgruntlement, twice as handsome) as Tom, lounging by the rail; obviously he was waiting for Alice. And of course, the one time she actually wanted to speak to him, he ignored her.

"Excuse me," she said, pausing in front of him. He didn't seem to hear her, so she said, more loudly, "Mr. Rookwood!"

There was no ignoring the use of his name. He did his usual not-looking-directly-at-her thing. "Did you wish to speak to me?"

"Yes, I did — I mean, I do," she said. "But — but not right now. In private."

His brows drew down. "Is it really necessary?"

"Yes, it is!" she said crossly. "Believe me, I wish I didn't have to." She turned on her heel.

Alice greeted Kit with a scold that sounded more like a caress. "There you are, you bad thing. I thought you'd be at the dock."

"Oh, eager beaver Tom hustled me aboard before I could tell him to take a powder," Kit said — loudly enough so that she would be sure to hear, Grace guessed. She resisted the impulse to turn back and flip his jaunty boater off his head and took Mrs. Rennell's arm to lead her off to look for a quiet place for her to sit.

"Up on deck's the best place for her," said the uniformed steward she found a few minutes later, when she asked him if Mrs. Rennell could retire belowdecks. He cast a knowledgeable eye over her pale face and nodded. "Out in the fresh air's the ticket. Here, I'll set her up in a nice sheltered spot and bring her some ginger water. That'll settle her stomach."

"You're a dear," Mrs. Rennell said as she collapsed into a wicker armchair set under one of the canopied sections of the deck. "I do hope dear Alice won't feel indisposed too." She peered at the low rail enclosing the deck. "That doesn't look very high. I shouldn't like for her to fall in if it should get stormy."

It might do her some good if she did, Grace thought. "I don't think she will, Mrs. Rennell," she said aloud. "Alice doesn't get sick, and she won't fall in." She took off her light canvas coat and tucked it over Mrs. Rennell's lap.

"Such spirits," Mrs. Rennell sighed. "She's a remarkable girl, isn't she?"

"There you are!" Tom Livingston appeared next to them. "Would you care for the grand tour before we start?" He tucked Grace's arm in his. "Will you excuse us, ma'am?"

Grace let him lead her away, though she felt bad at leaving Mrs. Rennell alone. Tom, however, had no qualms. "I wasn't going to let you spend the day stuck with the landlubbers," he explained.

Just then the smokestack emitted a mighty gout of smoke, and another. Grace watched them roil into the sky before vanishing, and another wave of dizziness hit her. "Mrs. Rennell may not be the only landlubber here," she said, hanging on to his arm with both hands.

"Are you all right?" Tom looked concerned—and a touch disappointed.

"I hope so—yes, I'm sure I'm fine." She smiled at him reassuringly—perhaps a little too much so, for he covered one of her hands with his free one.

"You look delicious," he murmured. "I wish all these people weren't here, because by George, I swear I'd kiss y—"

"Oh, we're moving!" Grace said. A deep rumble shook the boat and it began to move. A strange sensation, as if the floor was rising and falling under her feet, made her hold on to Tom's arm again. She hoped he wouldn't take it as invitation to act on his last unfinished sentence.

To her relief, he didn't. "Isn't it grand? Best feeling in the world! Come on, let me show you the rest of the *Princess*."

By the time Tom had finished showing her all over the 126-foot length of the *Princess*, however, she wasn't sure she agreed that being on a boat was the best feeling she'd ever experienced. A headache had begun to pound at the back of her head, accompanied by intermittent waves of dizziness. This wasn't seasickness, was it? Her stomach was fine—she felt in no danger of doing anything unfortunate on Tom's blazer after all. But something definitely wasn't right.

By then they'd left the harbor, on their way toward the open ocean. Grace knew that the plan was for them to discreetly shadow the racing yachts for a few hours before returning to the harbor, where a fortifying tea would be served at anchor. Most of the ladies had gathered under the two canvas awnings to keep out of the sunshine; Grace looked at two of them in chaise longues with envy. "Tom, can't we sit down for a moment?" she interrupted him.

"Still not feeling quite the thing? Here." He guided her to a pair of chairs under the forward awning and settled himself in one, pulling it a little too close to hers.

Grace sat down gratefully. She let Tom talk away at her about the *Princess Eleanor*, inserting yeses and nos at the appropriate places while hoping that her head wouldn't fall off. After a few moments she got the feeling that someone was watching her, and saw with a start that Mrs. Fish was seated a few chairs away, watching her with amusement.

"Well, look who's here. Come here and talk to me, sweet lamb. You—go," she added to Tom. "You can't monopolize her *all* the time, you know." She laughed her loud laugh.

Grace clutched her chair's arms, but it was not possible to ask *the* Mrs. Fish to come over here instead, no matter how headachy one felt. "You can explain the races to me when we get there," she said to a mutinous-looking Tom and rose from her seat. He nodded, mumbled something polite to Mrs. Fish, and left.

Grace sat down next to Mrs. Fish and waited until he was out of earshot before leaning toward her. "I'm going to try to talk to Kit Rookwood about Alice this afternoon."

"Good idea. Do it before your chum climbs the rigging and shows us all her bloomers," Mrs. Fish said with gleeful relish.

"Please, no." Grace shuddered. "I'm afraid he'll try to avoid me. He doesn't like me for some reason. I expect he'll stick to Alice like a burr."

"Hmmph." Mrs. Fish drummed her fingers on her knee. "Leave that to me. I'll make sure I get Alice out of his clutches, or him out of hers — I'm not sure which it is — for a bit, once we're out doing whatever it is we're supposed to be doing on this overgrown canoe." She squinted at Grace. "You don't look right, sweet pet. Got the collywobbles, do you?"

"No, just this horrid headache."

Mrs. Fish was still examining her. "You don't have to talk to him today. You could always hit him over the head with a tennis racquet at the Casino tomorrow and drag him into a bush to talk to him."

Grace smiled again but shook her head. "No. I want to get it done today. I'm sure I'll feel better shortly." The mental image that Mrs. Fish had summoned of Alice climbing the smokestack was all too plausible. Colonel Roosevelt had made sure all his children, including Alice, were champion tree climbers.

Mrs. Fish was as good as her word. A half hour later, when they'd joined the fleet of boats that had sailed out to watch the races, she jerked her head and stood up, taking Grace's arm. "Now," she commanded.

Grace let her waft her along as they left the shelter of the awning and headed toward the yacht's rail, where many of the guests, including Alice and Kit, had gathered, field glasses raised, to watch the ponderously graceful sailboats as they glided past each other at the race's starting line, jockeying for the best position when the starting cannon sounded.

Mrs. Fish surveyed the crowd. "Wouldn't it be much more exciting if they crashed into each other?" she called in a loud voice. This earned her an equal mixture of titters and mutters; it also caught Tom Livingston's attention. He made a beeline for them, his eyes fixed on Grace.

Mrs. Fish saw him too. She immediately steered Grace to where Alice and Kit stood by the rail so that he followed along in their wake. When she was behind Alice, she stopped, made sure Tom had joined them, then turned to him. "Oh, good. You've got a pair of those spyglasses things." She held her hand out expectantly and, when Tom gave them to her, peered through them briefly, then nudged Alice on the shoulder and handed them to her. "Look at that, lamb," she commanded, then turned to Tom. "Here, you. Which of them is which?"

Grace wanted to chuckle at the adroit way in which she'd managed to occupy both Alice's and Tom's attention, but didn't waste any time. She took Kit's arm, making him start, and tugged on it.

He frowned at her, and for a moment she was afraid he would refuse to come with her. Then he shrugged and let her detach him from the group.

Grace led him to the other side of the boat, as far away as possible from the gaggle of spectators. How should she begin? Find some polite way to lead up to the topic or jump right in? If only her head would stop hurting…

"Mr. Rookwood—" she began.

He made a harsh, impatient sound. "Will you stop calling me that?"

She looked at him in surprise. He was staring past her with a ferocious scowl on his face. "I—I didn't think it mattered what I called you," she said.

"It matters." He continued to look out toward the horizon for the space of a few breaths, then said, in his old, bored tone, "So? What's all this about?"

Grace swallowed, though her mouth was dry. "Alice. I'm worried about her."

He shifted his stance so that he was facing her, gazing over her shoulder as he always did. "Why? She seems fine to me."

"I'm sure she does," Grace couldn't keep herself from saying tartly. "That's the problem. You and she— People are starting to talk. Mrs. Fish told me about last week at the Harbor Fête, and the Casino, and—and the other night at Mrs. Wilson's." A fresh wave of dizziness washed over her.

"I see." His voice had acquired a mocking edge. "Do you think I'm out to compromise her virtue?"

"I don't know," she retorted. "I haven't decided yet if you actually care about Alice or are using her to while away a dull summer. But she's *my* dearest friend, and I won't stand by and let you break her heart. Or ruin her life."

He lifted one eyebrow. "Don't you thing you're getting a little melodramatic?"

Grace wanted to stamp her foot, but it would make her head feel worse. "No, I'm not. Her father's the vice-president of the United States, and if his daughter is running around like a—a hoyden before she's even come out, it might make trouble for him. If you really cared about her, you'd want to protect her reputation."

Kit smiled—cruelly, she thought. "Spoken like a true Puritan maiden."

"Stop it! We're not talking about me or your stupid teases. We're talking about—we're—" She trailed off as the pain in her head redoubled, so that it hurt to even hear or see. Kit's face swam before her, his hair getting confused with the sunshine. She closed her eyes because the brightness was too much.

"Grace, are you all right?" she heard him say.

She opened her eyes and forced them to focus on him. Well, what do you know—he hadn't called her a Puritan maiden. He'd even called her by name—though she was surprised it was Grace and not Miss Boisvert. Still, that could be counted as a victory of sorts.

"I'm quite well," she said as steadily as she could. All right, then—talking didn't seem to be doing the trick. Much as she disliked the idea, she would have to commence plan B. If only she could see straight—

"Please…let's not argue." She reached out and touched his sleeve, forcing herself not to clutch at it to stay upright. "We both care about Alice…don't we?" She raised her eyes to his and let her hand linger on his arm.

He stared back at her—*at* her, this time—for the space of three or four breaths. She moistened her lips and kept her eyes on his, remembering Alice's instructions on the train but adding all the force of her dryad self behind it, *willing* him—

"Kit," she whispered. Was it working?

He tore his gaze from her face. "Stop it," he said savagely and yanked his arm away. The sudden motion made her even dizzier than before, and she leaned back against the railing for support…and then there were clouds and sky mixing with the sunshine. Kit said something to her but she couldn't hear what it was, because she was falling…or was it the dizziness taking her again?

She hit something hard. It knocked the wind from her for a moment so that she gasped, and then she felt nothing at all.

Something held her. She felt it, from her right shoulder down across her chest to the other side, holding her up out of the cold wet. Or was it trying to pull her down? She cried out and tried to struggle.

"It's all right," someone said in her ear. "Don't fight me. I've got you."

That voice—she knew it. "K—Kit!" she stammered. And then she realized that the thing encircling her was his arm, and the cold wet was water, which seemed to be trying to drag her down into its depths by her skirt. Sweet Yggdrasil, she'd fallen off the boat! But how? She'd been trying to Captivate him—she remembered his eyes, staring into hers—but then he'd pulled away, and the sun had been too bright, and—

"Ssh." The arm surrounding her tightened gently. "It's all right—they're sending the launch after us. You're safe now."

He'd dived in to save her. *Kit* saved her. She closed her eyes; the salt water stung and made them well up with tears.

Within a few minutes, the launch was there. The crewmen pulled her aboard like a sack of soggy potatoes. Someone led her to one of the benches and draped a blanket over her shoulders. She sat blindly down, shaking.

The boat abruptly dipped sideways, and she looked up. Kit had pulled himself up over the gunwales of the launch and stood there, breathing hard. His white cotton shirt clung wetly to his chest and arms and his feet were bare, and she realized he must have taken off his jacket and shoes before diving after her. And then she noticed that he was returning her gaze.

"Are you all right?" he said.

She nodded.

One of the crewmen handed him a blanket. He wiped the water from his face with it and rubbed it over his head to dry his hair, then stood there, still looking at her.

"Thank you," she managed to whisper.

As she looked at him, his face seemed to darken. "What the

hell did you do that for?" he barked.

It felt as though he'd slapped her. "What?"

One of the crewmen standing nearby made a sound of protest. "Here, sir—I don't think the young lady meant to fall in—"

"She knew she wasn't feeling well. But she had to drag me over to the rail to talk instead of waiting till she wasn't about to collapse… Christ, we could have sat down in chairs like civilized people." Kit threw the blanket down and loomed over her, fists clenched like he wanted to hit her.

She stared up at him. His blue eyes were ablaze, and she felt her own begin to kindle under his furious gaze. "I'm sorry you had to jump in to save me," she snapped. "I'm sure you would have been just as happy to leave me in the ocean—or see me at the bottom of it."

He looked down at his feet and shifted as if the deck boards burned them. "I didn't say that—"

"You didn't have to." She turned her head and deliberately shifted on the bench so that her shoulder was to him, and found herself blinking hard. Curse the horrid salty ocean water that made her eyes sting so!

She felt him continue to stand there but refused to turn her head. After a minute, he moved away.

A nervously cleared throat a minute later finally made her look up. One of the crewmen—the one who'd remonstrated with Kit—stood there. "We'll be back at the boat in a trice, but is there anything I can do for you, miss?" he asked shyly.

Grace tried to bring his face into focus and couldn't, and realized that tears were still streaming from her eyes. No wonder he looked so apprehensive. "No, thank you…it's that I…I…" She rubbed her wet sleeve across her face, and inspiration struck. "I lost my hat."

He looked relieved; that was evidently an acceptable reason for a young lady to be sobbing her eyes out. "I'm sorry, miss. Once we've got you back, maybe the skipper will let us go look for it."

To Grace's dismay, the entire yachting party seemed to have gathered along the side of the boat to watch her being handed back up from the launch. Alice and Mrs. Rennell were there to greet her first, followed by Tom and his father.

Alice was grinning. "How's the water?"

Mrs. Rennell was still pasty-pale but determined to do her duty. "Poor child—were you overcome? I am sure that boats are no place for ladies of tender sensibilities."

Alice snorted. "Grace never gets the vapors."

"I am sure that poor dear Grace is unwell," Mrs. Rennell replied stiffly. It was probably the closest she'd ever come to disagreeing with Alice.

"Excuse me." Tom actually nudged Alice aside, giving her a cold look as he did, and tenderly draped another blanket around Grace. "I'm so sorry—I should have been there to take care of you. You weren't feeling quite the thing, Mrs. Fish says. I blame myself." He looked unhappy.

"It's all right. Kit took care of her." Alice's grin faded into a fond smile. "He's a hero, isn't he, saving you like that!" She turned away from Grace, no doubt to look for Kit.

Mr. Livingston cleared his throat. "I am sure Miss Boisvert would like to go down to the cabin to dry off and rest. The stewardess will be happy to help you, my dear. She's my captain's wife." He looked down at her kindly. "We'll steam back to Newport immediately."

"Oh, no!" Grace protested. "I don't want to ruin your party. There's no reason to go back."

Tom put an arm around her and began to guide her through the crowd toward the companionway leading below. "We'll do whatever you want," he murmured. "Don't worry, I'm here. I'll take care of you."

It was sweet of him, but the last thing she wanted now was

Tom gazing at her soulfully for the rest of the afternoon. "I should like a rest—or maybe a nap. My head—"

He looked disappointed but helped her down the companionway stairs into the saloon, where the large, capable Mrs. Joseph came hurrying forward to take charge of her. She took Grace to one of the guest cabins, made her take off her wet skirt and petticoats and shirtwaist, wrapped her in dry blankets, settled her into the berth, and made her drink a cup of hot, sweet tea.

"Coming down with the grippe, I'll warrant," she said comfortably as Grace sipped her tea. "Getting faint like that is always the first sign. You spend the next few days in bed, miss, and you'll be right as rain in no time. A bit of a dunk never hurt anyone, but you don't want to be playing games with the grippe. Now, drink that up and have a bit of a nap, and I'll see what I can do about making your clothes presentable by the time we get back to harbor."

Grace sank gratefully into the pillow as the woman tucked another blanket over her and drew the curtains over the cabin's porthole. But as much as she would have liked to sleep, the pain in her head would only let her clutch her blankets and stare into the dim cabin while tears she could no longer blame on seawater slipped down her cheeks.

SEVEN

Oddly, within a few minutes of returning to Mrs. Rennell's house, Grace's pounding head and dizziness had abated greatly. But she let the housekeeper and the maid fuss over her and order her into a hot bath with rosemary and chamomile in it, to keep her from catching cold after her unexpected swim. She stayed in it for a long time, hoping to soak out her chagrin and mortification in the fragrant water.

Her talk with Kit had accomplished nothing…and her attempt to Captivate him had ended in disaster. She couldn't shake the feeling that he'd *known* what she was trying to do, considering the way he'd pulled away from her so angrily. Humiliating was the only word for it. How could she ever face him again? Now she was back where she'd started, which meant that the only thing to do was to say something directly to Alice.

Why did Kit hate her so? What had she done to him, apart from beat him fair and square in a tennis match? He'd been so *angry* after he'd rescued her today; no one had ever behaved that way to her, even Grand-mère at her crossest. And yet the memory of their meeting still tugged at her—that *click!* of something between them, like the tumblers of a lock falling into place when the right key was inserted. He'd felt it too: she knew it. So what had happened?

Alice came into her room while she was combing out her hair and thinking about Kit. "I'm under strict orders to make sure you're in your bed," she announced and promptly made it impossible for Grace to be so by draping herself across it. "The fat lady on the boat told Mrs. Rennell you were dying of consumption or something."

"She thinks I'm getting the grippe, but I feel better now."

"That's what I said—you never get the vapors. *Now* will you admit that Kit is a paragon? The way he dove in to save you!"

Grace looked away; Alice was positively starry-eyed. "Did you see him?"

"No, but Mrs. Fish said she saw the whole thing. She said that you fainted and Kit tried to grab you but missed. Within a second he was ripping off his jacket and kicking off his shoes and diving after you." She frowned. "What were you doing with him, anyway? I thought you hated the poor boy."

"I don't. He hates me," Grace protested. "He practically said as much, once they'd pulled me out of the water. And anyway…" If she was going to warn Alice, it might as well be now. "The reason I was with him was because I wanted to talk to him about you."

Alice raised her eyebrows. "Why?"

Grace straightened her comb and brush on the vanity table, trying to think of a delicate way to phrase it, then gave up. "People are talking about you two. You were seen at the Casino that night up on the roof—"

"Yes, I know. Lots of people saw us. They didn't seem to mind. I even told you about it."

"Yes. But you didn't tell me about the rowboat race at the Harbor Fête—"

"Oh, *that*." Alice laughed. "It was just a lark. I would have told you except Mrs. Rennell was so busy fussing at Miss Hamm that I didn't have the chance."

"She wouldn't have been fussing at Miss Hamm if you hadn't run off. Nor did you tell me where you and he went the other night at Mrs. Wilson's house, during the concert."

This time Alice remained silent, but a rosy blush crept up her face. "We were seen?"

"You were seen leaving together and returning together, looking…um, disheveled."

The blush deepened. "Who said that?"

"I can't tell you. But it was remarked upon by several people, from what I was told. Alice, you know how stories spread. If it gets back to your family that you've been carrying on with a young man—"

Alice sat up and thumped her fist on the bed. "Oh, damnation! Why does the world have to blather about what I do—or what anyone does?"

"You don't seem to mind indulging in a bit of gossip yourself, at times," Grace reminded her.

"That's different. I like gossiping about other people, but I don't want them gossiping about me." At least she had the honesty to laugh a little shamefacedly. Grace rose and went to sit next to her.

"Then you've *got* to stop giving people reasons to gossip about you," she said earnestly. "That's what I wanted to talk to him about—to appeal to his better nature about you." No need to tell her what else she'd tried to do. "If he really cared about you—"

Alice stiffened. "You said that to him?

"What?"

"That bit about if he really cared about me." She leaned forward eagerly. "What did he say?"

"He didn't. That's when I fainted, or whatever I did."

Alice groaned and collapsed back onto the bed. "Couldn't you have chosen a better time to faint, for heaven's sake?"

"Thank you very much."

"Oh, I didn't mean it, and you know it." Alice sat up. "Kit is…that is, I…I think I love him." She looked down at her lap, blushing again.

Grace swallowed hard. This was worse than she'd expected. "But…really, Alice, you've only known him for two weeks."

She looked up, eyes narrowing. "It's not two weeks, it's sixteen days. You don't think that's time enough for me to know my mind? He's handsome and smart and much more interesting than any of the other boys I've met here. Certainly more so than Tom Livingston," she added.

Her barb missed its mark. "There's no need to pick on Tom Livingston," Grace said, a little sadly. "Kit Rookwood *is* handsomer and cleverer than most of the boys here. Perhaps a little too much so. I've been watching him. He's using all of your Captivation techniques…on you. The admiration, the reflecting back how you want to see yourself — don't you see? He's figured out exactly how to make you — "

"What makes you think he doesn't love me?" she snapped.

Grace hesitated. Alice's vehemence seemed all out of proportion…or maybe it wasn't. "I don't think anything. But I'm worried. I don't want him to hurt you."

"Then you can damned well keep out of my business!"

"Alice!" Mrs. Rennell had opened the door and put her head in, presumably to check on Grace. Her Pekinese face was tight with shocked disapproval. "Such language! Are you girls quarreling?"

Alice turned to her. Grace was sure she'd say something impatient and cutting, but she managed to hold her tongue. "I'm sorry, ma'am. I didn't intend to let that slip out."

"I should think not!" Mrs. Rennell came in. She still looked pale and worn from her bout of *mal de mer*. "Grace, you should be in bed. Alice dear, I asked you to make sure Grace—"

"She's getting there," Alice said shortly and climbed off the bed. Grace got into it; it was easier than protesting that, really, she was much better.

"That's better." Mrs. Rennell sat down on the edge of the bed. "I've cancelled our going to the Dyers' dinner tonight." She sighed. "I hated to do it—it's the *Dyers*, after all—but I don't think any of us are up for it."

"I am," Alice muttered from the window where she'd taken refuge.

Fortunately Mrs. Rennell hadn't heard her. "And I think you ought to stay in bed tomorrow, Grace, in case you are coming down with the grippe."

"Yes, ma'am," Grace agreed meekly. She was certain she wasn't, but it would be good to avoid society for a day or two. Was it all over Newport yet, how she'd ignominiously fallen off the Livingstons' yacht?

Mrs. Rennell patted her hand. "Poor child. Can I do anything for you?"

"You can tell her the news," Alice said, a little less grumpily.

"What news?"

Mrs. Rennell's hands fluttered, as they often did when she was nervous. "Oh, nothing, really. Dear Alice and I were talking, and I've agreed that it would be wrong for me not to do something to return all the hospitality we've received during your visit."

"The Livingstons were so kind to you today, Grace," Alice put in. "It would be positively churlish not to do something. And really, an evening event is the only possible answer. It doesn't have to be a ball. Just a lovely reception with music and dancing and a nice supper partway through the evening."

In other words, a ball. Grace shot Alice a suspicious look. "That sounds…very nice."

"Exactly." Mrs. Rennell's nods were almost frantic. "Just a

pleasant time among friends. Nothing your mothers could possibly take exception to."

Alice came to stand at Mrs. Rennell's shoulder, looking quite saintly. "I told Mrs. Rennell that we'd help her plan it, of course," she said. "We can't let her tire herself!"

Mrs. Rennell looked gratified. "You're a dear girl. But right now we should let Grace rest. Coming?"

"In a moment." Alice waited till Mrs. Rennell had left, then grinned at Grace from the doorway. "So what do you think? Am I brilliant, or what?"

"You're positively ruthless."

"Well, that too." Alice admitted. "We're getting our ball!" She pirouetted out the door.

Grace sighed and stared up at the ceiling. At least talk of the ball had distracted Alice from their conversation about Kit. She was so hopelessly infatuated that she couldn't even entertain the idea that he might be using her Captivation techniques on her. And who knew? Maybe he really *was* as nutty on her as she was on him.

But it seemed doubtful. Not once in their conversation on the boat had she discerned the least tenderness for Alice in his words or manner, which surely there would have been some sign of...wouldn't there? Drat the boy! Alice was...no, fragile wasn't the right word. Vulnerable—yes. As much as her Aunt Bye and her Lee grandparents had loved her, there was still a hole in her heart that they hadn't been able to fill. Grace was sure Alice was trying to fill it herself—with Kit. But it was hard to believe that Kit was up to the task—or even interested in trying.

The only silver lining was that Alice would now be preoccupied with planning her first ball. Maybe it would take her mind off Kit at least a little bit. But that was troubling, too—the way Alice had manipulated Mrs. Rennell into agreeing to hold one. It had been done contemptuously, almost—without regard to

Mrs. Rennell's scruples about her promise to their mothers. The poor woman had been forced to tie her conscience into knots at Alice's hints that not to hold a ball—sorry, an evening reception—would make her look mean and ungrateful. There wasn't much Grace could do or say now, but she did not like this new side of Alice.

∗ ⋅ ◦ ⋅ ⟨ ⋅ ◈ ⋅ ⟩ ⋅ ◦ ⋅ ∗

Grace stayed home the next two days while Mrs. Rennell told everyone she had indeed come down with a summer cold. The news that she was ill meant no one called—who wanted to risk catching a cold at the height of the season? But she hadn't been totally forgotten. Tom Livingston sent an enormous bouquet of roses, three of the latest novels, and his photograph, with a shy request that she might send him one of her when she was feeling better. Mr. Livingston also sent flowers and his own secretary to inquire after her health. Mrs. Fish slyly sent her a box of chocolates in the shape of a ship, and several other floral tributes arrived from young men she'd met over the last few weeks.

She also, much to her surprise, got back her adorable yachting hat that she'd assumed was lost forever, floating off into the depths of the Atlantic. It arrived remarkably un-salt-stained and unharmed in a plain box with no note, which also surprised her—Tom had taken the opportunity to send her long missives with the flowers and all his other offerings. Perhaps it hadn't been sent by him, but by the kind crewmen who'd taken care of her on the motor launch. She would have to ask Tom to thank them for her.

∗ ⋅ ◦ ⋅ ⟨ ⋅ ◈ ⋅ ⟩ ⋅ ◦ ⋅ ∗

The second day of Grace's enforced rest, Alice went with a group of friends to watch a polo match at Izzard's Field. On her return, Grace could hear her stomping up the stairs. She passed her own door and came straight into Grace's room without knocking.

"Well? How was the polo?" Grace closed the book she'd been reading and looked up at Alice. She probably needn't have asked. Alice looked as though her large hat was about to take flight, and her eyes were bright with anger or unshed tears. Or possibly both.

"Splendid." She took off her gloves with jerky motions, yanking on each finger as if she were trying to pull them off as well. Instead of throwing herself onto Grace's bed as usual, she began to pace.

Grace watched her for a moment. "Do you want to tell me what happened?"

Alice laughed shortly. "No, not really."

Grace waited. Whatever it was, it had definitely rattled her. Could it have something to do with Kit? She couldn't think of anything else that would have put Alice into such a state.

She was still pacing. "I overheard something. I don't know if I was supposed to—probably not, because the harpies were all talking behind their fans. I happened to be in the right place to hear their poison. I heard one of them mention your accident, so I stopped to listen, of course."

Grace groaned. Would she ever live down falling off the Livingstons' yacht? "What were they saying?"

"Don't worry, everything I heard about you was sympathetic. And then—" She paused to steady her voice. "Then one of them said, 'If it had been the Roosevelt girl who'd fallen, we'd know why she'd fainted, wouldn't we?'"

Grace frowned. "What's that supposed to mean?"

"Don't interrupt. Then another one said, 'Do you think Kit Rookwood would have gone to rescue her, or would he have been glad to get rid of the evidence?' And then they all laughed." Her face had turned a dull red.

"I still don't—oh!" Grace felt herself turn red as well. What an awful thing to imply! "Who were they? Do we know them?"

"I was behind them, remember? But I didn't recognize the voices." Alice had stopped pacing at last and sat on the edge of Grace's bed, staring down at her hands. "They made me want to go somewhere and wash their filthiness out of my ears. It was horrible."

Grace got up and went to sit next to her. "It was a perfectly rotten thing to say!"

"But not unexpected, right?" Alice smiled bitterly. "I suppose I should apologize for being such a beast to you when you tried to warn me about being seen with Kit too much."

"It's not necessary." At least now she wouldn't have to think about talking to Kit again.

"A real friend never says *I told you so*, right?" Alice gave herself a shake and stood up. "Well, I have to say that I've learned my lesson." She moved to the door. "From now on, *I don't get caught!*"

Grace laughed, but uneasily. "That's one way to look at it."

Alice paused, hand on the doorknob. "You think I'm joking, don't you? Well, I'm not. I'm not going to let petty, dirty-minded people control what I do, for fear that they might talk about me. Oh, stop looking so shocked. You and I spent plenty of time figuring out how not to get caught on some of our escapades in Chestnut Hill. Why is this any different?" She left, slamming the door behind her.

⁂

A blanket of stifling mugginess settled over Newport, too large and heavy for Grace to shift, and what little breeze there was blew warm and damp. Little Parker and Sarah were cranky and miserable with prickly heat rashes, and Mr. Rennell muttered at breakfast that he might as well have stayed in the city if it was going to be this damned hot here. Only the trees didn't complain about the weather.

So it was with alacrity that Alice accepted the invitation of a new friend, Mrs. Cornelius Vanderbilt Jr., for her and Grace be her guests at Bailey's Beach, where the fashionable went sea-bathing.

"Now, you mustn't let your Mrs. Rennell skimp on the champagne at her ball, Alice. That would be quite fatal, to serve an inferior one or, worse, to run out." Mrs. Vanderbilt fanned herself languidly as she gazed out over the water, where tiny wavelets washed in and out of the cove that formed Bailey's Beach. "You must go to Kessler's—not some cheap local merchant."

"Definitely Kessler's." Alice, cross-legged in the sand next to her, nodded wisely.

Grace, sitting next to her, wanted to laugh—what did Alice know about ordering champagne?—but kept her attention focused on the water as well. She didn't care for Mrs. Vanderbilt, who had all of Mrs. Oelrichs' and Mrs. Fish's snobbish grandeur and little of their fierce intelligence, and was obscurely annoyed that her given name was also Grace.

But Alice seemed entranced by her; for one thing, she was much younger than those ladies, being scarcely thirty, while having all their self-assurance. Grace could understand why Alice would be drawn to this stylish young matron. But she still didn't like her. There been a great deal of fuss around her near-elopement of a marriage, which even made it to the Boston papers. Perhaps Alice liked that whiff of disreputability too.

Mrs. Vanderbilt sighed. "And please don't let her do anything like bring her children down to introduce to everyone. It would be *too* grim, you know."

"Never!" Alice's scorn was palpable. "Though I wouldn't put it past her."

"Alice, you don't really think she would do that, do you?" Grace objected. "And she *is* throwing this ball for you, remember."

Alice pouted, but Mrs. Vanderbilt smiled serenely. "Which is why you want to make sure it's all as it should be. How awful to be remembered for an event everyone *laughs* at."

Grace, fuming inwardly, waited for a few minutes to pass and the conversation to move on, then stood up. "Anyone else care to join me for a dip?"

"No, you go," Alice said when Mrs. Vanderbilt shook her head. "I'll stay here."

Grace had been counting on that. Three was definitely a crowd right now. She crossed the smooth strip of sand, raked daily by the beach's caretakers, and waded into the water. The sun was hot on her shoulders, and her high-necked bathing dress stuck to her back. Couldn't bathing dresses be made of something other than wool flannel and not have both knee-length bloomers *and* a skirt? Not to mention the black woolen stockings that ballooned around her calves, full of trapped air—ugh! It wasn't fair that women had to bundle into layers of clothing in order to swim, while men could get away with short knit trousers above the knee (and no stockings!) and sleeveless knit tops.

She glanced enviously at a nearby group of young men, standing in knee-deep water while talking and laughing together, looking cool and unencumbered. One of them returned her look, and to her dismay she realized that it was Kit Rookwood.

He was standing with his arms crossed loosely on his chest, smiling at something that had been said, but his eyes were on her. She looked quickly away without acknowledging him. Why, of all people, did he have to be there? And why did he have to be so attractive standing there in his bathing suit, his smoothly muscled shoulders bare and his tousled hair kissed by the sun?

Now that he'd seen her, he'd know Alice was here as well, and she'd have to put up with him as well as Mrs. Vanderbilt. Which one would succeed in keeping Alice's attention? Her money would be on Kit, with his bare shoulders and throat. She'd be much better off staying in the water for as long as she could and avoiding the upcoming drama on the beach.

Except that as she paddled about, she couldn't help noticing that instead of looking for Alice he'd stayed with his friends, chatting...and watching her. Did he think she would require rescuing again? Well, she wouldn't.

She stayed in the water a full half hour till her teeth were chattering, but as she trudged back up the beach in her dripping woolen dress she somehow didn't feel at all cooled. Kit had stayed where he was, for which she supposed she ought to be grateful—there would be no flirting with Alice to have to watch. Could it be that he actually *had* listened to her, back on the Livingstons' yacht, and had decided to behave more circumspectly toward Alice?

"You look like a drowned cat," Alice said cheerfully as Grace rejoined her and Mrs. Vanderbilt on the beach.

"Thank you. Aren't you going to swim?"

"No, there isn't time now." Mrs. Vanderbilt drew her skirt aside so that Grace wouldn't drip on it.

Grace took the hint and dripped her way toward the changing rooms, pausing briefly on the sand to wring some of the water from her skirt.

"You're not dead, then!" a voice called. Grace looked up. Mrs. Fish stood on the board walkway above her, parasol raised.

"Not to my knowledge, ma'am," she replied. "Are you here to bathe? It's lovely." Well, the water had been, anyway.

Mrs. Fish shuddered. "I don't immerse myself in water that hasn't been heated and put into a tub first. Come up here and talk to me for a minute, pet."

Grace complied. Mrs. Fish examined her closely. "You manage to look beautiful even wrapped in wet flannel," she said. Then her eyes sharpened. "Clever girl, to stay home and play sick after that business on the boat. Unless you really were ill?"

"Thank you, I'm fine, really—and I was grateful for the rest. But I'm glad to see you." She lowered her voice. "I wanted to tell you that I think the conversation I had before I fell off that dratted boat did its work."

"Did it?" Mrs. Fish raised her eyebrows. "How do you know? Has young Rookwood run away to a monastery?"

Grace grinned. "No such luck. But he's here today. I know he saw me—he stared enough, the entire time I was in the water—"

"Ah, did he?"

Grace couldn't help making a face. "Yes. But what's important is that he made no move to go find Alice. I'm hoping that he's decided not to give the world any more reason to talk about the two of them."

Mrs. Fish squinted out over the beach. There was a funny little smile playing about her mouth. "Maybe," she said. "Or…"

"Or what?"

She shrugged. "Oh, nothing. Go get changed, lamb. You're making me feel wet, looking at you."

EIGHT

The following week was taken up with planning for the ball...or at least, all of the time when they weren't at luncheons or teas or playing tennis at the Casino. Alice seemed determined to cram an entire summer's worth of society into the remaining days of their stay and accepted every invitation. At least it kept her busy — so busy that she didn't seem to be thinking as much about Kit.

Though he certainly hadn't vanished from the scene. He played tennis with Alice twice that week and took her driving in a motor car, which she didn't stop talking about for hours. Grace began to worry that her self-congratulations had been premature and waited for another summons from Mrs. Fish, but none came.

And she herself was still feeling...not precisely ill, but not well either. "You look like you swallowed a quart or two of seawater when you fell off the Livingstons' boat and still haven't brought it up yet," Alice said to her a few mornings later. "You know, sort of gray and peaky. Are you all right?"

"I've felt better," Grace admitted. In fact, the only thing that made her feel close to normal was to spend as much time outside as possible, in the company of the trees of the Rennells' garden. They were mostly small ornamentals and did not have much to say, but their presence eased her discomfort a little…which made Grace think. She'd been so eager to immerse herself in the human world, and now here she was, grateful for the company of some Japanese cherries, a young horse chestnut, and a row of over-clipped arborvitae. You could take the dryad away from the trees, but you couldn't take the trees from the dryad. It was a sobering thought; was she like a fish removed from the sea, gasping for breath outside of her necessary element?

Every evening when Grace went to bed, it was with relief that another day had passed until their departure. She had even begun to think about begging off going to the Adirondacks with Alice in favor of going home. How lovely it would be to be among the trees of home, old friends that hadn't been planted in isolation or tortured into strange shapes…and what a relief to be home with her family, where she didn't have to be so careful.

Tom Livingston was still her shadow, along with a train of other young men who seemed to want to follow her around, even though she'd been careful never to be more than polite to them for fear that they'd end up as fascinated as Tom. He hadn't asked her out on the *Princess Eleanor* again, thank goodness, but he never seemed to be far away and had already asked permission to call on her in Chestnut Hill that fall, when he went to visit friends at Harvard. Grace could imagine what Grand-mère's reaction would be if he did.

So they helped Mrs. Rennell with plans for the ball, ordering the oriental lilies and spider chrysanthemums and pots of jasmine and palms to go with the Chinese lanterns that would be strung all over the house and garden, and a pagoda-shaped tent on the back lawn, where supper would be served. Even the footmen and waiters would be part of the décor, arrayed in red and black mandarin costumes. Grace worried a little that Mrs. Rennell was trying to be too "original" in her party theme, but Alice seemed to think it would be all right; Grace suspected she'd cleared it with Mrs. Vanderbilt, which was somehow vaguely irritating. Why hadn't Alice talked to her about it?

"Alice? Are you in there?" Grace stood outside Alice's bedroom door, knocking. Beside her was Mrs. Rennell's maid, Jeffries, looking affronted.

Mrs. Rennell had kindly sent Jeffries to help them get ready for the ball. Fortunately she'd mentioned it beforehand so that Grace was prepared and already had her hair done when the maid arrived. The last thing she wanted was to have a stranger fussing with it, lest she have missed any green when she'd last dyed it. But she'd let Jeffries help her with her dress — a pale celadon-green chiffon with beaded bodice that she and Mum had been careful not to let Grand-mère see — and sent her on to help Alice.

Except that Alice didn't want any help, or even to let Jeffries into her room. So Jeffries had summoned Grace for reinforcement.

"Of course I am," Alice called impatiently. "Where'd you think I'd be?"

"Jeffries is here to help you get ready — Mrs. Rennell sent her."

"I'm fine. Let her help you."

"I'm already done."

"Well, then she isn't needed, is she? Tell her to go away."

Grace looked apologetically at Jeffries. "I'm sorry. I do appreciate your help, though. Please thank Mrs. Rennell for us."

Jeffries sniffed and retreated down the hall to her mistress's room. Once she was out of sight, Grace rapped again. "She's gone. May I come in?"

A pause. "I'm in the middle of doing my hair, and I really can't open the door right now."

"That's all right. You don't need to open it for me." Grace turned the knob—or tried to. Alice had locked it.

"Alice," she said quietly.

"Oh, for heaven's—I'll be out in a few minutes. Go…go *do* something, will you?"

But she wasn't out in a few minutes, and it wasn't until most of the guests for the pre-ball dinner had arrived that Alice finally made her appearance. When she did, Grace understood why she hadn't wanted anyone in her room.

Where had she gotten that dress? Mrs. Roosevelt certainly hadn't bought it for her. Mrs. Roosevelt would never have allowed Alice anything like it. It was gorgeous, of course—satin with a tulle overskirt and draperies, embroidered with a sprinkling of beaded moons and stars…and all in deepest midnight black. Above the very low décolletage Alice's face was pale, but there was a feverish glint of excitement in her eyes.

Grace managed to excuse herself from Tom Livingston, whom Mrs. Rennell had kindly invited to dine with them, and sidled around the room toward Alice. Several guests were already glancing toward her and whispering.

"So that's why your door was locked," Grace murmured to her.

"Well, what do you think? I didn't want anyone telling me my dress was completely inappropriate for a girl my age, so it seemed easier to lock myself in until it was too late. It worked too. I'd pat myself on the back if I weren't afraid of falling out of my dress."

"Serve you right if you did. Where did you get it? Surely your stepmother didn't—"

"Are you joking? Mother would faint if she saw me in this. The other Grace—Mrs. Vanderbilt, I mean—helped me pick it out when I went shopping with her last week. Don't you wish you'd come with us after all that day?"

"Not really." Grace had refused because shopping with Mrs.

Vanderbilt had seemed like a singularly unappealing prospect. If she'd known, though—

"It's all right. I would have bought it anyway, even if you'd hated it." Alice hesitated for a second. "Well, do you hate it?"

Grace sighed. "You know it's beautiful. It's just that it makes you look like a thirty-year-old with an interesting past."

"Does it? Excellent!" She nodded toward the door. "Oh, there's Kit. Is it all right if I go and talk to him, Grandma?"

"Is that what this is about? Enticing—er, impressing Kit?"

Alice's glee slipped a little. "Maybe."

"Alice, we're seventeen! What do you want? Are you trying to get him to propose or something?"

Alice opened her mouth, then closed it. A succession of fleeting expressions crossed her face—uncertainty, anger, and finally, stubbornness. "If he does, you'll be the first to know," she said and strolled sinuously toward Kit.

Grace watched her despairingly. For all her intelligence, sometimes Alice did remarkably idiotic things. She craned her neck to see what Kit's reaction would be to so much Alice so provocatively displayed. For a brief second his eyebrows went up. Then he grinned, said something that made Alice chortle, and offered her his arm.

The dinner went without a hitch, to Grace's relief. Mrs. Rennell was handsome and surprisingly dignified in a gold Chinese brocade gown, and Mr. Rennell was an unexpectedly genial host and actually conversed with his neighbors at dinner. Grace kept an eye on Alice and Kit, seated together across the table from her, but they, too, behaved themselves, only whispering together a little more than was seemly. Perhaps tonight would be a success after all.

For the first part of the evening, it seemed like it would be. Though Mrs. Fish and Mrs. Oelrichs were unable to attend, Mrs. Belmont and her husband were there, as was Alice's new friend, Mrs. Vanderbilt, along with a party of houseguests whom she'd somehow forgotten to mention she'd be bringing. Mrs. Rennell was gracious about the extra guests, and when she discovered that one of them was a good-looking young vicomte visiting from France, she positively fluttered in excitement. Though the night was cloudy and a mist was slowly creeping in from the ocean—Grace had forgotten to talk to the weather in her anxiety over Alice—it only lent the Chinese lanterns scattered around the garden and illuminating the pagoda-tent a more lovely and mysterious glow.

Tom Livingston more or less fastened himself to her. "I don't care," he said when she gently hinted that perhaps claiming three dances before supper was a little much. "You're leaving in two days, and summer will be over as far as I'm concerned."

"Oh, Tom," she said, smiling. But underneath the smile she couldn't help feeling sad. He was such a nice boy, and she hoped some lucky girl would capture his fancy soon—a girl who could return his regard as she could not. She danced with several other young men and had Mrs. Vanderbilt's vicomte claim two of the post-supper dances on her dance card before she went into supper with Tom.

Alice had been dancing a great deal as well; the vicomte had already danced with her. Grace had seen him gazing soulfully down the front of her dress as they danced. But she'd also danced several times with Kit…and though Grace felt she ought to warn Alice to be more circumspect, how could she, after having let Tom dance with her so many times?

What she hadn't been doing, unlike Alice, was indulging in champagne. Mrs. Rennell had not committed the error of having insufficient champagne, and the costumed footmen were in constant motion through the ballroom (the two adjoining salons, thrown open into one room) with trays full of brimming glasses. Whenever she wasn't dancing Alice seemed to have a glass in her hand, and Grace often heard her laughter, higher and shriller than usual, from across the room.

But Alice was nowhere to be seen—or heard—at two a.m., when the orchestra took their break and the dancers wandered out to the pagoda for supper. Grace toyed with her food and let Tom's conversation wash over her while she scanned the guests in the gilded bamboo chairs, tucking into oysters and chicken crepes.

Alice wasn't among them. And neither was Kit. Very well, then; she would have to go find them and perhaps wring someone's neck…whose, she wasn't yet sure. She nibbled at a crepe until the guests began to drift back to the house, then pushed her chair back.

Tom leapt from his chair and held his hand out to her. "May I escort you back to the ballroom?"

She shook her head. "I need to run up to my room for a moment. Will you excuse me, please? I'll find you when I'm done."

He looked as though he would happily trail after her, given the least encouragement, but nodded reluctantly and led her back to the house.

Grace skimmed through the ballroom and ducked down the hall and to Mr. Rennell's library. She stood for several heartbeats on the threshold, listening, but it was uninhabited. Mrs. Rennell's crowded little morning room was likewise empty, so she turned back and ascended the stairs. The sewing room, guest bedrooms, and little parlor were all empty…as was Alice's room. Grace breathed a sigh of relief; it was unlikely that she would have gone to the third floor, which held more bedrooms and the nursery— hardly the place for a romantic rendezvous. If Alice wasn't in the house, then she must be somewhere in the garden. She descended to the first floor by the back stairs. Near their bottom was a door to the back garden, which she hoped she could slip out through unobserved.

No such luck; the door was propped open, and a pair of footmen were loitering outside it, passing a bottle back and forth between them. It was hard to say who was more embarrassed, she or they; she passed them with a brief nod and felt them watching her as she crunched down the gravel path.

The mist had thickened, and once out of sight of the footmen she paused for a moment, wishing she'd stopped in her room for a wrap. But she didn't want to brave the footmen at the back door again, and going in through the ballroom would put her in danger of being found by Tom or whichever young man she'd promised dances to after supper. If she were lucky, it wouldn't take her too long to find Alice — if she *could* find her, in her black dress — and when she did, a good scolding would warm her up. She smiled grimly at the thought.

First, there was the avenue of tall arborvitae planted in two staggered rows, which provided dozens of little alcoves to search, lit with gilded Chinese lanterns. She could ask their help — they'd gotten to know each other a little during her "cold." But most trees were bad at recognizing individual humans, or even telling the difference between men and women. She'd have to do the looking herself.

She was partway up the avenue on this side of the garden when a voice stopped her. "Madame — ah, mademoiselle! You are lost? May I assist you?"

Grace turned. Mrs. Vanderbilt's handsome young vicomte — what was his name? — was standing there. As the dim light from a nearby lantern illuminated her face, he smiled in recognition and held out his hand. "Ah! But I know you!"

Grace tried to conceal her impatience. "How do you do, monsieur le vicomte?"

"But you are supposed to be dancing with me, dear mademoiselle," he said, pretending to sound cross. He couldn't be any older than Tom Livingston, but there was a practiced quality to his speech that told her he was much more experienced.

"Well, as we're neither of us in the ballroom, perhaps we can forgive each other for missing our dance and make it up later?" If only he'd take the hint about *later*.

He didn't. "You are perhaps looking for something, out here all alone?"

"I'm looking for my friend Alice. Maybe you've seen her?" she added hopefully. "She's a little shorter than me, in a black dress?"

"In a black dress…" He brightened. "Why yes, I believe I have."

Grace sighed in relief. "Where? Can you tell me?"

"I shall do better than that." He held out his arm. "I shall take you to her."

"Thank you." She took it and let him lead her swiftly toward the end of the arborvitae avenue. In front of the last alcove, he paused under the lantern.

"But I thought it was here…" he said, sounding puzzled.

Grace stepped forward to examine its shadows more closely. "No, she's not here. Could she have—"

But a pair of hands suddenly circled her waist from behind, then slid up to cup her breasts. "It may be that I was mistaken," the vicomte breathed into her ear, then nuzzled it. "But while we are here, sweet mademoiselle, you are—*ow!*"

Grace whirled as he stumbled back from her, hopping on one foot and swearing to himself in French. Her heels were not that high, but they made an effective enough weapon when stomped firmly into a lightly shod instep. She took advantage of his momentary preoccupation to slip around the shrub and run lightly away.

"Mademoiselle—wait!" she heard him call. "Come back!"

"Not likely." She ducked behind the young horse chestnut at the end of the avenue. Holding her breath, she pressed herself against its trunk and held still, wrapping herself in the tree's shadow. He'd never be able to find her now, despite the lantern hanging a few feet away. She could do this in broad daylight and make herself all but invisible to human eyes.

Drat him! It was a good thing they were leaving Newport—she'd never be able to see the ghastly vicomte at the Casino or anywhere without wanting to slap him. She stood silently, listening to him wander around and call out to her in coaxing tones. She still hadn't found Alice, and now she'd have to dodge him while searching.

When it sounded as if he might have given up, she stepped carefully away from her hiding place and began to inch her way across the lawn toward the other row of arborvitae, glancing behind her in case the vicomte was lurking. Oh, when she found Alice, she'd—

"I beg your pardon!"

Grace nearly shrieked as someone walked into her and stumbled heavily. But the voice had not been the vicomte's.

"Are you all right, Henry?" said another voice.

"I bumped into something, but there's nothing there," the first voice said, sounding puzzled.

A man and a woman stood there, blinking in confusion in the lantern light, and Grace realized that she still held the tree's shadow wrapped around her. She retreated a few paces, shrugged it off, and stepped toward them. "I'm so sorry! I hope I didn't startle you."

The man shook his head slightly as if to clear it. He looked to be of hale middle age, with a comfortably plump figure and a receding hairline above his mild-expressioned face. A gold pince-nez perched on his nose.

"Not at all, my dear," he said gallantly. "These eyes of mine aren't quite as sharp as they once were, I fear...not that they were ever all that sharp. The question is, are you all right?"

"Poor child," the woman said softly. She looked to be of similar age to her companion, but had obviously once been a beauty and remained remarkably handsome, if a little vague-looking. Something about her face and fair hair seemed familiar.

"Not at all. I wasn't looking where I going," Grace said, a little desperately. At this rate she'd never find Alice—at least, not before someone else did.

Something of her worry must have shown on her face, for the man said, "My eyes aren't so dull that they can't see you're troubled. Is there something Mrs. Rookwood and I can do for you?"

"No, but thank—" Grace stopped. "Did you say your name is Rookwood?"

The man bowed. "Henry Rookwood, at your service, and Mrs. Rookwood," he said, a faint question in his voice.

"You couldn't—that is, you must be Kit's father and mother!" Grace knew she was staring, but couldn't help it. These pleasant people were *Kit Rookwood's* parents? They had to be; that was why Mrs. Rookwood had looked familiar. Kit obviously inherited his looks from her.

"Is Kit here?" Mrs. Rookwood sounded pleased. "We had another party to go to earlier this evening and just arrived and hoped we would see him—but he doesn't seem to be in the ballroom or that charming tent."

"Er, no. That is...well, I'm looking for my friend Alice, and...and I think Kit might be with her."

A rustling sound to the left made them all turn, and Kit himself emerged from behind a bank of enormous hydrangeas, looking rumpled but as elegant as ever in his evening clothes. "Grace!" he said urgently. "I thought I heard you— Oh!" He checked in surprised. "Father! You're here!"

"Where's Alice?" Grace demanded.

With the lantern to his back, it was hard to read his expression. "Wait a moment," he said and turned back to the hydrangeas. When he emerged again, he was carrying a limp Alice who lolled against his chest, eyes closed. Even from feet away Grace could smell the sickly sweet-vinegary scent of wine mixed with vomit that wafted from her.

"Alice!" she gasped. "What did you do to her?"

Kit's voice was flat. "She mostly did it to herself, thank you. Too much champagne, to start with. Then she fell off the bench she was dancing on, and things went downhill from there. I think she's asleep now."

"Oh, Alice..." Grace leaned forward to look at her face. She was pale and sweating, and her hair hung in damp straggles around her face.

"Christopher, I am not pleased." Mr. Rookwood frowned at his son.

"I'm sorry, sir." Kit looked uncomfortable. "Believe me, I didn't—"

Not far away, a woman's giggle, followed by a man's mumbled words, made them all fall silent. When it sounded as though the couple had wandered in another direction, Grace drew a deep breath. "We have to get her back to the house before someone sees her."

"I concur," Mr. Rookwood said. "But how will you get her home?"

"This is home—that is, we're guests here." Grace bit her lip, thinking. Alice looked beyond rousing, so she would have to be carried. If only she were strong enough to do it, she could maybe wrap a tree's shadow around them both and make it unseen back to the house that way...but she couldn't carry Alice, and the presence of the three Rookwoods made that impossible anyway.

"My son will carry her. It's the least he can do," Mr.

Rookwood said, breaking into her thoughts. "Let us keep to the edge of the lawn. Mrs. Rookwood and I will walk ahead, Kit will follow us, and you, Miss—er, Grace, was it?—will follow behind. If any of us should see someone coming, we'll clear our throats loudly, and that will be your signal to hide," he said to Kit, who nodded tightly.

"Oh, thank you!" Grace said. It was wonderful of them to not have made a fuss about Alice's condition. "Follow that line of bushes, and then we'll decide how to get her inside."

To her relief, they met no one as they made their way through the garden, though Grace was sure they would after Alice moaned loudly on two occasions. It would serve Kit right if she threw up all over his chest, but she didn't. At the end of the arborvitae avenue nearest the house, they paused so that Grace could decide the next step. The only way to get Alice inside without being seen would be through the back door. But if there were still servants loitering there…well, it would be a chance they'd have to take.

"I see," Mr. Rookwood said, when she explained how they would get into the house. "But may I suggested that just my son and Mrs. Rookwood bring her? Fewer people are less obtrusive, and as long as his mother accompanies them, no one could object to Kit's bringing Alice upstairs."

Grace hesitated. But Mr. Rookwood was right. Once they got her upstairs, she herself could go back inside without subterfuge and take care of Alice. "Very well," she said. "Inside that door, go up the stairs—they're a little narrow, so be careful—to the next floor. Alice's room is on the main passage, opposite a tall Chinese vase with pampas grass in it."

"Don't worry, dear. We'll get her there safely," Mrs. Rookwood said comfortably.

"Be careful," Mr. Rookwood said sternly to Kit. He nodded and shifted Alice's weight more securely against him. She stirred and gave a faint snore but didn't wake.

Grace led them to the door. To her relief, no footmen were there and the door was still propped open. After Kit and his mother vanished inside, she went back to Mr. Rookwood. "So far, so good," she said.

"Well, our role in this little adventure is mostly over. May I escort you back to the party?" He held out his arm to her.

"I don't *want* to go back." Not if it meant risking meeting the loathsome vicomte. Or even Tom Livingston.

"I can understand that," he said kindly. "But you do owe it to your hostess to inform her of Alice's condition—not in detail, if you don't wish!—and that you're both present and accounted for."

"I suppose you're right, sir," Grace said reluctantly and took his arm.

"Are you and your friend making a long stay in Newport?" he asked as they began to stroll back to the tent.

"We're leaving Thursday on the night boat to New York, but we've been here nearly a month." Thursday couldn't get here quickly enough.

"I see. Is New York home, then?"

"Oh, no! I'm from Boston, and Alice…" She swallowed. Was it really necessary to divulge who Alice was? Perhaps she could gloss over it. "I guess I didn't introduce myself, did I? My name is Grace Boisvert."

Mr. Rookwood's pace slowed for a moment. "Miss Boisvert, from Boston," he repeated softly. "How interesting."

When she looked at him inquiringly he patted her arm. "I am slightly acquainted with a Mr. Boisvert from Boston through the course of business. Could it be that you are related?"

"My father is Charles-Alexandre Boisvert, with Cabot, Boisvert, and Shaw."

"Ah, then I do know him. It's a fine old firm." As they passed a lantern, he paused and looked at her closely. "Yes…I can see him in you. It's always a pleasure to meet friends of friends—or daughters of them." He smiled, and the gold rim of his pince-nez caught the light and glinted with his smile.

Grace smiled back. What a nice man. She still wasn't sure how Kit could have come from such amiable parents. And thinking of her own papa made her feel better.

"I'd love to go home," she said. "But Alice and I are joining her family in the Adirondacks for a few weeks. That's why we're leaving for New York."

"The Adirondacks!" His face lit up. "I visited there as a boy and have always wanted to go back. Where are you staying?"

"The Tahawus Club, but please don't ask me where it is—I've never been there."

"You're in for a treat—the Adirondacks are a lovely place." He sighed.

Grace sighed too. "I think anywhere is preferable to Newport right now."

He nodded. "It can be overwhelming if you're not used to it. So now you're looking forward to taking a vacation from your vacation, are you?"

Grace laughed. "I think I am!"

They had arrived back at the terrace to the ballroom. Mr. Rookwood released her arm and bowed. "It was a pleasure making your acquaintance, Miss Boisvert, even under the circumstances. And I hope your friend feels better soon."

"Oh, the pleasure was mine! And…thank you, sir, for your help."

He gave a self-deprecating shrug. "It was nothing, and saved everyone some unpleasantness. Good night, Miss Boisvert." He bowed again, smiled at her, and turned away.

Grace managed to find Mrs. Rennell and whisper to her that she and Alice had had enough, and that Alice had already gone to bed. Mrs. Rennell looked anxious. "Is she all right?"

"Er…she may be a little off in the morning," Grace said reluctantly.

"Oh, dear." Mrs. Rennell's little face scrunched into its worried Pekinese expression. "I didn't know—did she have some champagne?"

"Er…a little." Then inspiration struck. "I think it was too much lobster salad, myself, though. Don't worry. I'm going up to her now. It was a lovely party, ma'am—don't you think it's gone well?"

Her expression cleared. "I think it has. I think it's gone very well!"

NINE

When Grace left the party and came upstairs, she found Alice had been sick on the floor next to her bed. She grimaced and cleaned it up as well as she could with the hand-towels in the bathroom—best not to call a maid, who might tell Mrs. Rennell about Alice's true condition—then managed to get Alice undressed and sponged off and into bed. She was a little more conscious by that time, enough to cooperate with removing her gown.

"Don't tear it," she mumbled to Grace.

"Too late. You took care of that yourself."

She groaned and half opened her eyes, trying to focus. "Oh…it's you. How'd I get here?"

Grace mopped her forehead again. "Why don't we talk about it tomorrow?"

By noon the following day, Alice had improved…somewhat. "I will never again, as long as I live, drink like that," she muttered to Grace, who brought her some plain black tea at lunchtime. The thought of anything more than that had nearly sent her back into the bathroom to retch over the toilet again.

"I should hope not," Grace said severely. "Not after what you told me about your uncle." Alice's uncle Elliot had had a severe problem with drink all his life before jumping out of a window while inebriated a few years before.

"Oh, God…no one knows, do they? Who saw me last night?" Alice removed the cold compress from her forehead and eyes and propped herself up against her pillows, looking blearily at Grace. "What happened, anyway? I gather you rescued me from—from something."

"I bumped into Kit's parents, and between all of us we managed to get you up here without anyone seeing, I think. Before that, I have no idea what anyone might have seen you doing. Kit said something about dancing on a bench—or rather, falling off it."

Alice shifted uncomfortably. "I don't remember anything about that, but I suppose it would account for my sore ankle. Kit's parents are here? Really? What are they like?"

"Nothing like Kit—well, he looks like his mother, who's quite lovely. But they're very nice people."

"'Very nice people—nothing like Kit.'" Alice grimaced. "You really don't like him, do you?"

Grace ignored that and rose from her chair by Alice's bed. "Why don't you nap now, and maybe you'll feel well enough later that I can help you start packing. We leave tomorrow afternoon, remember."

Alice turned her head away. "Oh, Kit…" That dreamy-eyed expression took over her face. "I don't want to go to Tahawus if it means leaving him!"

"Very well. I'll go up there by myself and tell your parents you've run away to join the circus.'"

Alice snorted. "Do you think they'd care if I did? That's an idea, though. Maybe Kit and I should run away together. Wouldn't that be romantic?"

Grace sighed and went to begin her own packing.

She didn't accomplish as much of it as she hoped to that afternoon. At four the doorbell rang. Grace ignored it; it had been ringing all afternoon with callers paying the requisite calls of thanks to the previous evening's hostess, and Mrs. Rennell had been in her element. But this time, the doorbell was followed a few minutes later by a knock on her door.

"Please, miss," said the parlor maid when Grace opened it. "Mrs. Fish is outside in her carriage and asks if you'll come for a ride with her."

Mrs. Fish—goodness! "Please have the footman tell her I'll be down as soon as I put on my hat." There was no time to change into a proper carriage dress; Mrs. Fish would have to take her as she found her. What could she possibly want? *Please* let it not have anything to do with Alice last night at the ball!

Mrs. Fish returned her tentative greeting with no sign of impending lectures. She directed the coachman to keep going until he heard otherwise, then turned to Grace. "So you're leaving us, I hear."

"Yes. I was going to call on you tomorrow to say goodbye and thank you for all your kind—"

"Well, you won't need to now, lamb, as I've done it for you." She looked at Grace appraisingly. "It's a shame you're leaving, y'know. You're about the only interesting thing that's happened this summer, what with Harry Lehr gone."

"Thank you, ma'am." Grace took a breath and blurted, "Though I can't understand why you'd find a girl just out of school interesting."

"It's the effect you've had on people. Very diverting, you know. If you'd been a twenty-five-year-old with your own house here and a husband in the city five days a week, you'd have been positively dangerous—and even more interesting." She laughed loudly as Grace blushed.

"It's only been Tom Livingston," she protested.

Mrs. Fish shook her head. "There's been any number of boys sniffing around when you haven't been paying attention—or when Tom hasn't growled at them to keep away. And what about Kit Rookwood?"

Grace couldn't restrain a faint snort. "Oh, no. I don't know about any other boys, but not him. He's Alice's pet, remember?"

Her jowly face creased in an incredulous smile. "You think so?"

"Well, don't you, after their behavior that we were worried about? He seemed to be better after I spoke to him, so maybe he does really care about her." Then again, after last night, she wasn't so sure. If he'd truly cared about Alice, he wouldn't have let her get herself into such a state. "And to be honest, he's been really quite horrible to me."

"Really?" But she was still smiling. "What's he done?"

Grace wished she hadn't said anything. The whole thing would sound so childish. "He...er, took exception to my being from Boston."

Mrs. Fish poked her. "Go on!"

"He called me a Puritan maiden and made disparaging comments about me and—" She stopped, for beside her Mrs. Fish was shaking with laughter.

"Oh, lord, lamb! It's just as I suspected," she gasped, groping for her purse and extracting a handkerchief from it.

"I don't see what's so funny. It was quite distressing," Grace said coldly.

"Did it stop?"

"Sort of. After the incident on the yacht, he began to avoid me."

"Hmm. Yes, that would fit," she said, nodding.

"Excuse me if I am about to be rude, ma'am...but would you mind telling me what you're laughing about?"

Mrs. Fish patted her arm. "Haven't you ever seen a twelve-year-old boy when he's sweet on a girl? What does he do but behave as beastly toward her as he can, because he can't think of any other way to get her attention?"

"Oh, no—"

"Listen, pet. I saw something that you didn't. I was watching when you fell off that boat. It was very interesting." She pursed her lips and paused dramatically, just long enough to make Grace shift irritably in her seat, then continued. "If I've ever seen anyone's heart in their face, it was Kit's then. He looked like he'd lost his only chance of salvation...and then he was kicking off his shoes and struggling to get his coat off and was in after you in a flash. I didn't think a body could move that fast. If he's not in love with you, I'm the queen of England."

Grace turned to look at her. Surely she was joking—she *had* to be. But Mrs. Fish's expression was, for once, solemn.

"I don't believe it," she said flatly. "I'm sure he rescued me quickly, but who wouldn't have if they were a strong swimmer? I think you're reading more into it than was really there."

"Well, I know what I saw, lamb. And I still don't think he gives a hoot for your Alice—though I can't think why he's been sniffing round her the way he has."

"Exactly! Why would he—unless he meant it?"

Mrs. Fish shrugged. "I don't know. It's curious...which is part of why I'm sad that you're leaving. I'm dying to see how it plays out." She laughed again and turned the conversation to other topics.

When the carriage paused again at the Rennells' gate to drop her off, Mrs. Fish shook her hand. "Enjoy your trip to wherever it is you're going out in the woods. If you're in New York this winter, my pet, call on me, please."

Grace smiled at her. For all her peculiarities, she'd come to sincerely like Mrs. Fish. "I certainly will, ma'am."

"You're a good girl. The Roosevelt chit's lucky to have you as a friend—but don't be too surprised if the loyalty only goes one way." She held Grace's hand a moment longer. "There's something about you," she said musingly. "Darned if I know what it is, though, beyond that lovely face of yours."

As her carriage clattered down the street, Grace watched it. For all her loud and outlandish behavior, Mrs. Fish was a perceptive woman. But she was wrong about Kit. *Completely* wrong.

⁎⋇ ⫷❈⬧❈⫸ ⋇⁎

They left the next day. Mrs. Rennell drove with them to the docks in Fall River to see them settled into their stateroom on the night boat to New York.

Alice had completely recovered from her misadventures on the evening of the ball, which hardly seemed fair. But leaving Newport seemed to be punishment enough. She was silently glum during the drive and barely responded to Mrs. Rennell's conversational sallies. Only when they were actually making their last farewells did she seem to wake up.

"I hope you'll consider coming again to Newport next summer, my dear." Mrs. Rennell tenderly embraced her.

"What?" Alice blinked. "Oh, next summer. Yes, I'll certainly see you at some point. Grace Vanderbilt has already invited me to stay with her."

Mrs. Rennell seemed unsure whether to scold or cry. "Oh...of course. Goodbye." She started down the gangplank, pausing partway down and turning as if she wanted to say something. But there were others behind her, and she was forced to hurry down the rest of the way.

"Did Mrs. Vanderbilt really invite you to stay with her next year?" Grace asked as they stood at the rail looking down over the dock. Poor Mrs. Rennell! At least she seemed to have gained a little social advancement that summer, thanks to Alice.

Alice didn't answer. She was too busy scanning the passengers and crew hurrying around below them.

"Alice?"

"He didn't come to say goodbye," she said bleakly. "He didn't come after the ball to thank Mrs. Rennell, and he didn't come today before we left."

There was no need to ask who *he* was. None of the Rookwoods had called on Mrs. Rennell yesterday, which was odd—and it was even odder that Kit hadn't come to say goodbye to Alice. Grace had expected a dramatic scene involving armfuls of roses and vows of undying devotion, which would have been ghastly…but it would have been preferable to the naked hurt in Alice's eyes. Once again, someone Alice cared about had let her down.

"I'm sorry," she said gently.

"You didn't quarrel with him again the night of the ball, did you?"

If only they had—it would have been of no importance to her and might have made Alice feel better. "We barely spoke the night of the ball. I mostly talked to his parents while we were trying to get you upstairs. Besides, I don't think he'd let my being here stop him from coming to see you." A shudder ran through her, making her clutch the railing. Oh, no—not again! She took a deep breath and turned away.

"Where are you going?" Alice called after her.

"My bunk," Grace said shortly. The headache and dizziness that she'd felt on the Livingstons' boat were creeping over her. Bed would be the best place to spend the hours till morning brought them to the city. Oh, why couldn't they have taken the train to New York?

She was indeed miserable all night. Alice got up several times to bring cold washcloths for her forehead. "You took care of me the other night," she said a little gruffly when Grace tried to thank her the first time she came. "I can return the favor, can't I?"

❖

They arrived in New York and caught the train north to Albany, Alice steering them confidently through the echoing train station to the correct platform. In Albany they caught the Delaware & Hudson train to the village of North Creek, which was as far as the tracks went into this part of the Adirondacks. The passengers on the train consisted mostly of men wearing what was probably supposed to look like informal hunting garb but had obviously been made by Brooks Brothers—wealthy bankers and lawyers and brokers, Grace guessed, en route to the great northern forests to stalk deer and catch trout and feel, at least for a little while, like rugged woodsmen. When they arrived in North Creek, she followed Alice down the aisle and out onto the platform…and drew a deep breath of surprise and delight.

Alice had sat in the window seat, and her enormous hat had blocked Grace's view. But she'd been distantly aware of an energy, a subtle, invigorating tinge in the air even through the usual train smells of coal smoke and tired upholstery and too many bodies close to her. And now, out here on this rather shabby platform, that tinge struck her with its full, sparkling force.

It was the scent of hundreds of square miles of trees, green and fresh and vigorous— the brown, mellow scent of oak and beech and maple and the crisper, astringent tang of pine and fir and balsam. They perfumed the air with an intoxicating richness that made her ache to dash into the forest and dance among the trunks and throw herself down in a deep carpet of pine needles and *breathe*. Everyone in Newport had endlessly congratulated each other about being able to spend the summer in the healthy ocean breezes, but only now did she realize that to her dryad blood, the salt air had been anything but refreshing. She lifted her chin and inhaled deeply, and a delicious giddy feeling made her want to laugh out loud.

And the trees themselves! She could feel them, sense the hum of their conversations, the sheer overwhelming number of them — far, far more of them than there were humans in this land. It was humbling and awe-inspiring…and exciting in a way she'd never felt before. Oh, what she wouldn't give to walk among them right now — to run her hands over their bark, rough and smooth, to let their slow thoughts reverberate through her like the notes of an organ, to breathe in their scent… A peculiar shiver ran through her at the thought of being there among them, *feeling* them with all her senses —

"You'll be the young ladies goin' out to Tahawus," said a gravelly voice.

Grace reluctantly tore her attention from the joyous trees. The speaker was a grizzle-headed man in a patched canvas coat who could have been any age between thirty and sixty. There was a sardonic but not unkindly glint in his eye as he surveyed her and Alice from the front seat of a covered, two-seater buckboard.

"I assume so," Alice said. "And our luggage. Are you our driver?" She motioned to where the porters were stacking their trunks and boxes and bags.

The man looked at the growing pile on the platform with an expression of stoical resignation. "Good thing they sent two wagons." He let out a piercing whistle. A young boy who somehow managed to look as weather-beaten and grizzled as his elder brought a wagon up, then stopped to gawk at them.

"If you're not doin' nothing, then you might put your back into loading this gear," the man said to him, then looked back to Alice and her. "Sooner you git in, th' sooner we'll git there."

"How far is it to the Tahawus Club?" Alice swung up into the seat after Grace.

The man chirruped loudly to the horses. They lurched forward, then broke into a steady trot. "Thirty-five miles to the Upper Works. I'm to take you to the Lower Works, and someone'll be down to fetch you the rest of the way," he said over his shoulder. "We'll stop at Aiden Lair to change the horses."

"Thirty-five *miles*?" Alice looked dismayed. "We'll be driving till night. And what are all those places—Aiden Lair, was it?—and the Lower Works, anyway? I thought we were going to the Tahawus Club?"

"Aye, miss, it'll be well on dark by the time you're gettin' there. Some folks prefer to stay at the Lower Works for the night and then go on up in the morning, but thems weren't my orders. Tahawus Club used to be the McIntyre Iron Works back 'fore the war—the club took over the company's old houses. There's the Lower Works and the Upper Works, and your folks are staying at the Upper Works. Aiden Lair's a fancy hotel for sports on the road north."

While he was speaking, the dirt road before them suddenly changed texture, and the horses' hooves and the buckboard's wheels clattered on a surface that Grace realized was wood—logs sunk into the dirt, perpendicular to the road.

"What the devil is that?" Alice exclaimed.

"Corduroy road." Their driver didn't bother to turn around. "Helps on the places where it gets muddy when it rains."

"Don't your teeth get shaken loose?" Alice asked, gritting hers.

"What teeth, miss?" His shoulders heaved, and Grace realized he was laughing.

Alice blinked at his back, then laughed too. But her smile didn't last long. "Grace?" she said quietly.

Grace dragged her attention from the trees. "Mmm?"

"What in blazes are we doing here? Two days ago, we were in one of the most civilized places in the country. And now, we're here. Look at it." She lifted a hand to gesture at the tree-covered mountains ahead of them, then grabbed the frame supporting the canopy over them as the wagon lurched over a slipped log.

"You don't like it?" Grace realized too late that it was a foolish question. After the excitement and glamour of Newport, how likely was it that Alice would be happy here? "It *is* beautiful, don't you think?" she added, rather lamely.

As she expected, Alice snorted. "For about ten minutes… which ended five minutes ago. What are we going to *do* here? I can only take so many scenic walks before I start frothing at the mouth with boredom. And I'm sure that whatever this Tahawus Club is, it's going to be horribly rustic and *picturesque*. Good God — you don't suppose we'll be living in tents, do you?"

"You liked sleeping in my brother's tent when he let us use it that summer," Grace reminded her.

"Yes, when we were what — twelve? For a night or two?" Her eyes narrowed. "You like it here, don't you? And I thought you were wanting to have *fun* this summer and meet people and do exciting new things."

Grace shifted uncomfortably in her seat, and not from the effects of the corduroy road. She *had* said that, hadn't she…and what had she ended up with? Had she had "fun" in Newport? What was Newport, compared to this?

"Excitin's what you want, is it?" Grizzle-head spat over the side of the wagon. "'Round here, we ain't fond of excitement. In the woods, if things get excitin', it means someone's likely to get hurt, or worse."

After that, they all remained silent until they arrived at Aiden Lair Lodge, a large, porch-wrapped building built right on the road. She and Alice got out to stretch their legs, have a quick glass of lemonade, and use the washroom while the horses were changed for the next leg of the trip.

Grace stared at herself in the mirror over the washbasin as she washed her hands. Their driver's words echoed inside her brain:

in the woods, if things get exciting, it means someone's likely to get hurt. Well, she was excited: her eyes were bright and wide, and a faint color showed in her cheeks. Even the tendrils of hair that had escaped their pins under the brim of her hat curled exuberantly, as if ready to bounce off her scalp and into the trees. But she couldn't think that anything would hurt her here in this wondrous place. Alice, however…poor Alice, to be longing to be back in Newport with Kit.

It was midafternoon now as they set out again, the road climbing more steadily. The sunlight had taken on a deeper, autumnal gold that lit the faint haze hanging over the valleys and touched a few maples already starting to show color on the hillsides with an extra gilding. Alice closed her eyes and somehow managed to doze sitting bolt upright, but Grace could only gaze raptly at each new vista every turn in the road gave her. The murmur of the trees that only she could hear seemed to grow louder with each passing mile.

"Likin' it, are you?" their driver asked at one point.

The man didn't miss much, did he? "Yes," Grace said simply.

He nodded. "It takes some people that way — the woods. Some folks have a real feelin' for them, even if they ain't seen 'em before." They resumed their silence — a companionable one now.

"I 'spect you'll be wantin' to walk in the woods up there by the old works," he said after a while.

"I expect I will." Nothing would keep her away from them.

"Well…" He hesitated. "You'll want to be careful, when you do."

"Are there bears up there? Or wolves?"

He shrugged. "The wolves are long gone, and the bears're mostly fat and lazy this time of the year. Just yell at 'em iffen you meet one, and he'll leave you alone all right. It ain't bears I'm thinkin' about, though." He hesitated again. "You may not believe me, but there's…*things* in the woods. Especially up by the tops of the mountains. They've been there a long time, prob'ly before even the Indians got here, and they're not especially fond of you nor me."

"I see." Grace looked at his back thoughtfully.

"You keep your eyes open, an' if things don't feel good, you go on back home. Chances are it'll be fine the next day. But you don't want to mess with them none. I've heard stories." He hunched his shoulders and fell silent.

What would he say if he knew that she was far more likely than he to sense any strange entities? "Thank you, and I will be careful," she said.

He nodded and didn't speak again until they drew up outside of a house in the middle of what looked like a tiny village. Another wagon was already there, probably waiting to bring them the last miles to the Tahawus Club. The sun had dropped behind a mountain to the west, but the sky still flamed with its dying light. They'd have some twilight left for the rest of the trip.

Alice yawned and stretched. "I can see why people like to stop here and continue on in the morning. I'm stiff as a board. And it's getting chilly too." She shivered as they climbed down from the wagon.

"Maybe we'll have time for a cup of something hot," Grace said. It was getting colder now that the sun was setting.

"I 'spect they might have a cup of tea for you in the house, but I wouldn't be too long about drinkin' it so's not to waste daylight. 'Scuse me —" As soon as they were clear of the wagon, their driver began to lead it around the back of the house. The horses perked up, sensing dinner and a soft bed of hay.

"Goodbye," Grace called after him. "And thank you."

He waved one hand and disappeared from view around the corner.

"Good riddance," muttered Alice. "I can't believe we've still got another leg to go on this hellacious journey."

The front door of the house suddenly flew open, and lamplight flowed out the doorway. A thin, boyish figure stood there, peering out at them. "Alice! Is that you?" His voice cracked.

"Ted?" Alice brightened and hurried up the porch steps. "What are you doing here?"

"Come to meet you, silly." He came forward to greet her. "How was your trip? Is your friend with you?"

"Fine, and yes." Alice punched him lightly in the arm. "And I'm not a silly. Show some respect for your elders, lad. How's Father? How's Quentin's ear? Did you come all alone? Grace!" she called imperiously over her shoulder. "Come meet my brother!"

"Father's not here yet. He's in Vermont on a speaking tour, but we hope he'll be here soon. Quentin's fine. And I'm not quite alone," the boy said. Grace caught a gleam of spectacles on his face as she climbed the stairs toward them. "Anyway, they wouldn't let us go without a driver who knows the road."

"Us? Is Mother with you?"

"No, not Mother." Ted grinned and stepped aside. A taller figure had come up behind him and stood outlined in the rectangle of light from the door. But even half in silhouette, there was something familiar about the set of its shoulders and the tilt of its head.

"Welcome to Tahawus, ladies," said Kit Rookwood.

TEN

"K*it!*" Alice shrieked and launched herself across the porch toward him.

He took a quick step backwards so that she could only catch at the lapels of his jacket rather than throwing her arms around his neck, as Grace was sure she'd intended to. "Miss Roosevelt—er, Alice." He glanced at Ted, but Alice didn't seem to notice.

"I can't believe you're— Oh, Kit, I was *furious* that you didn't come to say goodbye to me in Newport!" Her voice trembled. "But this is why, isn't it? You wanted to surprise me, you bad boy."

"So I guess you do know each other," Ted said, still grinning.

Grace stood rooted to the top step of the porch, staring. What was *Kit* doing here?

As if he'd felt her regard, Kit looked over Alice's head to her. "Miss Boisvert—Grace. How…how are you?"

What, no Puritan-maidening? Had he finally gotten tired of it? Grace opened her mouth to respond, but Alice beat her to it.

"She's fine," she said impatiently. "Oh, Kit." She buried her face against his chest.

Grace wished she could see his expression; the glow in the western sky didn't cast enough light to see it clearly. But there was a curious, un-Kit-like stiffness about the way he moved his arm to pat her shoulder, then stepped back half a pace to disengage from her.

A murmur of voices from the open door finally seemed to bring Alice to the awareness that she and Kit weren't alone. She let go of his jacket and straightened, but still gazed up at him with such adoration in her face that it was painful to see.

"Um...." Alice's brother shifted uncomfortably, and Grace took a deep breath and climbed the last step to the porch. *Somebody* had to behave rationally here, and it appeared to be up to her.

"Hello." She held her hand out to Ted. "I'm your sister's friend, Grace Boisvert. I'm happy to meet you. Alice has spoken of you so often."

Ted turned to her with a relieved expression. "Hello! I'm pleased to— Oh!" He stared at Grace for a few seconds, then took her outstretched hand and turned bright red. "She—you—that is, Alice talks about you too. But she never told us how pretty you are." He gulped and turned even redder if that was possible.

And then a woman came out onto the porch scolding them to come in and get warm by the fire, and Grace and Alice were bundled inside to gulp a quick cup of tea and get ready for the final leg of their journey.

Alice would barely let Kit stir from her side in those few minutes. "I can't believe you're here," she said again. "You must have left right after Mrs. Rennell's party! Grace, can you believe it?"

"Well, yes, since he is," she couldn't help replying a little impatiently. "I will admit, however, to being curious as to *why* he's here."

Alice looked at her as if she were crazy, but fortunately Kit spoke before she could.

"It's your fault." He smiled at Grace. She was put off-balance by that smile—she hadn't seen it aimed at her since the day they met. "After you told my father where you were going, he couldn't get it out of his head. He hadn't been to the Adirondacks since he was a boy and decided that now was as good a time as any to return."

"And you didn't say no," Alice put in demurely.

"No. I've never been here and neither had Mother, so here we are. I think you'll like the Tahawus Club—right, Ted?"

Ted nodded enthusiastically and started to explain to Alice what he and their younger siblings had been doing since their arrival, but Alice didn't appear to hear him. When a wiry, pleasant-faced man came in and suggested that they take advantage of the last of the daylight and get going, she waited while Ted and Kit went out, then pulled Grace aside inside the front door. "Kit's parents!" she whispered. "I forgot about them! What am I going to do?"

"Do about what? I thought they were lovely when we met at the party."

Alice made an impatient gesture. "Yes, because you actually met them. *I* was drunk as a lord and passed out. What are they going to think of me? And what if they say something about that night in front of my family?"

Grace started to tell her not to be silly, but there was a note of desperation in Alice's voice that she'd never heard before. "They really were very nice. I don't think they'd be so careless or mean," she soothed.

"But what if they don't like me?"

Grace was saved from having to reply by Ted sticking his head around the door. "Coming?"

Alice composed her face. "Yes, already."

"Good. It's getting dark and Mr. Kellogg wants to get going. If you get cold on the way, you can have my jacket." He looked at Grace, then turned red again and ducked back around the door.

Alice grinned at her. "Ted's found a new interest, I see. I think I'd better write to Tom Livingston and tell him he's got a rival."

"Oh, stop it," Grace replied irritably.

But Alice was already out the door. "Ted, you and Grace can sit up front," she announced, descending the stairs. "Kit and I will take the back."

Ted registered his approval by at once climbing into the seat next to Mr. Kellogg. "There's plenty of room here, Miss Boisvert," he called to her.

Kit helped Alice up into the rear seat. She smiled down at him and patted the seat beside her. "I want to hear all about how you came up here."

But to Grace's surprise, he turned and held his hand out to her. "May I help you up?"

She hesitated at the foot of the porch steps. "Don't you want to sit there?"

Again, it was hard to read his expression in the twilight. "I think it's best if you do. Up you go," he said cheerfully — determinedly so, Grace thought — and taking her arm, almost pushed her up into the seat. She landed heavily next to Alice, and the near horse stamped his foot and snorted.

"Kit Rookwood! I thought you were going to sit with me!" Alice protested.

He'd already crossed behind the wagon and was swinging himself up next to Ted, who looked as disappointed as his sister. "All set, Mr. Kellogg," he said to the driver, who nodded and told the horses to start.

As they started up the road, Alice sat as rigidly as one could when riding in a jolting wagon. "Why did he do that?" she muttered to Grace.

"I don't know, but can't we talk about it later?" Grace

murmured back. She was exhausted—sleep had been all but nonexistent last night on the ferry—but right now she was too exhilarated by the beauty of the trees' song, bidding the sun farewell for the night, to listen to Alice. Time enough for that tomorrow…if the thought of the great forest around her didn't keep her in a tumult all night.

Fortunately their horses were not as tired as she was and kept up a brisk pace through the growing darkness, to their driver's frequently expressed surprise. "They've already been down to Lower and back twice today," he commented. "I don't know where they're getting all this energy."

So it wasn't much more than two hours later that they drew up in front of a two-story frame building, made welcoming by the light spilling from its windows into the dark night. And then the front door flew open, and what seemed like a horde of children but was really only three boys and a girl came scrambling across the porch and up to the wagon, shrieking, "They're here! They're here!"

After that, much of the rest of the evening was a blur to Grace. Someone helped her down from the wagon—she didn't remember who—and she and Alice and Ted and Kit were dragged in to the building by the children, whom she realized were Alice's younger siblings.

"C'mon," said the tallest one, who was perhaps eleven or twelve. "Mrs. Hunter sent some dinner for you if you're hungry. It's on the stove."

"We're hungry," Ted said, then glanced at Grace and blushed again, but none of his brothers noticed. They entered a sitting room, the details of which were obscured by two rows of small shirts and trousers and pinafores hanging from lines stretched along its width.

"Alice." A handsome, calm-faced woman rose from an armchair to greet them—Alice's stepmother, Edith Carow Roosevelt.

"So you're here. And Miss Boisvert, it's a pleasure to see you."

"Hello, Mother." Alice dutifully kissed her cheek. Grace shook hands with her and found herself surveyed by cool gray-blue eyes.

"You are looking well. You will excuse our décor; the children spend a great deal of time playing in the river behind the house and get very wet as a result. May I present Miss Young, the children's governess?" A sturdy-looking woman who'd just walked into the room with a basket of mending nodded to her and smiled at Alice. "Mr. Rookwood, thank you for accompanying Ted this evening. I am sure we will see you tomorrow."

"Yes, I'm sure too." Alice smiled sweetly at him.

Kit nodded. "It was my pleasure, Mrs. Roosevelt. Good night." He nodded again to the rest of them and, for a brief moment, met Grace's eyes. Before she had time to react, he'd turned and left.

* * *

"Eating breakfast at eight in the morning is barbaric. The sun is barely even up," Alice grumbled the next day as they left the cottage with Mrs. Roosevelt, Miss Young, and the children.

"That's true," Grace agreed. "I'm sure that in Newport sunrise wasn't till half past nine at the earliest."

Alice stuck out her tongue. "You're Miss Up-and-at-'em this morning. You must be feeling better after the boat yesterday."

"Much better." In fact, Grace had been up since before sunrise; the early morning hum of the trees had been impossible to resist. She'd tiptoed out onto the porch, the cold boards burning her bare feet, to listen to their melodious murmuring, like an orchestra tuning before the start of a concert, and her heart had leapt. It was the sound of home, the sound she woke to every morning in Chestnut Hill, only a hundred times more powerful. Only now did she realize how much she had missed it in Newport. She'd nearly run out to the trees in her nightdress, but the slam of a door and flare of a light at a window in a building across the way had sent her back inside to hurry into a shirtwaist and skirt. Breakfast couldn't come soon enough so that she could get out to those trees.

They crossed the road to the clubhouse, where meals were served though all the surrounding cottages—she must remember to call them *camps*—had their own kitchens. Now in the full light of day she could see that the Tahawus Club was almost a small village, nestled among the surrounding hills. Mrs. Roosevelt had told them last night as they ate their warmed-over supper that many of the camps were left over from when Tahawus had been the "Upper Works" of the Adirondack Iron & Steel Manufacturing Company. The clubhouse was originally the boarding house; it was a substantial two-story structure that bore no resemblance to the elaborately timbered Adirondack cottages Grace had seen pictures of in illustrated magazines. It was fronted by a deep porch, where several rockers were set in a row, looking out to the mountains to the east.

She and Alice followed Mrs. Roosevelt across the porch and into the clubhouse. The dining room was commodious, with white-clothed tables scattered around the room. A pair of enormous mounted bucks' heads stared glassy-eyed down at them from opposite walls.

"Here are some familiar faces!" A figure rose from one of the tables.

"Mr. Rookwood." Grace smiled and went to shake his outstretched hand. "It's a pleasure to see you again. Good morning, ma'am," she added to Mrs. Rookwood, who smiled pleasantly up at her. She glanced at Kit, who'd stood as well but remained silent. He nodded to her—cautiously, she thought.

"You see what you inspired me to do?" Mr. Rookwood waved his hand. "It's even better than I remembered, so you'll have to put up with being thanked. We were lucky that my friend Mr. Jennings was willing to lend us his camp here for a week or two. Ah, Miss Roosevelt—good morning! How was your journey from Newport? Well, what do you young ladies think of the Adirondacks? Had you imagined such splendor? But I'm letting my enthusiasm run away with me while you're probably wanting your breakfast. I'm sure I'll find an opportunity to bore you later." He beamed at them and remained standing until they'd joined Mrs. Roosevelt and the children at their table.

"There, that wasn't so bad, was it?" Grace murmured to Alice while their young waitress went around the table pouring milk for the children. "I told you that Mr. and Mrs. Rookwood wouldn't tell on you."

Before Alice could respond, it was time to place their orders, and then the chatter of Alice's siblings took all their attention—beside Ted there was Kermit, a dreamy-looking boy of twelve, sturdy ten-year-old Ethel, and Archie and Quentin, who looked angelic but were anything but, Alice had warned her. It wasn't until breakfast was over and they were back out on the porch of the clubhouse that she and Alice had a chance to talk.

"I think I'd like to do a bit of exploring, go for a walk," she said to Alice. "What about you?"

"Hmm?" Alice was gazing through the front door into the dining room, where Kit stood talking to his father, looking very earnest.

"I'd be happy to show you around," Ted said quickly. "I've been all over the place now—"

"Except that you've already promised you'd take Kermit and Ethel fishing at the lake this morning," Mrs. Roosevelt inserted as she passed them on her way down the stairs.

Ted seemed about to protest, then brightened. "Would you like to go fishing with us? Then you'll still get your walk in."

Grace smiled, but the last thing she wanted right now was

company. "May I go with you next time?"

"Yes, please! There's some good fishing up at—" His voice cracked, and he blushed and ducked down the stairs after his mother.

"Good morning!" Alice trilled.

Grace turned and saw that Kit had emerged from the clubhouse. "You didn't seem convinced of that earlier," she teased.

"Coffee can work wonders." Alice sidled close to Kit as he joined them. "Isn't it a lovely day?"

"Yes," Kit said simply. Grace found herself studying him. Less than a week ago he would have made some flirtatious response to Alice and probably said something to her about it being sinful for Puritan maidens to enjoy good weather. What had changed since they'd left Newport?

"Anyway," Alice continued, "I'd go with you, Grace, but Kit and I already have plans to go for a walk."

When had they had time to make those plans, since they hadn't had a moment alone together? Grace stole another glance at Kit. For a second he looked as surprised as she felt, but his expression quickly smoothed.

"We could all go together—" he began.

Alice cut him off. "No. Grace walks too fast." She was already partway down the stairs. "I'm going to change my shoes," she called and, pausing on the bottom step, lifted one foot clear of her skirts and waved it at him. It was encased in a peach satin bedroom slipper. "Come on, Grace. I'll be back in two minutes!"

Up in their room, Alice knelt on the floor and dug through one of her trunks. "I *know* I've got some boots in here somewhere."

"I'd hate to see what your slippers will look like if you don't."

Alice grinned. "They'll be torn to shreds, and then Kit will be duty-bound to carry me back from our walk. So maybe I won't bother with boots after all." Her grin faded as she sat back on her knees. "Grace, did Kit seem…I don't know. A bit…off?"

So she'd noticed too. "In what way?"

"I don't know, or I wouldn't be asking. It's like…" Alice hunched her shoulders.

Like he wasn't the same boy she'd been kissing in broom closets all over Newport? "We're not in Newport anymore," she said. "It's different here."

"You're telling me," Alice muttered. "I wish we were back there right now."

"Don't forget that both his and your parents are here," Grace said. "It's a little hard for a boy to flirt with a girl when their mothers are watching, don't you think? Not to mention that he's here among strangers, rather than among friends in Newport."

"I suppose," Alice said, but her expression had lightened. "I'm sure that when we're alone, he'll be himself again." She paused. "He's being a lot nicer to you if you've noticed."

"Maybe it's no fun to tease me here because his mother might not approve of his picking on girls."

Alice laughed. "Oh, Grace. You can always talk me out of a bad mood." She turned back to her trunk and crowed trium-phantly a minute later. "Here they are! Well, have a good walk. I know I will." She hurried downstairs.

Grace watched Alice and Kit through the window until she saw which direction they were going so that she could take the opposite one, then slipped out of the camp. Why on earth had Kit suggested they all walk together? The last thing he'd seemed to want in Newport was to be in her presence. At least here in the forest it would be easier for them to keep out of each other's way.

⁕ ⁕ ⁕

As she started up the narrow unpaved road, she could hear happy shrieks from the creek that ran behind their camp — Archie and Quentin, probably trying to drown each other. It was a good thing that their governess looked like an unflappable person.

She'd passed the last camp now, and the road was petering out into a footpath before it disappeared into a wall of trees. She paused to gaze up at it, then plunged into the forest.

Out of the sun, the temperature dropped several degrees. The ground was thickly carpeted with last year's leaves—maple and beech and yellow birch—and above her, the trees that had shed them stood tall and sturdy yet graceful, their branches intertwining like the arms of dancers in a *corps de ballet*. Here, close to the edge of the clearing, was a tangle of young trees and honeysuckle, but within a few feet, the lack of sun reaching the forest floor banished any undergrowth but occasional ferns and mosses. Somewhere farther up the mountain a crow called, and several replied, their raucous *ca-a-aws!* ringing and echoing in the trees.

She left the footpath and ventured deeper among the trunks and had to remind herself to breathe. The air was rich with the scent of green leaves and bark, but there was a dry, bitter edge to it that spoke of the coming of autumn; the trees were turning their thoughts to preparing for the winter's rest. But it was something more than the air—there were just *so many* trees. Arriving in North Creek yesterday, she'd been struck by their sheer numbers. Now she was among them as individuals, and it made her feel both exhilarated and shy at the same time. She wanted to rush from tree to tree, stroking their skins and listening to each slow voice, to drink them in.

The trees were aware of her too. They were watching her, and she felt…what? Surprise, yes…and puzzlement? She hesitated, then approached a sturdy beech and pressed her hands against its smooth, silvery bark. The touch sent the same odd shiver through her that she'd felt yesterday at North Creek. "Greetings, friend," she murmured.

The beech's leaves rustled. *You speak in our words*, it said.

How can that be? I have never known a man to speak.

Trees were never very good at picking up the differences between people, including their sex. "I'm not a human. Have you never met any of my kind?"

The tree was silent for a long moment. *No, you are not a man. You don't feel like a man, though you have the appearance of one. But you are not a Changer or a Shadow nor anything else I have met before. You speak with the language of trees, and you feel…akin. How can that be?* it said again, almost to itself.

Did the trees here not know dryads then? Perhaps none had visited this part of the Adirondacks…and these trees were native to America, not Europe, so they would have no ancestral knowledge of them.

"We *are* akin," she said to the beech. "My kind come from another land, where a goddess gave birth to us many years ago to protect and cherish her trees. Some of us live in this land now — I am from far to the east of you, near the ocean. It is an honor to visit your forest, cousin."

She felt the tree mulling this over. *Akin to us, yet you look like men. Do you live among them?*

"We live among them, but they don't know us. At least, not anymore." What must it have been like all those centuries ago, when dryads were known and respected? They probably didn't have to dye their hair, for one thing. "What are those other…er, beings? Changers and Shadows?"

Do you not know them? They also walk the forests. The Changers can take what shape they wish, but their spirits are wild and strange. The Shadows do not have any form at all. They like the high places and the dark places, and sometimes they are angry and rush through our branches like a black wind. We do not know what they are. The tree sounded as if it didn't want to know either. Grace remembered what their driver from North Creek had said about things in the woods. Could this be what he meant?

"Should I fear them?" she asked. "I've never heard of them before."

Be wary of Changers, yes. I do not know if you should fear them. They take advantage of the weak when they can and count it a pleasant pastime, though they respect strength and are drawn to power. The Shadows—

"Ah, is that you, Miss Boisvert? They are beautiful, are they not?" a voice called. "I think the trees here are more beautiful than anywhere, and I've traveled a bit in my time."

Grace started and whirled around. Mr. Rookwood was striding up the path she had just left, puffing as if he'd been walking quickly and wiping his brow with a folded handkerchief. He joined her under the beech and stared up its trunk into its canopy sixty feet above them.

"Oh, yes, they are!" she said effusively. "I was just admiring this beech—its bark is so smooth! They don't grow like this back at home."

He stretched out a hand to touch it, but his mild blue eyes were focused on her. "I hope you don't mind that I came looking for you, Miss Boisvert. I thought it would be the perfect opportunity to catch you alone."

She let her hand drop to her side. "Is there something wrong?"

"Oh, no. I merely wished to ask if we had conducted ourselves properly this morning. The circumstances of our first meeting with you and your friend were somewhat, ah, irregular, but Mrs. Rookwood and I didn't feel it necessary to bring them up at breakfast in front of Mrs. Roosevelt."

"You handled it perfectly, sir. Believe me, Alice was very grateful for your discretion." She hesitated again, then said in a rush, "She really didn't intend to drink so much that night. It was her first ball, you see, and she was so excited—"

He held up a hand. "No explanation is necessary, Miss Boisvert. It's been a few years since I was seventeen, but I can still remember how easy it was to occasionally get carried away and to not want my parents to be possessed of all the details when I did. If we had concerns that Miss Roosevelt made a habit of it, we would certainly have spoken to her mother in private. But I'm sure it was a one-time event. I expect her condition the following morning taught her that too much champagne has its consequences."

Grace nodded. "She was…not at all well that day."

He chuckled. "Poor thing. But some people learn best not to play with fire by getting burned once or twice, and there's no getting around it for them." He looked at her. "I don't get the impression you're one of that type, Miss Boisvert."

"You're very kind, but I'm not sure I can claim any virtue. I've never yet found a fire I wasn't able to resist sticking my hand in, but who knows? Perhaps I haven't found one bright and tempting enough yet."

Mr. Rookwood laughed. "You sound as if you regret that fact. But I've no doubt that you're a very level-headed young woman." He gave his forehead one last pat with his handkerchief and folded it away. "There. I've caught my breath now, so will you walk with me for a bit? This path goes on up to Lake Henderson and beyond to Mount Marcy itself, but I don't think we need go that far."

She fell into step beside him. "Is Mount Marcy one of the higher mountains in the area?"

"My dear Miss Boisvert! It's the highest peak in all of New York, and right here in our backyard, so to speak. The view from its summit is quite spectacular, I understand. You younger folk should get up an expedition to climb up there some time during your visit."

Grace thought of the beech's description of the Shadows and Changers. She'd be happy to leave the mountaintops to them, thank you very much. "Perhaps Kit and Alice will organize one."

"Do I sense a lack of enthusiasm for mountain climbing on your part?" His eyes twinkled behind his pince-nez. "Then again, I'm not sure how enthusiastic my son would be either. So tell me, how did you and Miss Roosevelt meet Kit?"

"At the Casino. We...happened upon each other."

"Oh? That sounds like there's a story behind it."

Grace scuffled her feet through the leaves to the side of the path. "Not particularly. At least not an interesting one. I bumped into him dusting off a ball boy who'd fallen down the stairs." It was unsettling to remember that day and what her first impression of Kit had been, and how it had changed. What would Mr. Rookwood say if she told him about Puritan maidens? She somehow didn't think he'd be pleased.

"And Miss Roosevelt? She seems quite...taken with Kit."

"Oh, she and Kit took to each other at first sight." Discussing this with an adult—and especially the father of one of the subjects under discussion—was decidedly odd. But there was something about Mr. Rookwood's open friendliness that mitigated the oddness.

"Hmm." He was silent as they strolled up the footpath through the trees. Overhead, small birds sang and twittered, and a crow—or was it a raven?—croaked at them conversationally as it flew from a nearby tree to one deeper in the woods. Mr. Rookwood glanced up at it.

"Kit can be a very charming young man," he finally said. "He takes after his mother in that respect. I fear that he's not always aware of how potent that charm can be to susceptible young women—"

Like Alice, Grace thought.

"—and unintentionally leads them to believe that his heart is more engaged than it actually is."

Grace stared at the ground as they walked. Could Kit not have been aware of the effect he had on Alice? After all, she herself had a similar problem this summer with Tom Livingston. And it might explain why Kit was drawing back from Alice now—perhaps his parents had had a talk with him after the incident at Mrs. Rennell's ball. On the other hand, lurking in broom cupboards with Alice hardly seemed unintentional. But she could hardly say that to Kit's father.

"I think I understand, sir," she said aloud. "I don't know if there's much I can do about it, though. Alice is, er, one of those people who learns by getting burned."

"I had guessed that," he replied a little dryly. "But I'd never ask you to do anything about it. Just be aware, for her sake, if—or when—disappointment comes."

"Yes, sir," Grace said, but inwardly she quailed. They were here till at least the fifteenth of September. What would life be like if Alice no longer had Kit to keep her mind off her boredom? At least she'd be going to Washington after that, where there would surely be a great deal of excitement to help her forget.

"How long do you stay in Tahawus?" she asked.

"My friend Mr. Jennings was vague on that topic—I understand he hadn't planned to come up here this fall, so we have the use of his camp for as long as we wish. My brother is looking after our business while I visit here, though he plans to pay us a short visit as well. And when we return, Kit will be joining us in the office." He turned to look at her. "What of you, Miss Boisvert? Back to school after this?"

"I don't know. I would like to go to college next year, but I believe my parents would like us to travel for few months in Europe before we decide anything."

"It's not a bad plan. Travel can be as educational as any classroom or professor, as I found out after I graduated college with perhaps too inflated a view of my abilities." He told her an anecdote of his visit to the West Coast as a young man, and then another, and kept her entertained as they went on a little farther, then turned and retraced their steps down the path. When they reached the edge of the camp clearing, Grace hesitated. "I—I think I'll go back and walk a little more."

Mr. Rookwood looked stricken. "And here I've been depriving you of your solitude among the trees. Will you forgive a thoughtless old man who's too delighted to have found a new audience for his stories?"

Grace laughed. "It was a pleasure to hear them, sir. And…thank you," she added. "About Alice—and all."

"Not at all, Miss Boisvert." He looked at her, head to one side. "Tahawus suits you, I do believe. You—pardon me for saying this—you look to be in much better frame here than in Newport."

Oh, dear. She had better check her hair when she got back to the camp. "I am finding the air here very…agreeable."

"I'm very pleased to hear that." He lifted his hat to her. "Enjoy your ramble!"

Grace returned his polite bow, then turned back to the woods. He really was a nice man; she'd be able to reassure Alice that the secret of their first meeting in Newport would remain a secret. And as for his delicate warnings about Kit—oh, bother Kit Rookwood! He was ruining a trip that should have been pure fun for her and Alice.

Above her, a purring, clicking sound made her glance up. The crow that had followed them—or was it another one?—looked down at her. "Well, and what do you want?" she said to it.

It jumped up into the air and cawed loudly, flying ahead of her and landing on branches, keeping a close eye on her as she walked. She'd always liked crows. The trees at home said they were proud and touchy but curious and intelligent observers and a useful source of information. Too bad she didn't understand their speech. "No, I'm afraid I'm not edible," she said to it. Maybe next time she ought to bring some breadcrumbs when she walked in the woods.

The crow chuckled and walked up and down the branch for a minute, then leapt out of the tree toward her. For a second Grace thought it was attacking her, but instead it soared past her head, so close that she felt the air displaced by the beating of its wings against her face as it climbed up into the air and disappeared into the sky.

"Well!" she said, squinting after it. That had been odd. She went to the tree in which it had been perched. "What was that bird that sat on you? Was it really a crow?" she asked.

The maple stirred under her hand. *You are the tree-cousin*, it said.

Well, that was quick. These trees didn't miss much, did they? "Yes, I am. Please—was that a bird?"

Sometimes it is. It takes other shapes as well, but I have mostly seen that one in the shape of a crow. They each have their preferred forms.

Their preferred forms… "A Changer," she murmured.

Yes. It is curious about you. You are not something we have seen before.

"Can they talk? Why didn't it talk to me if it's so curious about me?"

Because they do not yet know if you are dangerous. The tree hesitated. *It might be best if they continued to wonder. So long as they fear you, they will keep their distance and watch.*

"Hmm. Thank you." Grace let the tree satisfy its curiosity about her with a few more minutes of questions, then went back to camp to think about the very different conversations she'd had that morning with both man and tree.

ELEVEN

Alice was practically floating around the camp, smiling dewy-eyed at nothing, when Grace finally returned from her walk.

"And?" Grace asked. Not that she had to ask—Alice's happiness was almost ridiculously obvious. "Did he propose?"

"Of course not, goose! But everything's fine." Alice sighed ecstatically. "It was so romantic, walking among the trees with him. You were right—he feels we ought to behave a little more circumspectly while we're here with our families…and what's more, he…well, he says he cares too much for our friendship to not treat me with respect. Isn't that so *noble* of him? It's exactly what my father would have been like, I'll bet."

"Mmm," Grace said noncommittally. Of course, it was also what he might say if he were trying to start separating himself from her, just as Mr. Rookwood had suggested he might. But no matter the reason, at least she wouldn't have to worry about them being caught canoodling in a woodshed by Mrs. Roosevelt.

All through dinner that night at the clubhouse Alice gazed soulfully at Kit, who did not, Grace noticed, return her gaze.

Instead, she caught him looking at *her*, twice. It was disquieting, as he'd always seemed to avert his eyes from her in Newport. Well, so long as he maintained his new politeness toward her, she didn't care if he stared at her till his eyes fell out.

⁌ ❄ ⁍

To Grace's surprise, Alice did not get up for breakfast the next morning. "Ask them to send me a tray," she mumbled, burrowing deeper into the blankets. "I'm too relaxed to get up."

"Even to see Kit?"

"I'll see him later." She smiled mistily. "That's why I'm so relaxed. I'm not all anxious over him anymore. It's such a relief—you've no idea. You go on."

"Where's Sister?" Ted fell into step beside Grace as she joined the children on the walk over to the clubhouse.

"Sleeping late today and wanting a tray sent up to her later."

"Huh. What a slug-a-bed." He looked at her sideways. "So I guess that means you won't be busy with her this morning."

"It looks that way," she agreed.

He didn't say anything further until they were seated at table, when he turned to his mother. "I wondered if we could go fishing again today up at Lake Henderson."

"Oh, can we?" Ethel said eagerly. "Kermit, don't you want to go again?"

Mrs. Roosevelt sipped her coffee, then nodded. "Very well. Archie and Quentin will stay here with Miss Young."

"But I wanna fish!" protested Quentin.

"You're too little. If you were to fall in, you'd get eaten by a pickerel. Grace will come with us though, won't she?" But Kermit was looking at his elder brother as he spoke, rather than her.

"Yes, please do come with us, Miss Boisvert." Ted turned pink behind his spectacles, and she knew immediately that he'd put his brother up to inviting her. "We've got a pole for you and every-thing—or if you don't actually want to fish, you don't have to."

"I can put your worms on for you," Kermit volunteered. "Unless Ted says we're using flies today."

"I worm my own hooks all the time at home, but thank you for the offer. I'd love to come with you." Going fishing with three younger Roosevelts would be more fun than watching their older sister sigh after Kit. Hopefully Alice would get through this phase soon so that they could have fun together again, just like they always had.

"She puts her own worms on," Kermit said, awed.

"Well, so do I," said Ethel. "What's so great about that?"

"'Cause you're not a young lady."

"Am too!" Ethel punched him in the arm.

"One would never think so," Mrs. Roosevelt commented dryly. "Do not feel you have to accompany the children if you don't want to," she said to Grace.

"No, I really would like to go."

"Of course she wants to come with us!" Kermit said indignantly. "Don't scare her off, Mother!"

"Come where?" Kit was there suddenly, though Grace hadn't noticed him enter the dining room. But no, there were Mr. and Mrs. Rookwood, making their way to their table. Mr. Rookwood smiled and nodded to her.

"Fishing at Lake Henderson," Ethel told him. "We're going after breakfast."

"What a coincidence—so am I." Kit's flashing grin lit up his face. "Maybe we should consider joining forces. I expect you know where all the good spots are," he said to Ted.

No. Oh, no. Grace felt her smile turn rigid on her face.

"We've found a few, haven't we, Kermit?" Ted looked flattered. "Kermit took a brook trout the other day that was at least two pounds. We'd be glad to show you a good place or two."

"I'll catch up with you after breakfast then. Good morning, ma'am. Miss Young." He nodded to the adults politely and went to join his parents.

Grace ate her oatmeal and pancakes and bacon without really tasting them. Kit's presence would ruin the day, but she couldn't back out now. She'd simply have to find herself a fishing spot as far from Kit as possible.

She walked the half mile up to the lake with Kermit and Ethel, carrying the basket of sandwiches and lemonade that Mrs. Hunter made for them, answering their questions about Newport and enjoying their chatter. Ted and Kit walked ahead, Ted occasionally glancing wistfully back at them.

On reaching the lake, Ethel and Kermit jumped into one of the club dinghies pulled up on shore and rowed toward the middle of the long, narrow ribbon of water, squabbling amiably about whose favorite spot they'd head for first. Ted turned to Grace. "Do you want to fish from shore or from a boat?"

"Oh, you must show Kit where your good places are. I think I'll try that gravel bank over there." She nodded toward a low, rocky spit a short distance away, partly shaded by overhanging trees.

Ted looked crestfallen. "No one ever catches anything there. Out on the lake is much better."

Oh. He'd wanted to take her out on the lake, hadn't he? A row would be pleasant, but if Ted had developed a crush on her, it might be awkward.

"Why don't we go out there after lunch?" Kit put in. "I'd like to try my luck from shore first as well. Anyplace you suggest?" He clapped Ted on the shoulder, who swallowed his disappointment manfully and nodded.

Grace picked her way carefully along the water's edge to the gravel spit and put her line in for a few minutes, for form's sake, then set her pole down and retreated to the shade of the trees. She didn't try to engage them in conversation but spread out her jacket on the low bank beneath them and sat down, eyes closed, the better to listen to the murmur of their thoughts and speech. Their cadence was so different from the trees at home—faster, more complex, full of unfamiliar notes and words...

Once again, that shiver lanced through her, this time leaving her almost light-headed. She dug her fingers into the soil of the bank to steady herself—

The shiver deepened. Her fingertips tingled, and suddenly it felt as if they'd grown inches—no, *feet*—wiggling into the ground, branching out into dozens of tiny fingerlets burrowing purposefully into the dirt—taking root, drawing her down, drawing her *in*. The murmur of the trees grew louder in her ears, and her heartbeat took up its rhythm—

A new sound—the uneven crunch of footfalls on gravel—broke that rhythm. She gasped and opened her eyes.

Kit stood at the water's edge a few feet away, his pole on his shoulder, gazing down at her. The sun outlined him in gold but left his face in shadow. "I'm sorry," he said. "I didn't mean to startle you."

She drew in an uneven breath. "What are you doing here?"

"I...wasn't having much luck where I was and thought I'd see if yours was any better. No, please don't get up. I didn't mean to disturb you."

Well, he had—bother the boy! Something had been happening—the trees...but it was gone now. Grace started to scramble to her feet. "I really ought to try a few more casts so Ted isn't disgusted with me."

"I doubt he'd ever be that." There was a smile in his voice. He set down his pole and stepped forward to offer his hand, but she'd already risen. They stood awkwardly facing each other for a few seconds. Kit broke the silence.

"I— Actually, I'm glad I found you alone. I wanted to have a word with you." The smile in his voice had been replaced by something less assured.

Grace had been dusting her hands on the sides of her skirt and had to force herself not to clutch the fabric. "A—a word?"

"Well, more than that." He stared down at his feet, then took a deep breath and looked her in the eyes. "I wanted to say that I'm sorry."

"What?"

He still held her gaze. "I'm sorry for how I behaved toward you in Newport."

"Um…" She had to look away; his eyes were too intense. The Kit she'd known in Newport was gone; this was a different young man. Or had *that* Kit been real? Who was Kit?

"Will—will you accept my apology?" he asked into the once-again awkward silence.

"I—I don't know. You were…" She hesitated, then squared her shoulders and met his eyes again. "You were perfectly horrible to me. A lot of the time you seemed to go out of your way to be unpleasant. If you hate me so, why couldn't you just have left me alone?"

He looked down at his feet again. "I know," he muttered, swallowing hard once or twice. Dear Yggdrasil…was the never-at-a-loss Kit Rookwood fighting back *tears*?

Well, good. She'd shed a few of her own, back in Newport. "So you're sorry," she said after a moment. "What difference does that make now?"

He raised his head. His face was pale and there was a suspicious brightness in his eyes. "I hoped that if—if you would accept my apology, then we could try again. Start from the beginning, and see if…if it couldn't be different this time. If this time, we could be friends."

The uncertain look in his eyes transported her back to the afternoon at the Casino when they'd met over a bucket of scattered tennis balls. Was it possible to pretend the subsequent weeks hadn't happened and go back to that moment in time when something—some knot—had tied itself between them?

"Being…friends involves trust," she said slowly. "I'm not sure I can bring myself to trust you, even if I do accept your apology."

He looked both pleased and startled. "You do?"

"There's not much else I can do if I'm trying to be the person my parents raised me to be. But you more or less ruined Newport for me. It'll be hard to get over that." She hesitated. "It might help if you could tell me why you were so—why you behaved as you did."

His gaze fell. "I can't. It— I can't. I'm sorry."

Well. That was that, then…but she wished he would. And she wished she could ask him about Alice, too, while they were at it. But it would be too difficult—and he would rightly be able to say that it wasn't any of her business. Except that she couldn't help feeling that it was—

He held out his hand. "Could…could we shake on it?"

She looked down at it, tanned and strong, and remembered how their hands had met once around a dropped tennis ball. She took it. "Can I…I have to ask—why? Why are you doing this now?"

A ghost of a smile touched his mouth. "So that I can live with myself, and maybe get a good night's sleep again."

That was unexpected. "Would you have bothered apologizing if we weren't here together for the next few weeks?"

"Yes." No more smile now. "I would have followed you back to Boston if necessary."

She realized that their hands were still clasped in a handshake and made a small movement to disengage them. But he held on. "Thank you. I'll do my best to earn your regard." To her astonishment, he bent slightly and raised her hand to his lips.

Before Grace could do more than draw in her breath, the now-familiar sound of someone crossing the gravel bank was heard, and Ted materialized on the rocky shore to her right. "There you are! Did you get any strikes here? I'll bet— Oh!" He fell silent, staring at their joined hands.

Grace snatched her hand back. "No, I—I didn't," she said quickly. "But I didn't try very hard, and…and—"

"Is it time for lunch already?" Kit consulted his watch. "I expect Kermit and Ethel will be back shortly. Let's eat and go out in the boats after that. My luck with the fish wasn't any better than yours."

There was an extra conspiratorial quirk to the look he gave Grace. He was never at a loss, was he? Here she was blushing and stuttering at being caught holding hands with him, and he was not at all ruffled. Yet he'd been close to tears not long before—at least, she thought he had. Had they been real? Back to that old refrain again: who was the real Kit? She might have accepted his apology, but she was a long way from trusting him.

Kermit and Ethel returned shortly with tales of fish too small to keep and too large to have landed, and they ate their sandwiches in the shade of a group of swamp maples close to the water's edge. After they had finished she went out in one of the boats with Ted, Kit following behind them alone in another. Sitting in the aft of the boat and watching his stern young face, she knew she had to say something. She waited until they'd pulled a little away from Kit and said quietly, "I expect you're wondering what Kit and I were talking about when you found us."

The stern expression deepened into a scowl. "It's none of my business."

"No, it's not. But it isn't anything that needs to be kept secret either. He was apologizing to me, and we shaking hands over it."

The scowl on Ted's face shifted into surprise. "What was he apolo— I'm sorry."

"No, you may ask. He and I did not get along well in

Newport—in fact, we were more or less at daggers-drawn with each other. He acknowledged that it was his fault and asked if we couldn't try to get along better in future."

"Oh." Ted kept the boat far enough ahead of Kit that they couldn't be overheard. "I thought he… Well, I thought he and Alice… And when I saw you standing there like that, I wondered if…" He subsided into an embarrassed silence.

"If he was two-timing your sister," Grace finished for him. "No, he's not." She had no idea what it was he was doing with Alice, but it wasn't that. "It's a relief for me to know that he won't be horrible to me anymore."

"Horrible to you! How could anyone possibly be horrible to you? I mean, you're—" His voice cracked, and he turned bright red and rowed so hard that Kit shouted, "Hey! Are you trying to lose me?"

"I—I'm glad you told me," Ted said quietly a few moments later, when he'd rowed out his discomfiture. "Though I'm kind of… Kit's a brick, or at least I thought he was."

"He doesn't have to stop being one," she said. "The fact that he apologized to me definitely raises him in my estimation."

"That's true," he said, brightening. "I say, here's one of the places I wanted us to try. Do you want to do a cast or two?"

"No, but you should. Here, why don't we switch? I can keep us in place, and you can fish."

Ted tried to demur, but she wouldn't let him, so they carefully switched places and she took the oars. She was glad to be able to sit quietly as they floated—funny that being in a rowboat on a pond didn't trouble her the way being on larger boats did—and watch the others fish while she thought her own thoughts.

So Kit had apologized. She wasn't sure whether to believe his statement about needing her forgiveness in order to live with himself; if that were the case, then why had he behaved so badly in the first place? At least his Puritan-maidening at her wouldn't continue, which was a relief. As for their becoming friends…well, she'd have to wait and see; if he were civil to her, then she'd be civil to him.

And then there was what had happened before Kit found her. Her hands tightened around the oars, remembering the feeling of her fingers seeming to take root in the ground. She had never felt anything like that before; if Kit hadn't interrupted, what else might have happened?

A muffled exclamation from across the water made her look up. Kit was half standing in his boat, his rod bent in a tight arc toward the water.

"He's got one!" Ted whispered. "Looks like a proper one too."

It took over a tense forty-five minutes of playing his line, but he brought it in—a lake trout that Ted estimated to be all of five and a half pounds.

"That's a granddaddy of a fish," Kermit said admiringly when they were all ashore again, walking back to the club.

"You don't suppose he left behind a wife and children, do you?" asked Ethel, wide-eyed.

"Mrs. Fish will find herself another husband," Ted said. "There are lots of fish in the pond. Let's hurry so Kit can give it to Mrs. Hunter to cook for his dinner."

Grace smiled, remembering the Mrs. Fish she knew who adored her husband and made sure they had dinner alone together at least once a week despite her busy socializing. She should write her a note; she would be amused to hear Kit was here but behaving himself as far as Alice was concerned… Then she remembered their final conversation in her carriage, not quite a week ago, about Kit. She drew her breath in so sharply that Ted, walking beside her, asked if something were wrong.

"Not a bit," she assured him. At least, she didn't think there was…and surely Mrs. Fish had been wrong about Kit. Of course she had.

As soon as they were back from the lake, Kit and children went to the clubhouse with Kit's fish. Grace slipped away from them to meet Alice, striding across the rough lawn toward her.

"There you are! Where was everyone all day? I thought I would die of boredom." She slipped her arm through Grace's and steered her to the hammock behind their camp.

"I went fishing with Ted and Kermit and Ethel and Kit." Grace felt herself color on the last name and hoped Alice wouldn't notice.

"He went fishing with *you children*?" Alice's voice teetered between disbelief and outrage.

"The fact that you're a month older than me doesn't mean you can lump me in the child category."

Alice ignored her. "Why didn't anyone invite me?"

"Because you were still in bed?"

"That's hardly a reason. Kit should have..." She let her sentence trail off and flung herself into the hammock, swinging it so violently that the trees supporting the hammock groaned in protest, but her face had softened. "Oh, Grace...is he mad at me?"

Grace stopped it and settled gingerly next to her. "Why should he be? I thought everything was moonlight and roses between you?"

"Oh, it is," Alice said quickly. "I..." She shrugged.

"I didn't get the chance to tell you, since you slept late—Mr. Rookwood told me that Mrs. Rennell's ball would remain a closed topic as far as he and Mrs. Rookwood were concerned. Wasn't that nice of him?" Maybe that would make her feel better.

It did—slightly. "That's good," Alice said, but sighed as she spoke. "I still wish Kit had called me to go fishing with you."

"You didn't do everything with him in Newport," Grace reminded her gently.

"I know. But things are different here." She sighed again. "I can't explain it right now."

Hmm. Grace studied her averted profile. Evidently everything *wasn't* moonlight and roses between them. "Alice, are you sure about him?"

Alice's eyes narrowed as she turned to look at Grace. "What do you mean?"

Oh, bother. She probably shouldn't have said that. But Mr. Rookwood's warning yesterday morning would not leave her alone. "I mean…what if you've been a—a pleasant diversion for him—you know, squiring the vice-president's daughter around Newport—and now that you're up here, it's time to move on—"

Alice jumped up, nearly dumping her out of the hammock. "You don't know anything about it!" she snapped. "Just because you never liked Kit doesn't mean you can say things like that!" She marched back toward their camp.

Grace thought about following her but decided not to. Better to let her think it over alone for a while. Alice might be stubborn, but she was also fair-minded. Where Kit was concerned, though… She sighed and relaxed back into the hammock, swinging it gently…and stiffened.

Something was watching her.

Very casually, she sat up, glancing around her as she did. There was no one in sight, though she heard the strum of a banjo from one of the camps and a murmur of laughter from somewhere else. But whatever was watching her wasn't laughing. It didn't feel like the regard of the trees she'd felt earlier while walking. She rose carefully and went to one of the trees supporting the hammock, resting her hand on it as she pretended to remove a pebble from her shoe.

"Something watches us, my friend," she murmured. "Do you know what it is?"

The tree's leaves fluttered in a sudden chill breeze. She felt its surprise at her speech—and she felt fear, too, both its own and hers, as that cold wind ruffled past them, and was gone. With its passing, the feeling of being watched abruptly vanished. But she didn't wait to see if it would return; the lengthening shadows reaching eastward suddenly made indoors seem much more inviting, even with an angry Alice there.

She tiptoed into their room to find Alice sitting cross-legged on her bed, raptly gazing down at a bowl of water lilies.

"Aren't they lovely?" she said, not looking up.

"Very. Where did they come from?"

Alice reached out to stroke a satiny white petal. "They were on the floor in front of our door, but I'm pretty sure I know who brought them."

"Oh?"

"Well, isn't it obvious? They're a peace offering from Kit, for not calling me to go fishing with you. I'm sure he sneaked in and left them here for me. Who else could they be for?" She smiled dreamily. "I wonder if I could spend the winter with Auntie Bye in New York again? Kit will be there, working for his father. It would be quite perfect. You could even come visit us—me."

Grace ignored the change of pronoun. "I thought your aunt would be in Washington this winter?"

Alice's gaze never left the lilies. "Don't ruin a good dream, please!"

After supper that night, as they walked back to the camp, Ted fell into step beside Grace and cleared his throat. "Um…I was wondering…"

"Yes?"

"Did…did you like the water lilies? There were hundreds of 'em down at the other end of the lake, and they…they reminded me of you—" He swallowed.

The water lilies Alice thought Kit had brought her. "They were lovely. Thank you."

"We can go get more if you like. There really were hundreds of them—no, thousands!"

Grace smiled. "I'll bet there are, but these will last for a few days, I'm sure."

"Well, tell me when they fade, and I'll get you more." His voice broke on the last word. He tried to turn it into a cough, then broke into a run to catch up with Kermit and Ethel. Grace watched him, still smiling, then sighed. Oh, Alice.

TWELVE

Alice was up for breakfast at eight the next morning with everyone else, though she didn't look happy about it.

"I didn't sleep at all well last night," she complained to Grace as they walked to the clubhouse through a fine mist. "But I don't want to miss out on any fun with Kit."

"I'm sure he'd take you fishing if you asked him," Grace said.

"Yes, but that presupposes that I *want* to go fishing. I'm happy to see fish boned and cooked and reposing on my plate with some chopped parsley and a wedge of lemon, but not in any other state." Her brows drew down. "Don't you think it might have been nice for him to have given that fish he caught to me, by the way?"

Grace coughed to hide the exclamation that had almost slipped out. "Ahem…I think he had Mrs. Hunter prepare it for his parents."

"Well, I suppose that's all right." But her continued frown said otherwise. It stayed on her face until they entered the dining room and she saw Kit.

"Good morning!" she cried gaily as she hurried toward him,

all signs of peevishness gone. "I thought we could take a picnic lunch and go explore the old ironworks today."

"That sounds interesting." Kit smiled, but Grace saw that his eyes were on her. "What do you think, Grace? We could bring the children too."

"What?" Grace was taken aback. "I didn't think—"

"Absolutely not," Alice said. "Er—that is, isn't there a lot of old machinery down there? I wouldn't want to bring them if there's a chance someone could get hurt, and they can be awfully rambunctious."

"And besides," she said to Grace an hour later, after she'd come back from fetching the lunch basket Mrs. Hunter packed for them, "the children have no sense of decorum. If Kit and I can't go alone, at least you know enough to find something else to occupy you when we want to be private."

Grace bit her lip to keep from pointing out that Kit had told Alice that he didn't want them to "be private" anymore. Instead she replied, a touch acerbically, "Thank you. I'm glad to know I've learned my place, ma'am."

Alice laughed. "Silly. You know what I mean. Let's go!" Kit was waving to them from the bridge by the Rookwoods' camp.

Kit, however, didn't seem to understand when Alice wanted to be alone with him. He resisted all of her attempts to lag behind Grace on the walk down to the abandoned ironworks and strolled between them, swinging the lunch basket and addressing his conversation impartially to both of them.

Grace wondered afterward if it wasn't Alice's growing indignation that caused her to pay less attention than she should have when they were wandering about the abandoned ironworks. She'd moved away on her own to give Alice the chance to be alone with Kit that she'd hinted so broadly about and was peering up the enormous blast furnace—it looked rather like an ancient Near Eastern ruin, somehow translated to a woodland setting—when she heard a sharp cry.

She found Alice half-sprawled on the ground next to a low mound of rusted metal. She hurried over, trying to block out visions of her best friend impaled on a jagged iron spike. "Alice! Are you all right?"

"I'm fine… Confound it, I think I tore my blouse!" To Grace's relief, Alice had gingerly raised herself on her forearms and turned onto her side, looking more annoyed than injured. "It's one I bought in Newport. Where's Kit?"

"I don't know, and it's a good thing you didn't tear anything more vital than your blouse." Grace bent over her. "What were you doing, anyway?"

"Trying to follow him down there." She gestured to a ruined stone building below the blast furnace. "But I caught my foot on something. *Kit!*" she shouted.

Grace winced; Alice had yelled nearly in her ear. "Here, give me your hand. Let's get you up and make sure you're all right."

Alice shook her head. "You're not strong enough to pull me up. Call Kit again."

"Oh, all right. Kit!" she called, and turned back to Alice. "You didn't hit your head, did you?"

"No, nothing like that. It's just my— Oh, Kit!" She collapsed back onto the ground, eyes fluttering shut, and pressed the back of her hand against her forehead, like a swooning heroine in a melodrama, as Kit came striding up the hill.

"Are you all right?" he said to Grace. "I heard you call—"

"I'm fine. It's—" She gestured toward Alice.

He frowned and crouched beside her. "What happened?"

A slight line appeared between her eyes. "Oh, Kit, I fell and I can't get up! Am I hurt? I feel so dizzy and strange… Is there much blood?"

Incredulous, Grace stared down at her. What was she saying? Twenty seconds ago she'd been fretting about whether her blouse was torn. Had she hit her head after all, and was only now feeling the effects? She looked at Kit and saw that his eyes were twinkling with suppressed amusement.

"No, not too much blood that I can see," he said gravely. "Of course, it might already be soaking into the ground—"

"*What!*" Alice sat bolt upright, feeling her side. "Where? How much?"

"There we go!" He stood up quickly and had pulled Alice to her feet before she could say another word.

She glowered at him as she set her hat straight on her head. "I might really have been hurt, you know."

"But you weren't. You tripped over something, I expect. You should be careful—there's a lot of old junk lying around." He looked at Grace. "Shall we find a place to sit and have lunch? There's a pretty creek down there. I think it's what powered the machinery."

"Lunch already? I'm not very hungr— Ow!" Alice staggered and grabbed Kit's arm.

"What is it?" Alice had gone pale this time.

"My ankle! It hurts like the devil."

Kit was no longer smiling. "Can you put any weight on it— Oh, never, mind." He bent and scooped Alice up in his arms.

She gave a small shriek that quickly turned to a laugh and put her arms around his neck. "Kit! What are you doing?"

"Looking for a place to sit you down so we can look at your ankle. I expect you twisted it when you fell." He spotted a low pile of rocks by the blast furnace and climbed toward it. He set Alice down on a large rock and knelt to examine her ankle, pressing it gently through the thin leather of her low boot.

She winced. "Ow! I think I twisted it. What am I going to do?"

"You're going to sit here with Grace while I go for help. You can't walk a half mile back up to the club on a bad ankle, even if it's only a wrench."

"Why don't you just carry me home?"

"Because I can't walk a half mile back to the club without dropping you." He spoke pleasantly enough, but Grace could hear the impatience in his voice.

"You disarranged my hat again." She adjusted it and looked up him through her lashes. "Why doesn't Grace go get someone?"

Kit shook his head. "I can go faster."

"Yes, but— Oh, never mind." Alice folded her arms on her chest and scowled at her foot.

Kit looked at her for a second, then turned away. "I'll be back as quickly as I can," he said to Grace. "Will you be all right?"

"Yes, of course."

He nodded and picked his way back up to the road, then broke into a run.

"Well!" Alice said crossly. "I like that—leaving me all alone with a broken ankle."

"Last I checked, I'm still here," Grace said. She knelt at Alice's feet. "Do you want me to take your boot off? I can get some cold water from the stream to bathe—"

"Oh, for heaven's sake! All I did was lose my footing and twist it—"

"So not broken, then." Grace touched it gently.

"No, not broken," Alice snapped. She glared at Grace for a moment, then her face relaxed into unhappiness. "Grace, what am I going to do?"

"You don't need to do anything. Kit'll fetch someone with a wagon, and we'll get you home quite easily. I'm sure that your mother—"

"That's not what I meant!" Alice hung her head and stared miserably down at her lap. "It's Kit. He hates me, doesn't he?"

Grace rose and sat down next to her. Overhead a large black bird circled them lazily, dark against the high, thin clouds, then landed on the ruined blast furnace and stared down at them. "No,

I don't think he hates you. But you were acting like an idiot, you know."

Alice groaned. "Oh, God, I know. I couldn't help it. I said the first things that came into my head, and they were all wrong. I could hear that they were wrong even as I said them, but I couldn't stop them coming out of my mouth. There's something wrong with Kit."

Grace frowned. "But I thought you said that you'd settled everything between you—"

"Well..." Alice would not meet her eyes. "I *thought* we had. Two days ago he said he loved me more than ever, but he hasn't been acting that way. I swear he's been going out of his way to avoid me."

"Oh, but surely you're—you're imagining things. He was here today with you, wasn't he? And the only reason he left was to get help—for *you*."

"Yes, but—" Alice began, then closed her mouth.

Grace could guess what she'd been about to say—if he'd really cared about her, he would have insisted they come here alone together...or have stayed with her and sent Grace for help. Which was wrong-headed, but how could she explain that to Alice?

"Well, why don't you ask him? I'm sure he'll tell you you're imagining things," she said.

Alice shook her head sadly. "I know he will. But it won't be true," she said. "He's changed."

Yes, he had...and she was as confused about it as Alice. The way he'd said, 'Will you be all right?' before he left—as if it mattered to him—had taken her aback.

Alice didn't say anything more until the *clop-clop* of an approaching horse sent Grace to see who was coming. It was Kit and Mrs. Roosevelt in a buggy. Kit hopped out and ran to them while Alice's stepmother turned the buggy at a wide place in the road. "Your chariot awaits, ma'am," he said cheerfully to Alice, who looked anything but cheerful.

"Mother's going to kill me," she muttered as Grace helped her stand.

"No, she won't. Why should she? And Ethel loves playing nurse—you've said so yourself. She'll take care of you."

"Hmph." Alice was in no mood to be comforted.

Grace and Kit between them helped her to the road and into the buggy. Mrs. Roosevelt watched their progress silently and, as they boosted Alice into the seat, only asked, "Are you all right?"

"Yes," Alice replied shortly. She looked down at Kit and opened her mouth, then closed it again.

"We'll see you back at the club," Mrs. Roosevelt said, loosening the brake and giving the reins a shake. Alice looked back at them once before the buggy was lost to view around a curve in the road.

"Well." Grace sighed. "I guess we ought to get going as well."

"Yes, I suppose so," Kit said. "Except that we've got a lunch waiting for us down by the creek that it would be a shame to waste. Why don't we eat it and then go back?"

Grace hesitated. "Alice wouldn't like it."

"Alice will be busy getting her ankle bathed in ice water and wrapped and fussed over for the next two hours. She'll be fine." He paused, then added, "I promise I won't bite."

The words were spoken gently, but Grace caught the unmistakable hint of challenge in them. She drew in her breath. "I'm not afraid of you."

"I know. You never were." He smiled then, a lopsided half grin. "If it makes you feel any better, I'm terrified."

"Of what?"

"Of saying the wrong thing. I've had plenty of practice at that."

To her surprise, Grace laughed. She felt almost giddy—reaction to Alice's accident, probably, and the strangeness of not having to be rigidly on her guard with Kit anymore.

"So will you eat lunch with me?" he asked.

She nodded, and they picked their way down the slope to the creek, where he'd left the lunch basket. She resolved to find a tree to sit against, in case she needed reinforcements—not that a tree could help her if Kit turned unpleasant, but its presence would be comforting.

But Kit led her to a large, flat rock that jutted out over the creek. He spread a blanket over it and gestured for her to sit. "Will this do?"

"Er, yes. Sandwich?" She peered into the basket. "I think they're all chicken—no, there's a ham as well. Which would you like? There's hard-boiled eggs, too, and some grapes and cookies. Mrs. Hunter must like Alice. She didn't pack such a nice lunch for us yesterday."

"Ham, please." He somehow looked younger, but that might be because he was more informally dressed than she'd ever seen him in Newport. He wore a collarless white shirt with a sweater draped over his shoulders and brown corduroy trousers with boots—a far cry from the tennis flannels and evening jackets that suited him so well. Not that he didn't look as handsome as he always did. Before she could stop and make herself tongue-tied, she asked, "Do you like it here? Or would you rather be back in Newport?"

He took the paper-wrapped sandwich and bottle of lemonade she handed him. "Yes, I do like it. Newport is a lot of work—as you probably noticed—even though I'm used to it by now since we've summered there since I was small. It's different here. The people who come here are as wealthy and powerful as the people in Newport, but they don't have to show the entire world that they are."

"Which makes them more so," she said. "The strongest lion is the one who's so sure of himself that he can lie in the sun and nap most of the day. It's the weaker lions who have to fight and show off to each other."

"So this is where the strongest lions come to nap. Speaking of lions, when does Colonel Roosevelt arrive?"

"I don't know. I believe he's on a speaking tour in Vermont, but I think he's expected in a week or so."

Kit nodded. "I like them," he said. "The Roosevelts, I mean. They're like...well, they're like that lion's cubs we were talking about—all pouncing and growling and having a grand time of it. Do you have any brothers or sisters?"

"One of each." If anyone had told her it would be so easy to talk to Kit Rookwood even half an hour ago, she would not have believed it. "An older brother—he's just finished his freshman year at Harvard—and a younger sister. She's horse crazy."

"Lucky," he said softly. "I don't have any. I don't think I've understood what I missed until recently."

Grace tried to think of what it would have been like to be an only child, and couldn't. Grand-mère would probably have fussed her to death. "What makes you miss them now, when you didn't before? I would have thought it would be lonely, growing up alone."

"I never knew that it was lonely. If you've never had something, you can't miss it. But now..." He shrugged. "I'm expected to join my father's business and take it over someday, and I'm not sure that I want to. If I'd had brothers, there wouldn't be so much pressure."

Pressure? Mr. Rookwood seemed like such a gentle person that it was hard to imagine him trying to force Kit to do anything. "Maybe in time it will become more attractive—or you'll change your mind."

"Maybe." He looked at her. "We're doing well, aren't we? I haven't said anything to make you want to run away yet—at least, I don't think I have."

For some reason, Grace felt herself blush. "No, you haven't. But we should finish up soon." The last thing she needed was Alice thinking she'd taken a liking to Kit. Well, not that she might not start to like him, maybe a little, if he continued to be as agreeable as this.

As they repacked the remains of lunch in the basket and made their way back up to the road, the crow perched on the blast furnace let out a solemn croak.

"Are you still there?" Grace called up to him. Was it the Changer that had watched her the other day?

"Friend of yours?" Kit's smile had a humorous quirk.

"A recent acquaintance, unless it's one of his cousins," she replied lightly.

Kit squinted up at the bird. "Hello, cousin," he said softly. The crow peered down at him, made a low, whickering sound, then hopped into the air and flapped away.

They walked back to the club in silence. But it wasn't an uncomfortable one, Grace realized when they were nearly there. As they drew abreast of the bridge across the brook that led to the Rookwoods' camp, Kit halted. "Well," he said.

"Well," Grace echoed. What was she supposed to say now? Her gaze fell on the lunch basket he still held. "Here, I'll take that back to the clubhouse. It's across the way from us." She reached for it. As he handed it to her, their fingers brushed. She pretended not to notice. "See you this evening," she said.

He nodded and then smiled at her with his beautiful, sun-coming-out-from-behind-clouds smile. "Thank you for eating lunch with me and not hating it," he said and turned quickly away, hands in pockets as he strode across the bridge.

"You're welcome," Grace said quietly to his back, then continued up the road. She hadn't hated it. She'd been nervous, yes…but so had he. It had put them both on their best behavior, but that was all right. Who knew, maybe they could actually become friends. Maybe sometime, if they did, she'd ask him again about Alice and Newport.

The rockers lining the porch of the clubhouse were full at this hour of the afternoon, occupied by a cadre of older female guests, maiden aunts and grandmothers, most of them, engaged in reading the newspapers that had arrived from the Lower Clubhouse. The "Porch Ladies," Archie had christened them. They reminded Grace of a row of justices with their black dresses and white hair and air of passing judgment on all that passed before them.

"How is Miss Roosevelt?" one of them asked as Grace climbed the stairs.

Goodness, news traveled fast…but they would have had a ringside seat, watching Alice being helped down from the buggy right across the road from them. "Resting comfortably, I trust," she said brightly, passing through their ranks on the way back to the kitchens.

"It's not safe, poking about those old ruins," she heard one of them say.

"And you would have been there like a shot when you were seventeen, Elvira, especially if there were a young man involved," a second voice answered, followed by a chorus of creaky chortles.

Grace left the basket with a girl peeling a large pile of potatoes and took a deep breath, preparing herself to run the gauntlet of Porch Ladies again. But they were once again engaged with their newspapers and let her go without comment.

Alice was not so forbearing. Grace found her on the parlor sofa with a hot-water bottle filled with ice on her ankle and Ethel hovering nearby.

"About time," Alice snapped at her. "I though you'd be right behind us."

"You were being driven, remember?" Grace pulled up a chair. "How is your foot?"

"Sadly wrenched," Ethel piped up. "But we're keeping it well iced and wrapped so that it doesn't swell too badly."

"And it will be a wonder if my toes don't fall off from lack of blood," Alice growled.

"She's a rotten patient," Ethel told Grace. "Worse than any of my brothers. They usually at least show a little *gratitude*." She left the room with her nose in the air, then stuck her head back in the door. "Would you like some lemonade, Grace? Youngie and I made it a little while ago."

"I'd love some, thank you." Grace waited till she'd disappeared again, then looked at Alice sternly. "You don't have to be such a bear, you know. She's only trying to help."

Alice looked sulky. "What do you expect? Of all the stupid things to have done… I'm going to be stuck here on the sofa for a good two days, you know."

"And then you'll be fine," Grace said. "And you needn't be stuck on the sofa. You can go sit on the porch or even hobble down to the brook. Or go sit with the Porch Ladies," she added mischievously.

Alice snickered. "In a black dress and a pince-nez? I'll bet I could tell them a thing or two that would turn their hair white, except it already is." She sighed. "Does Kit think I'm a complete idiot?"

"No, not at all. He didn't even mention y—" Grace stopped abruptly, but Alice finished for her.

"He didn't even mention me?" she said, and let her head fall back against the sofa cushions. "That's even worse."

"What was there to say? You hurt yourself, and your mother brought you home."

"It's clear you've never been in love. So what took you so long to get back?"

She wouldn't let go of that, would she? "We ate lunch. It seemed a shame to waste it."

"*You ate lunch?*" Alice sat up and grabbed Grace's wrist. "Oh my God, I'd forgotten… The sandwiches? You ate them?"

Had she gone mad? "Some of the sandwiches, and the grapes and the—"

"Which sandwich did Kit eat?" Alice asked urgently.

Grace frowned. "Um—it was ham, I think. I had a chicken."

"And did you give it to him, or did he take it out of the basket himself?"

"I gave it to him. Why?"

Alice sank back into the cushions. "No. Oh, no." She threw her arm across her eyes.

"Alice, what is the matter with you?" Grace demanded.

"That sandwich—it was special."

"Special how? Did you put rat poison in it?"

"I—I made magics on it," Alice whispered. "I'd asked him what kind of sandwich he wanted and he said ham, so I made a magic on the ham sandwich that he would remain eternally devoted to the person who handed it to him. It was supposed to be me." She moved her arm and stared bleakly at Grace.

Grace sighed. "Do you really believe that…that your magics actually *do* anything?"

Alice's eyes narrowed. "They've always worked before."

"Could that be because it was going to happen anyway? Come on, Alice. We're supposed to be young ladies now, not little girls playing make-believe. Just because I gave Kit a ham sandwich doesn't mean he will love me or even like me. Yes, we've called a truce because he apologized to me for Newport—"

"He did? When? Why didn't you tell me about it?"

"It was only yesterday—at the lake, for heaven's sake—"

"On your fishing trip? So what else haven't you told me about?"

Grace stared at her. "What is wrong with you? There is nothing—*nothing*—going on between us. We're barely learning how to speak politely to each other. And nothing's going to happen because of a sandwich."

"What if it does?"

The last threads of her patience snapped, and Grace stood up. "If Kit decides he likes someone else because of an imaginary magic spell, then whatever he felt for you couldn't have been very strong, could it?"

"How dare you?" Alice cried, rising as well—or trying to. With a pained squeal, she collapsed back onto the sofa. "Now see what you did?"

"*I* didn't do anything," Grace said coldly. "When you can talk about things rationally, I'll come back and sit with you." She stalked to the door and nearly collided with Ethel, backing out of the kitchen with a tray of glasses and a plate of cookies.

"Here we are—" She stopped short. "Grace?"

"I'll be down shortly," Grace said and climbed the stairs to their room to give her temper a moment to cool.

THIRTEEN

After breakfast the following morning, Grace paused on the porch of the clubhouse to survey the day.

With her sore ankle, Alice had remained in bed. She'd been subdued all evening and had gone to bed early, ignoring Grace as well as she could considering they shared a bedroom. They did not discuss the angry words they'd exchanged that afternoon. Grace hoped that a good night's rest and being served breakfast in bed would help shake her from her mood. Whether it would shake her from her conviction that her magics would now force Kit to fall in love with Grace was another question.

Oh, why had the Rookwoods had to come to Tahawus? Everything would have been so much simpler if they hadn't. Alice would have pined for a while, but she would have gotten over Kit eventually. It would be sorely tempting to write home and ask Mum to fabricate a reason for her to leave early if matters became too unpleasant…except that she couldn't abandon Alice when she was so unhappy. That wasn't what a friend did.

However, this morning she was not going to think about Alice or Kit. Wrapped against the chill morning mist in one of Ted's heavy sweaters that he'd been incoherently delighted to lend her and armed with her sketchbook, she was bound for a good long walk in the woods and the company of the trees.

"Are you an artist, Miss Boisvert?" Mr. Rookwood had come to stand next to her on the porch.

Grace glanced behind her, but it was too early for the Porch Ladies to have taken up residence. "Not much of one," she confessed. "But I thought bringing a sketchbook would make my wandering around in the woods appear a bit less frivolous."

"Excessive frivolity does not appear to be one of your faults, at least as far as I have seen." He gazed up at the hills. "I had planned a walk myself up to the lake. Would it trouble you if our paths coincided for a little while?"

"Not at all, sir."

"Thank you." He held up a fly rod and willow creel. "Here is my sketchbook if you won't tell anyone. I have no intention of actually catching anything, but they permit me to stand on the shores of beautiful lakes and contemplate the scenery while appearing industrious."

Grace laughed. "Your secret is safe with me."

"How is Miss Roosevelt this morning?" he asked as they started up the road.

"Asleep, actually, which is why I'm taking my walk now. She'll need entertaining later," Grace said, then wished she hadn't. That made Alice sounded like a spoiled child.

"It's difficult for a healthy young person to be forced into inaction," Mr. Rookwood said. "But I expect she'll be back on both feet in a day or so, yes? The injury isn't severe?"

"She'll be fine." At least, her ankle would.

Mr. Rookwood was silent after that, which allowed her to listen to the morning. The trees had enjoyed the rain the night before and were humming happily, and the forest felt peaceful and free of that watchful sensation she'd noticed the other day.

"When you're out walking, you do tell someone where you're planning to go, don't you?" Mr. Rookwood asked suddenly. "I was thinking of Miss Roosevelt and what a terrible thing it would have been if she'd been alone when she fell."

"I don't, but I will," she said, more to placate him than anything else. After all, what could hurt *her* in the woods?

"I'm relieved to hear you say that." He hesitated, then said, "I was talking to one of the hunting guides—Mr. Dumont. You've met him? He had some interesting stories to tell about these woods."

"Like old legends? That sounds intriguing."

"Yes, I suppose it does—except he didn't seem to think they were legends at all. It sounds as though a lot of his stories were about things he himself had seen."

It was hardly surprising that a man whose livelihood took him into these woods on a daily basis should have noticed something of the unseen world within them if he were at all observant. "I should love to hear them."

"This is perhaps not the best setting for a retelling." He glanced around at the still, misty trees. "Perhaps another time?"

She smiled. "Of course."

"Thank you." His return smile was sheepish. "And now you probably think me a superstitious old fool, but I've seen a few things myself that I can't entirely explain as I've admired the scenery at the lake. This is a rich and wonderful land we are visiting, Miss Boisvert. I hope my brother will enjoy it when he arrives."

"Oh, is he coming?" She thought about Alice's need for distraction—maybe Kit had some attractive cousins. "Will he be bringing his family?"

"No, my brother never married, alas. He's been taken up with business over the last weeks, though, and will appreciate a bit of relaxation. Well, this is where I leave the path. I've found my own secret fishing hole where the fish never trouble my contemplation." He smiled at her—she caught an echo of Kit's lopsided grin in it—before setting off down a tiny side path.

She watched him go until he was lost to sight among the trees and mist, and wondered what stories the guide had told him about the woods. For a second, the chill of the morning cut through Ted's borrowed sweater, making her shiver. Then she shrugged and continued up the path.

Not far from where she and Mr. Rookwood had parted ways, she struck into the trees and found a small, almost perfectly circular hollow hidden by a rise and dotted with birch and sugar maples and one beautiful and (at this elevation) unusual balsam fir at the center of the hollow. It was perfectly gracious when she spoke to it, but there was something about it—a quality of *other*—that made her wish she could climb one of the nearby mountains where the balsams grew up to the tree line and learn more about them. She dawdled for a long while there—it reminded her somehow of Mum's grove back in Chestnut Hill—then, as it was approaching dinnertime, climbed back up its side and made for the path back to Tahawus…and stopped in her tracks.

An enormous rock lay in the center of the path where there hadn't been one before. It was like a playful giant had tossed it from the top of a nearby mountain, except that it was rough and lichened, as if it had always been here.

She didn't move, but studied it carefully for a few minutes. There were no freshly broken branches to show that it had somehow rolled here from someplace else… "Which means it got here in some other fashion," she said aloud. "Perhaps it flew here? On wings, maybe?"

There was a silence during which even the birds seemed to stop singing in the trees around them…and then the rock wasn't there. In its place was a crow, which flew up to a branch and gave forth a burst of what could only be described as laughter.

"Too clever!" it croaked. "Couldn't scare you that way."

Grace jumped a little, even though she'd been expecting something like this. She took a tentative step toward it. "No, it didn't scare me," she said. "It was too ridiculous to be frightening. Why do you want to scare me?"

"To see what you are." It examined her, head to one side. "*Tree-cousin*, the trees are calling you. I don't know what that is."

A puzzled quality came through the crow's—or Changer's, she supposed—harsh voice. "Well, I don't plan on being afraid of you," she said.

The crow vanished. Suddenly in front of her was a large black bear, standing on its hind legs and growling at her with its mouth drawn into a snarl.

Grace blinked and drew in her breath, but only for a second. "Well done."

The bear dropped to all fours and a red fox suddenly took its place. It sat to scratch behind one ear, then grinned at her, tongue lolling.

"Yes, I can see you have the animal kingdom down pat," she said.

The fox was gone. A mighty balsam fir, eighty feet tall, hovered over her. And then it was gone, and Alice stood there. "Where have you been?" she demanded. "I've been looking all over for you!"

Grace laughed. "Full marks for the balsam, but I think you need to work on humans a little more."

Alice vanished and the crow was there, pacing back and forth. "What was wrong with the human?" it demanded, for all the world like a diva criticized for a poor performance.

"The eyes. It looked like Alice, but the eyes were dead. I suspect you may not think very highly of them, but humans do have souls and spirits, and you can see it in their eyes if you look."

The crow gave a derisive squawk. "I don't get close enough to them to see that—if it's true, tree-cousin."

"The proper term is dryad, in case you wanted to know." She went to a rock and sat down.

"So?" The crow flew up to a low branch and looked at her thoughtfully. "So what can you do, dryad?"

Not much, Grace thought to herself. But she couldn't tell it that. "Would I be wise to tell you all that I'm capable of, Changer? But I can do this." She felt above her for a cloud, and pulled it down so that they were engulfed in thick, white mist. "Would you like some rain? I can bring that too, though it takes a little longer to call the clouds."

She couldn't see the crow well through the mist, but heard it mutter, "You called it. Can you send it away?"

The cloud sank into the ground around them, leaving a heavy dew on everything. Grace wished she could shake the moisture off like a dog emerging from a lake, but it wouldn't be dignified. "Well?" she asked.

The crow had no similar concerns about preserving its dignity; it ruffled its feathers and shook itself off energetically. "You show me, dryad!"

Grace smiled to herself and called under her breath to the tree the crow perched on. Abruptly, the branch on which it was perched jerked sharply to one side. The crow squawked as it started to tumble, then caught the air with its wings and floated down to the earth.

"Ha! I should have known that you could tell the trees to do that," it said. "And yet, you would pass for a man."

"Only if I keep my hat on," she muttered. Being among the trees like this was making her hair grow out green much more quickly. If she didn't find an hour soon to be alone with her bottle of Mademoiselle's Secret, she'd have to start wrapping her head up in a kerchief. And thank goodness the Changer didn't seem to want any further demonstrations of her power; she didn't think it would be impressed to hear her recite the song the balsam he'd been perching on had taught her or watch her cure a nasty case of oak gall.

"What did you say?"

"Nothing," she said. "Are there many of you in the forests here?"

"Some," it said vaguely. "We come and we go."

"What about the Shadows? Are they—"

The crow jumped and let out a harsh caw, which it tried to pretend it hadn't. "Hush! We don't speak of them," it said, and Grace could have sworn that it looked nervous.

"Do you fear them?" she asked, not really expecting an answer. But the crow surprised her.

"Everything fears them. How can you not know them?" it asked.

"Because I've never seen one before where I live." And there certainly hadn't been any fearsome entities in Newport, unless you counted Mrs. Vanderbilt. "I think I've seen them—or one of them—well, not *seen*, really, more like felt—"

"They aren't seen if they don't want to be," the crow whispered hoarsely. "But you know they're there. There have been a lot of them here—they've come down from the mountains, for some reason, even with the moon in fullness—and they hate moonlight. I've seen them on the lake over there." It jerked its head in the direction of Lake Henderson, not far away. "Don't go there if you don't want to meet one."

Good heavens—and the children went fishing there alone all the time—not to mention Mr. Rookwood at his non-fishing hole. Was that where Mr. Rookwood had seen the mysterious things he'd hinted at? Should she warn them not to go there? Still— "Why should they trouble us?"

"There's something they find interesting. Maybe it's you, dryad." The crow cackled. "I like you. You are not foolish, like the humans. I'll be watching you."

"Haven't you been already? Was that you I saw down at the blast furnace the other day?"

"It may have been. Or maybe not." The crow flapped up to a higher branch, then promptly gave itself away. "You were with a human."

"My friend Alice? Or Kit Rookwood?"

"I don't know what you call each other," the crow said testily. "You ate food with it." It paused. "I wanted some but you didn't leave any."

It was talking about Kit, then. "Maybe I'll bring you a sandwich sometime. What about the human?"

"I don't know. But it watches you. It wants something from you."

These Changers were observant. Yes, Kit wanted her friendship...and so? "I think I'd guessed that." She rose from her rock.

"Where are you going?" the crow demanded.

"Back to camp." She hesitated. According to all the old tales she'd read, it was not done to ask a supernatural creature its name, and she had the feeling that the old tales had it right. "I expect that I'll be seeing you around, Crow," she added, with a small bow.

To her amusement, the Changer dropped a creditable curtsey. "You will, dryad, you will." With that, it took wing and was gone.

⚯

Alice's mood seemed much improved that afternoon—so much so that she agreed to let Ted and Kermit chair-carry her out to the brook behind the camp and set her up in a lawn chair under an umbrella to watch the children paddle and splash. The morning's chill mist had long since vanished and the afternoon was golden and sultry. And to the further improvement of Alice's mood, Kit came too. She gazed down at his form stretched out on the rough-mown grass with approbation but said, "How lazy you are, Kit. Shouldn't you be doing something energetic and outdoorsman-like right now?"

"We could get a tennis game up. They mowed around the net this morning so the playing will be good—except that Sister can't right now, can she?" said Ted, looking disappointed. "Do you play, Grace?"

She was glad he'd finally heeded her requests not to call her Miss Boisvert. "Yes, I—"

"You'd better believe she does," Kit broke in, sitting up. "She beat the socks off me two games out of three when we played once in Newport—and I barely squeaked by in the third."

Alice laughed. "It was no more than you deserved."

But Grace stared at Kit. That horrid game! It had been the start of his rudeness to her...and now, here he was, praising her playing and behaving as if none of the strange undercurrents of that morning had ever happened.

"I'm hot," she said abruptly. "I think I'll join the children in the brook."

"Don't let them push you in," Alice cautioned. "They've been known to."

"Only with Father, and he likes it," Ted said. "They won't dare duck her, though Quentin might splash."

Grace could feel his eyes on her as she untied her boots and pulled off her stockings. Glancing up, she saw that Kit watched her as well. Their eyes met, but unlike in Newport, he did not look away. She stood up quickly and went down to the water's edge.

"Hey, it's Grace!" Ethel shouted. She could out-shout all of her brothers. "C'mon, Grace! We're having races!"

Miss Young smiled at her from the bank where she was folding squares of newspaper donated by the Porch Ladies into boats. The children were launching them, then running alongside on the banks to see whose would go the farthest.

"All the way to Albany and New York City!" Ethel announced. "That's what Mr. Hunter said. He said this creek's part of where the Hudson River starts."

"So we could get in a boat right here and go there if we wanted?" Archie's eyes gleamed.

"No, you could not," Miss Young said firmly.

"I'd like mine to go to China," Kermit said in his dreamy way. "I'd sail it home filled with porcelain dragons and a pair of lion dogs for Mother."

"What would you eat? China's awfully far away, you know," said Ethel.

"He could eat the dogs!" Archie collapsed into the water with glee at his own wit.

"That's a terrible thing to say! Youngie, did you hear that?" Ethel waded purposefully toward her brother. Miss Young rose immediately to intervene, and Grace took the opportunity to retreat downstream to be alone.

Except that she wasn't for very long. As she picked her way among the slippery rocks, holding up her skirt, she heard a small splash behind her and turned. Kit had followed after her, his trousers rolled up his calves. She restrained the urge to run down the creek bed and waited for him.

"It's like ice!" he called. "Aren't you freezing?"

"It's a mountain stream. Of course it's cold."

He came to stand next to her. "Are you all right?" he asked abruptly. "The way you jumped up like that—you weren't offended by what I said about your tennis playing, were you?"

Grace began to amble down the stream again so that she could stare down at her feet and not have to look at him. "It brought back unpleasant memories."

He followed after her. "I'm sorry. I didn't think. I guess I got carried away, telling Ted…but you were magnificent that day, you know."

She would not let his praise turn her head. "I didn't want to play you, but I was determined to win. I was angry with you for intentionally losing to Alice. It was so — so *obvious*."

"I didn't want to play you either," he said. She noticed that he didn't respond to the second part of her statement. "But since Alice was making us, I desperately wanted to beat you too."

She stopped walking and turned to face him. "I know you did. Why?"

He didn't look away. "Because I had some…inner demons I needed to best."

"What do you mean?"

He shrugged, then broke into a smile and bent to scoop something out of the brook — a newspaper boat, waterlogged but still floating. "I wonder whose this is? Let's see who claims it."

She followed him back up the creek. All the children claimed it, of course, so a fresh round of boats had to be folded and launched.

Alice was frowning when they rejoined her on the bank. "Why did you go so far and leave me here?" she demanded.

"I had to go after Grace and make sure she didn't slip and fall. One sprained ankle's enough in camp, don't you think?" He grinned his old saucy grin at her, and she visibly melted.

"Scamp. You're supposed to stay here and keep my spirits up to speed my recovery," she scolded, but with a smile.

Grace wasn't reassured. Alice wouldn't start harping about her misfired sandwich magic again because Kit had followed her down the creek, would she?

⚜

To Grace's (and, she supposed, everyone else's) relief, Alice was up and hobbling within a couple of days with a walking stick Ted made for her. But she'd decided she preferred getting a breakfast tray to coming down to breakfast, so Grace was able to keep mornings after early breakfast for her solitary walks. Almost daily, she visited the quiet hollow she'd found and listen to the whisperings of the trees and relax in a way she couldn't at the camp. Or at least mostly relax. On two or three occasions now she'd felt that eerie, cold, watching sensation, the same as that afternoon in the hammock behind the camp, and felt a chill breeze that seemed to come from nowhere and vanish just as inexplicably. It didn't quite make her afraid, but it wasn't pleasant either. It certainly wasn't going to keep her from the woods.

But it made her nervous for the children. When one morning a few days later a misty rain began to fall before breakfast, the younger children cast only a few wistful looks outside before settling down with books by the fire. Ted and Kermit, however, donned waxed cotton coats and set out to go fishing on Lake Henderson.

Grace stood on the porch and watched them trudge up the path, dodging puddles. The Changer's warning about Shadows lurking at the lake made her want to run after them and ask them not to go, but she couldn't do that without explaining why. And she could only imagine what they would have said if she'd told them to watch out for cold gusts of wind. She would have gone with them herself—though what she could do against a Shadow, she had no idea—but she had promised Alice a few games of checkers.

"Good morning, Miss Boisvert. Are you walking this morning or remaining sensibly by the fire?"

Grace turned. Mr. Rookwood, also bundled in a waterproof coat and hat and with a fishing pole on his shoulder, was smiling at her from the road. "Mr. Rookwood! Would you... May I speak with you for a moment, please?"

"Certainly." He came up onto the porch and set down his pole. "I don't know why I'm going to the lake today, except that fish are supposed to like rain and I have a reputation to live up to. I hope that I don't catch one or I shall be forced to find a new spot." He took off his hat and shook it over the railing.

Grace couldn't help smiling. "That would be a terrible shame, sir."

"To be truthful, I doubt it will come to that. My friend, you appear distressed. May I help you?"

He wouldn't think she was being silly, would he? But no, he himself had said... "A few days ago you said something about maybe having noticed some...strange things in the woods—and at the lake—and I...well, I wanted to ask that if you happen to be at the lake when any of the children are there, and you sense that something might not be right—"

"That I would keep an eye out for them? Of course I will." He looked at her keenly. "Should I take this to mean that you've seen something yourself? By the lake or in the woods?"

Grace hesitated. "Um..."

He held up a hand. "If you don't want to talk about it—"

"I...still haven't made my mind up about it—what I should think. I don't know if it's good or bad, or if terms like that even apply to it."

He was silent for a minute, staring out at the mist-shrouded mountain. "Good and bad. Black and white," he said quietly. "It's a gray day...but it's a gray world, isn't it? Not only the weather, I mean, but everything. These...things we've seen—even they're gray, somewhere between real and not real. I don't think there isn't anything in the world that isn't gray... Forgive me, Miss Boisvert. Mountains make me philosophical, it seems."

"Not at all," she said politely. "Papa once said something like that to me, before I left for Newport—that life was not black and white."

"Did he?" Mr. Rookwood smiled. "He's a wise man, your father."

As he spoke, a buckboard came jolting up the road. It drew to a stop in front of one of the camps down the road, and the three young men it contained jumped out, joking and laughing with each other. One of them tipped the driver, and then they climbed the stairs and went inside. Further sounds of laughter and greeting could be heard before the door closed behind them. The driver brought the buckboard round to the stables behind the clubhouse.

"Newcomers," Mr. Rookwood commented. "It will be pleasant to see some fresh faces about."

"Especially young male ones!" Grace said vehemently. Would having three presentable young men around improve Alice's mood? Then she noticed Mr. Rookwood looking at her oddly and laughed. "I'm not excited for my sake," she explained. "I was thinking more about Alice. Maybe having some new faces around will help take her mind off—" Flustered, she stopped as she remembered to whom she was speaking.

"Off my son," he finished. "Yes, I can see that. How do matters go there?"

She remembered their conversation the day after her arrival and decided to be frank with him. "Not very well. I—I have the feeling Kit is trying to disengage from her, but she doesn't want to admit she knows it. It's quite uncomfortable all around."

"I can see that it might be." Mr. Rookwood looked pensively out at the mountains again. "Well—I won't keep you any longer, Miss Boisvert. Rest assured that I'll keep an eye on matters up at the lake." He put his hat back on, gave her a reassuring smile, and ambled off into the rain.

FOURTEEN

Alice pretended to yawn when Grace told her over their checkers about the new arrivals. But she wore a Newport shirtwaist to lunch and, by meal's end, had the three young men presented to her and invited to tea that afternoon. She invited Kit, too, in an offhand way that made Grace suspicious.

After lunch, she took Alice's arm as they walked back from the clubhouse. "Let me guess. You're plotting some Captivation this afternoon on those poor boys, in an effort to make someone jealous."

Alice shrugged. "What if I am? It will make for an amusing afternoon since I'm unable to enjoy the delights of catching slimy fish with the children, tramping around and admiring trees and rocks the way you do, or trying to shoot defenseless woodland animals like my brother." Ted had gone off hunting with one of the guides after returning from fishing that morning. "And if someone should happen to get jealous, it's no more than he deserves. It will be a — a salutary experience for him."

And an unlikely one. But Grace didn't say that out loud.

The rain tailed off shortly after lunch, so the tea was on the porch. The young men — Mr. McNaughton, son of the family who had lent the Roosevelts their camp, and two Mr. Robinsons, students at Harvard's School of Law — clustered around Alice in a manner that Grace was sure she found gratifying. She sat holding court with her injured foot propped on a chair and clad in one of her lace-trimmed peach satin slippers.

When Kit arrived — attired in a Newport suit, Grace noticed — Alice gave him a curt greeting. He smiled in response, introduced himself to the other young men, then took a chair by Grace where she perched on the railing in the corner of the porch, determined to make sure Alice took the limelight.

"They seem like a nice crew," he said. "I gather that my nose should be thoroughly out of joint by now."

Grace frowned down at him. "You don't have to joke about it." She hesitated, then added, "Alice is miserable, you know."

To her relief, he didn't change the subject. "I'm sorry. Yes, I know that, and I honestly hope that she'll find one of them to be a much more engaging companion than me."

"I don't want her hurt any more than she has been. She's very vulnerable under all of her — her Aliceness."

"It was never my intention to hurt her."

Grace glanced over at Alice, whose attention was completely taken by her guests. "What *was* your intention, then? Because you hurt her badly."

He wouldn't meet her eyes. "It was just a flirtation."

"*Just* a flirtation?" Grace wanted to box his ears. "Your 'just a flirtation' was her practically planning your wedding."

"I'm sorry." He swallowed hard. "I…I never meant it to go that far."

If anything, his admission made her angrier. "That's even worse! What did you do, plan it all out beforehand? Oh, I wish we'd never set foot in Newport!"

"Grace…" His voice was pleading. "If I could do Newport again, it would be completely different. I wish to God I could."

"Why couldn't it have been different the first time?"

"I—I can't tell you."

"Why not?"

"Not now. Not yet. But I will. I'll explain all of Newport. I owe it to you." He reached out and touched her hand.

His touch stilled the words on her lips. She stared down at him, and this time he met her eyes. "I promise," he whispered.

Grace couldn't look away. There it was again—that *something* drawing her to him, just as it had the day they met—

"Grace!" Alice called. "Did you hear that?"

Grace nearly toppled from her perch. Kit put up a hand to steady her. "What? No, I'm sorry I didn't. What was it?"

"Good heavens, don't fall off the porch. There's to be a dance over at the Hewitt Lake Club, and we're all invited!" Alice's eyes sparkled.

"I'm sorry your foot should be injured right now, Miss Roosevelt," one of the Robinson boys—Grace thought it might be Beverley—said.

"We-e-ell, I expect it might be feeling better in a few days' time if you wish real hard." She grinned and waved it at him.

A dance! Well, if it put Alice into a better mood, then Grace was all for it. "Where is it?"

"A little way from Aiden Lair," Mr. McNaughton said. "The moon will be half-full—plenty of light to come home by."

"A moonlight ride sounds perfectly romantic." Alice smiled dreamily at no one in particular.

Grace's confusion over her cryptic conversation with Kit receded as she thought about driving through the woods at night. Even with a half-moon, would they be safe when there were Shadows potentially about? Crow had said that they hated moonlight, but was the light of a half-moon enough to keep them at bay?

While Alice hopped on her injured foot to make it stronger in time for the dance and frowned over her wardrobe, Grace spent the next two days haunting the woods, looking for Crow. She was sure she saw two other Changers, though they didn't speak to her. One took the form of a small cloud, which wasn't the most articulate of shapes, though it did return her tentative bow before drifting past her. But she also felt that cold watching sensation that seemed the calling card of a Shadow, and had tried not to run away in a blind panic from it.

"Why should I tell you how much moonlight will keep a Shadow away?" Crow asked when she finally found him—she couldn't help thinking of the Changer as a "he" though she doubted they possessed genders—perched on the balsam in her hollow as if he had always been there.

"Because I brought you a ham sandwich?" Grace surveyed him with arms folded across her chest.

"I would have liked chicken better," he said, though he'd made short work of the sandwich when she'd offered it.

"Why doesn't it surprise me that you'd be a cannibal?"

He cackled. "But I'm not really a bird."

"If this is your favorite shape, you must have some bird-like tendencies," Grace said. "Now—do you really not have any idea about how much moon there needs to be to keep the Shadows away, or will I have to bring you a chicken sandwich in order to get an answer out of y—"

Crow vanished, and a tiny salamander took its place on the side of the tree. Grace was about to scold him when a whoosh of icy air rushed past her, making branches thrash and filling the hollow with a dark coldness.

She fell to her knees to keep from being blown over. Her canvas jacket and twill skirt did nothing to halt the chill that cut through them as if they weren't there. The cold wind swirled around her, and she felt it examining her with a remote, contemptuous interest before it blew out of the hollow and up the hillside. Small twigs and leaves fell from the trees around her as it passed. Leaning to pick one up, she saw that it was edged with frost.

"Crow," she said when she could breathe again. She climbed to her feet, trying not to cry. A feeling of despair and emptiness had been left in the wake of the cold, and her teeth chattered, no matter how she tried to stop them.

He popped back into crow shape. "Do you still want to know how much moonlight will keep a Shadow away, dryad?"

She shook her head. It seemed like a ridiculously naïve question now. "What was it doing?"

"Just passing through," Crow said. "It seemed angry, though. And it saw you all right."

"Grace!"

She looked up. Kit was sprinting down the side of her hollow. Crow muttered something under his breath and turned into a salamander again.

"It's—I'm all right," she said as Kit reached her.

He didn't seem to hear. Grabbing her shoulders, he pulled her roughly against him. "Grace," he muttered into her hair. "Oh, Grace."

She rested her head against his chest and gave a little sigh. His warmth and solidity felt so very good... The icy despair the Shadow had left in its wake began to recede. "It was so cold..."

His arms tightened around her in response. "You're sure you're all right? It didn't hurt you?"

"I'm fine. It...scared me."

"It scared me too." His heart pounded under her ear, strong and steady. She would happily stand here for the rest of the day listening to it, warm and safe—

"Miss Boisvert!"

Kit jerked and let her go. Mr. Rookwood was hurrying down the slope to them, looking worried. He still clutched a fly rod—had he and Kit run here all the way from the lake?

Grace realized that her hat had been knocked off. She stooped to retrieve it and nearly fell over. Kit caught her arm; she wished he would hold her again, but with Mr. Rookwood's arrival, the moment for it had passed.

"The wind—we felt it at the lake." Mr. Rookwood was panting for breath. "Kit said— thought you—walking here—" He examined her anxiously. "Did it— Did you—?"

"It was here," she said. "But it didn't stay long."

"If it had wanted to hurt her, she wouldn't be here." Crow had abandoned his salamander guise once more and glared at them as he glided to the ground, ruffling his feathers. Then he jumped into the air and took wing, flapping his way out of the trees and out of sight.

Mr. Rookwood leaned against a tree. "A...friend of yours?" he asked, wide-eyed.

Kit's hand fell from her arm as he stared after Crow.

"Um...an acquaintance, anyway." How was she going to explain Crow to them?

But they didn't ask. Instead, Mr. Rookwood stared thoughtfully at the ground for a long moment. Grace started to shiver; Kit took off his jacket and wrapped it around her.

"Miss Boisvert," Mr. Rookwood finally said. "I don't pretend to fully comprehend the nature of...of whatever it was we all felt, but it frightens me. You...seem perhaps to have a little more experience with these things—"

"Oh, no," Grace interrupted. "I don't know any more about them than you do. And Crow, the thing you saw—he simply sort of...introduced himself to me, and—"

"I don't blame him," he said gallantly. "But it makes me

apprehensive. I confess to feeling somewhat *in loco parentis* as your father is not here, and the thought of you wandering alone in these woods when entities like what we've seen—"

"Shadows," she supplied.

He nodded. "Shadows then. Miss Boisvert, I'm asking you not to walk alone here anymore. Kit or I would be happy to accompany you whenever you wish to walk, and I for one would breathe easier knowing you'll never be alone. Kit?"

"I'm at your command." He gave her his lopsided smile. "That is, if Ted doesn't shoot me. Or his sister."

"I must confess that some hurt feelings are of secondary importance to me," Mr. Rookwood said sternly.

"Thank you, but…well, what difference would it make if there were ten of you with me if a Shadow was intent on harm?"

He sighed. "You're right, of course. But I still request that you consider it. And now, I for one could use a cup of strong, hot coffee, and I expect you could too. Shall we go find one? Mrs. Hunter always has a pot on at the clubhouse."

"Yes, please," she said meekly.

Grace couldn't help being on edge when they set out for Hewitt Lake on Friday afternoon, even though the sight of them all in evening clothes (Alice in her demure yellow silk and not the black dress, thank goodness) clambering into the wagons and setting off down a rough Adirondack road was amusing enough. She and Alice sat in the rear of the wagon where the jolting was the worst, but it allowed Alice to twist around in her seat and exchange gestures and snatches of conversation with the Robinson boys in the wagon close behind them.

Alice's friendship with the Robinsons had flourished over the last days to such a degree that Grace hoped that she'd gotten over

Kit after all. At least, her chatter was full of them, while Kit figured hardly at all. It was a relief to have her more herself again—at least mostly. Grace had caught her once or twice staring into space with a lost, desolate sort of expression, but she'd immediately brightened when she'd noticed Grace looking at her.

Where Kit *had* figured prominently was her own life. Though she hadn't promised Mr. Rookwood that she would avoid walking alone, Kit seemed to have a mysterious faculty for knowing when she was setting out and meeting her where the road went into the woods. In the silences during their walks she often thought about how he'd held her after the Shadow had blown through the woods and wondered if he did too.

But no Shadows blew anywhere on either their walks or on the road to Hewitt Lake, though Grace felt sure something was watching them. Crow, perhaps? She spotted several crows along the way, but none gave any sign that it might be anything but a bird.

The Hewitt Lake clubhouse was larger and more elegant than theirs at Tahawus, a fact that struck Alice. "I hadn't noticed how poky our place is till we came here," she muttered to Grace as they entered the spacious dining room, cleared of tables and chairs for the dance. "Why couldn't Father have been invited here instead? Oh, look! Aren't those some of the boys we met on the train to North Creek?" She limped toward a group of young men, who greeted her uproariously.

Grace did not follow. Watching for Shadows and worrying about what might happen on the drive home had destroyed any sociability she might have felt. But Ted, his voice cracking with nervousness, asked her to dance, and she could not refuse. After that she found a place to sit in a corner, half-concealed by a large stuffed bear, forepaws raised before it in a threatening manner. It seemed like an odd decoration for a dining room, but it was perfect to hide behind.

"Thank goodness Archie and Quentin aren't here. They'd try to take it home." Kit somehow materialized next to her. He patted the bear's shoulder.

She'd nearly forgotten how good he looked in evening dress, so used to him was she now in soft-collared shirts and corduroy trousers. "They'd probably succeed, and there would go my hiding place. Why aren't you dancing?"

"Why aren't *you?* Women are in the minority tonight. You're depriving all the sports of a partner."

"They'll have to do without me. Please don't let me keep you from joining the dance."

She saw a glint of mischief in his eyes. "Actually, you *are* keeping me from dancing. Because I want to dance with you."

He wanted to dance with her? A bubble of nervous laughter rose in her throat. "I told you, my feet are both left ones tonight. I'm just…I would make a wretched partner."

"You're thinking about what we might meet in the woods on the way home, aren't you?" he asked more gently.

"Yes."

"I see." He paused. "Will it make you feel any more like dancing if I give you my solemn promise that our drive home will be completely uneventful?"

She shook her head, nettled. This was not a joking matter. "It's very kind of you, but you shouldn't make promises you can't keep."

"I never make promises I can't keep…well, almost never." He grinned his old lopsided grin at her.

She didn't smile back. "Which may be why I can't quite bring myself to tru— Oh, never mind. Go dance with Alice and make her happy. Leave me here to worry in peace."

"I already asked her. She refused."

"She *did?*"

"She told me she was already promised for the next dozen

dances, but that maybe she could squeeze me in at the end of the evening."

Good heavens. Was Alice still trying to make him jealous, or had the advent of the Robinsons begun to mend her broken heart? "That's...a surprise."

"So you see that I'm quite free." He bent forward and, before she could protest, grasped her hands and pulled her to her feet.

"Kit, stop! You—you can't just drag me—"

"I'll have you know I'm considered an excellent dancer and will not step on your toes or tear the hem of your dress or anything like that."

"Kit—"

"Or is it that you're *afraid* to dance with me?" he asked softly.

She couldn't refuse now without making a spectacle of herself. But as he led her into the crowd of dancers, she began to wonder if he wasn't right. And when he put his hand on her waist and pulled her close, a fluttery sensation filled her middle. But it wasn't fear she felt.

She tried to will her heart to stop racing, but it would not cooperate. It pounded so loudly in her ears that she wondered if he could hear it too. When he'd held her back at Tahawus after the Shadow had passed, she'd been able to convince herself that her reaction to his embrace was gratitude. That excuse would not work here and now. What she was feeling right now, in the middle of a crowded dance floor, was sheer *want*.

She wanted the dance to last forever, to always feel his touch. She wanted it to end right now so that she could pull his face down to hers and kiss him. She'd wanted him since that moment in Newport when they'd met over a scattered bucketful of tennis balls.

All the weeks of pretending *not* to want him rushed through her in a flood, and she stumbled. His hand tightened on hers, keeping her upright, but he didn't speak. Did he sense what she was feeling? If she were to look into his eyes right now, what would she see?

Don't look, part of her mind told her. *You don't need to know.* So of course the very next moment, she lifted her eyes to his…and her breath grew short.

He knew. He knew because he felt it too. It was there in the way he gazed down at her, his eyes heavy and hooded, as if he were a second away from devouring her.

She moistened her lips. "Kit…"

He shook his head. "Later," he whispered and pulled her a little closer. His breath warmed her ear. She wished she could close her eyes and let her head rest on his shoulder, let the music carry them on and on and on, wrapped in each other's arms.

She and Kit Rookwood…it was ridiculous. Impossible. Alice and Newport loomed large between them.

But not right now. For as long as this dance lasted, they were together.

❦

Grace was awake long before breakfast the next morning. She slipped out of bed, dressed hurriedly, and tiptoed down the stairs and outside, leaving Alice gently snoring. She herself wasn't sure she'd even slept; they hadn't arrived back at Tahawus from the dance till after one. Alice had chattered cheerfully the entire drive home, which their driver, Mr. Kellogg, dryly thanked her for as "it kept the horses awake." Grace was grateful for it too; it had kept her from having to say a word.

Out in the dimness of the predawn, she stopped to listen. The trees were softly rustling into wakefulness, murmuring to each other of the taste of the day. No cold Shadow wind blew nearby, alarming them. Thank heavens for that. She strode up the road and under their welcoming branches.

No cold Shadow wind had blown last night, either, though she'd sat bolt upright in the wagon listening for it above Alice's prattle and willing the westering half-moon not to set too quickly. Whether their absence had anything to do with Kit's promise — No, how could it? What could he — or anyone — do to halt or ward off a Shadow?

She made her way to her hollow, more by feeling than by sight, and sat down at the foot of the balsam, leaning back into its cradling branches. Its sleepy thoughts brushed across her. *You are well?*

"I am, thank you." Grace let her head fall back and sighed.

But not at peace.

"No, I… No."

When would she ever feel at peace after last night?

Just a few weeks before, Kit had been her tormentor and Alice's boyfriend…but now everything had changed. All those weeks in Newport she'd thought she hated him. Now she wasn't sure what she thought. Was it possible to loathe someone and, at the same time, be attracted to him? Or was that part of why she'd hated him — because he had chosen Alice rather than her?

Except, it seemed, he hadn't. It appeared Mrs. Fish been right, and all the while he'd been kissing Alice in broom closets, he'd been wanting *her*.

The thought brought that funny feeling back to her midsection. After their dance he'd brought her back to her seat behind the bear and then disappeared. She'd sat there for an hour with eyes half-closed, remembering every look, every touch, until it was time to leave. He'd hurried forward to help her up into the wagon, practically shouldering one of the Robinson boys out of the way to do so, but wouldn't meet her eyes. Perhaps he was as confused as she was.

So many questions, so few answers. And the biggest one was this: did she truly want to lose her heart to someone who'd pretended for weeks that he'd lost his to someone else and wouldn't explain why? And never mind the fact that he was a human and she a dryad; she couldn't even begin to address that overwhelming question.

"You trees have it much easier than we do. You don't fall in love," she said aloud.

No, said the balsam after a long moment. *Not as you do, if I understand what you mean by 'fall in love.' But we care for our seedlings and our siblings and want them to thrive and grow. Is that what you mean?*

"Um...maybe a little. Not quite. Or...yes, but more. It's that, along with a longing—a thirst—that never stops, and the two are all entwined in each other."

That sounds...strange.

"Oh no, it's...well, all right, maybe it is a bit strange. But it's also wonderful." She curled her fingers into the leaf mold, remembering the feeling of Kit's hands on her waist, on her hand—

—and then she drew in a sharp breath, because suddenly her fingers weren't her fingers. They were something else, delving purposefully into the soil beneath the leaves.

Or at least it felt that way. They drew her in, down, questing, branching, farther, faster... Her eyelids fluttered, but all her senses seemed to have been re-routed to her hands: sight, hearing, even taste all resided in her reaching, trembling fingers. The soil was rich, old, full of many lives; she drank it in like wine, and like wine it made her lightheaded and dreamy. It was like that moment by the lake when she'd gone fishing with Ted and the children—only more so. This time, the feeling was deeper— sweeter—*ahhh.*

She surged ever downward, drawing deep into the velvet darkness...until she touched one of the balsam's roots. A shuddering thrill ran through her at the contact, and she reached out eagerly then, thirsting...

What is it? What are you doing? the balsam demanded. It sounded mildly affronted and more than mildly bewildered.

Grace still waited, balancing on the edge—her breath, even her heartbeat seeming to wait with her—it was so close, she was sure...

Nothing happened.

Tree-cousin! Grace!

Far off, one of Mrs. Hunter's roosters back at Tahawus gave its shrill morning call. And everything—Grace's breath and heart and hands—were as they had been, as if they'd never waited for a rapture that didn't come, had never reached for the force that flowed in this forest and tried to melt into it.

She pulled her hands from the soil, and they were only her hands. She buried her face in them then and drew a long, shuddering breath that was almost a sob. Now she understood what had happened—or hadn't happened. She had tried— unconsciously, instinctively—to settle herself into this forest, to join with it, just as Mum was settled into their woods at home and as all adult female dryads did eventually with the forest they would call their own. Only these woods did not know dryads, did not know how to accept a dryad's magic and guardianship so that they would always be one. She had tried to force herself on it.

"I'm so sorry!" she mumbled into her hands.

What are you sorry for, Grace? the balsam asked. It still sounded confused.

"I...tried to make you— I wanted us— I didn't know what I was doing!" She felt hollow inside and so alone. Aside from her shame.

I do not know what you were doing either, the balsam said. But I felt you...I did not know that you could do this. What was it?

"It's—it's what my people do. We join with you. We take care of you." Except that not all forests knew dryads. Not all forests needed—or wanted—them to do it.

You wish to take care of us?

"I—think I've fallen in love with you." A sudden picture arose in her mind—a house in these woods, just big enough for her and Kit. She would walk through the woods by day with him, hand in hand, and by night, in their little house… She swallowed hard. It would be glorious. Heavenly. And utterly impossible.

The balsam was silent for a long moment. *I do not know that I understand, but I felt…something. Was it the love that you speak of?*

"It might have been." Her head ached, and she was suddenly so weary that she could have curled up at the balsam's foot and slept till noon. "I'm so sorry," she said again. "I think I'd better go."

You do not have to, unless you wish to. You are always welcome here, Grace.

That made her want to cry. She climbed to her feet, then touched one of the balsam's branches. "I…that is…thank you."

⁂

She made herself go to the clubhouse for breakfast rather than slinking back to bed. As early as she was, Mrs. Roosevelt and the children were already there.

"Mr. Roosevelt arrives today," Mrs. Roosevelt announced. She did not look as though she'd only slept a few hours the night before. "Ethel and I are off to meet him for lunch at my friend's camp, not far from the Lower Works. I am assuming that Alice…?"

"She was sound asleep when I got up," Grace confirmed. "I doubt she'll waken before you're ready to go."

"Indeed." Neither Mrs. Roosevelt's expression nor tone of voice changed, but Grace suddenly felt guilty on Alice's behalf.

No wonder she so often felt alienated from her family.

She waved Ethel and Mrs. Roosevelt off in the buggy and thought about escaping to the woods for a walk, but the memory of this morning was still too tender. So instead she made her way out to the hammock with a book as camouflage, but only stared blindly at its pages until she fell into an uneasy, fitful sleep.

Alice drifted out of the camp shortly before lunch, leaning heavily on her cane. Grace watched her advance with concern. "Did you overdo it last night?" she called when Alice was in hailing distance. "Your ankle, I mean."

Alice shrugged. "Of course I did. But it was worth it. If I limp around today, it doesn't matter." She collapsed sideways into the hammock next to Grace.

"Did you have a good time? We never got to talk last night. You were in bed and asleep before I even had my slippers off." She'd had the distinct feeling that Alice was feigning sleep in order to avoid talking, but she couldn't say that. "You were definitely the belle of the ball."

"It was nice to have a little liveliness, though it wasn't Newport." Alice yawned. "Did I see you dance with Kit?"

Grace tried to analyze her tone. Alice had seen them dance, but had she *seen* them? Had the electricity between them been visible to everyone? "Once," she said cautiously. "He said you were too busy to give him a dance and that one of us had to."

"Oh, yes. I suppose I did say that, poor boy." She sighed. "Really, he was too obnoxious about it—tried to insist and all—but I simply couldn't squeeze him in. I don't mind telling you that...well, he's starting to get a little tiresome."

Grace sat up. "But I thought you—"

"Oh, I'm still fond of him, of course, but...well, one moves on, doesn't one? Anyway, I came out to tell you it's time to get ready for lunch."

Grace silently followed her back to the camp, her thoughts

whirling. After last night's dance, Alice might well have gotten over her infatuation for Kit...or she might still be trying to make him jealous. It was impossible to discern which. But if it was the latter, why wasn't Alice confiding in her?

As they followed Miss Young up the clubhouse stairs a short while later, Grace heard someone call her name. She turned and saw Mr. Rookwood, closely followed by another man she'd not seen before. "Good afternoon, sir," she said, letting her voice rise questioningly.

"Good afternoon to you, my dear. May I present my brother, Mr. John Rookwood? He's just arrived from the Lower Works— ah, you too, Miss Roosevelt."

Grace remembered his mentioning that his brother was coming and smiled graciously at the man. Mr. John Rookwood appeared to be considerably younger than his brother, no more than forty. Though they shared a superficial resemblance, there was a restless edge about the newcomer that the elder Mr. Rookwood lacked.

"How do you do, sir? I hope you'll enjoy your visit," she said.

"How do you do, Miss Boisvert?" John Rookwood shook her hand, then seemed reluctant to let it go. Was it her imagination, or did he examine her with a keener interest than seemed warranted? He barely glanced at Alice as they were introduced; instead, his eyes darted back to her. "I hear you're fond of walking. I am as well. Perhaps you'll show me some of the more interesting places to walk here."

Alice gave the faintest of snorts.

"Grace and I will be happy to take you walking, Uncle John." Kit, who had hung back with his mother, suddenly stepped forward. Grace looked at him, astonished, but his attention was focused on John Rookwood.

"Of course. I'm sure you've discovered any number of pleas-antly out-of-the-way places in the woods here." His smile was affable, but there was an edge to his voice.

Grace winced, both from embarrassment and because Alice had grabbed her upper arm too hard, digging her fingernails in. She moved it, and Alice let go.

"Most places in these woods are out-of-the-way," Kit said. He met Grace's eyes for a brief moment, then turned away.

"Where is Mrs. Roosevelt today?" Mr. Rookwood asked. He looked uncomfortable too.

Alice took Grace's arm again. "Gone to meet my father. He arrives today as well. Isn't that a coincidence?" She bore Grace off to their table, where Miss Young and the children were already waiting.

"I'm not sure I care for Kit's uncle," she murmured to Alice when they were seated.

"That's too bad. He seemed to take an interest in you." Alice didn't bother to lower her voice. "So will you take him walking in the woods?" There was a strange note in her voice, but her face was expressionless.

"Not if I can help it." She glanced over at the Rookwoods' table. John Rookwood was staring at her, so she looked quickly away.

⋯⋯

When they heard a buggy stop in front of the camp a few hours later, Ted and Kermit and Archie and Quentin all went flying out of the house to greet their father, followed at a more dignified pace by Grace and Alice and Miss Young.

But no Colonel Roosevelt was climbing down from it, only a subdued Ethel and Mrs. Roosevelt, who looked distinctly upset.

"Where's Father?" Quentin shrieked.

"He—he won't be here for a few days," Mrs. Roosevelt said. She looked up at Miss Young. "There was a phone message from him down at the Lower Works. He's gone to Buffalo. President McKinley—"

"Father says that someone shot the president!" Ethel announced to them.

Mrs. Roosevelt's knuckles tightened around the handle of her purse. "Ethel."

Miss Young paled. "Who could want to do such a thing to such a good, gentle man?"

"Is he dead?" Ted asked, his eyes wide. "Because that would mean—"

"He is *not* dead," Mrs. Roosevelt said quickly. "Your father naturally went there to be of whatever service he could to the poor man and Mrs. McKinley. He promised to cable us tomorrow with further news."

"Who shot him?" Alice asked. Grace felt a quiver run through her as she spoke.

"Some dreadful anarchist, Father said." Mrs. Roosevelt began to climb the stairs.

Miss Young came forward and put her arm around her. She let the younger woman lead her inside.

Silently, all the children went down to the river behind the house. The younger ones went immediately to the brook, the president already forgotten, but Ted and Alice looked at each other. Slow grins stretched across their faces, and Ted let out a whoop, then clapped his hand over his mouth and looked guiltily toward the house.

Alice felt no such compunction. She dropped her cane and seized his hands. They did a dance on the spot, until Alice stopped, wincing. "When do you think it'll happen?" she said, accepting her cane back from Ted. "Maybe Father's already president!"

"Alice!" Grace couldn't help being shocked.

"Grace Boisvert, I defy you to state that if it were your father, you wouldn't be wondering the exact same thing," Alice retorted.

"We'll get to live in the White House!" Ted said, grinning.

Grace left them still chortling and went back to the house. She slipped upstairs and threw herself on her bed. She lay for several minutes, staring at the ceiling, then jumped up again and went to her bureau and took out some stationery and her fountain pen, and sat down at the small table by the window that served as her and Alice's desk and dressing table. She swept aside a handful of hairpins, a slingshot Ethel had made, and a jar of cold cream, and started to write.

Dear Mum and Papa,

I know I just sent you a letter a few days ago, but I had to write again.

You will have already heard, but the news about President McKinley has only reached us here via telegram from Colonel Roosevelt, who was supposed to have arrived today but has instead gone to Buffalo to be with him.

I've never met President McKinley, or even seen him. But the idea that someone walked up to him and shot him simply because he disagrees with the government he represented—I can't understand it. I can sort of understand (if not condone) a man who robs another because his family is hungry or even kills him for personal revenge. But this doesn't make any sense, and that makes me afraid. How is it possible to live in a world where such horrible, senseless things happen?

Something else bothers me that I thought of when Mrs. Roosevelt said that Colonel Roosevelt was going to see if he could be of any help. I desperately wanted to go too, but what good would I be? Of what use are dryads, really, wandering around and talking to trees, when there are real problems in the world that need fixing? Maybe it would be better after all if we stopped worrying so much about keeping our lines pure and thinking we're so special, and just blended into humanity. Who would miss us, apart from the trees, maybe? And it's not like they particularly need us or anything, even if we heal them when they're sick and talk to them. There are so few of us, and so many trees. I've learned how many trees there really are, here in the Adirondacks.

I am sorry if this is upsetting to you, but I had to say it. I miss having anyone with whom I can really talk. This has been a long summer.

Grace stared down at what she'd written. Perhaps she'd better put a note at the top not to show this letter to Grand-mère.

We had a new arrival today, though not as exciting as the advent of the Robinsons whom I told you about. I don't believe I've mentioned my friends the Rookwoods, have I? (She certainly hadn't, lest the mention by name of a human boy make Grand-mère worry.) We met in Newport and they came up here as well. Mr. Rookwood has been very kind to me in particular—he says he is acquainted with you, Papa, and that he feels he owes it to you to watch over me. His brother, John Rookwood, arrived to join them today, and though he does not seem quite as pleasant as the other Rookwoods, I'm sure the addition of a new face will enliven things.

Alice's ankle continues to mend, no doubt helped by frequent doses of Robinson. She and her brother Ted are excited at the possibility that they might find themselves the children of the president of the United States, and while I understand their excitement, I hope it doesn't come true, because that will mean that Senselessness won.

Please give my love to Dorothy and Grand-mère and Sandy—I assume he's finally home for the start of school?

Love,
Grace

FIFTEEN

The telegram that arrived from Colonel Roosevelt the next day after lunch contained rather more encouraging news.

"The president's surgery was successful," Mrs. Roosevelt told them. "After the bullet was removed from his abdomen—"

"His *stomach*," Archie said. "An abdomen is just a stomach. One of the Porch Ladies told me so."

"You know better than to interrupt," Mrs. Roosevelt said sternly. "And *abdomen* and *stomach* are not truly interchangeable. As I started to say"—she frowned at Archie—"if the president continues to mend, then we may hope to see your father soon."

Alice leaned toward Ted. "Not if I can help it," she muttered. "I made some magics last night. We'll see how long he lasts."

Grace glanced at them, then got up quickly and went outside.

A tension had settled on the camp. It was clear to Grace that Mrs. Roosevelt had no wish to see her husband become president and be subject to the same danger that had nearly killed Mr. McKinley. Though the younger children didn't quite understand that, they were anxious to have the colonel, their favorite playmate, join them. And Alice...though outwardly she seemed herself, she was like a string stretched far too tight across a violin. Last night while they'd gotten ready for bed she had asked Alice what was troubling her, hoping that she'd break down and talk about Kit and the Robinson boys and what she was truly feeling. Alice hadn't answered, but had blown out her lamp and gotten into bed. They had both lain awake a long time, not speaking, which had never happened before in all the years of sleepovers at each others' houses. The silence had hurt.

Grace knew that she herself was making her own contribution to the tense atmosphere. John Rookwood had twice invited her to go walking with him. There was something repellent about him—something in the way he looked at her that made her want to cringe away from him. Both times she'd been saved by the children, who'd already claimed her for tennis practice or fishing, but she wouldn't always have an excuse to avoid him.

Except that morning. The only sign of life around Tahawus was the swaying of the Porch Ladies' rocking chairs across the road at the clubhouse. There was no sign of the Rookwoods either—not even Kit, who took seriously his father's behest not to let her wander alone in the woods. There would be no better time than now to slip away for an hour or two of solitude.

It was a dull, cloudy day, and the woods were shadowed and still. When she reached her hollow, she paused, but it was deserted. She went to the balsam tree and touched a branch tentatively, remembering the last time they'd spoken. "Hello, friend."

Tree-cousin Grace. You have not been here for some days.

"I've not been alone long enough to come and see you." And she hadn't wanted to—to force herself on the trees here, as much as she'd longed to visit them.

Perhaps that is a good thing.

A lump rose in her throat. "I'm sorry. I should not have come—"

Listen. Can you not feel it?

A prickly feeling ran across the back of her neck. "It feels…quiet in here today. Quieter than usual. Is that what you mean? I thought it was because of the weather. I can feel that rain is coming—"

A loud flapping made her look up. A crow landed on her rock and looked at her. "Sandwich?" it croaked.

Crow! "I'm sorry. I didn't plan on coming here today, or I would have brought you one."

"A likely story." Crow cocked his head to one side. "You're brave to come here alone."

"Brave?" An uneasy sensation prickled between her shoulder blades.

"*They're* about." Crow said. "And they're restless."

They could only mean one thing. She looked quickly from side to side, waiting for a blast of cold wind. "Are you sure? It seemed awfully quiet—"

Crow let out a harsh caw. "Not quiet. Silent. I think it would be best if you left, dryad."

Grace began to think he was right. Thank goodness the children were all at the camp; not even Ted was out fishing today. But others might be.

"Crow, will you do something for me?" she said.

"I might."

"Will you fly to the lake and come back and tell me if there are any humans near it?" If Mr. Rookwood was fishing there, he should be warned.

"What's it worth to you?"

"I promise that I'll bring you a sandwich tomorrow."

"Done," he said promptly. And didn't move.

"Well?" she asked after a moment had passed.

"There's a pair of humans on the shore. I saw them on my way here. Only the two, though there are others farther away in the woods, hunting."

Grace sighed and began to climb up the side of the hollow. "You couldn't have just told me, could you?"

"I wanted the sandwich." Crow laughed and took off in a flurry of feathers.

As she moved through the woods toward the lake, she listened more carefully and understood what Crow had meant about the silence. The usual hum of the trees talking with each other was almost nonexistent. A breeze fluttered past her. She tensed, but it died away—a true wind and nothing else.

She was halfway to the lake when the crunch of footfalls on leaves made her halt. John Rookwood appeared on the path before her, fly rod-less and smiling to himself like a cat that had noticed the dairy door had been left ajar. "Miss Boisvert!" he exclaimed, doffing his hat. "Are you out for a walk? I'm returning from one myself, but I'd be happy to accompany you farther."

"Is Mr. Rookwood still at the lake?" she asked breathlessly.

"How did you know he was there?" For a fleeting second, she thought he frowned. "But yes, he is. I can take you to him." He crooked his arm to her. "Or perhaps it's something I might help you with. I'm always happy to be of service to charming young women."

Grace tried not to wrinkle her nose in repugnance. "N-no, but thank you." She took a deep breath. "And really, if you were on your way back to the club, you need not accompany me. I'm sure I can find Mr. Rookwood—"

"Grace!"

She turned. Kit was running up the trail toward them. As he came closer she saw that his expression was tight and angry.

"Where are you going?" he demanded when he'd reached them.

John Rookwood looked at him with a faint air of amusement. "Miss Boisvert wishes to find your father. I was taking her to him."

"I'll do it," Kit said flatly. "No need to trouble yourself, Uncle John."

"No trouble at all, as I was saying to Miss Boisvert."

They stood glaring at each other. Grace felt frozen in the face of their silent struggle.

Then John Rookwood laughed. "Very well, Kit. I shall relinquish the pleasure of aiding Miss Boisvert this time. Your servant, madam." He captured her hand and bowed over it in a courtly way that made Kit grind his teeth (she could hear him), then left, not looking back.

Kit scowled after him; Grace guessed he was trying to master his temper. "So…have you and your uncle always been so close?" she asked.

He was startled into a short laugh. "It's gotten worse in the last few years. I don't think he likes the idea of my joining the family firm. Grace—" He caught her hands in his. "Keep away from him. He's…he's not to be trusted," he finished, though she was sure he'd been about to say something else.

"Don't worry. I'd already decided I didn't much care for him— Oh!" She gulped. "All this drove it out of my head—we've got to get to your father. The Shadows are out again—they're near the lake—"

He let go of her hands and began to propel her down the path back toward the club. "In that case, you're going home."

"But Kit—your father!"

"I'll go warn him. If those things are around, I don't want you anywhere near them," he said sternly.

"Kit—"

"Grace." There it was again—the look she'd caught a glimpse of as they danced the other night…but this time it was more than a glimpse. "Please go," he added quietly.

She went.

Colonel Roosevelt finally arrived on Wednesday evening. The children were practically exploding with excitement, particularly Ted, who had brought down his first deer a few days before. As the buckboard pulled up, they went tumbling out of the house to greet him.

"What? Where did all these bunnies come from?" Grace heard a raspy baritone voice call amid the happy shouts. She followed Alice out onto the porch. It had rained heavily earlier in the day and a drizzle still fell, dripping from the eaves. The colonel could barely be seen among the children hugging him and tugging on his arms. But even in the growing dusk the famous gold pince-nez was visible, and the large, white teeth, displayed now in a delighted grin.

"Hello, Father," Alice called above the din. "Welcome to Cocktail Hall!"

The colonel's eyebrows rose. "What did you call it?"

"Oh, didn't you know? That's the camp's nickname. Someone told me at the dance last week." She smiled sweetly at them all.

Her father sighed. "Leave it to you to discover that, Sister." Then he caught sight of Grace, hanging back behind Alice. "Ah, your friend from Boston. How do you do, Miss Boisvert? How is your family? Your father was a few years my senior and already through Harvard, but we knew each other."

"It's an honor to meet you, sir. My father asked to be remembered to you."

"Why don't we let your father come in out of the rain?" Mrs. Roosevelt said. "Theodore, dinner is in less than half an hour, and we need to change."

"So we do, Mother. All right, you little ruffians, begone!" he said with mock ferocity but caught Ted's arm to hold him back while the others scattered. "I'm proud of you, son, getting your first deer. A clean shot, Mother tells me."

Ted gulped and nodded. "It was. They took a photograph—"

"Did they? We'll have to send copies to your aunts and—"

"Theodore," Mrs. Roosevelt said.

It was only one word, quietly spoken, but Colonel Roosevelt jumped guiltily. "Sorry, Mother. I'm coming." He darted up the stairs, flicked Alice's cheek with one finger as he passed, smiled at Grace, and went inside.

Grace took a deep breath after he'd gone inside. "He sort of drags all the air after him, doesn't he?" she commented.

Alice bristled. "He does not! He's—" Then she smiled sheepishly. "All right, he does. But no one's allowed to say things like that about him except me." Her mouth turned down. "I should have gone and shot a deer too. Then he might have been glad to see me."

Grace sighed. "Maybe 'Welcome to Cocktail Hall' wasn't the best way to greet him."

"Oh? Since when do you know my father so well?"

She met Alice's eyes levelly. "I don't. But you've told me how your uncle died."

Alice looked away. "I was only trying to be funny," she muttered. "No one understands me."

"I do," said Grace, holding out her hand. But Alice had already gone inside.

The other guests of the club seemed to share her opinion of Colonel Roosevelt. When they sat down to supper that evening, conversation in the room became loud and general. The colonel seemed to enjoy the attention and answered questions about the president's condition with such optimism that Grace felt better than she had for days. By the time the dishes had been cleared and coffee poured, the entire room was hanging on his words.

All except one person. Kit hardly looked toward their table all evening. He'd even shifted his chair so that his back was to them, which struck her as odd. But the colonel's conversation distracted her from pondering it for long.

"It's a shame that degenerate Czolgosz had to ruin the president's visit to the Pan-American Exhibition," he was saying. "Not to mention my vacation. I have lost time to make up here. What do you say to climbing a mountain, Mother? I've always wanted to go up to the top of old Cloud-splitter."

"A climb up Mount Marcy? That sounds like fun," Jim McNaughton said wistfully.

"Join us then! Anyone else?" The colonel's grin flashed around the room.

"If he's going, we are too," Beverley Robinson declared.

Grace looked at Alice. A family outing might be a good thing for her right now…and having her trio of swains along would surely make the prospect more attractive. "I would like to go," she said. "What do you think?"

No. Don't go, a small voice whispered. It made her start with surprise—who had said that? She glanced at Alice next to her, but it was clear she hadn't spoken; on her other side, Kermit was drinking his milk. Had she imagined it?

"Hmm," Alice said. When everyone reluctantly began to leave their tables, all of them—at least it seemed like it—stopping to speak with the colonel on their way out, she made her way to the Rookwoods. Grace trailed after her, warily.

"Kit," she called. "I want to talk to you."

He turned and waited for them politely, but something about the set of his shoulders told Grace that he wished he were anyplace but there. "Good evening," he said as they came up to him. "You must be pleased to have your father here."

Alice ignored that. "Come with us. To Mount Marcy, I mean."

His eyes flickered to Grace's, then fell again before she could read what was in them. "Thank you, but I don't like to intrude on a family party."

"It's no such thing. The Robinsons and Jim McNaughton are coming, and they're not family." She looked at him keenly from under lowered lashes.

"Then it isn't...but I'm afraid I still can't go. We have an expedition of our own planned—"

"Some fishing down on Schroon Lake." John Rookwood, who had come up behind Kit, clapped him on the shoulder. "Though your trip sounds much more intriguing. I'm tempted myself to jump ship and join you." He looked at Grace. She shivered.

"What *is* it with men and fish?" Alice rolled her eyes, then gave Kit her most winning smile. "Oh, come with us. You know you want to."

Kit didn't smile back. "Next time, maybe. Good evening." Abruptly, he turned away, pulling his uncle with him.

"Well!" Alice tossed her head. "Some gratitude. Anyone else would have been dying to go mountain climbing with the vice-president."

"That's not fair," Grace said. "If he'd already promised his father he'd go, he couldn't really back out."

"Hmmph." Then Alice smiled, unpleasantly echoing John Rookwood's expression. "I'm astounded that Kit's uncle didn't throw them over after all to come with us. I think you've got an admirer—"

"Don't. Just *don't*." The very thought of such a thing made her feel ill.

Alice sniffed. "Well, you're in a mood tonight." She turned and began to thread her way back to the knot of people around her father.

"Grace?" Kit had reappeared next to her. He glanced quickly around, then spoke in a low, urgent voice. "Grace—do *you* have to go on this trip?"

"What? Yes, of course I do. Why?" She looked at his bleak expression and remembered. "Oh, God, the Shadows."

He rubbed his forehead as if it hurt. "Yes, the Shadows."

"I didn't think—climbing Mount Marcy sounded like a fine idea when Colonel Roosevelt suggested it. But I *have* to go. Someone has to look out for everyone. I know I can't do anything," she said as he opened his mouth to protest. "But I can at least watch and—and warn." She glanced over to where Colonel Roosevelt stood. The crowd around him had thinned, and Mrs. Roosevelt had gathered the children in preparation for leaving. "It'll be all right. If things get bad, I can make us all come back to the club." She looked back at him. "Shouldn't you be careful as well where you're going?"

"I'll be fine—" He broke off as she raised an eyebrow at him, then grudgingly smiled back. "All right, point taken. But I still wish you would stay here…or better yet, go home to Boston."

"Boston!"

"If that's what it would take to keep you safe, yes."

She wasn't quite sure how to interpret that. But before she could decide, he glanced behind him. "I have to go. Be—be careful. I wish…" He shook his head, gave her one final look, and left.

They left the next day at noon in what seemed to Grace like a parade: in addition to her and the seven Roosevelts and Miss Young (Quentin had been left in the care of Mrs. Hunter), the Robinsons, and Mr. McNaughton, there were also two guides, Noah LaCasse and Ed Dimick.

"Are we going all the way to the top of the mountain right now?" Archie asked. "'Cause I can't see it." A fine, misty rain was falling, obscuring the hills and even the tops of the taller trees at times. "An' I don't know how we can climb it if we can't even *see* it."

"Don't worry, it's still there even if you can't see it. Right, Noah?" The colonel clapped the guide on the shoulder.

"Last I check, it was there." Mr. LaCasse's French-Canadian birth was evident in his accent. "Don't you worry, it's too big to lose." His moustache twitched in amusement.

Grace wasn't sure if she was worried or not about the fact that they couldn't see very far; poor visibility went both ways, though she doubted Shadows needed eyes to find them. She shivered, though she wore a sturdy wool serge divided skirt, riding boots, and both a snugly belted cardigan and a waxed canvas coat and hat to help keep off the rain.

It was five miles up to their first stop, Lake Colden, where they would spend the night before climbing to the top of Mount Marcy tomorrow morning. Despite the weather, everyone seemed to be in good spirits, though Grace wasn't convinced that Alice's weren't mostly a sham. To her relief, not much actually happened on their hike. Alice laughed and chattered to "her" boys; Archie used globs of pine sap to glue pine needles to his upper lip so that he could "look like Father and Mr. LaCasse;" Ted cut her a stout walking stick and bounced back and forth between walking with her and the adult men, whose company he felt entitled to join now that he'd proven himself as a hunter. Even the trees had little to say; their overheard murmurings were all about the autumnal taste of the drizzle that afternoon. At one point Grace was sure she had spotted Crow, but as she couldn't call out to him to make sure, it was difficult to discern whether it was her acquaintance or a more mundane bird.

The last part of the day's journey was via canoe across the lower part of Lake Colden to their campsite — two small, log-built cabins lined with rough bunks. Mr. Dimick took Ted and the Robinsons to cut balsam boughs to spread in the bunks, while Mr. LaCasse built a roaring campfire and made a start on preparing supper.

"Branches. We're sleeping on tree branches," Alice said, standing in the doorway of the cabin designated as the ladies' dormitory.

"I know." Grace grimaced, but for a different reason. Although trees didn't feel physical pain and wouldn't suffer to have limbs lopped off, she would rather have slept on bare ground.

"And I suppose we get to pee into a hole in the ground behind a tree somewhere."

"Yup!" Ethel said brightly, edging past Alice with an armful of balsam. "There's even a plank with a hole in it to sit on, but it's all slimy because of the rain. It's all right if you put some branches down on it first." She dumped her armful on a bunk and began arranging it. "Want me to show you where it is?"

Alice shuddered. "Thank you, but I'll just cross my legs."

Fortunately, supper was more pleasant than the sanitary arrangements. Mr. LaCasse was a skilled campfire cook and produced potatoes baked in the ashes and sizzling steaks and hot coffee. After they'd eaten and rinsed their dishes in the lake, Mr. LaCasse related some funny anecdotes about his life as a woods guide, and Colonel Roosevelt told ghost stories.

"If *someone* is not able to sleep tonight, he's staying with you," Mrs. Roosevelt said, nodding to a wide-eyed Archie sitting at her feet and clutching her skirt after the colonel had told a particularly gruesome tale.

"Nonsense. He knows that it's all moonshine," the colonel said heartily, but beckoned to the boy and held him on his knee, encircled in one arm.

"What about you, Mr. LaCasse?" asked one of the Robinsons, who appeared not to have heard Mrs. Roosevelt. "Surely you must have a spooky story or two about the woods, considering how long you've been guiding."

Mr. LaCasse had just finished filling his pipe. He put the end of a stick in the fire till it caught, then used it to light the tobacco.

"I have," he said after the pipe was drawing to his satisfaction. "More than one or two."

"Won't you tell us one?"

Mr. LaCasse silently puffed for several seconds. "No," he finally said. "This is not a good time nor place to tell stories like that. No telling what might be listening. But let me tell you about the feller I was guiding down Santanoni way, who was telling all and sundry about the two-foot bullhead he said he'd caught down in Lake Harris—"

Grace pulled her sweater more snugly together at her throat and was glad that Mr. LaCasse had declined to tell any of his "spooky" stories. Their campfire in the midst of the dark woods felt like a beacon; no stars or moon shone from above to distract unfriendly watchers from its light. She was grateful when it started to drizzle again, and they all retired to the cabins for the night. Even so, she lay awake listening to the night sounds of the woods long after Alice and Mrs. Roosevelt and Miss Young and Ethel and Archie had gone to sleep on their beds of balsam.

SIXTEEN

Grace blinked into the blackness. Why was it so dark and cold, and what was poking into her side?

And then she woke a little more and remembered where she was. She shifted the boughs beneath her, then pulled up the blankets that had slipped over the edge of her bunk, but it was no good. Something had disturbed her sleep, and it wasn't a tree branch.

She sat up and squinted around the cabin. Dryads had better-than-normal night vision, so she could see that everyone who was supposed to be there was in their bunks. Now that she was fully awake, she remembered that it had felt like someone had called her. Might one of them have called out in their sleep? But they all appeared to be slumbering peacefully. It must have been a dream…but she somehow had the feeling it hadn't been.

She slid carefully from her upper bunk so as not to disturb Alice below her, swiftly pulled on her skirt and sweater over her chemise and drawers, then tiptoed barefooted across the cabin floor to the door. Pushing it open, she peered through the gap.

A beam of light struck her full in the face, dazzling her. She gasped.

"I wasn't sure that you'd heard me," said Kit's voice quietly.

He closed the shutter on the lantern. "I'm sorry if I blinded you."

Grace clung to the door, glad she hadn't shrieked. When she could see again, she slipped outside. "What are you doing here? I thought you were going to Lake Schroon," she whispered.

"I came to talk to you. It's urgent," he added as she opened her mouth.

She hesitated. "All right. But not here or we'll wake everyone in camp."

He nodded and took her hand. He led her toward the lake, then along its shore, where it was easier to walk quietly in the soft, sandy earth, cold on her bare feet. It had stopped raining, but the sky was still low and heavy with clouds. A faint, uneasy wind rustled the branches of the heavily slumbering trees above them. Grace felt strange moving among them and not feeling their awareness of her, their usual quiet acknowledgement of her presence. It was like she had become invisible. Or a ghost.

When they were out of all possible hearing of the cabins, Kit stopped next to a young beech. He hung the lantern from a low branch and opened one shutter. His face was so somber as he turned to her that she was moved to ask, "Has something happened?"

"No." Then he laughed shortly. "At least, not yet."

This didn't sound like Kit. "Then what's so important that you had to come five miles on a mountain trail in the middle of the night to tell me about it?"

He was watching her face intently. "That I love you."

The unreal feeling that she'd had moving among the trees intensified. Or…no, she was dreaming. She had to be. She was back in the cabin, in her bunk among the balsam boughs, and in a moment she would turn over and awaken —

But the cold earth under her feet and the drip-drip-drip of moisture from the trees made it clear that she was not. "Are… Did you say what I think you said?"

He smiled a little, but the intent look in his eyes never wavered. "Yes, I said I love you. Don't sound so incredulous." He grasped both of her hands and drew them to his chest. "I fell in love with you about five seconds after I first saw you at the Casino. I couldn't tell you then. But you have to know now."

"But—but Alice—" she began.

"Oh, hang Alice! I don't give a fig for her. It's *you* I love." He gave her hands a little shake to emphasize his words.

She took a deep breath, and another. "But I *do* give a fig. Why did you make up to her and seem to hate me in Newport if…if neither was true?"

"Sometimes I did hate you, actually." He gave her a wry smile. "At least I tried to, because I wanted you so badly. Why do you think I tried so hard to beat you at tennis that day? I thought that if I did, then maybe I'd be able to get you out of my head. And I wanted to throttle poor Livingston and any other man who even looked at you, no matter how angry I made myself feel at you."

So *that* was why he'd been so rude to poor Tom all the time. "But Alice—"

"Can't we please forget about Alice for now?"

"No. She's my best friend, and you made her fall head over heels in love with you, and now she's miserable because she's afraid you don't feel the same way about her. What will she do when she finds out that it's true?" She lowered her voice. "Oh, Kit, why? Why did you do that to her?"

He had avoided her eyes while she spoke. At her question, though, he squared his shoulders and looked at her. "It wasn't my choice."

Grace drew in a quick breath. "You mean someone else told you to make up to her?"

He nodded, looking unhappy.

"Dear God! Kit, that's—"

"A rotten thing to have done. Do you think I'm proud of

myself, even though I didn't have a choice? And all the while I knew you were watching—and judging." He looked away quickly. "I'm sorry, Grace. If my telling you the truth means that you'll hate me, I…I don't know what I'll do."

Grace opened her mouth, then closed it. It was like she'd been looking at a picture, and then someone had turned it ninety degrees so that she realized it was completely different from what she'd thought she'd been seeing. Kit had been making up to Alice because he'd been told to—by whom? And why? *Why?*

"This is… I don't know what to say," she finally said.

"Don't say anything, then, except…oh, Grace, please…give me some time to sort this out. I'll make things right with Alice somehow. She'll probably hate me forever—and I'll deserve it—but it will be over. Will you wait for me? Because I'll wait for you…well, forever. I *love* you," he said again, quietly but firmly.

She shook her head. "I'm—It's—" And then a horrid thought struck her. "You don't… It isn't because I'm…well, *pretty*, is it?" Could he be another Tom after all, enchanted by her dryadness?

"Grace." He shook his head. "Give me more credit than that. Of course I like to look at you. But that's not who *you* are. I love Grace, not Grace's exterior." He tilted her chin up with one finger so he was looking directly into her eyes. "Please—this is important. You don't have to understand now, but listen and remember. Something's going to happen, and I want you to know that it's none of my doing—"

"What's going to—"

"Ssh." He touched her lips. "I can't explain now. It will also likely happen that people will say false things about me when I'm not there to defend myself. That's when you have to remember that I love you." He paused. "I'm asking you to trust me."

Trust him. "Kit," she whispered.

He glanced up at the sky. "I have to go soon. Oh, Grace."

He pulled her toward him, closer than they'd been at the

dance…and then his arms were around her and her cheek was resting against his shoulder so that she could hear his heart beating strong and fast, and they were pressed together, so warm that in another minute she would melt into him—or he into her. His breath quickened, and she felt his cheek against her forehead. "Oh, Grace," he said, so softly—and something inside her rearranged itself.

She knew her feelings for him had been changing; their dance at Hewitt Lake had shown her just how much. But wanting him was only part of the matter. Could she trust him, after he'd hurt and deceived Alice—and her too? He was asking her—begging her—his arms felt so good, so right…and yet, was she *sure?* Alice had had these arms around her as well and had probably felt the same way. Why couldn't he tell her what was going on? Until he did, she would wonder if his embraces of her, too, had been at someone else's command.

But she couldn't pull away.

She lost track of how long they stood there, but her icy feet eventually reminded her of their existence. She shifted them, and Kit pulled away. Without a word he led her back along the shore by slender beam of light from his lantern, until they were near the cabins. They stood by the banked campfire, close but not touching.

"Will you be able to get back all right?" she whispered to ease the tension.

He nodded wordlessly, looking at her. And then he set down the lantern and took her in his arms again. But this time he bent his head to hers, and then he was kissing her, gently and slowly so that she didn't pull away but stayed still, astonished by the feeling of his mouth on hers, firm and smooth and then softer, warm with his breath. It seemed to go on forever and yet it didn't, and when he drew his head back, her lips felt the chill night air and longed to be warm again.

He brushed back a stray wisp of her hair. "That's the third

time I've kissed you," he murmured. "Doesn't doing something three times mean it's true?"

She tried to concentrate, but her head felt like it had after she'd drunk a glass of champagne at her first party in Newport. "Wh — when were the other times?"

"I kissed your hand when we first got here. Remember?"

Yes — when they were fishing up at Lake Henderson, when poor Ted had been so shocked, but — "When was the other time?"

"When I dove off the Livingstons' boat to rescue you. You were unconscious, I think, and everyone else was so busy getting the launch out to us that they didn't notice a quick kiss right here." He touched her temple and smiled into her widened eyes.

"But you yelled at me right afterward!"

"Because you'd scared the hell out of me. You don't know what a struggle it was not to hug you to pieces in front of everyone on the launch after they'd pulled us aboard. I had to use that fear to make myself angry and stop myself."

So Mrs. Fish had been right. Grace opened her mouth, but he'd already released her, caught up his lantern, and started back down the path toward the lake. She watched him go, because at that moment she was incapable of motion. She wished she could call out to him to tell her more, to explain. What did all this mean? And what was going to happen that he couldn't tell her about?

She shivered and waited, but the night and sleeping trees around her held no answers to her questions. She crept back into the cabin and climbed into her bunk, onto the slowly bleeding balsam boughs, and lay awake until a gray, drizzly dawn slowly filled the woods.

⚬⚬⚬

They ate breakfast sheltering from the heavy drizzle under the imperfect umbrella of a tall balsam. Grace nibbled her biscuit and ham sandwich and stared across the water, wondering where Kit was. Was he lying in his bed back at Tahawus thinking of her, just as she was thinking of him, or had the Rookwoods already left for their fishing trip?

The heavy chill of the morning managed to subdue even the Roosevelt children, who ate their breakfasts almost silently. Mrs. Roosevelt watched them and finally announced, "I think we're going to leave the mountain climbing to you, Theodore. The children had their night in the woods, but I think that was enough for them."

"No it wasn't," Archie muttered, then sneezed. Miss Young looked at him anxiously.

"Well, I'm going on," Ted said. "I want to climb a mountain for my birthday." He was turning fourteen that day.

"And so you shall," Colonel Roosevelt said, clapping him on the shoulder. "Gentlemen?" He looked at the Robinsons and Mr. McNaughton.

"We're going on," Herman said. "It would take more than a little rain to stop me."

"Stout lad!" The colonel turned to Alice. "And you, Sister?"

Alice was drinking from her tin coffee mug as he spoke. She lowered it and met Grace's eyes for an instant before looking away. There was an expression in them that Grace couldn't decipher. "I wouldn't miss it for the world," she drawled.

A heavy mist settled in as they finished packing their canvas rucksacks and re-lacing their boots; combined with the rain, it reduced visibility to a matter of feet. But Mr. LaCasse was unconcerned. "I know the way," he assured the dubious Robinson boys. "You won't fall off the mountain while I'm with you."

Grace was pleased when Alice fell into step beside her, rather than with her entourage. She'd been oddly silent all morning, but that had suited Grace's own mood. She was still thinking about Kit, wondering what it meant…but underneath the thought ran a quiver of uncertain elation. He loved her. Did that elation mean she loved him too? Tom's declarations had never made her feel anything but a little sad—

"Ow!" Next to her, Alice had stumbled.

Grace caught her arm. "What happened?"

"My ankle. It hurts."

Her ankle! Of course it must hurt after walking five miles yesterday. "Oh Alice, I forgot! We probably should have stayed with your mother. Do you want to go back? I'm sure your father will underst—"

"No," Alice said shortly. She shook off Grace's hand and they continued walking in silence, while Colonel Roosevelt and the others chatted cheerfully ahead of them despite the rain and gloom.

Grace adjusted the brim of her hat so that it didn't drip down the back of her neck and squinted up at the clouds covering them, wondering if she could risk sending them off elsewhere so they could have a more pleasant walk up the mountain. But that would take time and concentration, which she wasn't sure she had enough of. The trail was steeper and more difficult than yesterday's, with rocks and roots and fallen branches and thick, sucking mud puddles slowing progress—hard enough for her but worse for Alice, and she had to be alert to help if Alice needed it.

Then there was the nagging memory of Kit's words—his "something" that might happen. Had he meant that it would happen now, today, or when they got back to the club? Why couldn't he just have told her what it was?

Finally, there was the worry that somewhere out there, the Shadows might be lurking, hating this human intrusion onto their mountaintop. But with the rain and fog, it was even harder to watch for them. Why hadn't she tried to dissuade them all from this trip after all, instead of blithely coming along? Alice's pace was slowing; already it was getting harder to see the rest of their party through the water-filled air.

"Are you sure you're all right?" she asked Alice after another half mile.

Alice didn't speak for a moment. "Oh, I'm dandy," she finally said. "Even though it appears I've lost something. Or maybe it was *stolen* from me." She looked sideways at Grace.

Grace frowned. "What are you missing?"

"For one thing, I missed some sleep last night. Someone woke me up. Someone putting on her clothes and sneaking outside, who left the cabin door ajar." Alice's voice was full of barely contained fury.

Oh. Grace stood still as understanding swept over her.

"So now I know why Kit's barely looked at me. When did it start? Here or Newport? Maybe at Mrs. Rennell's party when I was too sick to notice? Did you plan his coming here then?"

"It's nothing like that," Grace said desperately. How could she explain about her and Kit to Alice when she couldn't even explain it to herself? "I had no idea the Rookwoods would follow us up here. And I did *not* steal him from you. I *did* hate him. I don't anymore, but I still don't know what I feel about him—"

"Oh, I *see*. Is that why you were kissing him? To see if it would help you decide?"

"I didn't kiss him," Grace protested. "He kissed me."

Alice looked at her bleakly. "Is that supposed to make me feel better?" To her horror, Grace saw that she was crying—Alice Roosevelt, eldest daughter of the hero of San Juan Hill and one half of the Trouble Twins of Chestnut Hill, was crying.

"It just keeps happening. Everyone shuts me out—first my family, and now my best friend and the boy I loved. I should be used to it by now, shouldn't I?" She started to sob. "I've been holding it in all morning. Every time I looked at you, I wanted to hit you."

Grace watched her helplessly, standing in the rain with her

face buried in her hands and shoulders shaking. Oh, Alice. The flirtatious, brash young sophisticate she'd tried to be in Newport was gone, leaving a sad, angry girl. A tendril of mist drifted by, making her look ghostly and distant though they stood only a few feet apart—

"Where are the others?" she said, lifting her head.

"I don't care." Alice's voice was muffled against her hands.

"I can't hear your father or Mr. LaCasse or the boys anymore."

They both stood still, straining to hear. But the only sounds were those of the rain and a faint breeze rustling the leaves.

"They've left us!" Alice said, clutching her arm. "We're lost!"

"We're no such thing," Grace said bracingly. "Hush and let me listen some more. I thought I heard them just now."

She hadn't, but it suddenly seemed that pushing this rain and fog away might be a good idea after all. She took a deep breath and reached up to push the fog back up and the clouds and rain faster along their easterly path—

—and hit something. Something was blocking it, holding the bad weather here over them as firmly as if it had been nailed down. And the only thing that could do that was magic. But it was like no magic she'd felt before. There was a menacing edge to it that made her recoil and half raise her hands to ward it off.

"What are you doing?" Alice demanded.

"N-nothing." Grace made her voice sound as ordinary as possible. "Look, I know it's foggy, but I'm sure we can catch up if we hurry. The trail isn't too hard to follow." Something was wrong, and she didn't want to be alone out here with that layer of malevolent magic over them.

"I can't hurry. My ankle hurts."

"Don't you want to find your father? Can't you please at least try?"

"Why should I do anything for someone who steals her best friend's boyfriend?"

"This has nothing to do with me. Alice, *please* —"

"Hello!" a voice called. "Who's there?"

Grace whirled around and peered into the fog. That had sounded remarkably like— But it couldn't be. "Hello?" she shouted. "Here! We're here!"

Two shapes emerged from the dense whiteness behind them, from the direction of Lake Colson and their camp—two familiar shapes.

"Well, well," John Rookwood said. "What have we here?"

SEVENTEEN

"Mr. Rookwood!" Grace felt limp with relief. Of all the people who might have appeared, he was by far the most welcome, except maybe for Kit. She hurried to him, then stopped. "I thought you'd gone to Lake Schroon?"

He took her outstretched hands and gripped them reassuringly. "We had to postpone our trip. But what about you? Where is the rest of your party?"

Grace looked at John Rookwood and Alice. "Would you excuse us for a moment?" She pulled Mr. Rookwood a short distance away. "We got separated from Colonel Roosevelt and I'm worried," she murmured to him.

"So I gathered. What troubles you, my dear?"

"That." She gestured up at the sky. "There's something not right about it. Something is holding this weather in place over the mountain. It..." she took a deep breath. "It doesn't feel as if it means anyone well."

He stood with his hands behind his back, gazing down at the ground as she spoke, so that she could not see his face. Now he looked up, eyebrows raised. "You can feel that? How interesting.

To what do you ascribe this…ill will?"

"I don't know. I worry that it has something to do with the Shadows."

"I see," he said slowly. "Have you felt any of them this morning?"

"No. And maybe that's a good thing. It—"

"It certainly is!" John Rookwood had come up behind them. "We worked damned hard all night to put as many of them as we could find up there. You didn't give us much time."

Mr. Rookwood closed his eyes and winced. "John, I wish you would let me deal with this."

"And I wish you'd left it to me. We'd probably have been done by now and cozily back in civilization again." His eyes flicked over Grace.

Grace's body suddenly felt detached from her mind. Only her ears seemed to be capable of working as usual, but they had to be wrong. They *had* to be. "Mr. Rookwood?" she whispered, fighting down rising panic.

He glared at his brother before turning to her. "My dear Miss Boisvert." His voice was calm and soothing. "I see it is time I did some explaining."

"Y-you did this?" She gestured at the sky.

He gave a small cough. "Yes, we, er…did."

"But—how? Unless you're—"

John Rookwood made her an ironic bow. "We are Isham and Rookwood, Inc. at your service, magical consultants at large, offering our unique expertise to businesses and individuals alike who require—"

"Be quiet, John." Mr. Rookwood did not raise his voice, but his brother stopped speaking at once.

"Excuse me," Alice said loudly. "In case you've forgotten, I'm here too, and I'm getting wetter by the minute while you're standing there yammering."

"My apologies." Mr. Rookwood raised one hand and made a short, sweeping gesture, and suddenly it was not raining where they stood, though it continued to fall all around them. Alice's mouth fell open.

"Now then," he continued. "We are wizards, as I believe you were going to say. And as my brother said, we are business consultants who perform services for those who require them."

"For a thumping good fee," John Rookwood put in. Mr. Rookwood sighed.

"Services…with your magic," Grace said as calmly as she could. Mr. Rookwood — the Rookwoods — wizards!

"That is correct."

"Are you performing a service for someone right now?"

"We are completing one. The primary part has already been accomplished."

"Primary part?" John Rookwood said derisively. "Not if you ask me—"

"I didn't, John. We are not paid to have opinions. How many times do I have to remind you of that?" His expression remained unperturbed, but his tone had sharpened. "You will please escort Miss Roosevelt back to the cabins by the lake."

"But we were climbing *up* the mountain," Alice protested. "And anyway, we have to find my father. He'll be worried. Grace, tell him. He listens to you."

"He'll worry less if you're somewhere comfortable and dry with the rest of your family. After you're safe at the cabins, I promise that we will find him and let him know," Mr. Rookwood said kindly — too kindly. Grace heard the command in his voice and saw Alice's brow smooth and the tension in her shoulders release.

"All right," she said and docilely accepted John Rookwood's arm. A piece of whatever sheltered them all from the rain broke off and followed them.

Grace took a deep breath. "I heard what you did to her."

"I'm merely sparing her some anxiety and taking her out of harm's way. I wish to speak with you alone, and neither my brother nor your friend would have contributed to the conversation." He held out his arm to her. "Shall we start down as well? Mount Marcy is no place for a young lady today. Even if she *is* rather an unusual one." He raised one eyebrow at her and smiled.

Grace didn't move; indeed, it took all her will to remain standing. "You know what I am?" she asked in a small voice. No one—no one who wasn't another dryad, anyway—had ever known what she was.

He looked at her with concern. "Please don't distress yourself, my dear! You did nothing to compromise your secret—in fact, you are to be commended for your discretion. It's part of my business to be as well-informed as possible, which includes knowing that the Boisverts are one of the few remaining pure dryad families in the United States. No, I haven't actually met your father—you will, I hope, forgive me that small prevarication."

Grace remembered the night of Mrs. Rennell's party and how he'd examined her under the light of the torch…and remembered something else too. "Kit," she whispered. "He's… Is he…?"

"Yes, he is a wizard as well—and an excellent one." For a moment, a father's pride in his son shone in his face. "You don't know how pleased I am that he's old enough to join us as junior partner. He's a far better wizard—and far more level-headed— than my brother." He opened his mouth to say something more, then seemed to think better of it, instead taking her arm and gently guiding her back down the mountain path.

Grace let him because she was busy trying to readjust her view of the world…but mostly, she was thinking about Kit. "Does he know what I am?"

"Yes, though he didn't until I told him, that night in Newport before we all left." His voice was kind. "And no, he's never been affected by your dryad allure. He's too advanced for that, though my brother is not. I must apologize for his behavior at times around you."

Grace barely heard him. Kit knew! A surge of emotion welled up in her—excitement and something else. If he knew what she was and still loved her, then… "Where is Kit?"

"Around." Mr. Rookwood made a vague gesture. "As I said, we are at work right now. This is his first undertaking for us. He's keeping watch."

The glow dimmed. "You're working with the—the Shadows?"

"I've been studying them ever since we arrived. My 'fishing' forays on Lake Henderson provided me time for that, just as your sketchbook gave you time with the trees."

Grace remembered Crow telling her how the Shadows had been gathering at the lake. "I can't imagine what you'd want to do with them. They terrify me."

"I can't say I enjoy their company either." He smiled wryly. "But they will prove to be remarkably helpful, I think. They were quite interested in you, you know."

"In me?" She shuddered. "Why?"

"They were drawn to you from the first. They're always attracted by power, though they had never seen your particular type before. I, too, find it interesting. Very interesting."

Grace shook her head. "I have no power to speak of. You must know that if you know dryads. We look after our trees. That's all."

"Ah, I beg to differ, Miss Boisvert. You possess many useful magical skills. You have power over plant life. You can control the weather and hide in the shadows of trees, and—ahem!—you possess a certain attractiveness to human men that renders them easily swayed. You may have noticed my brother's reaction to you; I don't believe he's aware of it, but I noticed it immediately on your meeting. These are all qualities that would be of use in my line of work—and that list does not include the power of your own intelligence and personality, my dear. I've observed that you've got a Changer quite tamed."

"What? Oh, Crow? He's not tamed. He just likes to talk to me. Mostly I think he likes the food I bring him."

"Changers almost never interact with anyone else, including their own kind. To call them loners is vastly understating the case." He smiled at her astonished expression. "Furthermore, they don't need to eat. Yours has convinced you that it does so that you'll keep coming back."

"Good heavens!" So Crow liked her, did he? But that wasn't what was important right now. "Um…Mr. Rookwood, are you offering me a *job*?"

"Why be so surprised? I'm a successful businessman, as you might have gathered from your time in Newport. I know a good thing when I see it. In addition to your other attributes, you're level-headed and certainly know how to keep a secret." He gazed into the fog and added, "I'm sure Kit would be pleased if you joined us. You are young yet, but in time… Yes, I want you to join me, Miss Boisvert. I want you to become part of Isham and Rookwood—as a full partner, someday, if you so choose, along with Kit."

Full partner, with Kit. She bowed her head to conceal her expression. "May I ask, sir, what business it is you perform? Who hires you, anyway?"

"It varies, of course. Our current client is a repeat customer. You would certainly recognize his name if I said it. He takes a strong interest in current national and international affairs—it's his job, you might say." He smiled. "Others of our clients are less well known. They come to us and ask us to perform certain tasks. We decide if we can perform the required actions without compromising ourselves and our business and if they can be done to the clients' satisfaction. If so, we agree upon a price and a timetable. Our greatest asset is our discretion. We have never yet failed to complete a commission to a customer's satisfaction. If we feel we cannot successfully do our job, we won't accept the commission."

Something about his careful phrasing made her uneasy. "That's impressive, I'm sure…but what sort of things do you *do*?"

"Many things." He looked at her sideways and seemed to reach a decision, "For an example, there was an occurrence in Havana Harbor a few years ago that you might have heard about. That was one of ours."

An occurrence in Havana Harbor… She gasped. "You blew up the *Maine*?"

"My brother did. He enjoys travel and likes to take on our commissions in exotic locales. I'm more of a homebody, though in my defense it can be said that I'm some years older than he is, and besides, Mrs. Rookwood does not like me to be away from home for long," Mr. Rookwood explained apologetically, then gave a small laugh. "Not that Buffalo is a particularly exotic locale. John was not pleased with having to stay there as long as he did after we left to see the job done, but one does what one must do."

Buffalo? And then an icy shower, far colder than the rain around them, seemed to run down her back, and she stopped walking. "The president," she said. "You got that man to shoot him."

"Not quite. Czolgosz had already planned to shoot the president. We merely made sure he succeeded. That is how we work; we find a suitable tool at hand and use it. We rarely, if ever, find it necessary to intervene directly."

A sick feeling made her throat close up. She noticed that she still held his arm and snatched it away as if he were made of fire. Kindly, courteous Mr. Rookwood, whom she'd felt so comfortable and *safe* with, was a—a…

"I know what you are thinking," he said. "I am not a

murderer. I hold no opinion or rancor. I merely do what I am hired to do. That is all."

"But—"

"Do you remember not long ago how we talked about black and white and gray? In my world, there is no black and white. The world is full of judges, as you may have begun to notice, but there is a strange thing about them: one man's black is another man's white. I choose to see neither, Miss Boisvert. I see all gray."

Her breath was starting to come in gasps. She bent, hands on thighs, and fought to control it, all the while feeling his sympathetic gaze on her…and that was the worst part—that he did feel sorry for her. He was a pleasant, courtly gentleman who also happened to be a cold-blooded assassin-for-hire. And with his magical abilities, a very successful one…except—

"But it didn't work, did it?" she said, straightening and looking at him defiantly. "The president is still alive and is getting better. The colonel said so."

"The colonel is mistaken. His wound is not survivable. I expect that he will be dead by this time tomorrow if not sooner. Which still leaves the second part of my commission."

"The second part—?"

"I believe I already mentioned that there were two parts to our present commission. The president is dead, or will be soon. That leaves the vice-president." He watched her for a moment, as if to guess what her reaction would be. "I have a dozen Shadows caught in a web above us—they're what you felt when you tried to move the rain. When the moment is right, they'll be released…and their release will blow Colonel Roosevelt off the top of Mount Marcy. It will be a tragic accident, nothing more."

Grace gasped. "Does Kit know what you're doing?" But she knew the answer before he opened his mouth. She remembered how Kit had avoided shaking Colonel Roosevelt's hand and kept his eyes averted from him. Kit knew.

"Kit was a great help. He laid the groundwork for us by befriending Miss Roosevelt in Newport in order to gain access to the family, though I feel he could have managed her with somewhat more delicacy." Mr. Rookwood shook his head. "It was his first assignment, so a degree of fumbling was understandable, if regrettable. Now, may we go on? Time is not in long supply today."

She let him propel her along, her thoughts racing. Kit had told the truth—he *had* been compelled to pretend to fall for Alice. And he had warned her that something was going to happen…and that he was not a part of it. Mr. Rookwood obviously did not know that Kit had changed his mind about helping to murder poor Colonel Roosevelt…and she would not tell him, since she would not be part of it either. How could Mr. Rookwood do such terrible things? It was difficult to believe, no matter what she'd heard from his own lips.

"We're nearly back to the cabins." Mr. Rookwood's voice broke into her thoughts. "It will be necessary for John and me to return to the mountain quickly. I trust you'll be coming with us?"

"What if I say no?"

"Then I will be forced to lock you and Miss Roosevelt up for a few hours while we complete our commission. After that? I am not sure. I will have to discuss the matter with Kit and John. I had assumed your response would be something other than I suspect it might be." There was a slight questioning inflection to the end of his sentence.

"My answer is no," she said firmly.

"I see." He sighed. "I like you, Miss Boisvert. Believe me when I say that the offer to join us was not made lightly on my part…or on Kit's," he added.

A few minutes later they came to the cabins. There was no sign of anyone but Alice and John Rookwood; Mrs. Roosevelt and the children must have already started back to the club. John

Rookwood looked questioningly at Mr. Rookwood, who shook his head. He laughed harshly.

"Another task your son botched," he said. "You should have left her to me. I'd have had her properly in hand."

Grace froze. What had he just said about Kit?

"Enough, John." Mr. Rookwood sounded distinctly irritated this time. "Ladies, you will oblige us by going into one of the cabins."

Alice seemed to have woken up from the spell of docility Mr. Rookwood had cast on her. "I should like to know what is going on here, Mr. Rookwood. Your brother has been excessively rude and will not permit me to go anywhere nor tell me anything."

"My apologies, Miss Roosevelt. Will you kindly enter a cabin?" His voice was as mild as ever, but that commanding edge was back in it.

Alice stilled. "Yes, sir."

"You'll want Miss Boisvert to keep you company, I expect."

"Yes." Alice reached for her. Grace lunged to avoid her, but Alice grabbed her arm and began to pull her inexorably toward the cabin.

"Alice, wake up! Don't listen to him!" Grace tried to squirm out of her grasp. She had to get away from them—had to warn Colonel Roosevelt—

"Please do not resist, Miss Boisvert," Mr. Rookwood said quietly. "I do not think either of us would like to see this become…unpleasant."

"Alice!" She let herself go limp, hoping to break her grip. But Alice didn't even blink, and dragged her bodily into the cabin. The door closed behind them with a dull *thunk*, leaving them in gloom relieved only by the small blocks of light where the chinking between the walls' logs had fallen out.

"All right, we're in here! Let me go!" Grace fought to free herself until Alice stirred and seemed to waken.

"Wha — what are we doing in here?" She frowned at Grace. "Why are you lying on the ground? You're all muddy!"

Grace scrambled to her feet and went to the door. It wouldn't budge. She tried to push the latch-bar up, but it might as well have been glued in place.

"What is going on here?" Alice demanded.

"We're being kept out of the way." Grace suddenly remembered that Colonel Roosevelt was not only the vice-president but also Alice's father. She sat down wearily on one of the bunks. "I ruined it. I should have said that I would join them and then maybe I could have found a way to stop them, but I didn't think of it till just now —"

Alice sat down, not too near her, on the bunk. "Stop who from doing what?"

Grace opened her mouth to reply and quickly closed it. What could she say that Alice would understand…or believe? She had to say something… "The Rookwoods — they… They're not good people —"

Alice gave a bitter little laugh. "I already knew that. About one of them, anyway."

"I'm talking about Mr. Rookwood and his brother." She took a steadying breath. "They're…assassins. They arranged to have President McKinley shot and are going after your father next, right now. They…uh…they're going to try to push him off the top of the mountain and make it look like an accident. That's why they locked us in here. We've got to get out and stop them." She went to the door and gave it another experimental push. It didn't budge.

Alice rose too and paced back and forth — which was all of about five steps in the cramped cabin. "I don't believe it," she said.

"It's true. Do you think I'd make such a thing up?"

"I don't know anything anymore. For example, I thought you were my friend —" She turned away. "How do I know you're not making it up? You seemed awfully friendly with Mr. Rookwood."

Grace closed her eyes. Yes, she had been. That's why it hurt so much. "He lied to me. You're not going to like this, but Kit… His father told him to—to make up to you back in Newport. It was a way for them to try to get to your father—"

"Shut up!" Alice whirled around and gave her a shove. "Shut up, shut up, shut up!"

"Alice—"

"You lie. Everything is a lie." She dropped to the cabin floor and drew her knees to her chest, sobbing brokenly against them.

Oh, Alice. Grace bent toward her but didn't dare touch her. "I'm sorry. Maybe I shouldn't have told you that, but the Rookwoods— You have to know how bad they are. They really do plan to kill your father, and you've got to help me figure out how to get out of here so we can stop them." She hesitated. "We're the Trouble Twins, remember? We can do it."

Alice only sobbed more loudly. Grace stared down at her shaking shoulders, and despair washed over her. Alice would not—or could not—help her. She would be stuck here while the Rookwoods let the Shadows loose on Colonel Roosevelt. All her life, she'd have to live with the knowledge of her failure.

And something else troubled her, something that she couldn't stop hearing and re-hearing in her mind's ear: John Rookwood's voice saying *Another task your son has botched*. Had Kit been playing her too, just like he'd played Alice, because his father had told him to?

Kit had warned her about this very thing. Why should she believe anything John Rookwood said, especially about Kit, whom he seemed to dislike so much?

But the only time the ever-serene Mr. Rookwood had come close to losing his temper was when John Rookwood had said that. Was it because Kit had "botched" ensnaring her or because John Rookwood had said something about it in front of her?

Neither alternative offered any comfort. Which should she trust—Kit's word, or what she had seen?

"Kit...he never did love me... H-he played me like a piano, and I f-fell for every minute of it," Alice suddenly said through her sobs.

The eerie echo of her own thoughts startled Grace—and filled her with resolve. They had to get out of here, not only to save Colonel Roosevelt but to confront Kit. "Never mind him," she said and this time put her hand on Alice's shoulder. "Help me figure out how to get out of here. Your *father*, Alice. We have to help him."

Alice looked up at her through her tears. "You— You're serious? They're going to try to kill him?"

Grace restrained her impatience. "Yes, if we don't do something about it." She didn't try the door again; Mr. Rookwood had obviously sealed it with some powerful magic she had no chance of breaking. That left the log walls, the rough plank floor, and the roof, also of rough planks.

The logs were beyond her power to affect; dead wood was dead, even to a dryad. The floor was impenetrable. But the roof... If she lay on one of the top bunks, could she kick at the roof and loosen the planks? She climbed up into one; her toes barely brushed the roof's underside. Bother!

She rolled onto her side and thought for a moment, then started picking at the chinking between the logs. Whoever next slept in this bunk would curse her for letting a draft in, but she had to see—how near were the nearest trees? Did any have branches close enough to the cabin that might be able to help?

But the clearing around the cabins was too wide. Grace checked each side, but no tree was close enough to help unless it fell on the cabin—which was not a viable solution to their dilemma. Which just left— "Help! We're trapped!" she called out the crack.

"Don't do that! What if the Rookwoods come back?" Alice had risen and was staring at her.

"If the Rookwoods come back here, it means they won't be up on the mountain trying to kill your father. And maybe your mother and Mr. Dimock aren't so far away yet that they won't hear us."

"Oh." Alice crouched against the wall where there was an open chink. "Halloooo! Help!"

They moved from side to side of the cabin, calling from each direction. It felt futile, but Grace had to do *something*. And once or twice, while Alice called *hello!*, she herself called *crow!* She had no idea where Crow might be or if he would respond to her call, but it was worth a try.

They continued calling. Grace's voice started to give out but Alice's continued strong…until something thumped above them, followed by a scratching, scrabbling sound on the roof.

"What was that?" Alice whispered.

The scratching sound continued, and suddenly Grace felt a change in the air around them. She drew in her breath; the room was growing lighter. The cabin door was slowly opening.

"Grace, the door!" Alice was up on her knees.

Grace took a step toward it. Had Mr. Rookwood's spell failed? She couldn't believe that… Or was this a trap, and John Rookwood was standing just outside the door, ready to smother her with a silk scarf and drop her body off a steep part of the path?

Alice had no such concerns. She was out the door before Grace could warn her to be careful. "Hey!" she heard her call. "Anyone there?"

Grace tentatively followed her out. The rain had slowed again to a fine drizzle, but the fog was thicker than ever. There was no one in the clearing. Alice stuck her head in the door of the other cabin. "No one's here," she said wonderingly.

A loud *cra-a-a-awk!* made them both jump. A large black bird was perched on the ridgeline of the cabin above them. It watched them for a few seconds then flew up into a nearby tree, where it could be barely seen through the mist, and cawed again.

"Crow," Grace breathed. So he *had* heard her! Not only that; he'd managed to open the door. Mr. Rookwood had been right—the Changer was her friend.

"Yes, it's a crow," Alice said impatiently. "Hey, where are you going?"

Grace was already ten paces up the trail to Mount Marcy. "To try to save your father."

* * *

It was plain before they'd gone half a mile—to more or less the same place where they'd met the Rookwoods, Grace couldn't help noticing—that Alice was slowing them down. Her sprained ankle, overused yesterday, would not permit her to go at more than ambling speed.

They both stopped, though neither had said anything. Alice spoke first. "I don't know what I could do to help anyway. You at least have two working legs."

It was not a time to say anything but the truth. "I don't know if I have any chance either. But I have to try."

Alice nodded. "I... Thank you." Her face took on a slightly pinched look, as if she were trying not to cry. "It's not fair. He's *my* father. I should be the one to save him. That's something else you get to have that I don't."

Grace bowed her head, because there was nothing to say to that. "I should get going," she said eventually.

"Yes."

They looked at each other. "Good luck," Alice whispered fiercely, then turned away.

"Can you find your way back to the cabins in this fog?" Grace called after her.

"I think I know the way by now. I—I'll wait for you there until…until it's time to go."

Grace nodded. They exchanged one more look, and then both turned and set out on their separate paths.

EIGHTEEN

It was a few minutes before Grace realized that Crow had come with her. She could just see his dark shape through the mist, flitting from tree to tree as if he were showing her the way — which, she soon realized, he was. They had left the trail, marked by recent boot prints (the colonel's, or the Rookwoods'?) and gone straight into the trees, which grew shorter and tougher and scrubbier as she climbed. She assumed it was a quicker route up the mountain though it certainly wasn't an easy one, clambering past boulders and skirting ravines and pulling herself up steep slopes slippery with wet leaves. The rain waxed and waned and waxed again, and the mist swirled, growing colder as she ascended. Thank Yggdrasil that Crow seemed to know where he was going; though dryads had excellent senses of direction, she wasn't sure that she would have been able to find her way through this wilderness on a day like this.

Curiously, Crow would not speak to her. Granted, he was usually on the wing, and she imagined that talking while flying might not be an easy thing to do. But the times she spoke to him while he perched in trees, waiting for her, he only cocked his head at her, then flew on.

"Cat got your tongue?" she finally said as she rested for a moment after scrambling through a boulder field. "Why can't you turn into a mountain goat and carry me the rest of the way?"

He made a chuckling sound and flew to another tree, leading her onward. All she could do was hope that he wouldn't lead her into crossing paths with the Rookwoods…at least not before she was ready for them. Because she was going to have to confront them or the Shadows they'd gathered in the very near future.

She could feel the presence of the Shadows more plainly now, infuriated at their confinement. The sky above her crackled with energy like an approaching thunderstorm compressed into a small space. Did the colonel not feel it hanging above the mountain, or Mr. LaCasse—

A sick feeling flooded her. It wasn't only the colonel who was in danger. It was Mr. LaCasse. The Robinson boys and Mr. McNaughton. Ted. *All* of them might be blown from the mountain when the Rookwoods loosed the Shadows—a blast of cold wind, like the one she'd felt in the woods but multiplied twelve-fold, would strike them as they stood on Marcy's summit and sweep them away. Freak winds happened in places like this; it would be a terrible tragedy, especially in the wake of President McKinley's death, but it would be a comprehensible one.

So her task was straightforward enough—free the Shadows if she could, and at the same time keep them away from Colonel Roosevelt and the others. Straightforward…and all but impossible.

"Wait, Crow," she called, and stopped to reach out to touch the branches of the scrubby balsams around her, most of them no taller than she was. Their fresh, sharp scent was muted here, as if it was too precious a commodity to waste in releasing to the air. "I'm afraid," she whispered.

A ripple of surprise went through them. *You are the man who speaks to trees,* one of them said.

It is Grace Tree-Cousin, said another. *Our kin down below, where the water lives in lakes, have spoken of you. You are far from your sleeping place.*

Grace thought of the balsam in her hollow; no other tree in Tahawus had learned her name. "I'm chasing the Shadows. I have to stop them."

Another wave of surprise, tinged now with doubt, made her already shaky courage ebb further. *Stop them?* said a tree to her left. *They cannot be stopped.*

"But I have to!"

We know them. We inhabit this place with them. They dwell here because there is nothing to trammel them. They are angry now because something is holding them. We do not know what it is.

"I do," Grace said. "Some men are using them for their own evil purpose, and I have to stop them. Which means stopping the Shadows."

They cannot be stopped. They are too powerful. When they move over the land, it is in a great cold, toothed wind.

"I know. I've felt it."

The tree fell silent. Then a different one spoke. *We do not try to oppose them. When they roar over us, we hold firm with our roots and let them blow over our branches.*

"Cra-a-ak!" Crow said. It was clearly a warning.

"I have to go. I—I hope I shall speak with you again soon," Grace said and climbed to where Crow sat. "Are the Rookwoods here?" she asked nervously.

Crow did not reply, but flew farther up the slope and looked at her expectantly.

"Yes, I'm coming. I suppose I was talking too long, but couldn't you just have said so? I wish you'd talk to me. It's not like you, and it's giving me the willies."

So was the fact that the trees were growing shorter and

bushier, making her feel more and more exposed. She knew with the rational part of her brain that the dense fog provided cover even while it kept her from being able to see, but rationality was not winning. Then the trees stopped being trees and became waist-high, then knee-high scrub, growing in thick islands in the gray stone, and she knew she was nearly at the top of Mount Marcy.

Instead of flying, Crow now hopped along the bare rock, which alternated smooth, weathered, lichen-speckled expanses with patches of rough cobble and boulders. Grace followed him cautiously, listening for voices. Walking here was disorienting—she was on top of the highest mountain in the state with nothing around her but fog-filled air. Heights did not usually trouble her, but she found herself looking down at her feet as she walked to avoid vertigo.

"I hope you know where you're going," she muttered to Crow.

He seemed to. He took her to a sheltered spot against a low rock face. She huddled there, grateful for something solid to lean against. "All right, Crow," she said after catching her breath. "Now what?"

There was no answer but the ever-restless wind that swirled the fog around her and the angry, buzzing roar she sensed from above.

"Crow?"

Nothing. Had he abandoned her here, now when she most needed an ally? "Crow!" she called, a little more loudly.

But Crow had vanished.

For a long moment, she struggled not to cry as her fear threatened to overcome her. But what help would Crow have been as she faced the Shadows anyway? Now she was alone, just her and the Shadows and the colonel and the Rookwoods all about to converge in this place. It was time to decide what she would do when they did. If she found Colonel Roosevelt first, she could maybe warn him and the others to leave the mountain and take shelter, if he would listen to her…a large *if*, since running away was not his usual response to danger. And what if she *didn't* get to him before the Rookwoods did?

Think, Grace! If only there were some way to turn the Shadows against them. But first she had to free them—except that she had no idea how they had been trapped. She was only a dryad with a dryad's magic, not a powerful wizard.

For a few brief seconds the fog billowed and lifted, and she saw that she was actually still some way from the summit. Gritting her teeth, she left the shelter of the rock face and, step by step, shuffled her way up. She came to a patch of low, scrubby vegetation and crept into it, crouching near its edge in the lee of a boulder. She still couldn't see though the thick mist, but maybe up here she'd be able to hear if—

A hand fell on her shoulder. "My dear Miss Boisvert, you astonish me," Mr. Rookwood said behind her.

⁑⁂⁑

Grace did not scream, though it was a near thing. Instead she stiffened and did not stir, even to look behind her. "Mr. Rookwood," she acknowledged, rising to her feet, and was glad to hear that her voice barely shook.

He came around to face her. "As greatly as I esteem you, I did not think it would be possible for you to escape the closure I put on the cabin," he said, and she realized that he did not sound angry or even annoyed—only puzzled and perhaps a little admiring. Good—let him wonder how she'd gotten out. She did not answer, but shrugged her shoulders.

John Rookwood suddenly loomed out of the fog. "No sign yet. I— What the devil! How the hell did she get here?"

"I imagine she walked, John," Mr. Rookwood said. "I will

keep an eye on her while you keep looking for Colonel Roosevelt."

"I've got a better idea. I'll keep an eye on her and *you* go look. Maybe you'll be able to find Kit while you're at it. I'm damned if I'm going to work with him again anytime soon, Henry." He grinned at Grace. "We can make ourselves very cozy here."

"I daresay you could, but you won't. I will remain here. I concede that Kit perhaps isn't ready to take on more duties, though you may recall that he performed his earlier role in this commission more than adequately." He looked sternly at his brother. "Go."

John Rookwood went, muttering under his breath. When he had disappeared into the mist, Mr. Rookwood sighed. "Do you see what I have to work with? John is a competent wizard but sadly lacking in several other qualities, among them common sense and decorum. I would give a great deal to have someone working with me who possesses those qualities." He looked at her.

Hadn't he given up? "I'm afraid my answer is still no, Mr. Rookwood. My mind hasn't changed in the last few hours."

"I see," he said softly. "I had hoped your presence here meant..." He was silent for a minute. "Perhaps I have been approaching this the wrong way. I would be prepared to give a great deal to have you in my firm."

"There's nothing you could offer me that would possibly change my mind."

He raised an eyebrow. "Not even Kit?"

Involuntarily, she met his gaze—and could have kicked herself when she saw the quiet satisfaction there. She'd given herself away.

"I saw the two of you when the Shadow escaped us and blew past you that day," he said almost gently. "It was clear what your feelings—both his and yours—are. I think that I can presume to speak for Kit if I say that he would welcome partnership with you.

In all senses of the word."

But I don't know that I love him! part of her protested, even as another part gloated *Kit could be mine!* It was a third part of her, however, that finally answered him. "Mr. Rookwood, I'm afraid my gray vision is not as developed as yours, and I don't think it ever will be — not enough to do what you do anyway. And Kit… Why should I take Kit under these circumstances? If I ever… If Kit and I are ever together — and note that I said *if* — it will be because we choose each other. Not because you've given him to me."

To her surprise, he smiled. "You are still very young, Miss Boisvert. It's easy to forget that in light of your other qualities."

"What does my being young have to do with any of it?"

"'Gray vision', as you call it, tends to develop with age and maturity."

"No. My father or mother would never see as you do."

"Are you sure? Do not be so quick to make such assumptions, because you can never know what motivates a person at the deepest part of his or her soul. And as for Kit…there are no guarantees in life. The bird in hand generally *is* worth more than two in the bush — "

"Henry!" John Rookwood was there, his voice hoarse with excitement. "He's here!"

Mr. Rookwood's manner underwent an abrupt transformation, from the courtly gentleman to something harder and more stern. He pushed her down into the scrubby growth. "Watch her."

A faint scent of balsam drifted up to her, along with a wondering, *What manner of creature are you?*

Startled, she stared down at it and realized that what she had taken for some scrubby alpine plant was in fact a patch of balsam fir, growing as tall as conditions here on top of the mountain would permit it.

"I'll do better than watch her." John Rookwood turned toward her, bending as if he intended to hoist her over his shoulder. "There's a nice drop-off a few yards that way."

Grace froze.

"You will do as you're told," Mr. Rookwood said coldly. "Kindly restrain your penchant for violence. It is not an asset in our business, as I have frequently been forced to remind you."

"What are we going to do with her afterward? She's a witness. We can't let her—"

"We will worry about that later. I am confident that, given time—"

"She'll be joining us shortly?" John Rookwood finished, mimicking his brother's measured tones. "Well, I think you're wrong…and even if you aren't, I don't want to work with her unless you give her to me. Then I might reconsider." He gave her a look that made her skin crawl.

"She's not a pet dog to be given to anyone."

"Except your precious son, who doesn't know how to handle her. Sorry, Henry. I get her, or it's over the mountain with her."

"And if you do that, what about Miss Roosevelt? We must assume Miss Boisvert has told her what is going on here. I will not jeopardize the success of this commission with an unnecessary occurrence just to satisfy your vanity."

Occurrence. Throwing her off a mountain cliff to her death would be an "occurrence."

"No," she whispered and let her terror and grief and helplessness flood out of her at the gentle touch of the balsam.

The balsam absorbed her fearful thoughts. *I am low and cannot hide you, though I would if I could, for you are kin. I know others of my kind are tall, not far away, if you could reach them. But I can only do what I can do here.*

"We're wasting time," Mr. Rookwood suddenly said, cutting his brother off in mid-sentence. "If anything happens to Miss Boisvert while I'm gone, I will not be pleased, John. And in the meanwhile, you might take a moment to reflect on who owns the majority of this partnership." He disappeared into the fog. Scowling, John Rookwood leaned back against the boulder.

Grace leaned toward the balsam. "I have to do something!" she muttered.

But what? It was her same old complaint—what were dryads good for? What was *she* good for? She couldn't do anything useful.

Why not? asked the balsam. *Why is what you can do not valuable?*

"Because...well, it isn't. Dryads look after trees. What use is that against the Shadows?"

"What?" John Rookwood jerked his head toward her. She bent over her knees, pretending to sob, and heard him make a wordless, derisive sound.

We do not oppose them. We hold fast with our roots and let them blow over our branches.

The words of the tree she had spoken to on her way up the mountain floated through her head, and she caught her breath. They did not oppose the Shadows...but when the Shadows had passed, they were still there. She did not have to stop the Shadows—she only had to let them blow past her.

"Help me!" she whispered to the balsam around her, shifting so that she could untie her boots. "You weather the storms and wind here. Lend me your strength!"

Overhead, the Shadows seethed. She could imagine Mr. Rookwood out there in a sheltered spot, lying in wait for the colonel for the perfect moment to release the Shadows. They would sweep him off the mountain in their headlong rush from their fetters. She couldn't stop them—but if all she could be as a dryad was a guardian, then she would shield the colonel and the rest of them—and hope that she could hang on.

She finished wiggling her boots and socks off and climbed quickly to her feet. John Rookwood tensed. "Don't try to run away, dryad. All you'll do is give me an excuse to toss you overboard." Bloodlust vied with a different kind of desire in his expression as he looked at her.

"I'm not going anywhere," she said. Quite the contrary.

The rough balsam spread around her feet, clinging hard, rooting into the thin soil that was mostly particles of weathered rock. If it could root there, she could too.

She closed her eyes and pressed her bare feet down into it, toes wiggling into the rocky soil. *Please. Please...* This time, she knew she could not stay to become the forest's guardian. But she could borrow it for a little while, perhaps...

And just as she had on the bank of Lake Henderson and again in her hollow, she felt herself reach down through the rocky soil and into the mountain, deep and deeper, surging downward into its very heart. *Help me. Tree and soil and rock, give me your strength. Help me hold fast.*

And the balsam did. She felt strength flow into her, not only from the patch at her feet but from the waist-high scrub below and from the small trees she'd spoken to below that. She took a deep breath and felt it surge through her, glowing —

And then a sound — no, not quite a roar but a dark echo of one, as if a photographic negative could be sensed through the air — rolled over the mountain. It might well have been mistaken for a distant rumble of thunder, but she knew better. Mr. Rookwood had released the Shadows. Whatever was about to happen would happen soon.

"Ha!" John Rookwood had felt it too. He braced himself against the boulder and squinted up into the sky.

The temperature dropped. Grace flung her arms into the chill air and remembered the chestnut trees of home who had always watched over her. *I protect what is below.* Dryad. Guardian.

"What the hell are you doing?" John Rookwood grabbed for her.

She threw her head back and shouted "Here!" to the Shadows. Her feet rooted deep into the ancient stone of the mountain…and then her outstretched arms seemed to grow as well, branching out longer and wider until she was sure that she had twenty arms, not two—and they spread wide, weaving and intertwining, sheltering the top of the mountain and everyone on it.

And then the Shadows sensed her in return. Bursting out—how had Mr. Rookwood been able to restrain them?—they screamed down toward the top of Mount Marcy like an angry swarm of bees, wanting only to destroy anything in their path. And right now, she was the largest *anything* on the mountain, shining like a beacon with the power lent her by the trees and blended with her own.

She braced herself for the blow, for the freezing blast that cracked limbs and uprooted trees. It hit her like a wall of ice; winded, she could not even cry out. The blizzard gust whirled and shrieked, tearing at her with malevolent gusts.

She gasped for breath as her branches creaked and bent and strained under the onslaught. But they would not break.

With the Shadows' cold came their contempt for the living, their anger, the dark, despairing empty *want* that was at their core. It ripped at Grace just as their wind did, flaying her hope, her confidence, her self, till tears ran down her cheeks and froze on her skin. She was nothing; she had defied her family, deceived her acquaintances, destroyed her best friend's happiness—

But her roots sank deep into the mountain, and the trees around them whispered her name, not letting her fall into the blackness at the Shadows' heart. She wavered and ached. But she would not let go.

And then a great wind, a cold hurricane, seemed to rush down the side of the mountain, howling in defeat. Grace heard the rustle and clatter of the branches of tens of thousands of trees as it passed. Then all was still.

Grace opened her eyes, expecting to see her upraised arms turned into enormous branches spreading across the mountaintop, and saw that they were still arms clad in a waterproof coat, not bark. Above, the clouds had drawn back, taking the mist with them, and an endless panorama of tree-covered peaks could be seen around them like a great green, undulating sea. The sun emerged, lighting it all with a golden warmth.

And then she collapsed into the balsam beneath her.

John Rookwood dropped as well, taking cover behind the boulder. The Robinson boys stood not thirty feet away, backs to them, marveling at the view that had suddenly opened up with the clouds' dispersal. "What did you do?" he said from behind gritted teeth.

A large black bird descended from the sky and landed on the boulder above them and looked down at Grace gravely.

"Crow," she said, squinting up at him. "I did it."

John Rookwood frowned. "That's no crow. That's—"

But Crow exploded into flight, flapping up and out into the empty space between the mountains, and vanished from view. Grace watched him, then looked at John Rookwood.

"Go," she said to him. "There's no reason for you to be here."

"The hell there isn't!" He reached into his jacket and pulled out a small pistol. "I'm not going to let you get away with making a fool of me!"

Everything seemed to move very slowly. Grace looked at the pistol, at its dully gleaming steel barrel aimed at her throat, then followed John Rookwood's overcoated arm to his face. His features were distorted with anger and frustration. But the hand holding the pistol did not waver.

"Oh, yes, my delicious little dryad," he murmured. "Be afraid." He leaned forward and drew the muzzle of the gun along the edge of her jaw in an obscene parody of a caress.

She had thought she was herself again, no longer connected to the trees and their vast reservoir of power. But as she felt John Rookwood's pistol on her skin, a tide of anger rose in her.

"No," she mouthed. Then, more loudly, "No!" She met his eyes and let her anger burn into them. He opened his mouth to speak—and it stayed open.

She pushed the gun away. He let her, eyes still fixed on hers as if he'd been mesmerized…and she realized that that was precisely what had happened. It was like what she'd done to poor Tom Livingston back in Newport, but without any intention to Captivate—only to command. And with the trees' strength still thrumming within her, she realized she could make him do *anything*. Like stand up and flap his wings like a chicken. Or go and confess what he had done to Colonel Roosevelt. Or throw himself off the top of the mountain…

Her breath caught. John Rookwood was the most loathsome person she had ever met. If she made him jump off the rock face he himself had threatened to throw her over minutes before, Isham and Rookwood would lose one of its partners, and she would have prevented probably dozens or hundreds more presidents from being killed and battleships from being blown up. She would be doing the world a favor, and all it would take was one horrible man's death—

Black and white, Miss Boisvert? Or gray?

For a long moment she stared at him. If she did make him jump off the mountain, then she might as well find Mr. Rookwood and join Isham and Rookwood on the spot. She would be the same as him.

"Give that to me," she said quietly.

He handed her the gun, eyes still fixed on hers. A string of drool rolled out of his open mouth.

"Now—go. Do not let anyone see you. And leave this place as

soon as you possibly can."

Without hesitation, he dropped to all fours. He crawled to the shelter of another boulder, and another, away from the group nearby admiring the view till she could no longer see him.

She collapsed into the balsam scrub, welcoming its rough prickles, and found enough strength to tease a shadow from under it to conceal herself. She lay still for a long time, staring up at the milky, rain-washed blue of the sky. She heard Ted's eager, "There! Look over there!" and the colonel's repeated, "Beautiful country! Beautiful country!"

But she also felt the clouds that had been scattered by the Shadows' departure regathering, and in a matter of minutes the sun had vanished and a cold mist had descended—though it lacked the icy threat it had held before.

She listened to the colonel and his companions make their way off Mount Marcy's top as the weather closed in again. She would leave in a moment, too, when she felt less shaky.

She had stopped the Rookwoods from killing Colonel Roosevelt and John Rookwood from killing her—all with her puny dryad powers that suddenly didn't seem so puny. The trees here had helped her, though they hadn't been "hers"—imagine what power, say, Mum could command with the help of her little forest at home.

And it was suddenly much easier to imagine how Grand-mère must have felt, losing her forest in France after the Germans burned it down in the war. She herself was about to lose a forest she loved. She would have to leave the Adirondacks when the Roosevelts did, and she wasn't sure she would be able to say farewell to these trees without completely breaking down. If only she could stay…but this wasn't the ancient times when a dryad could choose her wood and live there as she pleased. And these woods did not know how to live with dryads; they would be just as happy without her. But she would never forget them. Never.

They had taught her what she was, without knowing it themselves.

When rain started to fall in earnest once more, she pulled herself stiffly to her feet. For a moment she gazed down at the balsam scrub at her feet, then bent and touched it. "Thank you for everything, cousin," she said softly.

Before she left, she threw John Rookwood's gun off the mountain.

There was no Crow to guide her as she left the top of Mount Marcy, but she was a dryad, and dryads did not get lost. It rained hard on and off, which chilled her and made her wool skirt abominably heavy, but it did wash the worst of the mud off.

She couldn't help, though, occasionally looking over her shoulder as she descended back into the trees. Mr. Rookwood must be still be somewhere on the mountain. For the first time, he had failed to complete a commission. Would he be angry? Vengeful? Somehow she doubted it; vengeance would not be an advantageous use of his time. But she still looked behind her every few moments until she regained the trail down to Lake Colden. Neither Mr. Rookwood nor his brother would risk being seen there, as they were supposed to be fishing on Lake Schroon.

And as for Kit... But she wasn't sure she was ready to think about Kit yet.

Alice was waiting for her at the cabins when she at long last stumbled wearily into the camp. "Well?" she demanded. "Where's my father? What happened?"

Grace bent to wring the water from her skirt. "I'm quite well. Thank you for asking."

"Grace!"

She sighed. "As far as I know, he's still up there somewhere with Mr. LaCasse and the boys. I thought I heard them say something about going down to a lake to eat lunch, but that was a while ago. Do you mind if I sit down for a moment?" She looked over Alice's shoulder at the open cabin door.

Alice stepped aside but followed her in, still firing questions. "Didn't you talk to him? How did you stop the Rookwoods? Where are they?"

"I don't know. Far away, I hope."

"They tried to kill my father, and you let them *go*?" Her voice was incredulous.

"What was I supposed to do to them?" Grace sat on the edge of one of the bunks, fighting the temptation to stretch out on it and nap for three hours. "I'm lucky I was able to keep them from hurting your father."

"You should have done something. You've done everything else, haven't you?"

"Alice, don't. Just…don't."

"Don't what? *Don't* is the only thing I've heard from you this summer, except maybe for the *you shouldn't haves*." Her mouth twisted. "The worst part is, you were right. We probably wouldn't be here right now if I'd listened to you about Kit."

The pain in her voice drained away any of Grace's annoyance. "Yes, we might have been somewhere else," she said gently. "And your father might be dead now instead of alive. The Rookwoods were determined to get to him."

"Maybe. But maybe not. Maybe I could have saved him in that case, instead of you."

There was nothing Grace could say that wouldn't make matters worse, so she stood up. "Let's go back to Tahawus. It's getting late."

It was a long, quiet five miles, punctuated by frequent rests when Alice's ankle began to hurt too badly. Only when they were nearly home did Grace speak. "I expect we'll be leaving in the next day or two. You'll be going to Washington."

Alice didn't look at her. "The president will die?"

"Mr. Rookwood seemed to think so."

She didn't respond for several minutes. "I don't want to go there," she finally said.

"But I thought you couldn't wait till you—"

"Well, I've changed my mind."

Grace waited a moment, then said, "You could come back to Boston with me. Your grandparents—"

"Do you think I want to do that either?" Alice stopped walking. "You've been my best friend for years. You tried to keep me from making an idiot of myself with Kit. You saved my father from being shot or pushed off the top of a mountain. You're also the one who Kit really loves and were able to save my father when I couldn't, and you'll have to excuse me if I can't stand the sight of you just now."

They didn't speak for the rest of the walk home.

NINETEEN

By nine o'clock the next morning, Grace and most of the Roosevelts were climbing into the wagons that would take them back to North Creek and then home.

Colonel Roosevelt was not with them. A runner had found him yesterday afternoon having lunch on Lake Tear of the Clouds, bearing the news that President McKinley had taken a turn for the worse. He'd departed for Buffalo last night after telegrams arrived confirming that the president was not expected to survive the night. Somewhere on a dark, rainy road between the Lower Works and Aiden Lodge, he had become the president of the United States.

Alice was also not with them. A letter had arrived from friends she'd made in New York last winter inviting her to stay at a nearby camp. Rather than going with her stepmother and the children to their home in Oyster Bay, she'd decided to leave directly for Santanoni.

Her goodbyes to Grace as she climbed into the waiting buckboard were hurried and perfunctory. "Well, so long," she called, not meeting her eyes. "Maybe I'll see you in Chestnut Hill sometime."

"I'll write." Grace tried, and failed, to catch her glance.

She shrugged, and the buckboard started down the rutted road.

Grace knew that she if she wrote to her friend, Alice might respond…or she might not. She mourned for her as they rattled down the muddy track to North Creek; the Trouble Twins, the weeks of living in each others' pockets and finishing each others' sentences were no more. It was probably bound to happen—her and Alice's lives were about to become very different. Alice would be living in the White House, eldest daughter of the president—and she? Back to Mum and Papa in Chestnut Hill…and who knew where after that. Right now, she wasn't capable of speculating on what even the next day would bring.

And all the while they clopped and bounced down the road, she was aware that she was leaving the trees she'd fallen so much in love with. She tried to fix them in her memory—the silhouette of their tops against the sky, their scent, the wind in their branches. She'd gathered a little bag of balsam needles from beneath the tree in her hollow; now and then she took it out and buried her nose in it.

The sleepy village of North Creek was nearly unrecognizable; it was full of hired wagons hitched every which way, and newspaper reporters milled in the streets, anxious to talk to anyone who might have a connection to the Roosevelts. They almost mobbed the wagons that she and the Roosevelts rode in. It took the few available members of the railway police, the village's chief constable, and a horde of volunteer deputies to keep them from overwhelming Mrs. Roosevelt and the children as they tried to climb down from the wagons and make their way into the train station. Most of the reporters assumed she was Alice and mobbed her too. Ted gallantly tried to fight them off until a voice she knew called, "Grace! Grace Boisvert!"

Grace gasped. "Papa!"

And there he was, pushing his way through the shouting newspapermen until he arrived, hatless, at her side. Grace would have liked to throw herself into his arms, but she couldn't in front of all these people.

He linked arms with her and pushed into the train station. "We're on the next train to Albany. Where are your bags?"

"I'll make sure they're taken care of, sir." Ted had followed them; he was taking his position as man of the family very seriously. And Grace suspected he wanted to say goodbye to her too. Once they'd found a not-too-crowded corner she held out her hand to him. "Thank you, Ted. It has been a pleasure meeting you—and fishing with you. I hope that if you ever come to Boston with your sister, you'll call on us."

He turned bright red but took her hand and shook it with quiet dignity. "Thank you, Miss Boisvert. You…" He gulped. "I liked fishing with you too!" And then, as if another word would be too much, he nodded respectfully to Papa, gave her one last look, and disappeared into the crowd.

"An admirer of yours?" Papa asked. But his teasing smile was halfhearted; he was examining her as if to reassure himself that she was unharmed and whole.

"Alice's oldest brother." The thought of Alice made her sad all over again. She took his arm and squeezed it. "Papa, why are you here? You couldn't have known I was coming home—I was going to wire you here to let you and Mum know to expect me. Did you guess that President McKinley wouldn't…that he…" She steadied her suddenly shaky voice. "That we would be leaving Tahawus sooner than planned?"

"No. But we got your last letter." He glanced around the crowded station as if to make sure that no one was listening.

"My letter?" She tried to remember what she might have said in it that would have brought him here all the way from Chestnut Hill. "I don't understand."

He took one more furtive look around them. "Henry Rookwood. I had a hard time dissuading your mother and grandmother from coming as well, armed with torches and pikes." He looked at her closely. "Did anything happen?"

Did anything happen? Grace wanted to laugh and then to weep. Weeping won.

He handed her his handkerchief when she soaked through her own, and when she was calmer, he herded her onto the Albany train and found them a pair of seats in the back of the last car. "Tell me," he said.

He listened without comment as she told him what had happened from their arrival in Newport up to last night, though she noticed his jaw tighten occasionally and the knuckles of his clasped hands whiten at a few points. It wasn't until she told him what she had done to protect the colonel from the Shadows that he spoke.

"Did you feel better about being a dryad then?" he asked gently.

Grace dabbed at her eyes with his handkerchief. "I don't know. I did what I could."

"That's all anyone can do in life, sapling," he said. "That and try to learn so that, the next time, you're better equipped to face what life gives you."

She nodded. "There's more," she said, and told him about John Rookwood and how she had contemplated making him hurl himself from the top of the mountain. "It was… I could have done it. I know I could." For some reason, she couldn't banish from her mind the image of his staring, open-mouthed face as he handed her his gun.

"But you didn't." Papa's voice was soothing, but his brows were drawn.

"No, I…" She swallowed. She wasn't sure she could tell him how tempted she'd been to actually do it. "I didn't know I could do such a thing. Mum never said…"

"I didn't know either. Some of you are more powerful than others, I know. You might be one of those more powerful ones. Your grandmother…" He hesitated, then seemed to decide not to finish that sentence. "The fact that you had just been using the trees' power might have enhanced your natural ability."

"Oh." Grace remembered how John Rookwood had stared at her the day they met. She had been with the balsam tree in her hollow a short while before; perhaps it had started then.

He sighed. "I just wish…"

"What?"

"I— There's nothing to be done about it, but I fear that once Henry Rookwood finds out what you were able to do to his brother, he'll—" He shook his head.

He'll not rest until he has you working for him, Grace finished for him in her head. *Or sees you dead.* She shivered, and Papa took her hand and held it tightly. He held it while she cried again, and after when she fell asleep on his shoulder. It felt good to let all the tension of the last few weeks out at last. Papa was taking her home, and at least for a little while she didn't have to think.

By the time they arrived in Boston that evening, she was drooping like an unwatered plant. Mum took one look at her and put her to bed. She stayed there all the next day, sleeping.

When she finally got up, she dreaded going downstairs to face the family. But everyone treated her like an extremely fragile vase. Mum brought her out to sit with her trees, who sang to her. Grand-mère did her hair for her (with Mademoiselle's Secret, no less) and rubbed her hands and feet with oil of lavender. Even Dorothy refrained from galloping around the house and brought her pears from the tree behind the house, which was an enormous sacrifice on her part as she usually tried to eat them all before anyone else could get to them. Grace assumed it was because Papa had told them what she had told him on the train. At first she was glad, because it meant she wouldn't have to relive it all by retelling. But when, after dinner the third day she was home, Papa suggested they gather in his study, her stomach flip-flopped.

Mum spoke first. She made Grace sit next to her on the sofa by the fireplace and held her hand while she spoke. "Darling, as you might have guessed, we've been talking about what happened. And the first thing we want to say is that we are extremely proud of you."

"You saved the president of the United States from a pair of very powerful wizards," Papa added. "I confess that I would like to have known who it was that gave them the commission."

"I would not," Mum said firmly. "I like being able to sleep at night, thank you. It's a pity that Colonel Roosevelt will never know what you faced to save him, though."

"Grace knows what she did," Grand-mère said calmly. "That is enough. I am more concerned with what is left."

They all fell silent. "The Rookwoods," Papa finally said.

Mum gripped her hand too tightly for a minute. "When I think of Henry Rookwood playing up to you like that—"

"He didn't, Mum. That was what made it so…so… He wasn't pretending." He really *was* that kindly man who'd pretended to fish so he could enjoy the peace of the lake…when he hadn't been using its solitude to practice drawing Shadows to him to capture and unleash on the unsuspecting Colonel Roosevelt.

"Yes, but to try to convince you to work for him—"

Papa cleared his throat. "Grace, we are concerned that he won't give up. You beat him. He's either going to want revenge or to try even harder to get you to join him."

"I don't think revenge is something he cares about. It wouldn't be a rational use of his time." John Rookwood, however, was much less rational than his brother. And as for their junior partner…but she could not yet face following that line of thought.

"Whether he is or not, we have discussed the situation and what the best course of action might be —"

Grand-mère made a dismissive gesture. "Talk, talk, talk! I do not know why we must have all this chatter as it is very simple. Grace must go to France."

Mum jumped in hurriedly. "Not if you don't want to, of course, darling, but we think there are a lot of good reasons why you should consider it. It will get you away from the Rookwoods, for one thing. And give you a change of scene, help you make some new memories to push aside the old ones."

Grace let them go on talking because it seemed to make them feel better. When they finally ran out of things to say and looked at her expectantly, she said, "Yes, I think I'd like to go. At least for a little while."

They didn't ask her why she'd capitulated so readily after refusing to go in July, so she didn't have to tell them about the note that she'd found by the front door that morning, written in a precise hand on thick and expensive but unmarked paper. There had been no return address on it and no signature, but it hadn't needed them:

My dear Miss Boisvert,

    It never occurred to me that you would try to stop me completing my commission, but I can see now that it was the logical outgrowth of your feelings. I blame myself for forgetting that some, especially the young, do indeed see in black and white. Be assured that my offer still stands, on whatever terms you wish, when you begin to see the world's grays more clearly. Please come to see me when you do.

Grace had thrown it and the business card enclosed with it (*Isham and Rookwood, Inc., Consultants* with an address on the Upper East Side of New York) into the fire without telling her parents. It would have upset them unnecessarily and anyway, it was her problem to deal with…

Except that the business card would not burn.

Grace gingerly picked it out of the ashes of Mr. Rookwood's note and frowned at it, then tried to tear it in half. It would not rip. Nor would it turn to pulp in water, or allow itself to be cut up with scissors. She finally hid it at the bottom of her trunk under some tissue paper, where no one would be likely to run across it, and tried not to think about it.

⬥ ❖ ❖ ⬥

It was decided that Grace and Grand-mère would leave in a few weeks' time on the steamship *Rousillon*, bound for Le Havre. Mum and Papa would stay at home, as Mum would not leave her trees until they were in their winter sleep, then bring Dorothy and Sandy to meet her and Grand-mère in Paris at Christmas, after which they would sail home together.

A new flurry of packing and shopping commenced, though not quite as much shopping as had taken place before she left for Newport. Mostly it was for clothing to wear on the voyage itself. Grand-mère had plans for a great many trips to the fashion houses of Paris once they arrived, establishments whose clothes would make their Boston-made fashions look quite inferior.

Paris! She'd packed her French books and would practice her conversational skills as much as she could on the boat so that she didn't embarrass herself too badly when they arrived. It wouldn't be the height of the social season, though society never truly slumbered there. There would be plenty of opportunity for them to see the sights and meet Grand-mère's old acquaintances

...though she had made Grand-mère promise that she wouldn't try to marry her off to anyone while she was there. Boys were not anything she could face just now.

The prospect of a week on the ocean, however, almost made Grace change her mind about going.

"Pfft," Grand-mère said when she told her about her experience on the Livingstons' boat. "Of course you felt very bad. Dryads do not like to lose contact with the soil."

It might have been nice if Grand-mère had told her that back in July before she'd left for the yachting capital of the country. "But what will we do? We can't spend a week or ten days feeling so wretched."

"We will not feel wretched. Leave that to me."

"What will you do?"

But Grand-mère only pursed her lips and looked mysterious. Grace tried hard to not want to growl at her.

Mum kept her outside among her trees as much as possible. "I get the feeling you suffered for their company in Newport," she said one sunny afternoon a couple of weeks after her return as they reviewed Grace's packing list on a bench under her favorite oak.

"I didn't realize how much until we got to the Adirondacks. When we stepped out onto the platform, it felt like I hadn't breathed for weeks." She tried to ignore a stab of longing for the trees of Tahawus. "Even Alice noticed."

"That's not too surprising. You two know each other so well." A pause. "Have you heard from her since you got home? I don't recall having seen a letter."

"No." Grace stared down at the list in her lap without really seeing it. She'd written to Alice twice — short notes to let her know she was home and to ask how her family was — but there had been no response. "I... We... I don't know if she even... Oh, Mum, she hates me now!" She collapsed against Mum's shoulder.

"I wondered if something had happened between you." Mum sighed. "Regrettably, this is something that can occur when childhood friends grow up. Their worlds broaden and they move onto other interests, and former bonds can weaken, even among dryads. Or new friendships eclipse old ones. Especially male ones." There was a faint questioning edge to her voice.

Trust Mum to have picked up on that. Grace had told Papa that Kit had intentionally pursued Alice at his father's command, but nothing further. And certainly nothing about him and her. "She was pretty badly hurt by Kit," she said. "I can't blame her. I would have been hurt too. I just wish…"

"That he hadn't come between the two of you?"

"Mum! How did you —"

Mum actually smiled. "Because I can't think of any other reason why she would have come to learn he didn't really care for her unless he realized he could no longer pretend he did. And the most likely reason for that is that he'd come to truly care for someone else."

"But what if his father had told him to pretend to care for someone else instead of Alice?" she whispered, because her throat was suddenly too hot and tight to speak normally.

"Do you think he did?"

"I don't know! He told me that…that he loved me but that other people—I assume he meant his uncle—would tell lies about him, and… I don't know what to think!"

Mum held her tightly. "Do you care for him?"

"I don't know. When we first met, before he knew who I was, we—" She brought her hands together, fingers entwined. "He felt like that. But what if it wasn't real?" Her dreams every night had been haunted by his smile, his eyes, his hands. She wondered if, wherever he was, he was dreaming of her as well…or if he had already forgotten her.

Mum was silent for some time. Then she sighed. "I am so glad that you decided to go to France. Getting away for a few months will give you some perspective, I hope."

"Yes, Mum."

But she had been trying hard to gain some perspective *now*. Alone in her room, she'd thought about Mr. Rookwood and what he'd offered her. If she'd said yes, he would probably be arranging her life for her now — college, she expected, to get to know now the people who would become Isham and Rookwood's clients in the future. Kit would be waiting for her when she graduated, and then —

Oh, Kit. Questions tormented her. What had happened to him after he'd left her that night by the lake? Had he been up there on Mount Marcy, helping his father and uncle to try to kill Colonel Roosevelt? And if he had been helping them, then what should she feel about him?

The problem was that she didn't know if France would be enough to push him from her thoughts…or if she even wanted to push him out. Her time with him had been left unfinished, unresolved, a melody with the final, completing chord yet unplayed. She had been left waiting to hear what those notes would be…and yet, in a way, she didn't want to. Kit was a Rookwood and a human; she was a Boisvert and a dryad. Between those two extremes was a divide that any final, closing chord would surely get lost in.

• • ❖ • ❖ ❀ ❖ • ❖ • •

Indian summer had settled over New England, and even the nights were so unseasonably warm that Grace had left her windows open to the soft air. On this night two days before their departure for France she lay in bed watching the sheer curtains wave in the gentle night breeze, thinking about what was left to pack. Until, that is, something large landed with a thud on the sill of one of her open windows.

She sat up. There was a scratching noise, as of claws gaining purchase on wood. Then a large, dark something leapt from the sill and into her room. It sat for a second, then shook itself and took a step or two. It was a large black bird.

Grace fumbled for the matches on her bedside table and lit the candle there. The bird stood still and looked at her, head to one side.

"C-Crow?" she whispered.

The bird leaned forward and extended its wings as if it were about to take off...and then it was gone. In its place stood Kit Rookwood.

Grace cried out then—a high, breathy gasp. Kit did not move but watched her from where he stood by the window. "Grace," he said quietly, questioningly.

"K-Kit—wh-what—" It was a good thing she'd left the candle on the bedside table. She was shaking so hard that she might have dropped it.

"It's not something I do in front of just anyone," he said. "And no, it's not a crow. It's a raven. There are differences, though I can understand that some people don't know what they are." He looked at her, and his old lopsided smile spread across his face, though his eyes held a different expression. "Alice said once that you had your underclothes made in France and the thought has haunted me ever since—with good reason, I see."

Grace hastily retreated back under the bedclothes...and realized that Kit wasn't wearing anything at all. *Of course not*, said one part of her mind. *How could he go from a raven's form to a man's wearing a stitch of anything?* A slightly less rational part wanted to spend the next half hour drinking the sight of him in, for he was beautiful—broad shoulders tapering down to narrow hips and long, straight limbs, and...

The rest of her, however, panicked. "You can't stand there

naked in my room!" she whispered frantically.

His smile widened. "Um...I am."

Grace closed her eyes, reached for the quilt folded at the foot of her bed, and threw it toward him. "If you don't wrap yourself in that now, I'll scream."

"It used to take a lot more than that to make the Grace I know scream," he said, a little reproachfully, but she heard him move and then the soft susurrus of fabric. "There. I look like an early American Roman senator. Happy?"

Grace opened one eye a crack. He was standing over her, the quilt draped around him toga fashion. "Not too close!" she squealed and huddled back against the headboard.

He sat down on the edge of her bed. "Now you're being silly. I'm not going to bite you, though I can't promise I won't do anything else."

"Kit!"

He laughed softly. "Tell me something. Who are you more afraid of—me or yourself?"

She sat up straighter. "I'm not afraid."

"*That's* the Grace I know," he said and then fell silent, looking at her. "I've missed you so badly," he finally said.

A dozen things that all wanted to be said swirled in her mind. One finally floated to the top. "Where is your father?" she whispered.

"At home in New York with my mother," he said. "My uncle's there, too, as far as I know. No one is going to hunt you down. Father still has high hopes for you, and he won't let Uncle John trouble you."

Grace closed her eyes. His words were both a relief and frightening. "Isn't he afraid I'll...tell?"

Kit smiled. "Who would believe you?" His smile faded. "Are you all right?"

"I'm fine."

"No—I mean, are you all right since you got home? Since Mount Marcy."

Grace gripped the blankets hard for a moment. The mere mention of Mount Marcy could make her feel dizzy sometimes. "You know what happened there."

"I was there."

She frowned. "You were? But I never saw you!"

"Grace." He was shaking his head. "I was right when I said that some people don't know the difference between ravens and crows. Who do you think let you out of the cabin at Lake Colden?"

The events of that day began to rearrange themselves in her mind. "But I thought it was Crow!"

"I doubt your Changer friend could have undone the spell my father put on that door. And if I could have become a mountain goat and carried you the rest of the way, I would have," he added with another crooked smile. "But raven is the only shape I can take."

Grace remembered her joking complaint. So it *was* he who'd led her up the mountain. No wonder "Crow" wouldn't talk to her. She took a deep breath. "Why did you help me and not your father? They were looking for you—you were supposed to be on watch for them."

"I know. They can't shift—I get it from my mother's side, though she herself doesn't have any magic—so being able to turn into a raven made me useful to them for this job. For a few other jobs, too. Like looking for hats that got lost overboard in Newport."

Grace remembered the unsigned parcel containing her hat. That had been him too…

"Only I'm still not sure I want to help my father and uncle." He leaned toward her. "I told you before that I'm not happy about joining my family's firm."

She nodded. Now she understood why.

"They've been grooming me for this all my life. And…" He looked down at his hands. "I love my father, no matter what he's done. He was the best father I could imagine having, and I don't want to disappoint him. But I love you too. I don't know what I'm going to do."

Grace swallowed. "You know what your father said — what he offered me."

"He knows a good thing when he sees it. Whatever you did to Uncle John up there left Father nearly speechless with excitement and twice as determined to have you work for him. And I know what he said about you and me." He looked a little sheepish. "I think he figured out how I feel about you, even though I tried not to let him see it."

"How…" Grace hesitated, then steeled herself. "How do you feel about me?"

"Give me two seconds and I'll show you." He started to slide forward on the bed but stopped when she cowered back from him. "What is it?"

"How do I know you love me? Your uncle —"

"You're going to believe anything *he* said?"

"He said…when your father told him I wouldn't join them, he said that you'd botched the job and he should have been the one to…to recruit me. How do I know you weren't doing to me just what you'd done to Alice?"

He sat back and closed his eyes for a minute as if composing himself, then looked at her. "Grace, what did I tell you that night by the lake? I asked you not to believe anything you might hear about me, because it was likely to be a lie. Or at least not the whole truth."

"Did your father tell you to try to make me love you?"

He hesitated, then nodded. "Except that he didn't know that I was already in love with you. When he told me, it was…it was like he was giving me permission to do what I'd already wanted to do anyway, you know?" The smile that had touched the corners of his mouth vanished when she remained silent. "You still don't believe me, do you?"

"I don't know," she whispered. There was so much between them—Alice and Newport, secrets and lies. She wanted to believe him, wanted to reach out to him and feel his arms around her and his mouth on hers. But she couldn't. Not until she was *sure* that it was right.

And there was something else too. Mum's warnings about human-dryad unions had all made perfect sense back in July. But only now did she understand with her heart as well as her mind what they truly meant. Could she love Kit, knowing how transient their life together would be for her? Would she be brave enough to?

"Um...so, how is Alice, anyway?" he asked a little uncomfortably.

Grace felt uncomfortable too. "Oh, she's... You know Alice, she's always..." She took a breath. "I don't know how she is. She won't respond to my letters. She saw you kiss me that night, and...well, you can imagine what she said to me. She's glad her father is safe, but...but I don't think we'll ever be able to be friends the way we were before. If at all."

Kit leaned forward and held his hand out to her. She hesitated, then leaned forward, too, and took it. "I'm sorry that you and she...that your friendship had to be one of the casualties of all this," he said. "I was afraid of it as soon as I realized you weren't Alice, that morning at the Casino."

Grace hunched her shoulders. "I've been thinking...maybe it would have happened anyway. She would have gone to Washington no matter what, and we would have moved into different worlds."

"Grace." He squeezed her hand. She looked up and saw that he was looking at her intently.

"You may have lost Alice, but you gained me. I love you," he said. "Whether you believe it or not, I do. I debated asking you to run away with me tonight, but I realize now that I can't. It wouldn't be fair. I want you to *know* that you love me, and not have doubts. Go to Europe—yes, I know that you're going. The trunks are a bit of a giveaway, and I've been hanging out in trees eavesdropping. Go to Europe so that you can see what you could have there and if it's what you want…or if maybe it's me you love after all." He shook his head and laughed softly. "No one ever told me that being noble would be so damned hard. Two-thirds of me still wants to carry you off with me someplace where no one will find us."

"Kit…" Once again the image of the two of them living in the depths of the Adirondacks, just them and thousands of acres of trees, filled her with longing.

"Grace." He held his arms out to her. She hesitated—then wiggled out from under the covers and into his embrace. He held her close, stroking her bare shoulder, but did not attempt any further intimacy. They sat just so for a long time, and she breathed in the scent of his skin and the beat of his heart, and felt—not only in her fingers or toes, but through all of her—that sense of rooting, of thirsting, of filling and being filled that she held felt among the trees in Tahawus. Only this time it was not a tree or a forest that she was settling into, but Kit.

And then her breath caught as a flood of the same feeling filled her. This time, she was being settled into as well.

She closed her eyes and let it—*him*—wash over and through her till it was hard to know where she left off and he began. They didn't speak, because words weren't necessary between them. Not anymore.

At some point, though, Kit stirred. "I have to go, Grace," he said. "It will be morning soon."

Grace sat up reluctantly. "Where are you going?"

"Home. Don't worry, they haven't disinherited me. Uncle John would probably have liked to, but Father has decided that I just need a little more time before I'm ready to join them. He's nothing if not patient."

She'd already noticed that. "He wrote to me."

"My father? I'm not surprised. What did he say?"

"He congratulated me…and said that he would be waiting for when I changed my mind."

Kit sighed but didn't say anything further. He kissed her gently, then rose and walked to the window. "Will you write to let me know that you're there and all right? I doubt your family will be pleased if I write to you."

"Yes, I will." She fought back the strong urge to get out of bed and throw her arms around him and keep him with her.

He let the quilt slip from his shoulders and stood with his back to her. His naked back was smooth and elegantly muscled, down his buttocks and into his thighs. "I won't say goodbye, my love, because it isn't, is it?"

"No," she said quietly.

He nodded and turned so that he could look at her over his shoulder. "I love you, Grace," he said, and then the raven was back. It hopped up onto the windowsill and vanished into the night.

Grace waited a minute, then climbed stiffly off the bed. She went to the window and picked up the quilt, still warm from his body, and wrapped it around herself before lying down again. She cried a little, then fell asleep and dreamed of a night filled with swirling black feathers.

<hr>

"Grace! Wake up! You've absolutely gotta see this!" Her sister Dorothy, hair in braids and wearing one of her hand-me-down nightgowns, was shaking her shoulder.

"What?" Grace half opened her eyes. It was light out, but by the angle of the sun she could see it was still very early.

"Outside! Come on! You won't believe what they're doing!" Dorothy was practically dancing.

She sat up and rubbed her eyes. "What are you talking about?"

"The crows! Come *on!*"

That made her move. She nearly tripped on the quilt she still clutched around her but followed Dorothy to the open window — and stood transfixed.

A soft autumn mist obscured much of the sky and the surrounding trees, but the lawn below them hummed with activity. At least a dozen crows milled about, fluttering and flying and croaking to each other. There were hundreds of small white objects on the lawn with them, and more crows were arriving with white things clutched in their beaks.

"Look!" Dorothy said. "It's the flowers from the arbor!"

Grace stared and saw that she was right. The crows were plucking the creamy white blossoms of the autumn-blooming clematis that Mum called bridal wreath that cascaded from a pergola near the doors to Papa's study. They were carrying them back to the grass below Grace's window. "What are they doing?" she whispered.

"I don't know. Ooh, look at that big one!" Dorothy pointed.

A larger crow was perched on the bench set in a flower bed at the edge of the grass. Or might it be a raven? She looked at it hard and heard a voice in her mind say, *There's a difference, though I can understand that some people don't know it.* It let out a solemn croak, and all the crows began to stalk around the lawn, each with a blossom in its beak. They scurried around for a few minutes so that Grace couldn't see what they were doing and then, almost as one, took off into the sky.

Below her, the blossoms had been arranged to form the words *I love you.*

"Wow!" Dorothy gasped. "How did they do *that*?"

The raven—for she was sure it was a raven—croaked again as it flew to the arbor. It plucked a larger spray of flowers, then flapped up to Grace's windowsill and dropped it there. Grace met its dark eye as it looked at her, head to one side. Then it, too, took off into the morning fog.

"That…was…incredible!" Dorothy's eyes were wide. "Is that crow in love with you?"

"No," Grace said. After all, it wasn't a crow.

"Then why did it—"

"I don't know. Why don't you get dressed and go out and have a look? And…um, you might want to pick those up. Grand-mère wouldn't be happy to see that the birds have been at her pergola."

She waited till her sister had scampered off, then bent and tenderly picked up the sprig of bridal wreath. She was gazing down at it when another sudden thud made her look up. A large black bird was sitting on her window sill, looking at her interestedly. For a moment she caught her breath, but in the next realized that this was no raven, but a crow. "Oh," she said, disappointed.

"Oh? Is that all you have to say, dryad?" it croaked.

"Crow!" She stared at it in surprise, then laughed and leaned against the side of the window. "What are you doing here?"

"Waiting for my sandwich. You left without bringing me one."

"You came here all the way from the Adirondacks just for a sandwich?"

"Why not? I like sandwiches." He looked at her with one eye. "And I wanted to see what happens. What you do next."

"Well…not a lot, I'm afraid. I'm leaving for Europe in a few days."

"So? Things might happen there too. Do they have sandwiches in Europe?"

Grace grinned. "I'm sure they do."

"Hmm. Doesn't get you out of the one you still owe me."

"I'll bring one out as soon as I get dressed." Mrs. Toole might take a little convincing to produce a chicken sandwich at this hour of the morning, but Grace expected she could manage it.

"All right. I'll be waiting, dryad." Crow leapt from the window and coasted to the lawn.

Grace watched him for a moment, then looked at the sprig of bridal wreath still in her hand. She lifted it to her nose and breathed deeply of its sweet scent, then carried it to one of her trunks. She pulled a small, leather-bound journal from the tray on its top and tucked the spray into it, then went to get dressed.

AUTHOR'S NOTE

I've always been fascinated by Alice Roosevelt...well, by the whole Roosevelt family, really. President Theodore Roosevelt more than earned the oceans of ink that have been expended on him and his life, and Alice's brother Ted received the Congressional Medal of Honor for being the only general (and, at 56, the oldest soldier) to land in the first wave of the invasion at Normandy on D-Day in World War II. He marched up and down the beaches, walking with a cane, meeting each incoming troop transport and putting heart into the troops as well as organizing and directing traffic after the original invasion plans fell apart: without him, D-Day might not have been the decisive success it was.

But Alice...I have a love/hate relationship with her. Once her father became president in September of 1901 after the death of President McKinley (who really was shot at the Buffalo World's Fair by an anarchist), she became a news item and rarely left the front page; her escapades and partying were on an epic scale. Her father once famously said, "I can do one of two things. I can be president of the United States, or I can control Alice. I cannot possibly do both." She behaved very badly on many occasions and did some pretty unforgiveable things to a lot of people in her lifetime, but she was front and center in a time when women were supposed to be wallpaper, and you have to admire her for that.

I've wondered for years how Alice became Alice. For all the

privilege of her upbringing, her childhood and youth often seem rather sad to me: her mother died a few days after giving birth to her, and her father basically handed her over to his older sister to raise and went to Dakota Territory to be a rancher. Then at age three she was removed from that aunt's care—who had been the only mother she knew—to live again with her father and his new wife, who were more or less strangers to her. That has to have left a mark on young Alice…and I couldn't help wondering if, just maybe, some other unrecorded event might have done more damage…like, say, an unhappy first crush…?

Most of the external history in this book actually happened. Alice was a frequent visitor to her grandparents' home in Chestnut Hill, Massachusetts. She and the rest of her family did indeed stay at the Tahawus Club in the Adirondacks in August and September of 1901 and climb Mount Marcy on a foggy, drizzly day…and the clouds did disappear for a little while on the mountain's top the morning that the Roosevelts climbed it. Colonel Roosevelt got word, while picnicking by Lake Tear of the Clouds that very day, that President McKinley's recovery had received a setback, and he did indeed become president that night while hurrying through a driving rain to the train station in North Creek. It was enormous fun to fit Grace and dryads and Kit Rookwood and his family into and around these facts; sometimes it was startling how well they fit underneath the actual history. The only historical messing about I did was Alice and Grace's visit to Newport: Alice was not there in July of 1901, but did visit there in 1902 and many subsequent summers as the guest of Grace Vanderbilt, and got up to many shenanigans while there, of course. But as far as I know, the firm of Isham and Rookwood does not exist.

As for settings… The rickety remains of the Tahawus Club still stand (with some efforts being made in recent years to preserve the site), and Mount Marcy is still climbed by hundreds of

Adirondack hikers every year—hopefully without visitations from Shadows. The "cottages" of Newport, Rhode Island—including Tess Oelrichs' Rosecliff and Mamie Fish's Crosswinds (I adore Mrs. Fish—she truly was a character)—still stand, and many of them belong to the Newport Historical Society which has preserved them as museums; if you ever get a chance to visit Newport, they are totally worth seeing. The Casino remains a Newport landmark, as well as the home of the International Tennis Hall of Fame.

And now, a multitude of thank yous are in order. My gratitude to Jerold Pepper of Adirondack Experience (formerly the Adirondack Museum) for answering my queries on transportation between the Tahawus Club and North Creek, to Meredith Miller of the International Tennis Hall of Fame for notes on the Casino, and to Andrew D. Davis of Tricoastal Marine for questions about steam yachts; any errors in *Evergreen* on those subjects are mine alone.

Since books are not written in a vacuum, enormous thanks for your time, patience, and brains to Ena Jones, Rebecca Barnhouse, and Reka Simonsen, all of whom read this story in whole or in part and offered valuable input on making it better—I am deeply in your debt. Sherwood Smith went over it with her fine editor's eye and made it even betterer (ahem!)…and don't let Amy Knupp of Blue Otter Editing see me writing that way, because she did so much work toward making this manuscript sparkle. Thank you both for your help—you made this a better story and taught me to be a better writer.

And for that gorgeous, gorgeous cover, thank you to Ravenborn/Anika Willmanns.

Finally, thank you to the three safety nets I have below me, ready to catch me if I fall (redundancy is a beautiful thing): my wonderful colleagues at Book View Café, with whom it is a pleasure to work, and the equally wonderful Jen Clark Estes,

Larissa C. Hardesty, Ena Jones, Katie Kennedy, Robin Lemke, Cyndi Marko, Deena Lipomi Viviani, and Holly Westlund, with whom it is a pleasure to play, giggle, comfort, advise, and be writers together…and most of all to my amazing, amazing family. I love you so much.

Marissa Doyle

P.S. The further adventures of Grace in France among the dryad families of Brittany and back in New York to witness the launch of the Emperor of Germany's new yacht—and prevent Isham and Rookwood's most audacious "commission" yet from being carried out—are being planned. No release date yet, but if you have any comments about Evergreen or what you'd like to see in its sequel, drop me a line at marissa@marissadoyle.com —I'd love to hear from you!

About the Author

Marissa Doyle graduated from Bryn Mawr College and went on to graduate school intending to be an archaeologist, but somehow got distracted. Eventually she figured out what she was *really* supposed to be doing and started writing. She's channeled her inner history geekiness into a successful young adult historical fantasy series (the Leland Sisters), and is now also happily writing fantasy of various types for teens and adults. She lives in her native Massachusetts with her family, including a bossy but adorable pet rabbit, and loves quilting, gardening, and collecting antiques. Oh, and coffee.

Please visit her at her website, www.marissadoyle.com, and at her history blog, www.nineteenteen.com.

Thank you so much for reading *Evergreen*. If you enjoyed Grace's story, please consider telling your friends who also might enjoy it or posting a review on the site where you purchased it or on a book discussion venue like Goodreads or LibraryThing.

Connect with me
(because I love hearing from readers!)

Website: www.marissadoyle.com
Blog: www.nineteenteen.com
Facebook: www.facebook.com/marissadoyleauthor
Twitter: www.twitter.com/marissadoyle
Pinterest: www.pinterest.com/mdoyleauthor
Bookbub: www.bookbub.com/authors/marissa-doyle

Sign up for my newsletter and get the latest info on sales, new releases, and other fun stuff!
http://eepurl.com/bVDwlf

About Book View Café

Book View Café Publishing Cooperative is an author-owned cooperative of over fifty professional writers, publishing in a variety of genres such as fantasy, romance, mystery, and science fiction.

BVC authors include *New York Times* and *USA Today* best-sellers; Nebula, Hugo, and Philip K. Dick Award winners; World Fantasy Award, Campbell Award, and RITA Award nominees; and winners and nominees of many other publishing awards.

Since its debut in 2008, BVC has gained a reputation for producing high-quality e-books, and is now bringing that same quality to its print editions.